# SELECTED

RAINER MARIA RILKE was perhaps the greatest poet writing in German in the twentieth century. Born in Prague on 4 December 1875, he passed much of his unhappy youth in military academies before he matriculated at university, first in Prague and later in Munich and Berlin. His first volume of poetry, *Lives and Songs*, was published in 1894 and by 1900 he had completed another seven. Two visits to Russia with Lou Andreas-Salomé (inspiring *The Book of Hours*, 1905) are the first of many journeys he was to make, to Italy, Scandinavia, Spain, North Africa, and Egypt, before he settled in Switzerland in 1919. He married the artist Clara Westhoff in 1901, and they had a daughter, Ruth, before separating a year later.

Rilke's lyrical prose tale about the *Love and Death of the Cornet Christoph Rilke* (1906) achieved cult status, but his poetic breakthrough came with the publication in 1907 and 1908 of two volumes of *New Poems*, written after he moved to Paris in 1902, where he worked for, and wrote on, the sculptor Auguste Rodin. His only novel, *The Notebooks of Malte Laurids Brigge*, appeared in 1910. At the outbreak of war in 1914 Rilke was in Munich, and he fulfilled military service in an archive in Vienna. By then he had begun the *Duino Elegies*, although these were not completed until February 1922, in the Château de Muzot in the Valais. The same month saw the composition of the whole of *The Sonnets to Orpheus*. Rilke died of leukaemia on 29 December 1926, aged 51.

SUSAN RANSON is the translator of *Rainer Maria Rilke's 'The Book of Hours'* (New York and Woodbridge, 2008) and author of *John Hopkins, Metrical Psalmist: Co-author of the First National English Hymn Book, 1562* (Norwich, 2004).

MARIELLE SUTHERLAND is the author of *Images of Absence: Death and the Language of Concealment in the Poetry of Rainer Maria Rilke* (Berlin, 2006) and of essays and articles on Rilke, Bertolt Brecht, Peter Handke, and Rolf Dieter Brinkmann.

ROBERT VILAIN holds the Chair of German at the University of Bristol. He is the author of *The Poetry of Hugo von Hofmannsthal and French Symbolism* (Oxford, 2000), and co-editor with Karen Leeder of *The Cambridge Companion to Rilke* (Cambridge, 2010) and *Nach Duino: Studien zu Rainer Maria Rilkes späten Gedichten* (Göttingen, 2010).

# OXFORD WORLD'S CLASSICS

*For over 100 years Oxford World's Classics have brought readers closer to the world's great literature. Now with over 700 titles—from the 4,000-year-old myths of Mesopotamia to the twentieth century's greatest novels—the series makes available lesser-known as well as celebrated writing.*

*The pocket-sized hardbacks of the early years contained introductions by Virginia Woolf, T. S. Eliot, Graham Greene, and other literary figures which enriched the experience of reading. Today the series is recognized for its fine scholarship and reliability in texts that span world literature, drama and poetry, religion, philosophy, and politics. Each edition includes perceptive commentary and essential background information to meet the changing needs of readers.*

OXFORD WORLD'S CLASSICS

RAINER MARIA RILKE

# Selected Poems

*Translated by*
SUSAN RANSON *and* MARIELLE SUTHERLAND

*Edited with an Introduction and Notes by*
ROBERT VILAIN

OXFORD
UNIVERSITY PRESS

# OXFORD
## UNIVERSITY PRESS

Great Clarendon Street, Oxford OX2 6DP

Oxford University Press is a department of the University of Oxford.
It furthers the University's objective of excellence in research, scholarship,
and education by publishing worldwide in

Oxford New York

Auckland Cape Town Dar es Salaam Hong Kong Karachi
Kuala Lumpur Madrid Melbourne Mexico City Nairobi
New Delhi Shanghai Taipei Toronto

With offices in

Argentina Austria Brazil Chile Czech Republic France Greece
Guatemala Hungary Italy Japan Poland Portugal Singapore
South Korea Switzerland Thailand Turkey Ukraine Vietnam

Oxford is a registered trade mark of Oxford University Press
in the UK and in certain other countries

Published in the United States
by Oxford University Press Inc., New York

Translations © Susan Ranson and Marielle Sutherland 2011
Editorial material © Robert Vilain 2011
First published as an Oxford World's Classics paperback 2011

British Library Cataloguing in Publication Data

Data available

Library of Congress Cataloging in Publication Data

Data available

Typeset by RefineCatch Limited, Bungay, Suffolk
Printed in Great Britain
on acid-free paper by
Clays Ltd, St Ives plc

ISBN 978-0-19-956941-0

# ACKNOWLEDGEMENTS

AT Oxford University Press, Judith Luna's kind and knowledgeable guidance has been invaluable to the editor and translators at all stages of this project. In addition, Marielle Sutherland would like to thank Professor Karen Leeder and Frank Preut for their valuable advice, and Susan Ranson her daughter-in-law Regina Uebelmann for help generously given. Both translators have, naturally, consulted each other frequently during the two to three years of translation and are mutually indebted for many clarifications and suggestions.

Robert Vilain is highly indebted to Revd Richard Haggis (Oxford) for advice on biblical and religious questions, and to Karen Leeder for her expert knowledge and sensitive readings of Rilke from which he has learned so much during collaboration on two other Rilke projects completed in 2010 and during a series of seminars devoted to Rilke's late work held in Oxford in 2006. Above all he is grateful to Patience Robinson for her tolerance of the intrusion of Rilke into domestic life over nearly half a decade (so far).

Susan Ranson would like to thank the Editorial Director of Camden House, an imprint of Boydell & Brewer Inc., Rochester, New York, for permitting us to reproduce sixteen of her translations from *Rainer Maria Rilke's 'The Book of Hours': A New Translation*, 2008.

# CONTENTS

*Abbreviations*                                                                    xii

*Introduction*                                                                     xiii

*Note on the Text*                                                                 xxxv

*Note on the Translation*                                                          xxxvi

*Select Bibliography*                                                              xl

*A Chronology of Rainer Maria Rilke*                                               xlvi

## SELECTED POEMS

### From *Offerings to the Lares*

*Der Träumer* (II)  2                    *The Dreamer* (II)  3

### From *Advent*

'Das ist mein Streit'  2                 'This my struggle'  3

### From *In Celebration of Myself*

'Meine frühverliehnen'  2                'Songs I was granted in youth'  3
*Gebet*  4                               *Prayer*  5
'Der Abend ist mein Buch'  6             'The evening is my book'  7
'Ich fürchte mich so vor der            'I am so afraid of people's
    Menschen Wort'  6                        words'  7
'Nenn ich dich Aufgang oder             'Shall I name you a rising or a
    Untergang?'  6                           setting?'  7
'Kann mir einer sagen, wohin'  8         'What is the furthest I shall
                                             reach'  9

### From *The Book of Hours*

'Wir dürfen dich nicht eigenmächtig      'So arbitrarily we may not
    malen'  8                                paint you'  9
'Wir bauen an dir mit zitternden         'We build you with our
    Händen'  8                               trembling hands'  9
'Ich finde dich in allen diesen          'I find your trace in all these things,
    Dingen'  10                              in all'  11

'Ich kann nicht glauben, daß der kleine Tod' 10

'I cannot think that little figure Death' 11

'Was wirst du tun, Gott, wenn ich sterbe?' 12

'What will you do, God, when I die?' 13

'Wie der Wächter in den Weingeländen' 12

'Just as the watchman of the vineyard lands' 13

'Ich war bei den ältesten Mönchen' 14

'I lived with the ancient monks' 15

'Lösch mir die Augen aus: ich kann dich sehn' 14

'Put out my eyes: I see you still the same' 15

'Du bist die Zukunft, großes Morgenrot' 16

'You are the future, sovereign morning red' 17

'Die Könige der Welt sind alt' 16

'The emperors of earth are old' 17

'Jetzt reifen schon die roten Berberitzen' 18

'The barberries already ripen red' 19

'Denn wir sind nur die Schale und das Blatt' 18

'For we are only rind of fruit, and leaf' 19

'Herr: Wir sind ärmer denn die armen Tiere' 20

'Lord, we are poorer than the poor beasts' 21

'Denn sieh: sie werden leben und sich mehren' 22

'For see, they will live, flourish, multiply' 23

'Nur nimm sie wieder aus der Städte Schuld' 22

'But bear them away again from urban evils' 23

'Die Städte aber wollen nur das Ihre' 22

'Cities turn their force full on their own' 23

## From *The Book of Images*

*Eingang* 24

*Entrance* 25

*Die Heilige* 24

*The Saint* 25

*Aus einer Kindheit* 26

*From a Childhood* 27

*Der Knabe* 26

*The Boy* 27

*Menschen bei Nacht* 28

*People at Night* 29

*Der Nachbar* 30

*The Neighbour* 31

*Pont du Carrousel* 30

*Pont du Carrousel* 31

*Einsamkeit* 30

*Solitude* 31

*Herbsttag* 32

*Autumn Day* 33

*Abend* 32

*Evening* 33

*Die Heiligen Drei Könige* 34

*The Three Kings* 35

*Das Lied des Aussätzigen* 38

*The Leper's Song* 39

*Von den Fontänen* 38

*About Fountains* 39

*Schlußstück* 40

*End Piece* 41

## Uncollected Poems 1906–1908

'Sinnend von Legende zu Legende' 42

'Musing upon legend after legend' 43

*Ehe* 42

*Marriage* 43

*Fortgehn* 44                          *Leaving* 45
*La Dame à la Licorne* 46              *La Dame à la Licorne* 47
*Marionetten-Theater* 46              *Marionette Theatre* 47
*Der Goldschmied* 50                  *The Goldsmith* 51
'Wie dunkeln und rauschen             'In the instrument how they
  im Instrument' 50           darken and rustle' 51
*Requiem für eine Freundin*           *Requiem for a Friend* (extract) 53
  (Auszug) 52

## From *New Poems*

*Früher Apollo* 56                    *Early Apollo* 57
*Liebes-Lied* 56                      *Love Song* 57
*Der Ölbaum-Garten* 58                *The Garden of Olives* 59
*L'Ange du Méridien* 60               *L'Ange du Méridien* 61
*Die Fensterrose* 60                  *The Rose Window* 61
*Gott im Mittelalter* 62              *God in the Middle Ages* 63
*Der Panther* 62                      *The Panther* 63
*Die Gazelle* 64                      *The Gazelle* 65
*Das Einhorn* 64                      *The Unicorn* 65
*Der Schwan* 66                       *The Swan* 67
*Der Dichter* 66                      *The Poet* 67
*Blaue Hortensie* 68                  *Blue Hydrangea* 69
*Die Kurtisane* 68                    *The Courtesan* 69
*Die Treppe der Orangerie* 70         *The Orangery Steps* 71
*Römische Fontäne* 70                 *Roman Fountain* 71
*Das Karussell* 72                    *The Merry-go-round* 73
*Spanische Tänzerin* 74               *Spanish Dancer* 75
*Orpheus. Eurydike. Hermes* 76        *Orpheus. Eurydice. Hermes* 77

## From *New Poems, Second Part*

*Archäischer Torso Apollos* 80        *Archaic Torso of Apollo* 81
*Leda* 82                             *Leda* 83
*Die Insel der Sirenen* 84            *The Island of Sirens* 85
*Ein Prophet* 84                      *A Prophet* 85
*Eine Sibylle* 86                     *A Sibyl* 87
*Die Bettler* 86                      *The Beggars* 87
*Leichen-Wäsche* 88                   *Corpse-washing* 89
*Der Blinde* 90                       *The Blind Man* 91
*Schlangen-Beschwörung* 90            *Snake-charming* 91
*Schwarze Katze* 92                   *Black Cat* 93
*Lied vom Meer* 94                    *Song of the Sea* 95
*Venezianischer Morgen* 94            *Venetian Morning* 95
*Spätherbst in Venedig* 96            *Late Autumn in Venice* 97
*Die Laute* 96                        *The Lute* 97
*Das Rosen-Innere* 98                 *Rose Interior* 99
*Dame vor dem Spiegel* 98             *Lady at the Mirror* 99

x                    *Contents*

*Die Flamingos* 100               *The Flamingos* 101
*Rosa Hortensie* 100              *Pink Hydrangea* 101
*Der Ball* 102                    *The Ball* 103
*Der Hund* 102                    *The Dog* 103
*Buddha in der Glorie* 104        *Buddha in Glory* 105

## Uncollected Poems 1912–1922

'Ach, da wir Hülfe von Menschen        'Ah, as we waited for human
    erharrten' 106                         help' 107
*Auferweckung des Lazarus* 106         *The Raising of Lazarus* 107
'Tränen, Tränen, die aus mir           'Tears, tears breaking out of me' 109
    brechen' 108
'So, nun wird es doch der              'So it must surely be the angel,
    Engel sein' 108                        drinking' 109
'Hinweg, die ich bat' 110              'O leave me, you whom I asked' 111
'Du im Voraus' 110                     'You, beloved' 111
*Wendung* 112                          *Turning* 113
*Klage* 114                            *Plaint* 115
'Es winkt zu Fühlung fast aus          'Almost all things beckon us
    allen Dingen' 116                      to feeling' 117
'Ausgesetzt auf den Bergen             'Cast out, exposed on the
    des Herzens' 118                       mountains of the heart' 119
*An Hölderlin* 118                     *To Hölderlin* 119
*Der Tod* 120                          *Death* 121
*An die Musik* 122                     *To Music* 123
'In Karnak wars. Wir waren             'It was in Karnak. We had
    hingeritten' 122                       ridden there' 123
'Wunderliches Wort: die                'Odd, the words: "while away
    Zeit vertreiben!' 128                  the time"' 129

## Duino Elegies

*Die erste Elegie* 130                 *The First Elegy* 131
*Die zweite Elegie* 134                *The Second Elegy* 135
*Die dritte Elegie* 140                *The Third Elegy* 141
*Die vierte Elegie* 144                *The Fourth Elegy* 145
*Die fünfte Elegie* 150                *The Fifth Elegy* 151
*Die sechste Elegie* 156               *The Sixth Elegy* 157
*Die siebente Elegie* 158              *The Seventh Elegy* 159
*Die achte Elegie* 164                 *The Eighth Elegy* 165
*Die neunte Elegie* 168                *The Ninth Elegy* 169
*Die zehnte Elegie* 174                *The Tenth Elegy* 175

## The Sonnets to Orpheus

Erster Teil, Sonette I–XXVI 182        Part One, Sonnets I–XXVI 183
Zweiter Teil, Sonette I–XXIX 210       Part Two, Sonnets I–XXIX 211

## Uncollected Poems 1922–1926

*Odette R* . . . . 244

*Zueignung an M* . . . . 244

*Für* Nike 246

*Der Magier* 248

*Eros* 248

*Vergänglichkeit* 250

'Weisst du noch: fallende Sterne, die' 250

*Wilder Rosenbusch* 250

'Welt war in dem Antlitz der Geliebten' 252

'Nicht um-stoßen, was steht!' 252

'Gestirne der Nacht' 254

*Handinneres* 254

'Nacht. Oh du in Tiefe gelöstes Gesicht' 254

*Schwerkraft* 256

*Mausoleum* 256

'Wasser, die stürzen und eilende' 258


'Irgendwo blüht die Blume des Abschieds' 260

'Urne, Fruchtknoten des Mohns' 260

*Herbst* 260

'Rose, oh reiner Widerspruch, Lust' 262

*Idol* 262

*Gong* 262

*Gong* (II) 264

*Eine Folge zur* ›Rosenschale‹ 264

*Ankunft* 266

*Geschrieben für Karl Grafen Lanckoroński* 266

*Für Erika* 268

'Komm du, du letzter, den ich anerkenne' 270


*Odette R* . . . . 245

*Dedicated to M* . . . . 245

*For* Nike 247

*The Magician* 249

*Eros* 249

*Transience* 251

'Do you remember: falling stars that leapt' 251

*Wild Rose* 251

'World was there in my beloved's face' 253

'Overturn nothing that stands!' 253

'Night's constellations' 255

*Palm of the Hand* 255

'Night. O you so deeply freed' 255

*Gravity* 257

*Mausoleum* 257

'Waters that plunge and the quick-sliding' 259


'Somewhere the flower of farewell blooms' 261

'Urn, opium-poppy ovary' 261

*Autumn* 261

'Rose, O pure contradiction, delight' 263

*Idol* 263

*Gong* 263

*Gong* (II) 265

*A Sequel to the 'Bowl of Roses'* 265

*Arrival* 267

*Written for Count Karl Lanckoroński* 267

*For Erika* 269

'Come, you the last that I shall recognize' 271


*Explanatory Notes*                                                273

*Index of German Titles and First Lines*                           345

*Index of English Titles and First Lines*                          352

# ABBREVIATIONS

*B* I, *B* II    *Briefe in zwei Bänden*, ed. Horst Nalewski (Frankfurt am
              Main and Leipzig, 1991)
*DE*          *Duino Elegies*
*KA*          *Kommentierte Ausgabe*, 4 vols. plus a supplementary
              volume, ed. Manfred Engel et al. (Frankfurt am Main,
              1996 and 2003)
*SW*          *Sämtliche Werke*, 7 vols., ed. Ernst Zinn (Wiesbaden,
              1955–66 and 1997)

# INTRODUCTION

RAINER MARIA RILKE (1875–1926) was one of the leading poets of European Modernism, as important and as influential as T. S. Eliot, Wallace Stevens, and Paul Valéry, and certainly one of the greatest twentieth-century poets writing in German. His poetry is arrestingly beautiful, but it is also amongst the most challenging and thought-provoking ever written, in any language, at any time. It is not possible to read one of his poems without being halted, interrogated, and made to re-read and revise or refine an initial impression. These are poems that require and repay frequent re-reading, and if the capacity of a work of literature to sustain endless returns and fresh approaches is a mark of its quality, then Rilke's poetry must stand out as being exceptional. The satisfaction that many readers gain from it derives paradoxically from not being satisfied, not achieving full understanding, knowing instead both that there is more to be grasped and that one has none the less achieved an insight into one of the most extraordinary, complex, and subtle intellectual and aesthetic worlds that modern culture has to offer.

Some of the challenges of reading Rilke derive from the fact that his approach to poetry was never static or fixed. There is no single Rilke, no straightforward style or set of aesthetic precepts to which he adhered. He constantly subjected his own writing to the severest scrutiny, changing even some of his most basic assumptions and beliefs when he felt they were no longer valid. The different Rilkes in the complex series that constitute this man and his poetic personality often look back and incorporate their predecessors: very often his poetry is about itself, its origins and its development—it is thus 'poetological' poetry. Like all writers of any significance, Rilke changed as he developed, and although his creative growth was not simple or naively linear, it is none the less possible to think of it in a number of identifiable stages or periods whose transitions (whilst by no means abruptly separating styles) were usually marked by crises, turning-points, moments of inspiration, breakthrough, or release.

Watersheds were sometimes also marked by journeys or changes of place and dwelling—from Germany to Paris in late August 1902, for example, a long visit to Egypt in 1911, and his discovery of the

Château de Muzot in Switzerland late in 1921. After his childhood in Prague, which was disrupted by his parents' divorce and extended, unhappy periods boarding in military academies, this modest house near Raron in the Canton of the Valais was the nearest thing that Rilke ever had to a permanent home. In his constant physical and geographical displacement, and in his need to rely on the material support of wealthy or aristocratic patrons who often housed him for months on end, Rilke manifested a particularly acute form of the cultural malaise of rootlessness, restlessness, and unease that dominated the late nineteenth and early twentieth centuries in Europe. Friedrich Nietzsche's announcement of the 'death of God'[1] expressed in lapidary form the loss of faith in a divinely sponsored universe experienced by a whole generation, and reflected a broad crisis of moral and cultural values. The First World War was the most obvious and the most catastrophic form of a deep-rooted upheaval and turbulence, delivering a hammer-blow to already crumbling social structures and exacerbating the individual's disjunction from any traditional sense of community and collective. Whilst the war also saw the deployment of some of the most violent products of mechanization and industrialization, science had long before initiated a more rationalistic, teleological view of the world, and many felt that its rapid development was demystifying the processes of nature, sidelining the numinous, and subordinating intrinsic value to purpose and function. Years of crisis they may have been, but the first two decades of the twentieth century gave rise to a remarkable concentration of cultural masterpieces none the less. The single year 1922 in which Rilke's *Duino Elegies* and *Sonnets to Orpheus* were finished saw the completion or publication of T. S. Eliot's *The Waste Land*, James Joyce's *Ulysses*, Virginia Woolf's *Jacob's Room*, Franz Kafka's *The Castle*, Paul Valéry's *Charmes*, T. E. Lawrence's *The Seven Pillars of Wisdom*, the bilingual edition of Ludwig Wittgenstein's *Tractatus Logico-Philosophicus*, and Friedrich Murnau's *Nosferatu*.

It is in this historical and cultural climate that Rilke's poetry developed, and this brief introduction will trace that development using a broadly accepted modern taxonomy that divides his work into four phases. The poetry (and some short prose works and dramas)

---

[1] First in *Die fröhliche Wissenschaft* (*The Gay Science*, 1882) and later in *Also sprach Zarathustra* (*Thus Spake Zarathustra*, written 1883–5).

written between *Lives and Songs* (1894)[2] and the first version of *The Book of Images* (1902) is seen as his 'early work'. The *New Poems* (1907 and 1908) and the novel *The Notebooks of Malte Laurids Brigge* (1910) are the work of a 'middle period'. The *Life of the Virgin Mary* (1913) and the *Duino Elegies* (1923) form the major achievements of a 'late period' in which relatively little was brought to completion. Finally, *The Sonnets to Orpheus* (1923) and four collections of poetry in French are designated 'last works'. Each period also naturally includes some important individual poems not published by Rilke in collections or cycles.

This is a useful paradigm not least because it makes apparent continuities that might otherwise remain hidden. The 'middle' period, for example, includes a number of important texts—like *The Book of Hours* (1905), *The Book of Images* (1906), and the drama *The White Princess* (1904)—that are revisions of works conceived and sometimes already published in the early years. The 'late' *Elegies* were completed in a short burst of activity in February 1922 in the middle of the month in which the *Sonnets* ('last' works) were being composed—so whilst they are chronologically virtually simultaneous, poetically they point in quite different directions: the editors of the *Kommentierte Ausgabe* (annotated edition) of Rilke's works are rightly at pains both in the structural divisions of the volumes and in their explanatory notes to indicate how much more in common the *Sonnets* have with the poetry written at the very end of Rilke's life than with the aesthetic represented by the *Elegies*, which bring to a close a project rooted in the early years of the second decade of the century.

The present edition provides as full and as representative a selection of Rilke's verse from all these periods as space permits. Rilke was tremendously prolific—in the modern standard edition in German the poetry fills almost a thousand (monolingual) pages, and even this does not include all the early work—so for the purposes of this introduction and survey the selectiveness has necessarily had to be somewhat fierce. Nevertheless, the *Duino Elegies* and *The Sonnets to Orpheus* are complete here, and a significant number of the most important 'uncollected poems' are included, some translated for the first time. Whilst the selection is inevitably based to an extent

---

[2] The dates given in parentheses in this Introduction are the dates of publication, not those of the genesis or completion of a work.

on personal preference (especially in the choice of the *New Poems*), it
is also reflective of an assessment of what is essential or indispensable
to convey both Rilke's poetic achievements and his development as a
writer from precocious youth to an astonishing maturity.

To this end also, the Introduction and the Notes make frequent
quotation from Rilke's letters. Over almost thirty-five years he cor-
responded with nearly five hundred people—fellow writers, family,
and lovers, as well as friends, mentors, and acquaintances from the
highest echelons of the European aristocracy to teenage children and
domestic staff. The total number of his letters has been estimated at
more than 17,000—which almost matches the near-legendary out-
put of Voltaire, who lived twenty years longer than Rilke. All Rilke's
letters are about himself, intimately, even when they are also about
someone else, a place, or an object, for they all respond openly to the
world as a source of insight into the self. These letters deserve to be
treated as coeval with the more conventionally literary works, partly
because of their craftedness and beauty, but chiefly because they
reflect upon, clarify, and extend many of the themes and images of
the poetry and prose. The boundaries between different forms of
writing were certainly fluid for Rilke, and some collections—such as
the *Letters to a Young Poet* (ten letters to Franz Xaver Kappus giving
advice on love, life, and poetry) and the fifteen *Letters on Cézanne*—are
virtually regarded as creative works in their own right.

Rilke was a tremendously productive poet in his earliest years,
although a relatively small proportion of this work is now read widely.
He was himself somewhat ambivalent about its qualities, sometimes
nostalgic for its popularity but usually vehemently dismissive of
what he called 'rehearsals' ('Proben') for poethood.[3] Between 1894
and 1899 he produced more than a book a year. Romantically, even
sentimentally, they bear traces of his early reading—indeed in *Lives
and Songs* (1894) they are sometimes so obviously derivative of the
canonical works of nineteenth-century German poetry that no real
Rilkean voice is discernible. However, the best of them develop
a more individual style and represent a conscientious apprenticeship
in the technicalities of a variety of stanza forms, metrical schemes,
and the possibilities of rhyme; there are even early hints at Rilke's

---

[3] Letter to Robert Heinz Heygrodt of 24 December 1921 (*B* II, 196).

fondness for cyclic composition. Most of the poems in *Offerings to the Lares* (1895) are transfigurations of the monuments and topographical features of Rilke's native city of Prague and the Bohemian countryside surrounding it, or are about local artists and historical figures. The 'lares' are Roman gods of house and hearth, and the collection as a whole is shot through by an affection for 'Heimat' ('home' or 'homeland') that even at this early stage Rilke feels is under threat from the modern world.[4]

*Advent* (1897) is dedicated to 'my dear father under the Christmas tree' and contains many other personal dedications to poets, friends, and benefactors, including Hugo von Hofmannsthal and Peter Altenberg from Vienna, the Belgian Symbolist dramatist Maurice Maeterlinck, and the Danish poet and novelist Jens Peter Jacobsen. Its affinities with the contemporary artistic movement known as *Jugendstil* in German (art nouveau elsewhere in Europe) are most obvious in the fondness for surface and plane in the way the outside world is depicted (giving it a somewhat two-dimensional character) and in the choice of motifs, particularly in the first part ('Gifts'), where the inspiration from local topography that was discernible in earlier volumes gives way to stylized parks, pools, and castles populated by peacocks and swans in a world reflecting a mysterious and largely absent poetic self.

The shift from a longing for a dream-world towards a focus on that self is evident in the very title of Rilke's next published volume, *In Celebration of Myself* (1899)—two other volumes, the cycle *Christ: Eleven Visions* and *In Celebration of You*, remained unpublished in his lifetime. In the case of the latter, suppression was at the request of its dedicatee, Lou Andreas-Salomé, with whom Rilke had begun a four-year sexual, emotional, and intellectual relationship in 1897 that he later described as his 'second birth'.[5] This marked a watershed in many respects—he changed his name from René to Rainer, for example, and even altered his handwriting style. Inspired in part by Nietzsche's affirmation of life, despite its dangers and threats, *In Celebration of Myself* does not abandon the motivic and aesthetic repertoire of decadence and *Jugendstil* but depicts the self as on

---

[4] The 'Lares' remain important to Rilke throughout his life; cf. the letter to Hulewicz quoted below (pp. xxv–xxvi).

[5] Rilke and Lou Andreas-Salomé, *Briefwechsel*, ed. Ernst Pfeiffer (Frankfurt am Main, 1975), 243.

the threshold of a breakthrough to 'life' in its true fullness, and the collection as a whole is marked by a mixture of promise and frustration. It also introduces a powerful series of figures and images that will be developed over many years: the angel, girls, the Virgin Mary, the night, and God.

God, the Virgin Mary, and angels are perhaps surprising themes for a poet who was not a Christian (despite being received popularly as a religious writer for most of his life) and who was usually at least sceptical of, often overtly hostile to, aspects of Christian doctrine, worship, and morality. The very notion of a transcendent deity is alien to Rilke, whose debt to Nietzsche's discrediting of the traditional Christian God is evident in many of his early diary notes, as is his substitution of art for God: 'Religion is the art of those who create nothing', he wrote: 'They become productive in prayer: they give form to their love, their thanks and their longing, and thereby free themselves. . . . The non-artist must have a religion (in the deepest sense of that word), even if it is only one that rests on a common historical consensus. Being an atheist in his eyes is the same as being a barbarian.'[6] The highest form of productivity for Rilke is that of the artist, although the artist is seen not as an ivory-tower-dwelling aesthete hostile to the forces of life but as the highest potentiation of that life. Christ has been described as the symbol of Rilke's unanswered prayers in childhood, 'the interloper and intruder who denied life and mortal love and stood between himself and his mother',[7] who had sent him to a Catholic school in Prague before he was 7. The Christ of this collection, too, preaches not the God of the Jews and Christians but a new God of the here-and-now. Christ cannot himself create this God, he can only encourage the children to remember their innocence and openness and create him out of themselves.

In Rilke's next collection, *The Book of Hours*, these figures are supplemented by a Russian monastic icon painter—the speaking voice of the three cycles that this volume contains—and by St Francis of Assisi. A book of hours is a devotional book, a small breviary containing prayers, biblical texts, and psalms for the devout to use at certain times of the day in ways echoing the more rigorous schedule

---

[6] Rilke, *Tagebücher aus der Frühzeit*, ed. Ruth Sieber-Rilke and Carl Sieber; re-edited by Ernst Zinn (Frankfurt am Main, 1973). Quoted in *KA* I, 737.

[7] Siegfried Mandel, 'Introduction' to Rilke, *Visions of Christ: A Posthumous Cycle of Poems*, trans. Aaron Kramer (Boulder, Colo., 1967), 16.

of the monk—and the first version of Rilke's *Book of Hours* gestured towards this by embedding his poems in a brief contextual commentary. But despite appearances, Rilke's God here is not the God of Christianity; he replaces transcendence with inwardness and immanence, the notion of a supreme *being* with that of a force *becoming*, seeing God as an expression of a Nietzschean elemental power suffusing the whole of life, not intrinsically meriting but often dependent upon the faith of the believer for his own very existence. There are points, too, at which the object of Rilke's/the monk's devotion is not God but Lou Andreas-Salomé. Rilke's God undergoes many changes and developments as his poetics progress: the journey that he took to Egypt in the first three months of 1911 was important not only for the rich fund of imagery it bequeathed to his poetry from the *Elegies* on, but because Egyptian culture demonstrated what seemed to him a much healthier attitude to death, seen not in a rigidly antithetical relationship with life as it is in Christianity but as a continuation of it. The Orpheus of the *Sonnets* is in many ways also a myth specifically replacing the redemptive role of Christ. When Rilke writes 'O you great god who are lost to us! Infinite trace!' (*Sonnets*, I. XXVI), the dissolution of Orpheus is a pantheistic substitute for the personal incarnation that Christ represents.

Christianity may not have been palatable to Rilke, but its art and architecture was frequently inspirational, as the first collection of Rilke's 'middle' and more mature period testifies. He outlined the focus of the *New Poems* in 1907 thus:

I am not proceeding from 'great things and thoughts' outwards but instead inwards towards the very place where everything, even inconspicuous or ugly things, even the things from which we would otherwise simply turn away, appeal to me like matters of great and eternal significance and make indescribable demands upon me. This is the place where the artist, whose nature is to be an observer in many areas of life, can in this capacity experience the *whole* of life, that is to say, the whole world for and of itself, as if it were running through the middle of him with all its manifold possibilities. For me Paris has been . . . an immeasurable education because it has held up to my gaze and my senses the remotest and most extreme circumstances of spiritual experience, ones that cannot be verified any longer, condensed to the point of being incomparably seeable (seeable even from afar).[8]

---

[8] Letter to Karl von der Heydt, 21 February 1907 (*B* 1, 241).

These poems are often seen as belonging to the German tradition of 'Dinggedichte' ('thing-poems') that flowered in the hands of nineteenth-century poets such as Eduard Mörike and Conrad Ferdinand Meyer, and it is true that Rilke's poems do treat a wide variety of objects. Often these are works of art or architecture—Far Eastern or classical Greek and Roman statues, friezes, a lute, a coat of arms, a reliquary, medieval cathedrals, paintings, steps, a balcony, squares, towers, and fountains—but they include also more everyday things such as a ball, an orange, lace, a bed, a merry-go-round, or a bowl of roses. Some are about living things, animals and birds—the famous panther, a gazelle, a swan, a dog—and plants such as the blue and the pink hydrangea. Others are about things in an even more extended sense, about places and times—landscapes, parks, and graves, Venice in the autumn, the countryside around Rome, a dance—or events from history, myth, or personal experience or report (from the Last Count of Brederode avoiding capture by the Turks, or the Day of Judgement, to the death of a lover). Many take people as their subject, real observed contemporaries (such as a group of acrobats or a blind man), and historical, biblical, or mythical figures (Adam and Eve, a courtesan, prophets, the Sibyl of Cumae, sometimes mediated via a work of art), and there are figures, too, whose individuality is less important than their situation (a convalescent, a poet, a lonely man, a lover, a child, an alchemist).

Readers will ask what these things are for or what they represent, and the answers are complex because this is what is 'new' about the *New Poems*. A minority can be read as symbolic in a relatively narrow sense—'The Swan', for example, is 'about' or is 'an image of' the awkwardness of life contrasted with the naturalness of death. But even here it would be inappropriate to speak in terms of a metaphor's traditional 'vehicle' (swan) and 'tenor' (life/death/dying), since the poem is just as much 'about' the swan itself, which is illuminated by the explicit existential comparisons being made. Most of these poems resist paraphrase in this way, however, not suggesting a meaning or significance external to the object or person but instead conveying intensely *what* their subjects are, *how* they are these things, and an *experience* in the reader of seeing them. Rarely are the 'things' of these poems static; they enact movement, processes, growth, observation. In this way a poem such as 'The Merry-go-round' enacts rather than describes both an experience *from* childhood and the experience *of* childhood.

Behind the *New Poems* lies a preoccupation with 'Anschauen' ('looking' or 'gazing') that Rilke articulated in a famous letter to his wife:

Gazing is such a wonderful thing, and one we know so little about. In gazing we are completely turned outwards, but at the very moment when we are most outward-turned things appear to happen within us that have waited longingly until they are unobserved, and whilst these things happen within us, without us, perfectly and strangely anonymously— their significance grows in the object outside, a convincing, strong name, their only possible name, in which we blissfully and reverently recognize what is happening within us without ourselves reaching out for it, com- prehending it only very gently, from some distance, under the sign of a thing that just now was alien to us and in the next moment will be alienated again.[9]

Rilke's *New Poems* enact this subtle mutual process. They are about the relationship between 'objects' and their perceiving subjects, a relationship that releases the inner dynamics of both. As the passage above makes clear, they presuppose that in the modern world, when 'things' (canonically exemplified by the panther) are 'alien', there is an urgent need for action to release such vitality; it is the task of the poet to do so and to capture it in poetry that will preserve it in a form of suspended animation, maintaining the dynamic without freezing or neutralizing the inner energies of the things perceived.

Rilke's is not a neo-romantic conception of the poet as magician, since the imperative derives from the things observed—it is the archaic Torso of Apollo that issues the command to change our lives, and it is the absence of its eyes that reminds and challenges us to re-perceive the world. And the poetry of the *New Poems* is not inspired outpouring but careful craft, the product of conscious 'sculpting' of inner reality into outer form as befits an aesthetic partly inspired by Rilke's close cooperation with Auguste Rodin. Rilke learned much about art from Rodin, ethically ('toujours travailler'—'never stop working'), conceptually (the idea that the aesthetic object intensifies and exceeds the objects of the natural world), and pragmatically (how best to look at and read inner realities from outer surfaces). Above all he learned of the tension between the stillness that appears to characterize a finished work of art and the vitality that it expresses

---

[9] Letter to Clara Westhoff, 8 March 1907 (*B* 1, 247).

and incarnates: 'Even the stones of ancient cultures were not calm.
Enclosed within the hieratically restrained gestures of ancient cul-
tic worship was the turmoil of living surfaces, like water held in the
walls of a container. There were currents flowing in the impassive
gods that were seated, and in those standing up was a gesture like
a fountain rising out of the stone and falling back into it again, filling
it with wave upon wave.'[10] The motif of the rise and fall of the foun-
tain persists in Rilke's own work until the end of his life, reflecting
both movement and artistic self-sufficiency, a combination of dyna-
mism with cyclic enclosure that in Rilke's hands is always reciprocal,
never contradictory.

Whilst crucial to his own development, Rilke's response to
Rodin was neither uncritical nor itself static and he gradually came
to see Rodin's art as too deliberately symbolic and too dependent on
independently existing thoughts and concepts for him. His expo-
sure to the work of Paul Cézanne over a fortnight in October 1907
(Rilke visited the memorial exhibition at the Salon d'Autumne in Paris
almost every day) confirmed his preference for things depicted with-
out preconceived messages or intentional significance. Visiting the
exhibition with Mathilde Vollmoeller, a German-born artist living
in Paris, he was astonished to hear her say of Cézanne that 'he sat in
front of things like a dog, just looking, without tension or ulterior
motive of any kind' (*KA* IV, 614). What he says of Cézanne's paint-
ing applies to his own poetry: 'It is natural, of course, to love all the
things you make, but if you show this, you make it less well; you *judge*
rather than *say* it. You stop being impartial, and what is best about
it, the love, remains outside your work, does not enter into it, stays
un-transformed alongside. That is how atmospheric painting arose
(which is no better than naturalist art): people painted "I love this
thing" instead of painting "here the thing is"' (*KA* IV, 616).

Despite a preoccupation with things, the *New Poems* are not
neutral or objective as has sometimes been claimed, although they are
not subjective (in the sense of sentimental) and they avoid the so-called
'lyrisches Ich' (personal narrative voice). Formally they embody
a variety of possibilities, from the 'Rollengedicht' (literally 'role-poem',
as if spoken by a dramatic character) and the dramatic monologue
to the sonnet, of which there are many. This last is a form usually

---

[10] *KA* IV, 417 (from Rilke's monograph on Rodin).

associated with the poetry of thought rather than that of objects, but in Rilke's hands it is transformed, rendered supple and fluid, its traditional stanza structures, rhyme schemes, and metrical conventions boldly varied and developed.

The other major work of Rilke's middle period, his 'novel' *Malte Laurids Brigge*, is formally and structurally even more adventurous. It begins by appearing to imitate the form of a diary, but very quickly abandons the expectations of linear chronological progression that that genre creates; the fragmentation of the structure is a deliberate reflection both of the disruption to the structures of perception by urban experience and of the vulnerability that results from childhood trauma that the novel explores. Malte is an insect without a carapace, 'like a beetle that has been trodden on, you are squeezed out of yourself' (*KA* III, 507). There is little that one might call a discursive 'plot', although there is an evocative 'narrative' provided by the presentation of the processes of experience in Paris and in Malte's past in Denmark. Malte, too, learns to 'see', even if his 'sight' is predicated on a negative aesthetic of the foul and the broken rather than that of beauty. He is likened to one 'who hears a glorious language and with feverish intensity undertakes the task of writing in it. But he had yet to face the consternation at learning how difficult this language is; at first he did not want to believe that a long life could be spent forming the first, short, bogus sentences that had no meaning' (*KA* III, 633).

The enormity of the existential and aesthetic task that Malte finds himself faced with at the end of the *Notebooks* pre-empts the extended period of crisis that Rilke entered after the publication of these and the *New Poems*. Difficulties with personal relationships proliferated—he had affairs with Marthe Hennebert, Magda von Hattingberg (known as 'Benvenuta', 'The Welcome One'), Lou Albert-Lasard, and Baladine Klossowska ('Merline'), all of which he began with high expectations that were then disappointed. Love and an intimate connection to another human being were almost a *sine qua non* for Rilke, the conditions under which intensity of experience and self-awareness flourished and for a time gave energy for poetic creation; at the same time, however, they also drained him of that energy and, by involving him in the responsibilities and entanglements of personal life, inhibited his sense of self ('life' turned into 'fate') and interfered with writing. The First World War and the revolutions in Germany that followed, which Rilke saw as the worst of the intrusions of mechanized, capitalist society into truly meaningful life, contributed to his depression. He was himself called up and after a miserable period of basic training served out his time in a military archive in Vienna. This of course did nothing to appease the demons that an adolescence spent in military academies had stirred up.

It is not surprising that Rilke struggled with his work after *Malte*: he wrote to Lotte Hepner that the novel had been about one big thing, which was 'how is it possible to live if the elements of our lives are so completely beyond our comprehension? If we are continually inadequate in love, insecure in our decisions, and incapacitated in the face of death, how is it possible to exist?'[11] The early work on the *Duino Elegies*, begun in a moment of inspiration during a visit to one of the castles owned by Princess Marie von Thurn und Taxis and her husband in the winter of 1912, was itself a source of tension: Rilke was aware of having seized upon important ideas and images that he was at that point unable to think through and bring to completion. It was a powerful inhibitor to other work—a project in 1916 to bring together a sequence of works written a few years earlier and to be entitled *Poems to the Night* remained incomplete, for example: despite also being linked closely with the material of the *Elegies*, this did not trigger the completion of the larger project either. Instead Rilke translated—Michelangelo, Louize Labé, Mallarmé—and wrote a large number of free-standing poems. In many of these he developed a more expansive concept of space (in contrast to the focused, centred, even 'centripetal' conception implied by the *New Poems*), moving away from the idea of shaping or outlining an object towards one in which experiences were conceived spatially as unbounded and unenclosed. It is at this time that Rilke develops the concept of 'Weltinnenraum' (literally 'world-within-space') in which human consciousness seems to meld with the world of objects, things, and landscapes that is by definition without subjective consciousness (see the poem 'Almost all things beckon us to feeling', p. 117).

The poem 'Turning' is perhaps the one that most clearly expresses the crucial change of vision that Rilke underwent during the crisis years. It sets the work of seeing against that of the heart, acknowledging the power of the aesthetic that underpinned the *New Poems* and the achievements of that period but stating clearly that 'gazing . . .

[11] Letter to Lotte Hepner, 8 November 1915 (*B* 1, 599).

has a limit', for the world so looked upon thirsts for the activeness of love as well as the receptivity of an open gaze. 'Work of seeing is done, | now do heart-work | on the images in you' is the injunction of the final stanza; that which has been 'won' (a reference perhaps to the ethic of work and craft Rilke inherited from Rodin) has not yet been loved, and that is the next step. 'Turning' shows incidentally how much common ground there was between Rilke and the Expressionist generation of writers, who were at much the same time proposing a shift from an essentially passive impressionistic world-view ('seeing') to a visionary and dynamically *ex*pressive one ('looking'), as articulated for example in Kasimir Edschmid's 1917 manifesto (*On Expressionism in Literature and on the New Writing*). Lou Andreas-Salomé (to whom Rilke sent the poem as soon as it was completed) subjected it to a psychoanalytical interpretation: she doubted that the turn—real though it certainly seemed to be—was as sudden as it was portrayed there because Rilke's own body, his eyes in particular, had been betraying it for some time: they had become painfully congested because of an increase in the internal pressure of the blood towards them as if the body wished to make them into sexual organs. Psychologically plausible or not, the reading articulates the very real sense of blockage and longing for release that beset Rilke during these years.

The sense of alienation and crisis that Rilke experienced was by no means unique. In the early 1900s, his compatriot Hugo von Hofmannsthal went through a personal 'Chandos crisis', the evaporation of his confidence in the capacity of language to shape and express experience and of the integrity of the self that can be said to be experiencing in the first place. Paul Valéry's so-called 'nuit de Gênes' of October 1892 resulted in his abandoning poetry until 1917. Rilke's alienation was far-reaching, and his sense of responsibility urgent. A well-known letter to his Polish translator Witold Hulewicz confirms how much he felt the world was at risk:

For our grandparents a 'house', a 'well', a familiar tower, even their own clothing, a coat, was still infinitely more, infinitely more intimate; almost every object was a vessel in which they found humanity already present and to which they added a store of humanity ['Menschliches hinzusparten']. Nowadays there are things forcing their way over from America, empty, insensible things, fake things, *substitute lives* . . . A house, in the way it is understood in America, an American apple or a vine from over there has nothing in common with the house, the fruit, the grape into which the hopes and reflectiveness of our forefathers had made their way. . . . The vitalized, directly experienced things that *share knowledge with us* are in decline and cannot be replaced any more. *We are perhaps the last ones to have known such things.* It is upon us that the responsibility falls not only to retain their memory . . . but their human and 'laric' value ('laric' in the sense of the house-deities).[12]

Another letter, written in 1915 about his experience of the area around Toledo in Spain, shows how deeply Rilke felt then that he needed support in this task:

The Spanish landscape . . . has driven my constitution to its extreme in that there external things themselves—tower, mountain, bridge— possessed simultaneously the undreamed-of, unsurpassable intensity of their inner equivalents through which one might have depicted them. External appearance and inner vision everywhere came together in the object, in each one of them a whole interior world was made apparent, as if an angel encompassing the space were blind and were looking inwardly into itself. This world, no longer seen by men but within the angel, is perhaps the object of my true mission.[13]

This angel, the angel of the *Duino Elegies*, is one of the most powerful poetic figures of the twentieth century, terrifying yet noble, unap- proachable yet magnetically attractive, a guarantor of the fact that 'a higher level of reality is recognizable in the realm of the invisible'.[14] In the angel and the other unique figures that populate these ten com- plex poems—including the allegorical *dramatis personae* of the jour- ney through the Land of Suffering in the tenth—Rilke achieves that rarest of things, the creation of a modern myth. There are grounds for fear, as Rilke explains in a letter about both the *Elegies* and the *Sonnets to Orpheus*:

Formidableness has shocked and horrified mankind: but where is there anything sweet and marvellous that on occasion does not wear this mask, that of the formidable? Life itself . . . is it not formidable? . . . Anyone who has not acknowledged the fearsomeness of life on occasion, even acclaimed it, will never fully take possession of the ineffable authorities of our exist- ence, he will pass by on the verges, and when judgement is made one day

[12] Letter to Witold Hulewicz, 13 November 1925 (*B* II, 376–7).
[13] Letter to Ellen Delp, 27 October 1915 (Rilke, *Briefe aus den Jahren 1914 bis 1921*, ed. Ruth Sieber-Rilke and Carl Sieber (Leipzig, 1937), 80).
[14] Letter to Hulewicz, 13 November 1925 (*B* II, 378).

will be neither alive nor dead. To demonstrate how formidableness and blessedness are identical . . .: that is the core meaning and conception of my two books.[15]

Rilke aims in the *Elegies* to give a full account of the human condition and mythopoeically to identify a means of addressing the problems of existence in the modern world that will give us grounds for a degree of confidence and optimism. The poems are elegies—laments, poems of regret for loss—but they are also hymns. They are a lament for the condition of the modern consciousness, for the state of alienation in which man now finds himself, and for his banishment from a potential wholeness or completeness or unity. But they also celebrate man's capacity, via poetry, to preserve the external by transforming it inwardly.

There is a second sense in which the *Duino Elegies* are elegiac, for they contain echoes of the classical verse-form known as the elegiac distich (pairs of lines consisting of a hexameter followed by a pentameter), in which dactylic feet were prominent. Lines 5 and 6 of the first *Elegy* constitute just such a pair, and there are others in seven of the ten poems. The *Elegies* as a whole are obviously not written consistently in this form (the fourth and the eighth, for example, are written largely in iambic pentameters, blank verse), but most have what Theodore Ziolkowski calls 'dactylic parlando' (where the musical term indicates 'speaking', as if in fluent speech rhythms), and the elegiac distich hovers suggestively behind the varied verse-forms of the *Elegies*.[16] This is more than a mere parlour-game that Rilke plays with the reader: behind his *Elegies* the ghost of the perfect form constantly reminds us of the tendency of the modern world, the modern poetic aesthetic, to fragment, to fail to complete, to hint at perfection, or at an ideal, rather than achieve it. The falling away from the traditional form is quite deliberate and it reflects the subject-matter of the *Elegies* very precisely.

The *Elegies* present two categories of creature that allow Rilke to demonstrate alternatives to the human condition—the angel and animals—but also a number of figures who occupy a transitional state between that of corrupted humanity and the ideally non-human:

[15] Letter to Margot, Countess Sizzo, 12 April 1923 (*B* II, 296).

[16] Theodore Ziolkowski, 'The Fragmented Text: The Classics and Postwar European Literature', *International Journal of the Classical Tradition*, 6.4 (2000), 549–62 (p. 560).

lovers, children, the young dead, and heroes. Animals exist in a condition of openness, where their access to the world, their ability to *see* in the world of the visible, is not impeded by consciousness. Angels are the opposite, 'super-conscious' beings, creatures of pure consciousness, 'spaces of being' (*DE* II, 14), who exist entirely within the realm of the invisible—itself a 'space', to be thought of not as the infinite extensiveness of the cosmos but as the intangible but clearly discernible dimension that we can see, for example, 'on the other side' of a mirror—and which is explored in one of *The Sonnets to Orpheus* (p. 213). The tragedy of mankind consists in being condemned to remain on this side of such a mirror. The dignity of mankind, however, lies in our capacity to perceive that this dimension does exist and, as the *Elegies* progress, they counsel a resolution not to try to attain it but to celebrate and transform the world we do inhabit, imbue the visible with significance so that it is no longer felt to be such a poor relation of the invisible.

Mankind is alienated from the world because of his reflexive consciousness, the irremediable division of subject from object—which is a cognitive version of the biblical Fall of Man. The poetic 'I' reappears in the very first line after its banishment from the *New Poems*, marking the obtrusive presence of consciousness. However, there are certain conditions under which this does not apply. Children, for example, enjoy in Rilke's poetics an almost mythic, pre-lapsarian innocence; in play they inhabit imaginary worlds (*DE* IV, 73). Those who die young make the transition from childhood directly into death virtually without passing through the corrupting stage of adult awareness of the imminence of decline and death. Lovers, too, enjoy a form of suspension from the subject/object division provided that their love is not 'transitive' (that is to say provided that they say 'I love' and not 'I love you'): the first *Elegy* celebrates Gaspara Stampa, a sixteenth-century Venetian poet whose love was unrequited, but throughout his life Rilke admired others in similar situations, such as Bettina von Arnim (whose passion for Goethe was not reciprocated) and the Portuguese nun Mariana Alcoforado who was deserted by her seducer. These lovers are, not coincidentally, all women; the third *Elegy* evokes the disruptive power of male sexuality. It is not coincidental either that they are all writers—either of poetry or of letters—and thus capable of perpetuating their heightened 'intransitive' condition for posterity.

These examples of alternative and transitional consciousness are evoked and explored in the first four *Elegies*. The last poem to be written, placed fifth in the cycle, marks a low point in the mental and emotional search that the poet is enacting, and laments the situation of the rest of mankind via the image of a group of street-tumblers based on a real family that Rilke had seen in Paris and on a very different and more troubling representation of such a troupe in Pablo Picasso's painting of that name made in 1905. Their performance is destined to flip over from inadequacy to empty facility without ever lingering on the ineffable point at which true artistry is achieved, skill imbued with effort and meaning. Rilke invokes the angel again to imagine a place 'which we do not know of'—in the sphere of the invisible, then—where lovers might demonstrate an act of 'Können' ('being able to', *DE* V, 97), but it is a hypothesis rather than a memory. The hero who forms the subject of the sixth *Elegy* is real but rare, a unique example of an imitable state of freedom from the confines of consciousness in an adult male; courage and the compulsion to act bypass reflection, and the inevitable early death preserves this condition from the inimical effects of a continued existence where such intensity could not be sustained. He is compared with the fig-tree, which appears to fruit without bothering to indulge in the self-aggrandizement of blossoming.

The structure of the cycle so far has created a situation in which possibilities have been examined for the fulfilment of the hope incarnated in the putative cry of mankind to the angel that opens the *Elegies* but, with its nadir in the fifth and only a glimpse in the sixth, this hope is unrealized. The seventh opens with the realization that the ambition to resemble the angel is wrong-headed: the cry of the first is echoed as that of a bird who sings not in order to ask for something ('wooing', *DE* VII, 1) but as a spontaneous act of self-fulfilment. There is an excitement in this poem accompanying the realization that inhabiting our own world is enough for us, provided that we transform it and make it internal. The angel is still present here, but Rilke is jubilantly confident that we do not need to emulate him; showing him what is ours is enough—at this point he still needs the gaze of the angel to 'save' the things of the world for posterity, but its function is itself metamorphosing as the act of showing to the angel is understood as that of poetic creativity.

With some psychological plausibility Rilke records in the next

poem a dramatically retarding moment of doubt, a resurgence of
the conviction that man's self-consciousness precludes his self-
fulfilment. But as the near-triumphant 'major key' of the seventh
is modulated suddenly into a plangent minor in the eighth, it is
followed by another uplifting as the ninth *Elegy* refines the insights
of the seventh and focuses on the very transitoriness of human life as
the fit object of man's (poetically) restorative activity. Its injunction
is to transform the visible into the invisible by *saying*, an idea that is
reinforced in a volley of reformulations: 'Here is the time of the say-
able', 'speak and bear witness', 'praise *this* world . . . to the angel',
'show him that which is simple', 'Tell him Things'. What is often
not noticed about this *Elegy* and the task it celebrates is that, even
though the poet refers to the angel only in the third person (whilst
addressing the earth in the second person at the end), the salvation
of the here-and-now and its reinvigoration with significance has not
yet been fully emancipated from the supervision of the angel ('preise
*dem Engel* die Welt' is the injunction), The purely intransitive act of
praising will not emerge until the *Sonnets*.

The most intractable division that affects our lives is that between
life and death, and the final *Elegy* shows us the crossing of that bor-
der. The poet takes us on an allegorical journey out of 'Mourning's
capital' through the landscape of lament, past the experiences of the
living (love, pain, and mourning), past erstwhile cultural achieve-
ments, into a place 'out that way' to see 'trees-of-tears' and 'flower-
ing melancholia fields' and into the 'peaks of Original Grief'. Rilke
insisted to Hulewicz that this landscape was '*not to be equated with
Egypt*', but was 'in a manner of speaking a reflection of the lands of
the Nile in the desert–clarity of the consciousness of the dead' (*B* II,
377), which Rilke wishes us to see not as the negation of life but as
one component of an indissoluble pair with it.

The angel fades away in the last of the *Elegies*, and in the other
cycle that emerged in February 1922, he is replaced entirely by a
quite different figure, Orpheus. A representative of transcendence
(albeit not transcendence in a traditionally religious sense) is suc-
ceeded by one of mediation; a being beyond our time and space has
no place in *The Sonnets to Orpheus*, whose presiding deity—and he is
a deity for Rilke, not the demi–god or even the mortal that most of the
ancients saw him as—is anchored to the earth addressed so intimately
at the end of the ninth *Elegy*. Even the grandiose poetic form of the

elegy that Rilke derived partly from previous German poets such as Friedrich Hölderlin or Friedrich Klopstock is replaced by the altogether tighter scheme of the sonnet whose origins lie in French and Italian literature and whose very right to exist in German was hotly debated in the early nineteenth century. And he restores to the sonnet form its traditional function of guidance and teaching (which the many sonnets in the *New Poems* had consciously moved away from), albeit with no less formal flexibility than in the period between 1903 and 1907. And yet the two works, as Rilke wrote to Hulewicz, are intimately related: 'the *Elegies* and the *Sonnets* are permanently supportive of one another—, and I regard it as an infinite boon that I was able to fill both these sails with the same breath: the little rust-coloured sail of the *Sonnets* and the *Elegies'* huge white sail-canvas' (*B* II, 378).

Just before Rilke began writing the *Sonnets* he composed a number of poems that probed the themes and poetics of what would become the new cycle whilst overtly turning away from those of the *Elegies*. They include one written on 1 February 1922 that begins 'When will, when will, when will lament and saying suffice?' (*KA* II, 276). Here the cry to the angel is definitively rejected as a mode either of communication or (which is the same thing) self-realization: 'Because the stars seem silent to us in the screamed-at ether, the most distant, the old and the oldest ancestors spoke to us! And we: we heard at last! The first hearing people.' The first of the *Sonnets* picks up the motif of listening and hearing, which is carried through explicitly in another eight poems in the two parts.

If the *Elegies* moved tentatively towards affirmation before grasping it enthusiastically, the *Sonnets* are wholly devoted to it. Praise and song are its existential modes—'singing is being', 'Breathing, you invisible poem!'—and it would not be an exaggeration to say that the whole sequence is an exploration of the ontology of poetry. And in contrast to the *Elegies'* aspirations to timelessness, an acceptance of the temporal and the fleeting is a precondition for the Orphic existence of the *Sonnets*. Rilke writes of an ideal Orphic world in which there is no difference in kind between inner and outer, visible and invisible, singing and silence, holding and loosing—ultimately between life and death, which are the components of what the cycle calls a 'double-realm'. *Sonnet* 2. XIII issues the injunction 'Be—and know also non-being'. Whilst this is part of the modern myth that

Rilke constructs, it is, of course, an important component of the
classical myth that he uses as a starting-point, both in the descent
of Orpheus into, and his re-emergence from, the underworld and in
Orpheus' own brutal death at the hands of the Maenads which he
overcomes as his head continues to sing after being severed from his
body.

Rilke saw these sonnets as more direct and plain than his previ-
ous work—'I think that there is no poem in *The Sonnets to Orpheus*',
he wrote to a friend, 'that means something other than what is com-
pletely articulated in it, although often under its most secret names.
Everything in the nature of an "allusion" to my mind contradicts the
indescribable *there-being* ["Dasein", or "existence"] of the poem.'[17]
And yet they cannot be described as an easy read. Many evoke
absence, emptiness, and silence, and the burden of meaning is trans-
ferred to the linguistic structures and patterns that are described
rather than being conveyed by clear semantic 'content'. The image of
the mouth, as well as that of the ear, recurs frequently, suggesting that
the dominant theme of the cycle is the exploration of the conditions,
nature, and qualities of poetic language as it says, speaks, and praises.
'Bezug' ('relation', 'link', 'connection') is a key concept throughout
and it stresses the fact of connectedness rather than the substance of
the things connected. This makes it very difficult to paraphrase the
poems or 'hold' them mentally, reduced to an intellectually graspable
substance. And yet this is the essence of the mission of transformation
that lies at their heart, the metamorphosis of the visible world into
language, despite but also because of the obstacles presented by tech-
nology, capitalism, the modern urban world, and a conception of life
as 'fated' or determined rather than freely self-expressing.

The letter to Hulewicz referred to above is concerned above all
with the *Elegies* and the *Sonnets*, and thus with Rilke's late work. It
reflects concerns that he has harboured for most of his life, however,
and one of the quotations from it above (p. xxv) echoes a passage
added to the Rodin monograph in 1907: the tragedy that Rodin's
monumental bronzes articulate derives from being 'born into a time
that has no things, no houses, no exteriors. The interiority that
characterizes our age is formless, ungraspable: it flows' (*KA* IV,
478)—and Rilke himself remarks on the link with his earlier works

---

[17] Letter to Margot, Countess Sizzo, 1 June 1923 (*B* II, 307).

in that letter. The *Sonnets* do have much in common with the *New Poems* in that both presuppose respect for the integrity of the material world, but the later works are far more abstract, more concerned with 'relations between' than 'localities in', and the primacy of seeing has been replaced by that of hearing—attending to the 'vibration' of the world, its musical harmonies and dissonances, but also and especially its harmonics.

The reader of this selection will soon notice how full Rilke's poetry is of interdependent images of giving and receiving, rising and falling, presence and absence, corporeality and immateriality; a tendency to simultaneous gain and loss or beginning within completion is true of his poetic development as well as of his images. The inspirational gain of those of the *Elegies* that he 'found' in January 1912 created the tension that prevented their fulfilment; their completion was dependent on a new beginning in the *Sonnets*. But perhaps the most radical of all the shifts in direction that Rilke's poetry underwent was one in the very last years of his life in some of his most difficult and intense poems, and it took place because the accomplishment of the poetic task of the *Sonnets* meant that it could not continue to be valid for future work. A prolonged period of engagement with the work of Paul Valéry began with Rilke's translation in March 1921 of Valéry's own 'breakthrough' poem, *Le Cimetière marin* (*The Cemetery by the Sea*), and continued with more translations, of both poetry and essays, in the winter of 1922–3. For Rilke, Valéry offered a model for poetry very different from that of Orphic transformation.

The affinity that Rilke sensed between himself and his French contemporary made itself clearly felt in his poetry after the *Sonnets*. The poem 'Dedicated to M . . .', written a year after the Valéry translations, speaks of the 'heart's swing', as part of which there is a 'prescribed return' into a new creative period: 'the loaded sling, | heavy with heart's curiosity, tautens | upward into the opposite. | Different again: how new!' (p. 245). In February 1924 'The Magician' also proclaims a shift in poetic stance, positing a radical opposition between the magician-poet and the world hitherto quite uncharacteristic of Rilke. The magician is distinct from the world he is conjuring, which is defined as 'All that *he* is not; the Other'. The conception of the poet as magician is in the Mallarméan pedigree, to which Rilke recognized that Valéry belonged, as a letter to Lou Andreas-Salomé of 29 December 1921 confirms. It is reflected stylistically, for example, in Rilke's increasing use of emphatic, single-word or short-phrase 'conjurations' to open his poems. And it manifests itself in a pre-occupation with sound in poems such as 'Gong' (which derives to some extent from the model of dense musicality that French Symbolist poetry offered) and in poems such as 'Mausoleum' in the tradition of Mallarmé's 'tombeaux' poems. Whether the aesthetic that leads to an ever more hermetic style of writing was a fruitful one or not is actually one of the questions asked by 'Mausoleum', as Judith Ryan points out: 'is [hermetic poetry] a precious container for meaning that is hidden deep inside, like the kernel in the fruit, or is it merely a surface which, when turned inside out, will prove to contain nothing?'[18] Rilke has moved almost immeasurably far from the world of his first *Jugendstil*-inspired collections, but characteristically has done so whilst retaining a focus on lasting, complex, and sustaining images—here the tension between surface and depth.

Rilke has always enjoyed a remarkable degree of passionate interest and loyalty—both private, from his many lovers and admirers (who all testify to the personal fascination he exercised, despite his some-what unprepossessing physical appearance), and public. The early story in prose, *The Lay of the Love and Death of Cornet Christoph Rilke*,[19] whose first version was written in a burst of inspiration over a single night, became a cult work soon after it appeared in 1906, selling 8,000 copies in the first few weeks, more than 200,000 by the time of Rilke's death in 1926, and well over a million today. Differently, but no less intensely, Rilke's poetry still commands astonishing devotion. There are enough reprints and translations of Rilke's works, and enough books and essays about Rilke, to sink a battleship. He is one of the most edited, translated, and analysed poets of any age, and those interested in him include poetry lovers of all sorts, from the amateur to the academic, literary and cultural historians, and a wide range of alternative groups who see Rilke as a form of guru or spiritual(ist) guide. He might not have been displeased with either role, but he would most certainly have regretted any attempt to divert attention from his work.

[18] Judith Ryan, *Rilke, Modernism and Poetic Tradition* (Cambridge, 1999), 217.
[19] A 'cornet' is a commissioned officer in the cavalry, and the bearer of the flag.

# NOTE ON THE TEXT

THE German text for almost all the poems in this selection is based on that in the most up-to-date critical edition of Rilke's works: *Kommentierte Ausgabe*, 4 volumes plus a supplementary volume, edited by Manfred Engel et al. (Frankfurt am Main: Insel, 1996 and 2003). However, this invaluable edition, with its informative editorial material and introductory essays and a wealth of background material from Rilke's correspondence, is not exhaustive. The texts of two poems in this selection, 'This my struggle' and *Gong*, are therefore taken from the earlier standard edition, *Sämtliche Werke*, 7 volumes, edited by Ernst Zinn (Wiesbaden: Insel, 1955–66 and 1997).

The German texts in *Selected Poems* follow Rilke's idiosyncratic punctuation exactly as it stands in the editions cited above. Rilke frequently uses 'double punctuation', with a comma, a full stop, or a semicolon either preceded or followed by a dash. Since this is alien to modern English usage and not usually crucial to the sense, we have not usually adopted these variations in the translations and have replaced them by one only of the original two points, usually the dash. Occasionally, however, such as when Rilke adds a dash to a full stop in the middle of a line (most noticeably in the fast tempo of the *Duino Elegies*, for example), a more marked pause seems to be called for so we retain the original punctuation in translation. This is the case, too, when Rilke is at his most idiosyncratic, punctuating at the beginning of a line, before any of the words themselves.

Another idiosyncrasy of Rilke's is his inconsistent use of suspension points. In the earlier work these often take the form of the three points familiar from modern English usage, but in the later work in particular they tend to vary between two and ten points (such as in the tenth *Duino Elegy*). Bilingual editions of Rilke, including this one, usually prefer to retain Rilke's usage, both in the original German and in translation.

# NOTE ON THE TRANSLATION

Two translators have been responsible for the English versions of Rilke's poetry in this edition. Susan Ranson translated the poems from five of Rilke's early collections, some of the *New Poems* and *New Poems, Second Part*, the *Duino Elegies*, five of *The Sonnets to Orpheus* (1. VIII, IX, and XVIII, 2. IV and VI) and all but one of the uncollected poems. Marielle Sutherland is the translator of the majority of *The Sonnets to Orpheus*, of the remaining *New Poems* in both parts, and of 'Turning' amongst the uncollected poems. The translators of the *New Poems* are identified by their initials alongside the titles in the Notes at the end of this volume. Both translators would like to express their warmest thanks to Robert Vilain for undertaking the editorial work on this volume.

If the reader's eye falls first on the introductory early poems of this selection an impression could be gained from their transparent language that Rilke may not be as untranslatable as has sometimes been claimed. Indeed, some of these earlier lyrics did much to translate themselves. However, in the *New Poems* an intricate, purposeful density of expression and description already asserts itself; the *Duino Elegies* add further difficulty by their subtle rhythm–changes, speed, and high mood, and by the need to interpret the expressions of Rilke's imagination in our more pragmatic English words; *The Sonnets to Orpheus* lift the mood even higher, almost beyond speech and translation at times, since their subject is the song of the human being's creative connection to earthly life and to the unknowable nature of extinction. The uncollected poems, here mostly from Rilke's last years, present dozens of arresting styles and challenges.

   The first task facing us was that of rendering into English intensely lyrical poetry written in an intensely German style. It has the richness of rhyme and luscious musicality that German much more easily allows; the concentration of meaning and extended syntax, clause heaped upon clause, that are clearer in German than in English; the affinity for trochaic and dactylic metres that German has taken from the ancients but that English on the whole has not. Then secondly we had to find ways of re-expressing Rilke's both compressed and

vaulting personal style. We will briefly discuss a few of these challenges
in more detail.

In his early work the young Rilke allows himself to be intoxicated
by sound as he discovers how easily he can drench the line in asso-
nance, alliteration, internal rhyme, and end-rhymes repeated many
more times than once. In English, which has fewer consonant combi-
nations and fewer long vowels, sounds are lighter and less 'velvet' in
their appeal. The translator may have to use various tactics to indicate
the original musicality: a little alliteration, as much part-rhyme as
possible, and repetition where it can work to good effect. (SR has
discussed this subject at greater length in her Translator's Note to
*Rainer Maria Rilke's* The Book of Hours (2008), pp. xxxvi ff.)

We have not felt bound to reproduce Rilke's regular full rhyme,
choosing instead to modify this for the ear attuned to more recent
English verse. SR prefers largely to abandon full rhyme in favour
of part-rhyme or a slight indication of rhyme only, though still in as
many lines as possible. MS, in the tightly compacted *New Poems* and
*Sonnets to Orpheus*, often stays closer to rhyme and tries to replicate
sounds depending on how insistent these seem to be within the mean-
ing of the poem. For example, in sonnet I. VI she tries to preserve the
richness of the assonances. Orpheus here infuses the vision of the
living with appearances of the dead, and Rilke sounds out this Orphic
fusion of the upper and lower realms of life and death by blending
flickering, lighter German 'i' sounds with longer, darker 'au' sounds.
In her version MS blends English 'i' with 'oo' sounds.

Some poems demand more rhyme in translation than others: for
the faithful translator the most difficult poems of all are those with
the shortest lines (e.g. *End Piece*; *Sonnets to Orpheus*, I. XVII–XIX and
XXII–XXIII). Only close replication of both metre and rhyme can
preserve them in English as the lyrical distillations that Rilke makes
of them.

Rilke likes to cast a poem of several stanzas as one sentence,
usually syntactically complex with many subordinate clauses and
with the main verb perhaps in the last stanza (*Sonnets*, I. XXIII again)
or even omitted altogether (*Roman Fountain*; *The Ball*). This device
creates an almost physical tension between the stanzas, which the
translator has no right to sever. In fact, German syntax naturally delays
subsidiary verbs and often even the main verb or participle until the
end of the clause or sentence; these poems show Rilke making vivid

poetic use of the delay and by doing so making demands on the translator: *Der Ball* ends on the verb 'zufallen', at the very end of the ball's own movement. In *Sonnet* 1. xxiii he uses the single-sentence style for tracing the trajectory of the plane climbing into the sky and in *Roman Fountain* for the downward flow of water in a fountain with several basins. We see the same style in *Early Apollo*, which fills us with such awaiting and anticipation of language and poetry in the god that at the full stop we are craving the next sentence.

Despite his tightly controlled poetic expression, Rilke allows open emotion to surface, indicated perhaps (in *The Garden of Olives*) by an untranslatable repeated 'Ach' or in semi-incoherent phrases or exclamations (especially in the *Sonnets*, but scattered throughout most of the later work). Moreover, German still has the expressive familiar form of 'you', equivalent to English 'thou'. 'Du' and the imperatives, presenting informal, even intimate, registers, occur frequently in Rilke, but they too are difficult to render simply in English ('Du, mein Freund'; and 'Sieh' in *Sonnets*, 1. xvi).

Time and again the translator is brought up short by Rilke's predilection for word-creation, which is already apparent in the early collections. We meet perplexing compounds and abstractions in 'frühlingfrierende Birke' ('What is the furthest I shall reach', p. 8), 'Flammenumflehter' (*Prayer*, p. 4) or 'aus allem draußen Aufgereihten' (*The Ball*, p. 102). His project of drawing into relation the opposing territories of concrete and abstract, subject and object, presence and absence, is linguistically manifest in the contrasts formed between abstruse vocabulary or phraseology and utterly simple, conversational usages (sonnets 1. xiv, 'tun sie es gern?', and 1. xv, 'Wartet . . . das schmeckt . . .').

Then there is the need to replicate Rilke's varied metres, while softening a few of the stressed beats to create the relaxed, less insistent rhythms of spoken language. (For instance, MS's line 'In reflections resembling Fragonard' (*The Flamingos*) no longer has five full stresses but only three or even two, and is for that reason a most beautiful pentameter — SR.) This is not an illogical aim: the reader, unaccustomed these days to such regularity as Rilke favours and perhaps even now attuned to Shakespeare's miraculously modern spoken rhythms, asks for no less.

But Rilke also offers many highly irregular metres (*Song of the Sea*; several of the *Sonnets*; *An die Musik*), and the *Duino Elegies* wander from tetrameters through pentameters to hexameters, from trochee to dactyl, iambus to anapaest, which gives them the extraordinary pull of fast-flowing rivers. We attempt to mirror these rhythms and in particular to respect Rilke's preference for the trochee and dactyl, which are not 'native' to English prosody as they are to the German. However, to travel too far in this direction would sound artificial in English and you will often find the iambus and the anapaest taking over in our versions. We found that even if a trochee is consciously written at the start of an English line, it often, by an unconscious switch of the stress, reads as an iambus, perhaps because in English there are naturally fewer feminine line-endings to precede and mark a trochee. It took us much time and trouble to clarify the trochees at the beginnings of lines and so avoid confusing the reader's sense of the metre; we may not have wholly succeeded, because metre is sensed subjectively. On the whole, whatever the difficulties, we did not think it right to smooth Rilke's metrical variations into English iambics, especially the variations on a larger scale.

Influenced by Hölderlin, Rilke occasionally drops into the classical hexameter; again we follow suit. And in two poems ('Oh leave me, you whom I asked'; *For Erika*) he adopts complex verse-forms, also with regular mid-line caesura; in the latter poem this is a classical ode-form. In the interests of accuracy and rhyme, SR's version cannot perfectly match the metre: this illustrates the kind of trade-off that translation exacts from the all-too imperfect translator.

We have both worked by the demanding principle that verse translation should attempt to render not only the central meaning of a poem but almost all its detail, although we were certain that shadowing the original *poetry* must always be our overriding aim. Conscious of both the temptations and the pitfalls of faithfully replicating a verse-form in another language, we have tried to offer at least hints and traces of regular rhymes and rhythms (at times more), within flexibility. We hope this does justice to the idea that 'translation is not the work, but a path towards the work . . . an apparatus, a technical device that brings us closer to the work without ever trying to repeat or replace it'.[1]

SR and MS

---

[1] José Ortegay Gasset, 'The Misery and Splendour of Translation', trans. Elizabeth Gamble Miller, in Rainer Schulte and John Biguenet (eds.), *Theories of Translation: An Anthology of Essays from Dryden to Derrida* (Chicago, 1992), 109.

# SELECT BIBLIOGRAPHY

## Editions (German)

Engel, Manfred, Fülleborn, Ulrich, Nalewski, Horst, and Stahl, August (eds.), *Rainer Maria Rilke: Werke: Kommentierte Ausgabe*, 4 vols. plus a supplementary vol. (Frankfurt am Main, 1996 and 2003).

Zinn, Ernst, with the Rilke Archive and Ruth Sieber-Rilke, *Rainer Maria Rilke: Sämtliche Werke*, 7 vols. (Wiesbaden, 1955–66 and 1997).

## Translations into English

Cohn, Stephen (trans.), *Rainer Maria Rilke: Duino Elegies*, preface by Peter Porter (Manchester, 1989).

—— *Rainer Maria Rilke: Neue Gedichte/New Poems*, introduction by John Bayley (Manchester, 1997).

—— *Rainer Maria Rilke: Sonnets to Orpheus with Letters to a Young Poet*, introduction by Peter Porter (Manchester, 2000).

Crucefix, Martyn (trans.), *Rainer Maria Rilke: Duino Elegies*, introduction by Karen Leeder (London, 2006).

Deutsch, Babette (trans.), *Poems from the Book of Hours: 'Das Stundenbuch', by Rainer Maria Rilke* (Norfolk, Conn., 1941).

Good, Graham (trans.), *Rilke's Late Poetry: Duino Elegies, The Sonnets to Orpheus, Selected Last Poems* (Vancouver, 2004).

Hamburger, Michael (trans.), *Rainer Maria Rilke: Turning-Point, Miscellaneous Poems 1912–1926* (London, 2003).

Kramer, Aaron (trans.), *Visions of Christ: A Posthumous Cycle of Poems*, ed. with an introduction by Siegfried Mandel (Boulder, Colo., 1967).

Leishman, J. B., and Spender, Stephen (trans.), *Rainer Maria Rilke: Duino Elegies* (London, 1939; pbk. 1975).

MacIntyre, C. F. (trans.), *Selected Poems by Rainer Maria Rilke* (Berkeley, 1940; new edn. 2001).

—— *The Life of the Virgin Mary* (Berkeley, 1947).

Mitchell, Stephen (trans.), *The Selected Poetry of Rainer Maria Rilke*, introduction by Robert Hass (London, 1987).

—— *Rainer Maria Rilke: The Notebooks of Malte Laurids Brigge* (London, 1988).

Paterson, Don, *Orpheus: A Version of Rilke's 'Die Sonette an Orpheus'* (London, 2006).

Pike, Burton, *The Notebooks of Malte Laurids Brigge* (Champaign, Ill., 2008).

Poulin, A., Jr. (trans.), *The Complete French Poems of Rainer Maria Rilke* (Saint Paul, Minn., 1979).

Ranson, Susan (trans.), *Rainer Maria Rilke's 'The Book of Hours': A New Translation with Commentary*, ed. Ben Hutchinson (Rochester, NY, 2008).

Shapcott, Jo, *Tender Taxes: Versions of Rilke's French Poems* (London, 2001).

Snow, Edward (trans.), *The Book of Images, Rainer Maria Rilke* (New York, 1994).

—— *Uncollected Poems, Rainer Maria Rilke* (New York, 1997).

Ward, Geoff (trans.), *Selected Poems of Rainer Maria Rilke* (London, 2010).

## Letters

SELECTIONS

Altheim, Karl, et al. (ed.), *Rainer Maria Rilke: Briefe*, 2 vols. (Wiesbaden, 1950).

Baer, Ulrich (trans.), *The Poet's Guide to Life: The Wisdom of Rainer Maria Rilke* (New York, 2005).

—— (trans.), *Letters on Life: New Prose Translations* (New York, 2006).

Greene, Jane Bannard, and Norton, M. D. Herter (trans.), *Letters of Rainer Maria Rilke, 1892–1910* and *Letters of Rainer Maria Rilke, 1910–1926* (New York, 1945–7; rpt. 1993).

Hull, R. F. C. (trans.), *Rainer Maria Rilke, Selected Letters, 1902–1926*, introduction by John Bayley (London, 1988).

Nalewski, Horst (ed.), *Rainer Maria Rilke: Briefe in zwei Bänden*, 2 vols. (Frankfurt am Main and Leipzig, 1991).

Norton, M. D. Herter, *Wartime Letters of Rainer Maria Rilke* (New York, 1940; rpt. 1964).

Storck, Joachim W., *Rainer Maria Rilke: Briefe zur Politik* (Frankfurt am Main, 1992).

INDIVIDUAL CORRESPONDENTS

Rilke and Andreas-Salomé Lou, *The Correspondence*, trans. Edward Snow and Michael Winkler (New York, 2006).

—— *Letters to Benevenuta* [= Magda von Hattingberg], trans. Heinz Norden, foreword by Louis Untermeyer (London, 1953).

—— [to Clara Rilke], *Letters on Cézanne*, ed. Clara Rilke, trans. Joel Agee (London, 1988).

—— *Letters to Merline (1919–1922)*, trans. Jesse Browner (London, 1989).

—— *Correspondence in Verse with Erika Mitterer*, trans. N. K. Cruikshank, introduction by J. B. Leishman (London, 1953).

—— and von Thurn und Taxis, Marie, *Briefwechsel*, 2 vols. (Zurich, 1951), trans. Nora Wydenbruck as *The Letters of Rainer Maria Rilke and Princess Marie von Thurn und Taxis* (London, 1958).

——, Zwetajewa, Marina, and Pasternak, Boris, *Letters, Summer 1926*, ed. Yevgeny Pasternak et al., trans. Margaret Wettlin and Walter Arndt (Oxford, 1985).

### Biographical

Freedman, Ralph, *Life of a Poet: Rainer Maria Rilke*, trans. Helen Sword (New York, 1996).

Holthusen, Hans E., *Portrait of Rilke: An Illustrated Biography*, trans. W. H. Hargreaves (New York, 1971).

Leppmann, Wolfgang, *Rilke: A Life*, trans. Russell M. Stockman; verse trans. Richard Exner (Cambridge, 1984).

Prater, Donald A., *A Ringing Glass: The Life of Rainer Maria Rilke* (Oxford, 1986).

Salis, Jean Rodolphe de, *Rainer Maria Rilke: The Years in Switzerland: A Contribution to the Biography of Rilke's Later Life*, trans. N. K. Cruickshank (London, 1964).

Schnack, Ingeborg, *Rainer Maria Rilke: Chronik seines Lebens und seines Werkes*, 2 vols. (Frankfurt am Main, 1975).

Schoolfield, George C., *Young Rilke and his Time* (Rochester, NY, 2009).

### Secondary Sources: English

Abler, Lawrence, 'From Angel to Orpheus: Mythopoesis in the Late Rilke', in Marjorie W. McCune et al. (eds.), *The Binding of Proteus: Perspectives on Myth and the Literary Process* (Lewisburg, Pa., 1980), 197–219.

Batterby, K. A. J., *Rilke and France: A Study in Poetic Development* (Oxford, 1966).

Bishop, Paul, ' "An solchen Dingen hab ich schauen gelernt": Rilke's Visit to Egypt and the *Duineser Elegien*', *Austrian Studies*, 12: *The Austrian Lyric* (2004), 65–79.

Boa, Elizabeth, 'Asking the Thing for the Form in Rilke's *Neue Gedichte*', *German Life and Letters*, 27 (1973/4), 285–94.

Bridge, Helen, 'Place into Poetry: Time and Space in Rilke's *Neue Gedichte*', *Orbis Litterarum*, 61.4 (2006), 263–90.

Catling, Jo, 'Rilke's "Left-Handed Lyre": Multilingualism and the Poetics of Possibility', *Modern Language Review*, 102.4 (2007), 1084–104.

de Man, Paul, 'Tropes (Rilke)' (originally 1972), in *Allegories of Meaning: Figural Language in Rousseau, Rilke, Nietzsche and Proust* (New Haven, Conn., 1979), 28–56.

Detsch, Richard, *Rilke's Connections to Nietzsche* (Lanham, Md., 2003).

Durr, Volker, *Rainer Maria Rilke: The Poet's Trajectory* (New York, 2006).

Gray, Ronald D., 'Rilke's Poetry' and 'Rilke and Mysticism', in *The German Tradition in Literature, 1871–1945* (Cambridge, 1965).

Heep, Hartmut, *Unreading Rilke: Unorthodox Approaches to a Cultural Myth* (New York, 2001).

Heller, Erich, 'Rilke and Nietzsche, with a Discourse on Thought, Belief, and Poetry', in *The Disinherited Mind* (Cambridge, 1952), 97–140.

Hutchinson, Ben, *Rilke's Poetics of Becoming* (Oxford, 2006).

Keon, Carol, 'Flowers as Pure Existence in Rilke's *Sonette an Orpheus*', *Modern Austrian Literature*, 15 (1982), 113–26.

Komar, Kathleen L., *Transcending Angels: Rainer Maria Rilke's 'Duino Elegies'* (Lincoln, Nebr., 1987).

Leeder, Karen, and Vilain, Robert (eds.), *The Cambridge Companion to Rilke* (Cambridge, 2010).

Luke, F. D., 'Metaphor and Thought in Rilke's "Duino Elegies": A Commentary on the First Elegy with a Verse Translation', *Oxford German Studies*, 2 (1967), 110–28.

McGlashan, L., 'Rilke's *Neue Gedichte*', *German Life and Letters*, 12 (1958/9), 81–101.

Mason, Eudo C., *Rilke* (Edinburgh, 1963).

Metzger, Erika A., and Metzger, Michael M. (eds.), *Companion to the Works of Rainer Maria Rilke* (New York, 2001).

Nelson, Erika M., *Reading Rilke's Orphic Identity* (Bern, 2005).

Paulin, Roger, and Hutchinson, Peter (eds.), *Rilke's 'Duino Elegies': Cambridge Readings* (London, 1996).

Pettersson, Torsten, 'Internalization and Death. A Reinterpretation of Rilke's *Duineser Elegien*', *Modern Language Review*, 94.3 (1999), 731–43.

Pettit, Richard, 'The Poet's Eye for the Arts: Rilke Views the Visual Arts around 1900', in Françoise Forster-Hahn (ed.), *Imagining Modern German Culture: 1889–1910* (Hanover, NH, 1996), 251–73.

Peucker, Brigitte, 'The Poetry of Transformation: Rilke's Orpheus and the Fruit of Death', in *Lyric Descent in the German Romantic Tradition* (New Haven, Conn., 1987), 119–65.

Phelan, Anthony, *Rilke: Neue Gedichte*, Critical Guides to German Texts, 14 (London, 1992).

Rolleston, James, *Rilke in Transition: An Exploration of his Earliest Poetry* (New Haven, 1970).

Ryan, Judith, *Rilke, Modernism and the Poetic Tradition* (Cambridge, 1999).

Segal, Charles, 'Rilke's *Sonnets to Orpheus* and the Orphic Tradition', *Literatur in Wissenschaft und Unterricht*, 15 (1982), 367–80.

Sheppard, Richard W., 'Rilke's "Duineser Elegien": A Critical Appreci-
ation in the Light of Eliot's "Four Quartets"', *German Life and Letters*,
20 (1966–7), 205–18.
—— 'From the "Neue Gedichte" to the "Duineser Elegien": Rilke's
Chandos-Crisis', *Modern Language Review*, 68 (1973), 577–92.
Stahl, Ernest L., 'Rilke's *Sonnets to Orpheus*: Composition and Thematic
Structure', *Oxford German Studies*, 9 (1978), 119–38.
Stewart, Corbet, 'Rilke's *Neue Gedichte*: The Isolation of the Image',
*Publications of the English Goethe Society*, 48 (1978), 81–103.
Sutherland, Marielle, *Images of Absence: Death and the Language of
Concealment in the Poetry of Rainer Maria Rilke* (Berlin, 2006).
Waters, William, 'Rilke's Imperatives', *Poetics Today*, 25.4 (2004),
711–30.
Webb, Karl E., *Rainer Maria Rilke and Jugendstil: Affinities, Influences,
Adaptations* (Chapel Hill, NC, 1978).
Wich-Schwarz, Johannes, 'From Ahasverus to Orpheus: Transformations
of Christ in Rainer Maria Rilke', *Christianity and Literature*, 57.1 (2007),
87–108.

### Secondary Sources: German

Bauer, Edda (ed.), *Rilke: Studien zu Werk und Wirkungsgeschichte* (Berlin
and Weimar, 1976).
Bauschinger, Sigrid, and Cocalis, Susan L. (eds.), *Rilke-Rezeptionen: Rilke
Reconsidered* (Tübingen and Basel, 1995).
Bradley, Brigitte L., *Rilkes Neue Gedichte: Ihr zyklisches Gefüge* (Bern and
Munich, 1967).
—— *Rainer Maria Rilkes 'Der Neuen Gedichte anderer Teil': Entwicklungs-
stufen seiner Pariser Lyrik* (Bern and Munich, 1976).
Demetz, Peter, Storck, Joachim W., and Zimmermann, Hans Dieter (eds.),
*Rilke: Ein europäischer Dichter aus Prag* (Würzburg, 1998).
Engel, Manfred, *Rainer Maria Rilkes Duineser Elegien und die moderne
deutsche Lyrik: Zwischen Jahrhundertwende und Avantgarde* (Stuttgart,
1986).
—— (ed.), *Rilke-Handbuch: Leben—Werk—Wirkung* (Stuttgart and
Weimar, 2004).
—— and Lamping, Dieter (eds.). *Rilke und die Weltliteratur* (Düsseldorf
and Zurich, 1999).
Fülleborn, Ulrich, and Engel, Manfred (eds.), *Materialien zu Rainer
Maria Rilkes 'Duineser Elegien'*, 3 vols. (Frankfurt am Main, 1980–2).
Gerok-Reiter, Annette, *Wink und Wandlung: Komposition und Poetik in
Rilkes 'Sonette an Orpheus'* (Tübingen, 1996).

Görner, Rüdiger (ed.), *Rainer Maria Rilke: Im Herzwerk der Sprache* (Vienna, 2004).

Götte, Gisela, and Danzker, Jo-Anne Birnie (eds.), *Rainer Maria Rilke und die bildende Kunst seiner Zeit* (Munich and New York, 1996).

Kahl, Michael, *Lebensphilosophie und Ästhetik: Zu Rilkes Werk 1902–1910* (Freiburg, 1999).

Leeder, Karen, and Vilain, Robert (eds.), *Nach Duino: Studien zu Rilkes späten Gedichten* (Göttingen, 2010).

Leisi, Ernst, *Rilkes 'Sonette an Orpheus': Interpretation, Kommentar, Glossar* (Tübingen, 1987).

Löwenstein, Sascha, *Poetik und dichterisches Selbstverständnis: Eine Einführung in Rainer Maria Rilkes frühe Dichtungen (1884–1906)* (Würzburg, 2004).

Solbrig, Ingeborg H., and Storck, Joachim (eds.), *Rilke heute: Beziehungen und Wirkungen*, 2 vols. (Frankfurt am Main, 1975–6).

Stahl, August, *Rilke: Kommentar zum lyrischen Werk* (Munich, 1978).

Stevens, Adrian, and Wagner, Fred (eds.), *Rilke und die Moderne: Londoner Symposium* (Munich, 2000).

Storck, Joachim W., 'Wort-Kerne und Dinge: Rilke und die Krise der Sprache: Zu den Gedichten 1906–1926', *Akzente*, 4 (1957), 346–58.

# A CHRONOLOGY OF RAINER MARIA RILKE

1875    René Karl Wilhelm Josef Maria Rilke born prematurely in Prague
        on 4 December. A sister born the previous year had died within a
        week of birth. René was often ill as a child, suffering from repeated
        fevers and headaches.

1884    Rilke's first poem is composed on 24 May to celebrate his parents'
        wedding anniversary, although they separate shortly afterwards
        and Rilke is brought up by his adoring but often absent mother.

1886    Admitted as a scholar to the Junior Military Academy in St Pölten
        (Lower Austria), which he loathes.

1890    Attends the Military Academy in Mährisch-Weißkirchen
        (Moravia), but suspends his studies after three months because of
        illness and leaves mid-1891 without qualifications.

1891    Enrols for a three-year course at the Academy for Trade and
        Commerce in Linz, but leaves within a year to take private lessons
        in Prague in preparation for the School Leaving Certificate.

1892    Death of his uncle Jaroslav Rilke, ennobled as Ritter von Rülicken,
        who leaves him a small legacy to support his studies.

1894    Shortly after his engagement to Valerie von David-Rhonfeld,
        Rilke's first collection of verse, *Lives and Songs*, is published.

1895    Takes School Leaving Certificate and enrols at the German Carl
        Ferdinand University in Prague, reading Philosophy, Literature,
        and History of Art. Engagement broken off. Publishes *Offerings to
        the Lares*.

1896    Changes degree programme to Law and Political Science, and
        from September moves to the University of Munich to study Art
        History alongside his friend the painter Emil Orlik. *Dream-
        Crowned* published.

1897    First visit to Venice. Begins an affair with Lou Andreas-Salomé,
        with whom he lives in Munich from June to September before
        moving to Berlin in October. Meets the poet Stefan George and
        the dramatist Gerhard Hauptmann. A collection of verse entitled
        *Advent* appears at Christmas. The drama *Hoar-Frost* is performed
        in Prague.

1898    Travels to Italy in the spring (Florence and Viarreggio); (Aug.)
        settles in Berlin. Makes first visit to the artists' community in
        Worpswede at Christmas. Completes drama *The White Princess*.

1899   Studies History of Art in Berlin and travels to Vienna (where he
       meets the poet and dramatist Hugo von Hofmannsthal and the
       dramatist Arthur Schnitzler). (Apr.–June) Makes his first journey
       to Russia with Lou Andreas-Salomé and her husband, the distin-
       guished Orientalist Friedrich Carl Andreas; meets Leo Tolstoy and
       Leonid Pasternak, and by the autumn the first part of the *Book of
       Hours* is complete.

1900   Second visit to Russia with Lou Andreas-Salomé, after intensive
       study of Russian language and literature; another meeting with
       Tolstoy. (27 Aug.–Oct.) Extended visit to the painter and graphic
       artist Heinrich Vogeler in the artists' colony at Worpswede, near
       Bremen, during which time Rilke meets the painter Paula Becker
       and the sculptor Clara Westhoff as well as other artists and the
       writer Carl Hauptmann. (Oct.) In Berlin, touched by bouts of
       depression.

1901   Lou Andreas-Salomé breaks off their relationship in late February.
       (28 Apr.) Rilke abandons his university studies and marries Clara
       Westhoff and moves into a small house near Worpswede; (12 Dec.)
       their daughter, Ruth, is born. Second part of *Book of Hours* written
       in mid-September.

1902   (July) *Book of Images* published. (28 Aug.) Moves to Paris; (Nov.)
       writes the first of the *New Poems*, 'The Panther'.

1903   The art-historical studies *Worpswede* and *Auguste Rodin* appear.
       Spends most of April in Viareggio where the third part of the
       *Book of Hours* is written. Resumes contact with Lou. Clara obtains
       financial support for a period of study in Rome, where she and
       Rilke move in September, to remain until the following June.

1904   (Feb.) Begins work on *The Notebooks of Malte Laurids Brigge*. Travels
       to Denmark and Sweden at the invitation of Ellen Key before
       returning to Oberneuland (near Bremen, Clara's hometown) with
       his family. Publication of second version of *Cornet*.

1905   Admitted to a sanatorium near Dresden for two months after a
       long-lasting acute flu-like illness. Visits Lou in Göttingen be-
       fore moving to Paris on 12 September, where he stays until late
       July 1906, initially living with Rodin in Meudon-Val-Fleury as
       his private secretary. *Book of Hours* published. Lecture tour to
       Dresden and Prague.

1906   Lecture tour to Berlin and Hamburg, interrupted by his father's
       death. Rodin terminates his arrangement with Rilke in May and
       Rilke moves to the rue Cassette, working on the *New Poems*.
       Friendship with Sidonie Nádherný von Borutin and the Belgian

poet Émile Verhaeren. (July–Aug.) Rilke travels to Flanders with Clara. By the end of this year, when he journeys to Capri to stay with Alice Faehndrich for five months, some two-thirds of the first part of *New Poems* are complete. Works on translating Elizabeth Barrett Browning's *Sonnets from the Portuguese*. Rilke's prose work *The Lay of the Love and Death of Cornet Christopher Rilke* (initially published in 1899) becomes a best-seller.

1907    Return to Paris at the end of May. (Oct.) Journeys to Prague, Breslau, and Vienna and visits to writers including Stefan Zweig, Richard Beer-Hofmann, Rudolf Kassner, and Hofmannsthal. (Nov.) Rilke reconciled with Rodin and travels to Venice in mid-December, when Part I of the *New Poems* is published. Almost daily visits to the Cézanne memorial exhibition in the Salon d'Automne are recorded in letters to Clara that are published posthumously.

1908    Visits to Oberneuland, Berlin, Munich, Rome, and Naples before a six-week stay in Capri and a return to Paris for a year in early May. By August Part II of *New Poems* is complete; published in November. Writes the Requiem poems for Paula Modersohn-Becker and Wolf Count of Kalckreuth, a Munich poet who had committed suicide.

1909    Travels to Provence in September and October. Beginning of Rilke's friendship with Princess Marie von Thurn und Taxis.

1910    Visiting his publisher Anton Kippenberg and his wife in Leipzig, Rilke dictates the completed version of *Malte* (published 31 May). Travels to Weimar, Berlin, Rome, and Castle Duino near Trieste before returning to Paris in May. (Sept.–Oct.) Rilke is the guest of Princess Marie and then Sidonie Nádherný von Borutin in their castles in Bohemia before leaving for North Africa in mid-November.

1911    Spends three months travelling in Egypt, including a journey along the Nile to Luxor, Karnak, and the Valley of the Kings, returning to Paris via Venice. There follows a period of depression and low productivity. Clara and Ruth move to Munich and divorce proceedings are instituted, at Clara's request, although not completed because of religious restrictions enshrined in Austrian law. (12 Oct.) Rilke leaves on a long car-journey through the South of France to Castle Duino, where he lives as the guest of Princess Marie until May 1912, beginning the *Duino Elegies* there.

1912    Completion of *The Life of the Virgin Mary* and further work on the *Elegies* (completing I and II, and portions of III, VI, IX and X). (May–Sept.) In Venice, where Rilke meets the ageing actress Eleonora Duse, and then a month in Duino. He journeys to Spain from 1 November, visiting Toledo and Cordoba before reaching Ronda on 9 December.

1913    Returns to Paris in February via Madrid, but from June spends five months travelling in Germany, sometimes with Lou, who introduces him to Sigmund Freud. Visits an exhibition of wax dolls by Lotte Pritzel. In Paris in the autumn, working further on the *Elegies* (III, VI and X).

1914    Correspondence with 'Benvenuta', the pianist Magda von Hattingberg. A period of self-analysis. (20 June) Writes the poem 'Turning', which signals a new aesthetic and the hope of a new poetic start. Reads Georg Trakl and Friedrich Hölderlin. At the outbreak of war Rilke in Munich, almost wholly without means, although he is supported by a number of wealthy friends, including Herta Koenig, who buys Picasso's *Les Saltimbanques* (1905), one of the inspirations for the fifth *Elegy*. He begins a relationship with the painter Lou Albert-Hasard that will last for two years, and is saved financially by a substantial anonymous donation from the philosopher Ludwig Wittgenstein. After a burst of initial enthusiasm, Rilke shocked by the wave of nationalism that sweeps Germany as the war gains momentum.

1915    Almost the whole year spent in Munich, where Rilke hears lectures by Norbert von Hellingrath (on Hölderlin) and the gnostic visionary Alfred Schuler. A very productive working period in October and November (including the fourth *Elegy*) is interrupted by his conscription into the Austrian infantry (*Landsturm*), despite his shaky health.

1916    Begins military service in Vienna (in the military archive), where he spends time with the painter Oskar Kokoschka and meets Adolf Loos and Karl Kraus. Whilst waiting for demobilization (on 9 June), spends time with Hofmannsthal in Rodaun near Vienna.

1917    Works as a reader for the Insel publishing house. Continues to attend Schuler's lectures on death rites in classical antiquity. Housed in Munich and Westphalia by a series of friends before moving briefly to Berlin (meeting Count Harry Kessler and Walther Rathenau).

1918    Finds an apartment in the Ainmillerstraße in Munich in May. Develops an unusual interest in politics. Meets with the artist Paul Klee and a number of Expressionist authors (including Alfred Wolfenstein and Ernst Toller). Initially enthused by the November revolution, he quickly becomes more sceptical. Relationship with Claire Studer (who later married the author Yvan Goll and claimed to have been pregnant by Rilke).

1919    When the Munich Soviet Republic is suppressed, Rilke's apart-
        ment is searched because of his previous contacts with Toller
        and Kurt Eisner. Translation of sonnets by Michelangelo (be-
        gun in 1912 and continued intermittently ever since), and of
        poetry by Mallarmé. Leaves what he called 'the prison of Ger-
        many' forever on 11 June, having been invited to Switzerland by
        the Hottingen Reading Circle. Meets the painter Baladine Klos-
        sowka (Merline). Travels throughout Switzerland and a long lecture
        tour in November, during which he meets Nanny Wunderly-
        Volkart, the wife of a wealthy industrialist, who becomes his most
        trusted friend for the rest of his life.

1920    After wintering in Locarno, Rilke spends two months near Basel, on
        the Schönenberg estate of his friends the Von der Mühlls. Changes
        his Austrian passport for a Czech one, which permits him to travel
        to Venice to see Marie Taxis and her husband. Visits Paris for
        a brief period of 'recovery' from the traumas of the war in October
        and moves into Castle Berg in Ischl for the winter.

1921    A tentative new start on the *Elegies* in Ischl is interrupted by
        a request for help from Merline in Geneva. Begins his translations
        of Valéry in mid-March and leaves Castle Berg in May. Moves into
        the little Château de Muzot near Sierre in the Valais on 26 July,
        helped by Merline, who returns to Berlin in November.

1922    Hears of the death of Wera Ouckama Knoop on 1 January. A 'work-
        storm' in February sees the completion of the *Elegies* (VI, IX, and
        X based on material already written, VII, VIII, and V from scratch)
        and the *Sonnets to Orpheus*. Receives Marie Taxis in Muzot for
        a reading of the new works on 7 and 8 June. Ruth Rilke marries on
        18 May (Rilke does not attend, but lights four candles for her in
        a chapel near Muzot). Further Valéry translations in March and
        April and throughout the winter of 1922–23.

1923    After serious health problems in May spends June–August taking
        a cure in Bad Ragaz or in a sanatorium on Lake Lucerne. Rilke's first
        grandchild, Christine Sieber, born on 2 November. Further visits to
        a clinic in Val-Mont near Montreux at the end of December.

1924    Back in Muzot from 20 January, Rilke begins writing a series of
        poems in French (*Vergers*), as well as a number of poems in German
        with versions in French as well (including 'The Magician'). Visited
        by Valéry on 6 April and begins a poem-correspondence with Erika
        Mitterer in May that will last until August 1926. Last meeting with
        Clara in May. *Les Quatrains Valaisans* written by early September. In
        Val-Mont from 24 November until early January the following year.

1925    Rilke's last visit to Paris (7 Jan.–18 Aug.), where he meets Maurice Betz and works with him on a translation of *Malte*. Meetings with André Gide, Charles du Bos, Jules Supervielle, and Valéry. Completion of *Vergers*. Is attacked in the German press for 'swanning about Paris' writing French poetry. Back in Muzot, he writes his will (27 Oct.), and a number of poems in a new style (including 'Gong' and 'Idol'). Is visited by Erika Mitterer in November, but has to return to Val-Mont shortly before Christmas, and remains there for five months.

1926    Conducts an extended correspondence with the Russian poets Marina Tsvetaeva-Efron and Boris Pasternak between May and September. *Vergers* and *Les Quatrains Valaisans* appear in June. Spends time in the summer with Marie Taxis and Frau Wunderly, and meets Valéry for the last time on 13 September (having just translated his dialogue *Eupalinos*). Rilke injures himself badly on a rose bush and no longer feels secure in his Muzot home, so moves into the Hôtel Bellevue in Sierre before being forced to readmit himself to Val-Mont where his condition is finally diagnosed as acute leukaemia. In enormous pain, Rilke writes his last letters to friends and dies on 29 December shortly after his fifty-first birthday. He is buried in the tiny churchyard of Raron, high on a hill, on 2 January 1927.

# SELECTED POEMS

## Aus: *Larenopfer*

### Der Träumer (II)

TRÄUME scheinen mir wie Orchideen. –
So wie jene sind sie bunt und reich.
Aus dem Riesenstamm der Lebenssäfte
ziehn sie just wie jene ihre Kräfte,
brüsten sich mit dem ersaugten Blute,                    5
freuen in der flüchtigen Minute,
in der nächsten sind sie tot und bleich. –
Und wenn Welten oben leise gehen,
fühlst du's dann nicht wie von Düften wehen?
Träume scheinen mir wie Orchideen. –                    10


## Aus: *Advent*

DAS ist mein Streit:
Sehnsuchtgeweiht
durch alle Tage schweifen.
Dann, stark und breit,
mit tausend Wurzelstreifen                               5
tief in das Leben greifen –
und durch das Leid
weit aus dem Leben reifen,
weit aus der Zeit!


## Aus: *Mir zur Feier*

MEINE frühverliehnen
Lieder oft in der Ruh
überrankter Ruinen
sang ich dem Abend sie zu.

# From *Offerings to the Lares*

## *The Dreamer* (II)

DREAMS:* as vivid in my eyes as orchids.*—
Like them brilliant and opulent,
like them drawing through the giant stem
of living sap the juices of their strength,
like them flaunting an absorbed life-blood,                    5
revelling in the fleetness of the minute,
then, in the next, pallid as the dead.—
And when, softly, worlds pass overhead,
do you not feel their winds, flower-scented?
Dreams: as vivid in my eyes as orchids.—                      10


# From *Advent*

THIS my struggle:
dedicated to longing,
to wander the paths of days.
Then sturdied, strong,
with thousand rootlets* grasping                               5
deep into the terrain
of life, through pain
to ripen far beyond life and
far beyond time!


# From *In Celebration of Myself*

SONGS I was granted in youth
I often sang in the peace
of climber-entangled ruins,
into the evening's ears.

Hätte sie gerne zu Ronden       5
aneinandergereiht,
einer erwachsenen Blonden
als Geschenk und Geschmeid.

Aber unter allen
war ich einzig allein;       10
und so ließ ich sie fallen:
sie verrollten wie lose Korallen
weit in den Abend hinein.


### Gebet

ERNSTER Engel aus Ebenholz:
Du riesige Ruh.
Dein Schweigen schmolz
noch nie in den Bränden
von Büßerhänden.       5
Flammenumflehter!
Deine Beter
sind stolz:
wie du.

Der du versteinst,       10
du über den Blicken beginnender
König, erkiese
dir ein Geschlecht,
dem du gerecht
erscheinst,       15
saumsinnender
Riese.

Du, aller Matten
Furchteinflößer,
Einer ist größer       20
als du: dein Schatten.

Rondeau*-fashion I'd sooner
one by one have strung them
for a grown, golden-haired girl
to accept as gift and gem.

Yet in this world I remained
singularly alone;                                          10
thus, I let them drop: like
unstrung corals they rolled away
far into the evening.

## Prayer

GRAVE angel* of ebony,
peace immense.
As yet your silence
stands unscathed
in fires that penitents'                                 5
hands flame round you!
And those who pray
are proud
like you.

King-into-stone,                                          10
beginning too high for our vision,
take to yourself some
race to whom
you shall be justice
manifest,                                                15
thought-hemmed
colossus.

You who instil
fear in the weary,* know:
One stands greater
than you: your shadow.                                   20

DER Abend ist mein Buch. Ihm prangen
die Deckel purpurn in Damast;
ich löse seine goldnen Spangen
mit kühlen Händen, ohne Hast.

Und lese seine erste Seite,                                5
beglückt durch den vertrauten Ton, –
und lese leiser seine zweite,
und seine dritte träum ich schon.


ICH fürchte mich so vor der Menschen Wort.
Sie sprechen alles so deutlich aus:
Und dieses heißt Hund und jenes heißt Haus,
und hier ist Beginn und das Ende ist dort.

Mich bangt auch ihr Sinn, ihr Spiel mit dem Spott,      5
sie wissen alles, was wird und war;
kein Berg ist ihnen mehr wunderbar;
ihr Garten und Gut grenzt grade an Gott.

Ich will immer warnen und wehren: Bleibt fern.
Die Dinge singen hör ich so gern.                        10
Ihr rührt sie an: sie sind starr und stumm.
Ihr bringt mir alle die Dinge um.


NENN ich dich Aufgang oder Untergang?
Denn manchmal bin ich vor dem Morgen bang
und greife scheu nach seiner Rosen Röte –
und ahne eine Angst in seiner Flöte
vor Tagen, welche liedlos sind und lang.                 5

Aber die Abende sind mild und mein,
von meinem Schauen sind sie still beschienen;
in meinen Armen schlafen Wälder ein, –
und ich bin selbst das Klingen über ihnen,
und mit dem Dunkel in den Violinen                       10
verwandt durch all mein Dunkelsein.

THE evening is my book. Its fine
purple damask* covers fasten
with gold clasps;* and cool-handed
I reach, unhasting, to release them.

And read the first tender words                5
in quick delight—and following them,
stiller, I read the second page;
and now already dream* the third.


I AM so afraid of people's words.*
Everything they pronounce is so clear:
this is a hand, and that is a house,
and beginning is here, and the end over there.

Their meaning frightens, their mockery-play        5
and their claims to know what's coming, what was;
no mountain thrills them now; their estates
and their gardens abut directly on God.*

I warn; I ward them off. Stay back.
It's a wonder to me to hear things sing.*           10
You touch them, and they stultify.
You are the very destroyers of things.


SHALL I name you a rising or a setting?*
For sometimes, tremulous before the morning,
I reach in awe for its roses' glow—
and sense a fear in its flute note
that days are dawning songless and too long.        5

Evenings are other: they are mild and mine,
tranquil, lit up by my long looking;
the forests sleep, cradled in my arms—
and I the ringing harmony above them,
bound to the darkness in the violins               10
by all the dark that is my being.

KANN mir einer sagen, wohin
ich mit meinem Leben reiche?
Ob ich nicht auch noch im Sturme streiche
und als Welle wohne im Teiche,
und ob ich nicht selbst noch die blasse, bleiche          5
frühlingfrierende Birke bin?


## Aus: *Das Stunden-Buch*

WIR dürfen dich nicht eigenmächtig malen,
du Dämmernde, aus der der Morgen stieg.
Wir holen aus den alten Farbenschalen
die gleichen Striche und die gleichen Strahlen,
mit denen dich der Heilige verschwieg.          5

Wir bauen Bilder vor dir auf wie Wände;
so daß schon tausend Mauern um dich stehn.
Denn dich verhüllen unsre frommen Hände,
sooft dich unsre Herzen offen sehn.


WIR bauen an dir mit zitternden Händen,
und wir türmen Atom auf Atom.
Aber wer kann dich vollenden,
du Dom.

Was ist Rom?          5
Es zerfällt.
Was ist die Welt?
Sie wird zerschlagen,
eh deine Türme Kuppeln tragen,
eh aus Meilen von Mosaik          10
deine strahlende Stirne stieg.

Aber manchmal im Traum
kann ich deinen Raum

WHAT is the furthest I shall reach
in life, and who can tell me? Whether
I'll still be* a wanderer of the storm
and living as a wave in the pool,
and whether even I'll still be the pale,                              5
spring-cold, spring-wind-trembling birch?


## From *The Book of Hours*

SO arbitrarily* we* may not paint you,
you who are dawn, from whom the morning rose.
We fetch our colours out of the ancient trays,
the same brush-strokes, and the very rays
with which the saint surrounded you and stilled you.              5

Images we build you in their thousands,
and set them up in dense walls* round you.
Our hands veil you in devotion, lest
you stand apparent to the heart that finds you.


WE build you* with our trembling hands,*
towering atom on atom.
But who can complete your plan,
you our cathedral?

What is Rome?                                                    5
All but scattered.
What is the world?
It will be shattered
before there are cupolas on your towers,
before the miles of mosaic floors                               10
give rise to your haloed head.

But at times in a dream
I have overseen

überschaun
tief vom Beginne                                        15
bis zu des Daches goldenem Grate.

Und ich seh: meine Sinne
bilden und baun
die letzten Zierate.


ICH finde dich in allen diesen Dingen,
denen ich gut und wie ein Bruder bin;
als Samen sonnst du dich in den geringen
und in den großen giebst du groß dich hin.

Das ist das wundersame Spiel der Kräfte,          5
daß sie so dienend durch die Dinge gehn:
in Wurzeln wachsend, schwindend in die Schäfte
und in den Wipfeln wie ein Auferstehn.


ICH kann nicht glauben, daß der kleine Tod,
dem wir doch täglich übern Scheitel schauen,
uns eine Sorge bleibt und eine Not.

Ich kann nicht glauben, daß er ernsthaft droht;
ich lebe noch, ich habe Zeit zu bauen:             5
mein Blut ist länger als die Rosen rot.

Mein Sinn ist tiefer als das witzige Spiel
mit unsrer Furcht, darin er sich gefällt.
Ich bin die Welt,
aus der er irrend fiel.                              10

                    Wie er
kreisende Mönche wandern so umher;
man fürchtet sich vor ihrer Wiederkehr,
man weiß nicht: ist es jedesmal derselbe,
sinds zwei, sinds zehn, sinds tausend oder mehr?

your gilded space,
from its deep foundations                              15
up to the highest golden groin.


And I see: my senses
paint and create
the last decorations.



I FIND your trace in all these things,* in all
that like a brother I am careful for;
you sun yourself, a seed, within the small
and in the great give yourself the more.


This the mysterious play of forces, then,        5
that serve in things, over and under ground:
that rise in roots, narrow into the stem,
and in the crown like resurrection stand.



I CANNOT think that little figure Death,*
over whose smooth pate we look at life,
will be our forced fate, our dark care.


I cannot imagine him a serious threat;
I am alive, have time to build; my blood        5
is red for longer than the roses are.


My mind is broader than the game of terror
in which he taunts us with his bitter tease.
I am the world
he fell from in his dire error.                         10


Like the wandering monks* whose each return
we come to dread, he echoes their disguise.
We do not know: is he the same each time,
or two, ten, or perhaps thousands strong?

Man kennt nur diese fremde gelbe Hand,                15
die sich ausstreckt so nackt und nah –
da da:
als käm sie aus dem eigenen Gewand.


WAS wirst du tun, Gott, wenn ich sterbe?
Ich bin dein Krug (wenn ich zerscherbe?)
Ich bin dein Trank (wenn ich verderbe?)
Bin dein Gewand und dein Gewerbe,
mit mir verlierst du deinen Sinn.                     5

Nach mir hast du kein Haus, darin
dich Worte, nah und warm, begrüßen.
Es fällt von deinen müden Füßen
die Samtsandale, die ich bin.

Dein großer Mantel läßt dich los.                     10
Dein Blick, den ich mit meiner Wange
warm, wie mit einem Pfühl, empfange,
wird kommen, wird mich suchen, lange –
und legt beim Sonnenuntergange
sich fremden Steinen in den Schoß.                    15

Was wirst du tun, Gott? Ich bin bange.


WIE der Wächter in den Weingeländen
seine Hütte hat und wacht,
bin ich Hütte, Herr, in deinen Händen
und bin Nacht, o Herr, von deiner Nacht.

Weinberg, Weide, alter Apfelgarten,                   5
Acker, der kein Frühjahr überschlägt,
Feigenbaum, der auch im marmorharten
Grunde hundert Früchte trägt:

Only the yellow hand* we recognize,                          15
nakedly reaching, alien—near—
there; and there;
near as from our own sleeve all along.

WHAT will you do, God, when I die?
I, your pitcher (if I should shatter?);
drink for your thirst (if I should scatter)?
I am your garment and your matter;
you have no meaning once I'm dead.*                           5

Then you will meet no intimate, warm
words, as when I was your retreat.
The velvet sandals that I am
will loosen, fall from your tired feet.

Your heavy cloak will slip undone.                           10
Your glance, for which my cheek has made
warm pillowing, will come, will spend
the live-long day in search of me—
and settle, as the sun dips,
into some lap of alien stone.                                15

What will you do, God? I'm afraid.

JUST as the watchman of the vineyard lands*
has his hut—keeps his watch—
so am I, O Lord, hut in your hands
and night, Lord, to meet your night's touch.

Vineyard, pasture and ancient apple orchard,                 5
field that will not neglect the turn of spring,
fig-tree, even set in marble-hardened
ground, a hundredfold in fruiting:

Duft geht aus aus deinen runden Zweigen.
Und du fragst nicht, ob ich wachsam sei;                    10
furchtlos, aufgelöst in Säften, steigen
deine Tiefen still an mir vorbei.


ICH war bei den ältesten Mönchen, den Malern und Mythenmeldern,
die schrieben ruhig Geschichten und zeichneten Runen des Ruhms.
Und ich seh dich in meinen Gesichten mit Winden, Wassern und
    Wäldern
rauschend am Rande des Christentums,
du Land, nicht zu lichten.                                   5

Ich will dich erzählen, ich will dich beschaun und beschreiben,
nicht mit Bol und mit Gold, nur mit Tinte aus Apfelbaumrinden;
ich kann auch mit Perlen dich nicht an die Blätter binden,
und das zitterndste Bild, das mir meine Sinne erfinden,
du würdest es blind durch dein einfaches Sein übertreiben.   10

So will ich die Dinge in dir nur bescheiden und schlichthin
    benamen,
will die Könige nennen, die ältesten, woher sie kamen,
und will ihre Taten und Schlachten berichten am Rand meiner Seiten.

Denn du bist der Boden. Dir sind nur wie Sommer die Zeiten,
und du denkst an die nahen nicht anders als an die entfernten,   15
und ob sie dich tiefer besamen und besser bebauen lernten:
du fühlst dich nur leise berührt von den ähnlichen Ernten
und hörst weder Säer noch Schnitter, die über dich schreiten.


LÖSCH mir die Augen aus: ich kann dich sehn,
wirf mir die Ohren zu: ich kann dich hören,
und ohne Füße kann ich zu dir gehn,
und ohne Mund noch kann ich dich beschwören.
Brich mir die Arme ab, ich fasse dich                        5
mit meinem Herzen wie mit einer Hand,

Fragrance seeps from your round boughs. You do not
question whether I have watchful eyes;                          10
fearless, loosed in juices, all your deeps
pass me unstopping as they rise.


I LIVED with the ancient monks, painters and tellers of myths,
the quiet scribes of histories and runes of renown.
And I see you in my visions, with waters and woods and winds,
rustling, just beyond Christendom,
you land, not for clearing.                                      5


I want to narrate you,* I want to observe and describe
not with red or gold, but with ink of apple-tree rind;
not even with pearls could you begin to be bound
to the page, and your tenderest image springing to mind
you would transcend by your merest existence, blindly.          10

All things that go to make you I would unassumingly name;
I would tell of the kings, the oldest, and lands whence they came,
and record their battles and deeds in the margins of my pages.

For you are the ground; your summers our lingering ages;
you remember your distant tillers as well as the near,          15
and whether the near have sown you the better and ploughed you
    the deeper;
and barely aware of the harvesting of the ear
you hear neither sower advancing above you nor reaper.


PUT out my eyes: I see you still the same;*
deaden my ears: I cannot help but hear you;
without my feet still I can walk towards you;
without my mouth still I evoke your name.
Break both my arms, and I will hold you fast:                   5
my stronger heart will grasp you like a hand;

halt mir das Herz zu, und mein Hirn wird schlagen,
und wirfst du in mein Hirn den Brand,
so werd ich dich auf meinem Blute tragen.


Du bist die Zukunft, großes Morgenrot
über den Ebenen der Ewigkeit.
Du bist der Hahnschrei nach der Nacht der Zeit,
der Tau, die Morgenmette und die Maid,
der fremde Mann, die Mutter und der Tod.    5

Du bist die sich verwandelnde Gestalt,
die immer einsam aus dem Schicksal ragt,
die unbejubelt bleibt und unbeklagt
und unbeschrieben wie ein wilder Wald.

Du bist der Dinge tiefer Inbegriff,    10
der seines Wesens letztes Wort verschweigt
und sich den Andern immer anders zeigt:
dem Schiff als Küste und dem Land als Schiff.


Die Könige der Welt sind alt
und werden keine Erben haben.
Die Söhne sterben schon als Knaben,
und ihre bleichen Töchter gaben
die kranken Kronen der Gewalt.    5

Der Pöbel bricht sie klein zu Geld,
der zeitgemäße Herr der Welt
dehnt sie im Feuer zu Maschinen,
die seinem Wollen grollend dienen;
aber das Glück ist nicht mit ihnen.    10

Das Erz hat Heimweh. Und verlassen
will es die Münzen und die Räder,
die es ein kleines Leben lehren.

arrest my heart: my brain will throb its beat;
ignite my brain with firebrand,
then I will bear you in my blood's heat.


YOU are the future, sovereign morning red
streamed out over the eternal plains;
cock-crow after the great night of time,
dew, matins at first morning, maid,
stranger, mother, and death's final name.                    5

You are the Self-transfiguring, looming
limitless upward out of fate, lone
figure uncelebrated, unlamented,
unwritten like the wildwood of the unknown.

You are the essence deep in things, holding          10
its ultimate word silent in your ban,*
the unchanging face of endless change, revealed
to coastland as the ship, to ship as land.


THE emperors of earth are old
and have no heirs. Their sons died young,
and their pallid daughters loosed their hold
on the crowns bequeathed them and yielded into
the hands of force the sickened gold.                    5

The people break it down to coin,
and in his furnaces the one
lord of the present beats it out into
growling machines doing his will—
but fortune is beyond them still.                    10

The ore is sick for its origins
and leaves behind it coin and wheel*
that teach only the petty life;

Und aus Fabriken und aus Kassen
wird es zurück in das Geäder                                    15
der aufgetanen Berge kehren,
die sich verschließen hinter ihm.


JETZT reifen schon die roten Berberitzen,
alternde Astern atmen schwach im Beet.
Wer jetzt nicht reich ist, da der Sommer geht,
wird immer warten und sich nie besitzen.

Wer jetzt nicht seine Augen schließen kann,          5
gewiß, daß eine Fülle von Gesichten
in ihm nur wartet bis die Nacht begann,
um sich in seinem Dunkel aufzurichten: –
der ist vergangen wie ein alter Mann.

Dem kommt nichts mehr, dem stößt kein Tag mehr zu,     10
und alles lügt ihn an, was ihm geschieht;
auch du, mein Gott. Und wie ein Stein bist du,
welcher ihn täglich in die Tiefe zieht.


DENN wir sind nur die Schale und das Blatt.
Der große Tod, den jeder in sich hat,
das ist die Frucht, um die sich alles dreht.

Um ihretwillen heben Mädchen an
und kommen wie ein Baum aus einer Laute,                5
und Knaben sehnen sich um sie zum Mann;
und Frauen sind den Wachsenden Vertraute
für Ängste, die sonst niemand nehmen kann.
Um ihretwillen *bleibt* das Angeschaute
wie Ewiges, auch wenn es lang verrann, –
und jeder, welcher bildete und baute,                      10
ward Welt um diese Frucht, und fror und taute
und windete ihr zu und schien sie an.

from bank and factory and till
unbidden into the mountain veins                                   15
of rock re–opened it will steal,
and behind it rock will close again.


THE barberries* already ripen red;
ageing asters fail, breath by breath.
He who is not yet rich* at summer's passing
will wait for ever to possess himself.

He who shall find he cannot close his eyes                          5
and know that a full multitude of visions
waits for no more than night before it rises
teeming in the darkness of his sleep—
is like an old man in a bygone time.

Nothing approaches him or jostles him;                             10
everything that befalls him is deceit.
You too, O God. And you are like a stone
dragging him day by day into the deeps.


FOR we are only rind of fruit, and leaf.
The great death, which each of us contains,
is that fruit round which the world turns.

And for its sake maidens bloom and issue
like trees from lutes;* boys aspire towards it                      5
coming to manhood; and women, confidantes
to youth, alleviate its adolescent
anxieties as no one else can do.
And for its sake, what we see *remains*
like the eternal, even if long run down,                           10
and everyone who built or painted became
world about this fruit, froze, thawed
and altered course towards it, shone on it.

In sie ist eingegangen alle Wärme
der Herzen und der Hirne weißes Glühn – :
Doch deine Engel ziehn wie Vogelschwärme,
und sie erfanden alle Früchte grün.

15

HERR: Wir sind ärmer denn die armen Tiere,
die ihres Todes enden, wennauch blind,
weil wir noch alle ungestorben sind.
*Den* gieb uns, der die Wissenschaft gewinnt,
das Leben aufzubinden in Spaliere,
um welche zeitiger der Mai beginnt.

5

Denn dieses macht das Sterben fremd und schwer,
daß es nicht *unser* Tod ist; einer der
uns endlich nimmt, nur weil wir keinen reifen.
Drum geht ein Sturm, uns alle abzustreifen.

10

Wir stehn in deinem Garten Jahr und Jahr
Und sind die Bäume, süßen Tod zu tragen;
aber wir altern in den Erntetagen,
und so wie Frauen, welche du geschlagen,
sind wir verschlossen, schlecht und unfruchtbar.

15

Oder ist meine Hoffahrt ungerecht:
sind Bäume besser? Sind wir nur Geschlecht
und Schoß von Frauen, welche viel gewähren? –
Wir haben mit der Ewigkeit gehurt,
und wenn das Kreißbett da ist, so gebären
wir unsres Todes tote Fehlgeburt;
den krummen, kummervollen Embryo,
der sich (als ob ihn Schreckliches erschreckte)
die Augenkeime mit den Händen deckte
und dem schon auf der ausgebauten Stirne
die Angst von allem steht, was er nicht litt, –
und alle schließen so wie eine Dirne
in Kindbettkrämpfen und am Kaiserschnitt.

20

25

Into it is given all the warmth
of hearts and hot white glowing of the brain;                    15
and yet your angels stream like flocking birds
and coming upon the fruit, found it green.*


LORD, we are poorer than the poor beasts*
dying their blind death. For we have all
less than entirely died.* Send us the One*
who guides into our hands the precious skill
to bind life in espaliers, where May                             5
comes early, and the year's fruit advances.

Dying is difficult and alien
for this: it is not *our* death but takes us
because we cannot bring our own to ripen.
So, in a storm, it strips us from the branches.                  10

We stand, Lord, year on year in your garden,
your trees for nurturing a sweet death;
but by the harvest we have grown sere,
and like the woman you have struck barren
close down, false to our promise, fruitless.                     15

Or is my arrogance too much? Are trees
in the end better? Are we only womb
and sex of women who yield all too freely?
Surely we have whored with eternity
and when we come to childbed bring forth                         20
only the stillborn foetus of our death:
embryo, bent, full of misery,
trying to cover with its mere hands
(as though in fear of the fearful) eyes unformed
still; and on its bulged forehead stands                         25
dread of its destiny unmet, unsuffered—
so die we all, like just so many whores,
in labour pains, and from caesareans.

DENN sieh: sie werden leben und sich mehren
und nicht bezwungen werden von der Zeit,
und werden wachsen wie des Waldes Beeren
den Boden bergend unter Süßigkeit.

Denn selig sind, die niemals sich entfernten          5
und still im Regen standen ohne Dach;
zu ihnen werden kommen alle Ernten,
und ihre Frucht wird voll sein tausendfach.

Sie werden dauern über jedes Ende
und über Reiche, deren Sinn verrinnt,          10
und werden sich wie ausgeruhte Hände
erheben, wenn die Hände aller Stände
und aller Völker müde sind.

NUR nimm sie wieder aus der Städte Schuld,
wo ihnen alles Zorn ist und verworren
und wo sie in den Tagen aus Tumult
verdorren mit verwundeter Geduld.

Hat denn für sie die Erde keinen Raum?          5
Wen sucht der Wind? Wer trinkt des Baches Helle?
Ist in der Teiche tiefem Ufertraum
kein Spiegelbild mehr frei für Tür und Schwelle?
Sie brauchen ja nur eine kleine Stelle,
auf der sie alles haben wie ein Baum.          10

DIE Städte aber wollen nur das Ihre
und reißen alles mit in ihren Lauf.
Wie hohles Holz zerbrechen sie die Tiere
und brauchen viele Völker brennend auf.

Und ihre Menschen dienen in Kulturen          5
und fallen tief aus Gleichgewicht und Maß,

FOR see, they will live, flourish, multiply
unconstrained by time, and numberless
grow like the woodland berries till they hide
the forest floor under their sweetness.

For they are blessed* who did not turn and run          5
but stood unmoved, roofless in the rain;
their hands will reap as long as there are harvests
and their fruit fill a thousandfold.

They will persist further than any end,
outlive the rich, whose meaning seeps away,          10
and at last raise themselves like rested hands
when those of other lands,
peoples and classes weary.*


BUT bear them away again from urban evils:
from the disturbed and angry environs fighting
their lives, the tumultuous existence
wasting them away in wounded patience.

Has the earth no place for them?* Whom does the thrill          5
of the wind seek? Who drinks of the brook's brilliance?
And in the deep of the pool's reverie
is there no space to reflect their door, their sill?
The poor, as we know, need only a small niche
in which to ground their whole world, like a tree.          10


CITIES turn their force full on their own,
wrenching things along in their slipstream; here
animals are snapped like hollow stems
and* communities razed whole in flame.

Subservient to cult and craze, their people          5
tip out of balance, lapse from the measured mean,

und nennen Fortschritt ihre Schneckenspuren
und fahren rascher, wo sie langsam fuhren,
und fühlen sich und funkeln wie die Huren
und lärmen lauter mit Metall und Glas.     10

Es ist, als ob ein Trug sie täglich äffte,
sie können gar nicht mehr sie selber sein;
das Geld wächst an, hat alle ihre Kräfte
und ist wie Ostwind groß, und sie sind klein
und ausgeholt und warten, daß der Wein     15
und alles Gift der Tier- und Menschensäfte
sie reize zu vergänglichem Geschäfte.

## Aus: *Das Buch der Bilder*

### Eingang

WER du auch seist: am Abend tritt hinaus
aus deiner Stube, drin du alles weißt;
als letztes vor der Ferne liegt dein Haus:
wer du auch seist.
Mit deinen Augen, welche müde kaum     5
von der verbrauchten Schwelle sich befrein,
hebst du ganz langsam einen schwarzen Baum
und stellst ihn vor den Himmel: schlank, allein.
Und hast die Welt gemacht. Und sie ist groß
und wie ein Wort, das noch im Schweigen reift.     10
Und wie dein Wille ihren Sinn begreift,
lassen sie deine Augen zärtlich los . . .

### Die Heilige

DAS Volk war durstig; also ging das eine
durstlose Mädchen, ging die Steine
um Wasser flehen für ein ganzes Volk.
Doch ohne Zeichen blieb der Zweig der Weide,

count their snail-tracks an advance, hasten
where they had used to go soberly, and learn
to glitter, putting on the minds of whores,
and set their glass and metal screaming.                    10

Day on day aped by an illusion,
they strain and fail to find real lives,
and money rises, draining them, violent
like the east wind, and they are the small,
held in abeyance, waiting for wine, for all                  15
the juice of animal and human poisons
to tempt them towards the transient.*

## From *The Book of Images*

### *Entrance*

WHOEVER you may be: at evening step forth
out of your room, where nothing is unknown;
your house, the last, stands before the distance:
whoever you may be.
Lifting fatigued eyes now barely able                         5
to free their gaze* beyond the worn sill,
you raise, slowly, a single black tree
to set against the sky: slight, alone.
And you have made the world. And it is wide
and like a word ripening on through silence.                 10
And as your will comes to grasp* its sense,
tenderly your eyes let it go . . .

### *The Saint*

THE people thirsted; seeing them, the only
thirstless girl went to implore
of stones the water for a whole people.
The willow twig she carried gave no sign;

und sie ermattete am langen Gehn 5
und dachte endlich nur, daß einer leide,
(ein kranker Knabe, und sie hatten beide
sich einmal abends ahnend angesehn).
Da neigte sich die junge Weidenrute
in ihren Händen dürstend wie ein Tier: 10
jetzt ging sie blühend über ihrem Blute,
und rauschend ging ihr Blut tief unter ihr.

## Aus einer Kindheit

DAS Dunkeln war wie Reichtum in dem Raume,
darin der Knabe, sehr verheimlicht, saß.
Und als die Mutter eintrat wie im Traume,
erzitterte im stillen Schrank ein Glas.
Sie fühlte, wie das Zimmer sie verriet, 5
und küßte ihren Knaben: Bist du hier? . . .
Dann schauten beide bang nach dem Klavier,
denn manchen Abend hatte sie ein Lied,
darin das Kind sich seltsam tief verfing.

Es saß sehr still. Sein großes Schauen hing 10
an ihrer Hand, die ganz gebeugt vom Ringe,
als ob sie schwer in Schneewehn ginge,
über die weißen Tasten ging.

## Der Knabe

ICH möchte einer werden so wie die,
die durch die Nacht mit wilden Pferden fahren,
mit Fackeln, die gleich aufgegangnen Haaren
in ihres Jagens großem Winde wehn.
Vorn möcht ich stehen wie in einem Kahne, 5
groß und wie eine Fahne aufgerollt.
Dunkel, aber mit einem Helm von Gold,

she weakened from interminable walking                               5
and came to realize one other suffered
(a sick boy, and one evening they had looked
long at each other in an understanding).
Then the young willow twisted in her hands*
and bent in thirst, like a beast to water;                          10
now she walked blossoming above her blood,
and murmuring, her blood ran deep beneath her.


## From a Childhood*

THE darkness was like riches in the room
in which the boy sat, secret in himself.
And when his mother came in, as in dreams,
a glass trembled on the quiet shelf—
she felt the room give her away and stooped                         5
to kiss her boy: 'You're here?' . . . Then half shy
they both turned their eyes to the piano,
for many an evening when she sang to him
the child was caught strangely in her singing.

He sat quite still. His big gaze                                    10
hung on her hand, bowed underneath the ring
and stepping as though in heavy blown snow
over the white piano-keys.


## The Boy

I WANT to be one of those who drive their wild
horses through the night, whose torches flare
streaming behind them in the great wind
of the chase, broken out like loosed hair.
I wish to stand as at a boat's prow,                                5
tall and set there like a flag unfurled.
Dark, but with a helm that gleams gold

der unruhig glänzt. Und hinter mir gereiht
zehn Männer aus derselben Dunkelheit
mit Helmen, die, wie meiner, unstät sind,                    10
bald klar wie Glas, bald dunkel, alt und blind.
Und einer steht bei mir und bläst uns Raum
mit der Trompete, welche blitzt und schreit,
und bläst uns eine schwarze Einsamkeit,
durch die wir rasen wie ein rascher Traum:                  15
Die Häuser fallen hinter uns ins Knie,
die Gassen biegen sich uns schief entgegen,
die Plätze weichen aus: wir fassen sie,
und unsre Rosse rauschen wie ein Regen.


## Menschen bei Nacht

DIE Nächte sind nicht für die Menge gemacht.
Von deinem Nachbar trennt dich die Nacht,
und du sollst ihn nicht suchen trotzdem.
Und machst du nachts deine Stube licht,
um Menschen zu schauen ins Angesicht,                        5
so mußt du bedenken: wem.

Die Menschen sind furchtbar vom Licht entstellt,
das von ihren Gesichtern träuft,
und haben sie nachts sich zusammengesellt,
so schaust du eine wankende Welt                            10
durcheinandergehäuft.
Auf ihren Stirnen hat gelber Schein
alle Gedanken verdrängt,
in ihren Blicken flackert der Wein,
an ihren Händen hängt                                       15
die schwere Gebärde, mit der sie sich
bei ihren Gesprächen verstehn;
und dabei sagen sie: *Ich* und *Ich*
und meinen: Irgendwen.

fitfully, and ten men behind,
dark like me, helmets like mine, shifting
from glass-clear to dark and old and blind.                    10
And one next to me sounds his trumpet,* summons
space ahead for us with its glittering shout,
and blows for us a black solitude
through which we chase like dreams. Behind us house
on house falls to its knees, the curved lanes                    15
bend steeply to meet us, opening out
to wide, evasive squares for us to seize:
our rushing horses like a storm of rain.


## People at Night

NIGHTS* are not created for crowds.
The night distances you from your neighbour,
and you do best not to seek him out.
And if you light up your place at night
for looking your fellows in the eyes,                    5
consider carefully whose.

People terribly distort
in the light that trickles from their faces,
and wherever they may meet at night
it is there before you, this world of theirs,                    10
swaying and heaped and fraught.
Their foreheads shine with a yellow glaze
that drives out any thought,
their eyes flame with the wine they absorb,
their hands carry the weight                    15
of the heavy gesture by which they follow
each other's talk,
and they say as they use it: *I* and *I*,
and they mean: anybody.

## Der Nachbar

FREMDE Geige, gehst du mir nach?
In wieviel fernen Städten schon sprach
deine einsame Nacht zu meiner?
Spielen dich hunderte? Spielt dich einer?

Giebt es in allen großen Städten       5
solche, die sich ohne dich
schon in den Flüssen verloren hätten?
Und warum trifft es immer mich?

Warum bin ich immer der Nachbar derer,
die dich bange zwingen zu singen       10
und zu sagen: Das Leben ist schwerer
als die Schwere von allen Dingen.

## Pont du Carrousel

DER blinde Mann, der auf der Brücke steht,
grau wie ein Markstein namenloser Reiche,
er ist vielleicht das Ding, das immer gleiche,
um das von fern die Sternenstunde geht,
und der Gestirne stiller Mittelpunkt.       5
Denn alles um ihm irrt und rinnt und prunkt.

Er ist der unbewegliche Gerechte,
in viele wirre Wege hingestellt;
der dunkle Eingang in die Unterwelt
bei einem oberflächlichen Geschlechte.       10

## Einsamkeit

DIE Einsamkeit ist wie ein Regen.
Sie steigt vom Meer den Abenden entgegen;
von Ebenen, die fern sind und entlegen,

## The Neighbour

STRANGE violin, are you following me?
In how many distant cities already
has your lone night communed with mine?
Do hundreds play you? Does only one?

Are there, living in every great city,　　5
people who would be lost by now
without you—in the city rivers?
And why is all this meant for me?

Why am I always neighbour* to those
who from anxiety force you to sing　　10
and even to say: life is heavier
than the heaviness of the sum of things.

## Pont du Carrousel*

THE blind man* stands there on the bridge, grey
as a nameless state's boundary stone, the one thing,
maybe, that is changeless, round which spin
distant stellar hours; the still midpoint
of constellations. For there is a wheeling　　5
and wandering round him, a flowing and parading.

He is the just man,* set down in bewildered
ways to stand in them immovable,
the entrance to the underworld, sole
and dark among a superficial people.　　10

## Solitude

SOLITUDE is like a rain.
It lifts from the sea to meet the coming evenings
and from remote, outlying plains towards

geht sie zum Himmel, der sie immer hat.
Und erst vom Himmel fällt sie auf die Stadt.                    5

Regnet hernieder in den Zwitterstunden,
wenn sich nach Morgen wenden alle Gassen
und wenn die Leiber, welche nichts gefunden,
enttäuscht und traurig von einander lassen;
und wenn die Menschen, die einander hassen,               10
in *einem* Bett zusammen schlafen müssen:

dann geht die Einsamkeit mit den Flüssen . . .


## Herbsttag

HERR: es ist Zeit. Der Sommer war sehr groß.
Leg deinen Schatten auf die Sonnenuhren,
und auf den Fluren laß die Winde los.

Befiehl den letzten Früchten voll zu sein;
gieb ihnen noch zwei südlichere Tage,                          5
dränge sie zur Vollendung hin und jage
die letzte Süße in den schweren Wein.

Wer jetzt kein Haus hat, baut sich keines mehr.
Wer jetzt allein ist, wird es lange bleiben,
wird wachen, lesen, lange Briefe schreiben             10
und wird in den Alleen hin und her
unruhig wandern, wenn die Blätter treiben.


## Abend

DER Abend wechselt langsam die Gewänder,
die ihm ein Rand von alten Bäumen hält;
du schaust: und von dir scheiden sich die Länder,
ein himmelfahrendes und eins, das fällt;

skies where it is held in constant store.
And falls* on cities from sky-reservoirs.                     5

Rains down in the hybrid half-lit hours
when city lanes and alleys turn to morning
and bodies slip apart in the sad
disillusionment of finding nothing;
and when human beings who hate each other          10
are forced to sleep together in a bed:

then, solitude runs with the rivers' running . . .

## Autumn Day

LORD, it is time. The summer was immense.
Lay your shadow on the sundials, turn
the urgent winds loose across the plains.

Ordain full ripening of the last fruit;
grant it but two days in the south wind,                      5
follow it to perfection, and compress
the last sweetness for the heavy wine.

Whoever has no home* will build none now.
Whoever is alone will long remain so,
sleepless, taken up with books and letters          10
and wandering back and forth along the ways,
restive, at the drifting of the leaves.

## Evening

SLOWLY the evening changes its array,
held for it in a belt of ancient trees;
you watch: and bands of landscape slip from you,
one heavenward and one that falls away;

und lassen dich, zu keinem ganz gehörend,      5
nicht ganz so dunkel wie das Haus, das schweigt,
nicht ganz so sicher Ewiges beschwörend
wie das, was Stern wird jede Nacht und steigt —

und lassen dir (unsäglich zu entwirrn)
dein Leben bang und riesenhaft und reifend,    10
so daß es, bald begrenzt und bald begreifend,
abwechselnd Stein in dir wird und Gestirn.

## Die Heiligen Drei Könige

Legende

EINST als am Saum der Wüsten sich
auftat die Hand des Herrn
wie eine Frucht, die sommerlich
verkündet ihren Kern,
da war ein Wunder: Fern     5
erkannten und begrüßten sich
drei Könige und ein Stern.

Drei Könige von Unterwegs
und der Stern Überall,
die zogen alle (überlegs!)     10
so rechts ein Rex und links ein Rex
zu einem stillen Stall.

Was brachten die nicht alles mit
zum Stall von Bethlehem!
Weithin erklirrte jeder Schritt,     15
und der auf einem Rappen ritt,
saß samten und bequem.
Und der zu seiner Rechten ging,
der war ein goldner Mann,
und der zu seiner Linken fing     20
mit Schwung und Schwing
und Klang und Kling

and you are left not quite a part of either,                    5
not quite as shadowed as a house in silence,
or certain in invoking the eternal
as that which grows to star each night and rises*—

and leaving you (for untold disentangling)
your life, immense, maturing and unsure,                    10
so that, by turns confined and comprehending,
it alternates as stone in you and star.


## The Three Kings*

Legend

ONCE, upon the deserts' edge,
the Lord's hand opened,
as though it were a summer fruit
announcing its kernel;
and then, a miracle:                    5
greeting each other from afar
three kings and a star.


And these three kings Itinerant
and the star Everywhere,
were travelling (imagine it!)                    10
(a Rex to left, a Rex to right)*
towards a peaceful stable.


And what they didn't bring with them
to the stall at Bethlehem!
Each step clattered out ahead,                    15
and he that sat the black horse rode
at ease in his velvet.
And he that rode upon the right
was like a man of gold.
And he on the left side began                    20
with fling and swing
and ting-a-ling,

aus einem runden Silberding,
das wiegend und in Ringen hing,
ganz blau zu rauchen an.                                         25
Da lachte der Stern Überall
so seltsam über sie,
und lief voraus und stand am Stall
und sagte zu Marie:

Da bring ich eine Wanderschaft                                   30
aus vieler Fremde her.
Drei Könige mit *magenkraft*,
von Gold und Topas schwer
und dunkel, tumb und heidenhaft, –
erschrick mir nicht zu sehr.                                     35
Sie haben alle drei zuhaus
zwölf Töchter, keinen Sohn,
so bitten sie sich deinen aus
als Sonne ihres Himmelblaus
und Trost für ihren Thron.                                       40
Doch mußt du nicht gleich glauben: bloß
ein Funkelfürst und Heidenscheich
sei deines Sohnes Los.
Bedenk, der Weg ist groß.
Sie wandern lange, Hirten gleich,                                45
inzwischen fällt ihr reifes Reich
weiß Gott wem in den Schoß.
Und während hier, wie Westwind warm,
der Ochs ihr Ohr umschnaubt,
sind sie vielleicht schon alle arm                              50
und so wie ohne Haupt.
Drum mach mit deinem Lächeln licht
die Wirrnis, die sie sind,
und wende du dein Angesicht
nach Aufgang und dein Kind;                                      55
dort liegt in blauen Linien,
was jeder dir verließ:
Smaragda und Rubinien
und die Tale von Türkis.

out of a round silver thing*
that hung rocking by its rings,
a thick blue smoking.                                        25
And then the star Everywhere
laughed a strange laughter,
and ran ahead and stood over
the stall, saying to Mary:


I bring a wandering company                                  30
from far-flung lands,
three kings of might, all of them
heavy with gold and topaz,
and dark and dim and heathenish—
but have no fear. At home                                     35
the three of them have daughters twelve
but none of them a son,
so they would ask of you your own
to be their sun in azure heaven*
and comfort for their throne.                                40
Yet do not think to take so soon
mere sparkle-prince or heathen sheikh
for your son's destiny.
For think: the road is long,
and they have wandered, herdsman-like,                       45
so far that God knows in what lap
their ripe kingdoms fall.
And whereas here, warm as west wind,
the ox snorts at their cheek,
elsewhere they may be poor as poor                           50
and headless, so to speak.
So with the light that is your smile
illumine the confusion,
and turn your face and turn your child
towards the dawn, for there it is                            55
that in its azure lines lies
what each abandoned for you:
Emeralda and Rubinia
and the Valleys of Turquoise.

## Das Lied des Aussätzigen

Sieh ich bin einer, den alles verlassen hat.
Keiner weiß in der Stadt von mir,
Aussatz hat mich befallen.
Und ich schlage mein Klapperwerk,
klopfe mein trauriges Augenmerk                              5
in die Ohren allen
die nahe vorübergehn.
Und die es hölzern hören, sehn
erst gar nicht her, und was hier geschehn
wollen sie nicht erfahren.                                   10

Soweit der Klang meiner Klapper reicht
bin ich zuhause; aber vielleicht
machst Du meine Klapper so laut,
daß sich keiner in meine Ferne traut
der mir jetzt aus der Nähe weicht.                           15
So daß ich sehr lange gehen kann
ohne Mädchen, Frau oder Mann
oder Kind zu entdecken.

Tiere will ich nicht schrecken.

## Von den Fontänen

Auf einmal weiß ich viel von den Fontänen,
den unbegreiflichen Bäumen aus Glas.
Ich könnte reden wie von eignen Tränen,
die ich, ergriffen von sehr großen Träumen,
einmal vergeudete und dann vergaß.                           5

Vergaß ich denn, daß Himmel Hände reichen
zu vielen Dingen und in das Gedränge?
Sah ich nicht immer Großheit ohnegleichen
im Aufstieg alter Parke, vor den weichen
erwartungsvollen Abenden, – in bleichen                      10
aus fremden Mädchen steigenden Gesängen,

## The Leper's Song

LOOK at me: one of those the world has abandoned.*
Here in the city I am not known;
leprosy* has befallen me.
Banging my rattle* as I go,
I beat the sad sight that I am                                    5
in anyone's ear
who passes me close by.
And those who hear it, woodenly, simply
look away, for what's happened here
they would prefer not to see.                                     10

Wherever my rattle makes itself heard,
that is my home; but you, Lord, may
be making the rattle sound so loud
that people will fear me further away
who now shrink from my neighbourhood.                             15
So I can walk and walk, without
chance of a glimpse of girl or woman
or child or man.

Animals I hope not to frighten.

## About Fountains

SUDDENLY I have knowledge of* the fountains,
those enigmatic trees of glass.*
Could speak of them as of my own tears,
when I was once gripped by great dreams
and shed tears that I have since forgotten.                       5

Did I forget* that heavens extend their hands
to many things, and into human thronging?
Did I not always see magnificence
in steep paths* of old parks, in evenings
of soft expectancy?—in pale songs                                10
  rising from throats of unknown girls and brimming

die überfließen aus der Melodie
und wirklich werden und als müßten sie
sich spiegeln in den aufgetanen Teichen?

Ich muß mich nur erinnern an das Alles,                    15
was an Fontänen und an mir geschah, –
dann fühl ich auch die Last des Niederfalles,
in welcher ich die Wasser wiedersah:
Und weiß von Zweigen, die sich abwärts wandten,
von Stimmen, die mit kleiner Flamme brannten,              20
von Teichen, welche nur die Uferkanten
schwachsinnig und verschoben wiederholten,
von Abendhimmeln, welche von verkohlten
westlichen Wäldern ganz entfremdet traten
sich anders wölbten, dunkelten und taten                   25
als wär das nicht die Welt, die sie gemeint . . .

Vergaß ich denn, daß Stern bei Stern versteint
und sich verschließt gegen die Nachbargloben?
Daß sich die Welten nur noch wie verweint
im Raum erkennen? –Vielleicht sind wir *oben*,            30
in Himmel andrer Wesen eingewoben,
die zu uns aufschaun abends. Vielleicht loben
uns ihre Dichter. Vielleicht beten viele
zu uns empor. Vielleicht sind wir die Ziele
von fremden Flüchen, die uns nie erreichen,               35
Nachbaren eines Gottes, den sie meinen
in unsrer Höhe, wenn sie einsam weinen,
an den sie glauben und den sie verlieren,
und dessen Bildnis, wie ein Schein aus ihren
suchenden Lampen, flüchtig und verweht,                   40
über unsere zerstreuten Gesichter geht . . . .

## *Schlußstück*

DER Tod ist groß.
Wir sind die Seinen

over out of the melody and becoming
real, as though they must reflect themselves
in the receptive wide–open pools?

I must remind myself of all the things                          15
that happened to fountains and to me—I too
shall feel that tumbled-over weight of falling*
in which the waters came to mind again;
and know of boughs bent and sagging down,
of voices flickering at low flame,                              20
of pools, vulnerable and dislodged, shunted
into monotonously squared banks,
of evening skies retreating alienated
before the charred western forests, darkening
their altered vault, acting as if persuaded                    25
that this was not the world they had intended . . .

Did I forget that star by stony star
hardens and closes off from nearer spheres?
That worlds in space must see as though through tears
to know each other?—Perhaps we are *above*,                    30
woven into the heavens of other beings
who watch us in the evening. Perhaps praises
from mouths of poets reach us. Perhaps many prayers
drift up to us. Perhaps these strangers' curses
target us in vain, we who are neighbours                        35
of One they place on level height with us
when left alone in grief, in whom they trust
and whom they lose, a God whose image,
like the fitful and exhausted traces
of light that flicker from their searching lanterns,           40
passes over our indifferent faces . . . .

## End Piece

DEATH is mighty.
Laugh as we may,

lachenden Munds.
Wenn wir uns mitten im Leben meinen,
wagt er zu weinen                                                    5
mitten in uns.


# Gedichte 1906–1908

SINNEND von Legende zu Legende
such ich deinen Namen, helle Frau.
Wie die Nächte um die Sonnenwende,
in die Sterne wachsen ohne Ende,
nimmst du alles in dich auf, Legende,                                5
und umgiebst mich wie ein tiefes Blau.

Aber denen, die dich nicht erfahren,
kann ich, hülflos, nichts versprechen als:
dich aus allen Dingen auszusparen,
so wie man in deinen Mädchenjahren                                  10
zeichnete das Weiß des Wasserfalls.

Dies nur will ich ihnen lassen und
mich verbergen unter dem Geringen.
Unrecht tut an dir Kontur und Mund.
Du bist Himmel, tiefer Hintergrund,                                 15
sanft umrahmt von deinen liebsten Dingen.


## Ehe

SIE ist traurig, lautlos und allein.
Sieh, sie leidet. Deine Nächte legten
sich auf ihre leisen leicht erregten
Nächte wie ein stürzendes Gestein.

Hundertmal in deiner dumpfen Gier                                   5
warst du ihr Vergeuder und Vergifter;
aber daß du einmal wie ein Stifter

we are all his.
Mid-life\*, when we are sure of the day,
Death weeps boldly                                              5
right in our midst.

## Uncollected Poems 1906–1908

MUSING upon legend after legend
I seek your name, you of the bright beauty.\*
As the summer-solstice nights extend
endless into stars, you take, legend,
all things up into yourself, and bend                           5
round me like the summer's deep blue.

But to those who do not know you, helpless
I can promise nothing beyond this:
that I accumulate you,\* out of all
things, as in your youth they sketched the whiteness            10
into impressions of the waterfall.

Just this I would wish to leave them, then would
hide myself beneath the low and trifling.
Outlining you they fail you, brush and word.
You are wide sky, deep background,                              15
gently framed in your familiar things.

### Marriage

SHE is silent, melancholy, alone.
Look how she is suffering. Your nights
lodged themselves over her calm, lightly
roused nights like a pitched stone.

A hundred times in your blunt desire                            5
you were her poisoner and squanderer,
but, in that you knelt once beside her

still und dunkel knietest neben ihr
macht dich männlich und geht aus von dir.


### Fortgehn

PLÖTZLICHES Fortgehn; Draußensein im Grauen
mit Augen, eingeschmolzen, heiß und weich,
und nun in das was *ist* hinauszuschauen – :

O nein, das alles ist ja ein Vergleich.

Der Strom ist so, damit er dich bedeute,                    5
und diese Stadt stand auf weil du erschienst;
die Brücken gehn mit Anstand der dich freute
gelassen her und hin in deinem Dienst.

Und weil das alles ausgedacht ist nur:
dich zu bedeuten – : ist es wie die Erde;              10
die Gärten stehn in dunkelnder Gebärde,
die Fernen sind voll deutsamer Figur – .

Und doch trotzdem, nun kommt es trotzdem wieder:
der Schmerz, der Schmerz des ersten Augenblicks.
Noch war es da – : auf einmal ging es nieder          15
oder flog auf oder war aus wie Lieder – :
das war so voll unsäglichen Geschicks – .

Wie wenn . . . .
                    (bin ichs zu sagen denn imstande?)
Sieh: diese Augen lagen da: Gewande,
ein Angesicht, ein Glanz ging in sie ein               20
als wären sie – – ja was ? – –:
                              der Canal Grande
in seiner großen Zeit und vor dem Brande –
– – – – – – – – – – – – – –
und plötzlich hört Venedig auf zu sein.

darkly, tranquilly, as in endowment,*
manliness new in you goes out to her.


## *Leaving*

LEAVING suddenly. Standing in the grey
world looking with sodden, molten eyes
out into what irrevocably *is*—

Oh, but that is a mere comparison.

The river turns to you in its direction;                5
the city rose up when you came to it;
decorous, as delighted you, the bridges
pass back and forth serenely at your wish.

And since all this is thought into existence
to signify you, it is like the earth:                  10
gardens dark with gesture, distances
filled with the meaning of the metaphor.

And yet, no matter what, it still returns:
pain, the pain left in me from that first
moment. Still there, whether ebbing low                15
or flying up or fading out like songs:
full of inexpressible destiny—

As though . . . .
                    (but can I even say this now?)
those eyes lay there: clothes—a face—a sheen
of light that slipped into them glancingly             20
as though they were—what?—
                                the Grand Canal*
at its most glorious and before the fire*—
— — — — — — — — — — — — — — —
and suddenly, Venice ceases to be.*

## La Dame à la Licorne

(Teppiche im Hôtel de Cluny)

für Stina Frisell

FRAU und Erlauchte: sicher kränken wir
oft Frauen-Schicksal das wir nicht begreifen.
Wir sind für euch die Immer-noch-nicht-Reifen
für euer Leben, das, wenn wir es streifen
ein Einhorn wird, ein scheues, weißes Tier,               5

das flüchtet . . . und sein Bangen ist so groß,
daß ihr es selber/ wie es schlank entschwindet/
nach vielem Traurigsein erst wiederfindet,
noch immer schreckhaft, warm und atemlos.

Dann bleibt ihr bei ihm, fern von uns, – und mild        10
gehn durch des Tagwerks Tasten eure Hände;
demütig dienen euch die Gegenstände,
ihr aber wollt nur *diesen* Wunsch gestillt:
daß einst das Einhorn sein beruhigtes Bild
in eurer Seele schwerem Spiegel fände. –                 15

## Marionetten-Theater

(Furnes, Kermes)

HINTER Stäben, wie Tiere,
türmen sie ihr Getu;
die Stimme ist nicht die ihre,
aber sie ziehn dazu
ihre Arme und Schwerter                                    5
ungemein und weit,
(findige Verwerter
dessen was grade schreit.)

Sie haben keine Gelenke
und hängen ein wenig quer                                  10
und hölzern im Gehenke,

## La Dame à la Licorne

(Tapestries in the Hôtel de Cluny)*
                        for Stina Frisell*

WOMAN and noblewoman: often we injure
the female fate, misapprehending, we whom
you would still consider immature,
and as we touch it, it becomes the shy
white animal that is the unicorn                          5

and flees . . . in fear so great that you yourselves
can find it/ slender in its disappearance/
only after an hour of intense
sadness: warm and panting, tremulous.

Far from us, you stay with it, gently                     10
follow the daily tasks of feeling hands;
and objects humbly serve you—but to fulfil
*this* wish your sole desire: that time may see
the unicorn detect his image, tranquil,
merged in the heavy mirror of your soul.                  15

## Marionette Theatre

(Furnes, Kermes)*

BEHIND bars, like animals,*
they* pile their actions in heaps;
the voice in which they phrase their words
is not their own, but they augment it
in flourishing their arms and swords                      5
through singular, wide sweeps
(and make the most ingenious use
of anything that bleats).

They have no articulations
and hang a bit woodenly                                   10
and on the skew in their harnesses,

aber sie können sehr
töten oder tanzen
oder auch im Ganzen
sich verneigen und noch mehr.                              15


Auch pflegen sie kein Erinnern;
Sie machen sich nichts bewußt,
und von ihrem Innern
gebrauchen sie nur die Brust,
um manchmal darauf zu schlagen                            20
als schlügen sie sie ein.
(Sie wissen, dieses Betragen
ist deutlich und allgemein.)


Ihre großen Gesichter
sind ein für alle Mal;                                     25
nicht wie die unsern: schlichter,
dringend und ideal;
offen wie beim Erwachen
mitten aus einem Traum.
Das giebt natürlich Lachen                                30
draußen in dem Raum,
aus dem die von den Bänken
sehn
wie sich die Puppen kränken
und schrecken und an Schwänken                            35
in Bündeln zu Grunde gehen.


Wenn einer es anders verstände
und säße und lachte nicht:
ihr einziges Stück verschwände
und sie spielten ihr jüngstes Gericht.                    40
Sie rissen an ihren Schnüren
herein vor die kleinen Coulissen
die Hände von oben, die Hände,
die immer versteckten, entdeckten
häßlichen Hände in Rot:                                   45
und stürzten aus allen Türen
und stiegen über die Wände
und schlügen die Hände tot.

but they are capable equally
and utterly of murder
and of the limits of the dance,
the most abject of bows, and further.                         15

They cultivate no memory,
no recognition; their one
useful bit of anatomy
their breast, for beating on
from time to time as the mood takes them,                     20
as though they would beat it in.
(They know this is an action
plain enough, and common.)

Their faces, much too large for them,
are once and for all;                                         25
not like ours, but simpler,
powerful and ideal;
open, as though they start awake
directly from a dream.
And that, of course, tends to set off                         30
the outside laughter, screaming
in from the benches, where onlookers
watch
the puppets as they injure
and scare each other, and crumple                             35
under the pranks to bundles.

If anyone saw it differently,
and sat there humourless,
they would dismantle their only play
to replace with their Judgment Day.                           40
Tearing at the strung wires,
they would drag out before the curtains
those hands that were always hidden away,
hands from on high—hands now unhidden,
hideous, lit up in red:                                       45
and pouring out of every door
would clamber up the backdrop wall
and batter them till they were dead.

### Der Goldschmied

WARTE! Langsam! droh ich jedem Ringe
und vertröste jedes Kettenglied:
später, draußen, kommt das, was geschieht.
Dinge, sag ich, Dinge, Dinge, Dinge!
wenn ich schmiede; vor dem Schmied                          5
hat noch keines irgendwas zu sein
oder ein Geschick auf sich zu laden.
Hier sind alle gleich, von Gottes Gnaden:
ich, das Gold, das Feuer und der Stein.

Ruhig, ruhig, ruf nicht so, Rubin!                          10
Diese Perle leidet, und es fluten
Wassertiefen im Aquamarin.
Dieser Umgang mit euch Ausgeruhten
ist ein Schrecken: alle wacht ihr auf!
Wollt ihr Bläue blitzen? Wollt ihr bluten?                  15
Ungeheuer funkelt mir der Hauf.

Und das Gold, es scheint mit mir verständigt;
in der Flamme hab ich es gebändigt,
aber reizen muß ichs um den Stein.
Und auf einmal, um den Stein zu fassen,                     20
schlägt das Raubding mit metallnem Hassen
seine Krallen in mich selber ein.


WIE dunkeln und rauschen im Instrument die Wälder seines Holzes.

## The Goldsmith*

WAIT! Slow down! my growl to every ring
and call to stop the chains. Out there, later,
comes what is to come. Over and over,
Thing, I repeat, Thing, and Thing, and Thing!:
cry of the working smith. Before him, nothing          5
has about it what it might become,
or its destiny for shouldering.
God's own grace creates us equal here:
me, the gold, the fire, the precious stone.

Ruby—calm, keep calm. Stop calling out!          10
Pain is in this pearl, and water-deeps
flow full inside the aquamarine.
Making contact with you in your sleep
terrifies me. For you start awake!
Is azure lightning what you seek? or bleeding?          15
Monstrous sparks dazzle from the heap.

Only the gold seems to be compliant,
mastered in the fire. But I must bend
and tease it to its purpose round the stone.
All of a sudden,* as it makes to clasp it,          20
the Thing-of-prey strikes in pure metallic
hatred, and sinks its claws into my hand.

IN the instrument how they darken and rustle, the woodlands
    of its wood.

## Aus: *Requiem für eine Freundin*

. . .

So starbst du, wie die Frauen früher starben,
altmodisch starbst du in dem warmen Hause
den Tod der Wöchnerinnen, welche wieder
sich schließen wollen und es nicht mehr können,          185
weil jenes Dunkel, das sie mitgebaren,
noch einmal wiederkommt und drängt und eintritt.

Ob man nicht dennoch hätte Klagefrauen
auftreiben müssen? Weiber, welche weinen
für Geld, und die man so bezahlen kann,          190
daß sie die Nacht durch heulen, wenn es still wird.
Gebräuche her! wir haben nicht genug
Gebräuche. Alles geht und wird verredet.
So mußt du kommen, tot, und hier mit mir
Klagen nachholen. Hörst du, daß ich klage?          195
Ich möchte meine Stimme wie ein Tuch
hinwerfen über deines Todes Scherben
und zerrn an ihr, bis sie in Fetzen geht,
und alles, was ich sage, müßte so
zerlumpt in dieser Stimme gehn und frieren;          200
blieb es beim Klagen. Doch jetzt klag ich an:
den Einen nicht, der dich aus dir zurückzog,
(ich find ihn nicht heraus, er ist wie alle)
doch alle klag ich in ihm an: den Mann.

    Wenn irgendwo ein Kindgewesensein          205
tief in mir aufsteigt, das ich noch nicht kenne,
vielleicht das reinste Kindsein meiner Kindheit:
ich wills nicht wissen. Einen Engel will
ich daraus bilden ohne hinzusehn
und will ihn werfen in die erste Reihe          210
schreiender Engel, welche Gott erinnern.

    Denn dieses Leiden dauert schon zu lang,
und keiner kanns; es ist zu schwer für uns,
das wirre Leiden von der falschen Liebe,

## From *Requiem for a Friend*

. . .

AND so you died, as women used to die:
you died, in your warm home, the old death
of women in confinement, who wish they could
re-close themselves but find they can no longer,                    185
because that darkness they have also borne
returns to them, presses on them, and enters.

For you, they surely needed mourning-women,*
weepers for reward, who can be hired
to howl the night through when it is so still?                      190
Old customs: bring them back! We have too few.
They pass like all the rest, argued out.
So you must come, in death, to voice with me
those missed laments. Can you hear me cry them?
I want to fling my voice out like a cloth                           195
over the fragments of your death, and then
tear at it until it rips to rags,
and all my cries would have to go about
tattered and shivering in that wrecked voice;
*if* it all ended with lament—but I accuse:                         200
not the man who took you from yourself
(I cannot find him; he is like anyone),
but in him others: I accuse all men.

   If, somewhere, a deep sense of having been
a child rises in me, still unrecognized,                            205
perhaps my childhood's purest child-being,
I will refuse it and without a glance
desire to make an angel out of it
to throw into the front rank of angels,
those who cry out to remind God.                                    210
   For now this suffering drags on too long;
it is beyond us all, too heavy for us,
this tangled grief sprung from a spurious love
that builds by habit on possession, just

die, bauend auf Verjährung wie Gewohnheit,          215
ein Recht sich nennt und wuchert aus dem Unrecht.
Wo ist ein Mann, der Recht hat auf Besitz?
Wer kann besitzen, was sich selbst nicht hält,
was sich von Zeit zu Zeit nur selig auffängt
und wieder hinwirft wie ein Kind den Ball.          220
Sowenig wie der Feldherr eine Nike
festhalten kann am Vorderbug des Schiffes,
wenn das geheime Leichtsein ihrer Gottheit
sie plötzlich weghebt in den hellen Meerwind:
so wenig kann einer von uns die Frau          225
anrufen, die uns nicht mehr sieht und die
auf einem schmalen Streifen ihres Daseins
wie durch ein Wunder fortgeht, ohne Unfall:
er hätte denn Beruf und Lust zur Schuld.

    Denn *das* ist Schuld, wenn irgendeines Schuld ist:          230
die Freiheit eines Lieben nicht vermehren
um alle Freiheit, die man in sich aufbringt.
Wir haben, wo wir lieben, ja nur dies:
einander lassen; denn daß wir uns halten,
das fällt uns leicht und ist nicht erst zu lernen.          235


Bist du noch da? In welcher Ecke bist du? –
Du hast so viel gewußt von alledem
und hast so viel gekonnt, da du so hingingst
für alles offen, wie ein Tag, der anbricht.
Die Frauen leiden: lieben heißt allein sein,          240
und Künstler ahnen manchmal in der Arbeit,
daß sie verwandeln müssen, wo sie lieben.
Beides begannst du; beides ist in Dem,
was jetzt ein Ruhm entstellt, der es dir fortnimmt.
Ach du warst weit von jedem Ruhm. Du warst          245
unscheinbar; hattest leise deine Schönheit
hineingenommen, wie man eine Fahne
einzieht am grauen Morgen eines Werktags,
und wolltest nichts, als eine lange Arbeit, –
die nicht getan ist: dennoch nicht getan.          250

. . .

in its own eyes, rampant with injustice.                                         215
Where is the man who has the right of possession?*
Who can possess what is not self-held
but now and then catches and throws itself
outward, blissful, like a child at ball?
As little as a captain may hold steady                                           220
the Nike* at the ship's bow as she lifts,
buoyed in her own secret divinity,
into the bright sea-wind: little as this
can any man among us call to him
the woman who no longer sees us,* walking,                                       225
safely, the narrow strip of her existence
as though through miracles—if he is not
to live calmly committed to a wrong.

    For *this* is wrong, if anything is wrong:
not to enlarge the freedom of a love                                             230
by all the breadth that we can summon up.
In love there is just this for us to do:
to let each other go; for holding on
comes all too easily and takes no learning.


Are you still here? Somewhere, in some corner?                                   235
You knew so much of this, and were able
to do so much, open to all things
as you walked outward, like the start of day.
Women suffer: love means being alone,
and in their work artists sometimes divine                                       240
that where they love they must transform. You
began both; both are in that quality
that fame disfigures when it takes it from you.
How far you were removed from fame. You had
lowered your profile, quietly drawn your beauty                                  245
into yourself, almost like a flag
to take in for the grey workaday,
and wanted nothing but your long task—
left unfinished; left, after all, undone.

. . .                                                                            250

# Aus: *Neue Gedichte*

## *Früher Apollo*

WIE manches Mal durch das noch unbelaubte
Gezweig ein Morgen durchsieht, der schon ganz
im Frühling ist: so ist in seinem Haupte
nichts was verhindern könnte, daß der Glanz

aller Gedichte uns fast tödlich träfe;                    5
denn noch kein Schatten ist in seinem Schaun,
zu kühl für Lorbeer sind noch seine Schläfe
und später erst wird aus den Augenbraun

hochstämmig sich der Rosengarten heben,
aus welchem Blätter, einzeln, ausgelöst              10
hintreiben werden auf des Mundes Beben,

der jetzt noch still ist, niegebraucht und blinkend
und nur mit seinem Lächeln etwas trinkend
als würde ihm sein Singen eingeflößt.

## *Liebes-Lied*

WIE soll ich meine Seele halten, daß
sie nicht an deine rührt? Wie soll ich sie
hinheben über dich zu andern Dingen?
Ach gerne möcht ich sie bei irgendwas
Verlorenem im Dunkel unterbringen                    5
an einer fremden stillen Stelle, die
nicht weiterschwingt, wenn deine Tiefen schwingen.
Doch alles, was uns anrührt, dich und mich,
nimmt uns zusammen wie ein Bogenstrich,
der aus zwei Saiten *eine* Stimme zieht.               10
Auf welches Instrument sind wir gespannt?
Und welcher Spieler hat uns in der Hand?
O süßes Lied.

# From *New Poems**

## *Early Apollo**

As sometimes when the fullest spring morning
glances sheer through still leafless branches,
so here: there is nothing at his head
to screen us from all poetry's radiance—

all—which else must strike us nigh-on fatal;*                    5
for as yet no shade is in his gaze,
his temples are too cool for laurel still,
and only later will rose-gardens* raise

their high stems from the ground of the eyebrow,*
sending petals singly and diffused                              10
to drift and ride upon the trembling mouth:

silent even now, unused and glinting
and only with its smile* drinking in
something, as though it were infused with singing.

## *Love Song*

How may I hold my soul that it refrain
from touching yours? How may I lift it clear
beyond the thought of you to other things?*
Oh—dearly I would wish to lay it there
beside the lost and dark and alien,                             5
in some deep, tranquil place too far from here
to answer, trembling, to your depths' trembling.
But all that touches us, your life and mine,
sounds as a bow upon a violin,
drawing the voice in which two strings are one.                 10
What is the instrument that holds us spanned?
And what musician* has us in his hand?
O sweet song.

## Der Ölbaum-Garten

ER ging hinauf unter dem grauen Laub
ganz grau und aufgelöst im Ölgelände
und legte seine Stirne voller Staub
tief in das Staubigsein der heißen Hände.

Nach allem dies. Und dieses war der Schluß.       5
Jetzt soll ich gehen, während ich erblinde,
und warum willst Du, daß ich sagen muß
Du seist, wenn ich Dich selber nicht mehr finde.

Ich finde Dich nicht mehr. Nicht in mir, nein.
Nicht in den andern. Nicht in diesem Stein.       10
Ich finde Dich nicht mehr. Ich bin allein.

Ich bin allein mit aller Menschen Gram,
den ich durch Dich zu lindern unternahm,
der Du nicht bist. O namenlose Scham . . .

Später erzählte man: ein Engel kam – .       15

Warum ein Engel? Ach es kam die Nacht
und blätterte gleichgültig in den Bäumen.
Die Jünger rührten sich in ihren Träumen.
Warum ein Engel? Ach es kam die Nacht.

Die Nacht, die kam, war keine ungemeine;       20
so gehen hunderte vorbei.
Da schlafen Hunde und da liegen Steine.
Ach eine traurige, ach irgendeine,
die wartet, bis es wieder Morgen sei.

Denn Engel kommen nicht zu solchen Betern,       25
und Nächte werden nicht um solche groß.
Die Sich-Verlierenden läßt alles los,
und sie sind preisgegeben von den Vätern
und ausgeschlossen aus der Mütter Schooß.

## The Garden of Olives*

HE walked up under the grey leaves, just
drained and grey on the dry olive-grove land,
resting his forehead, dense with dust,
deep in the dustiness of his hot hands.

After all that, this. And now the end.                    5
Now I must go, while I am going blind.
Why is it your will I must proclaim
you there, when I myself no longer find you?

I cannot find you now. Not in me, no.
Not in the others. And not in this stone.              10
I cannot find you now. I am alone.

I am alone with all this human pain
I came here to relieve, and in your name,
thou that art not. Oh nameless shame . . .

Later, the story went, an angel* came—.              15

Why an angel? It was the night that came,
leafing indifferently through the trees.
The disciples were stirring in their dreams.
An angel? Alas, it was the night that came.

The night that came was of no special kind;          20
it went as many others have.
Nights when dogs just sleep and stones just lie.
It was a sad one, just another night
that waits for morning to arrive.

For angels do not come to those who pray,           25
not so, or nights expand immense about them.
Those who lose themselves are cut loose soon.
Fathers leave them simply to their fate,
and they are excluded from their mother's womb.

## L'Ange du Méridien

Chartres

Im Sturm, der um die starke Kathedrale
wie ein Verneiner stürzt der denkt und denkt,
fühlt man sich zärtlicher mit einem Male
von deinem Lächeln zu dir hingelenkt:

lächelnder Engel, fühlende Figur,                              5
mit einem Mund, gemacht aus hundert Munden:
gewahrst du gar nicht, wie dir unsre Stunden
abgleiten von der vollen Sonnenuhr,

auf der des Tages ganze Zahl zugleich,
gleich wirklich, steht in tiefem Gleichgewichte,            10
als wären alle Stunden reif und reich.

Was weißt du, Steinerner, von unserm Sein?
und hältst du mit noch seligerm Gesichte
vielleicht die Tafel in die Nacht hinein?

## Die Fensterrose

Da drin: das träge Treten ihrer Tatzen
macht eine Stille, die dich fast verwirrt;
und wie dann plötzlich eine von den Katzen
den Blick an ihr, der hin und wieder irrt,

gewaltsam in ihr großes Auge nimmt, –                       5
den Blick, der, wie von eines Wirbels Kreis
ergriffen, eine kleine Weile schwimmt
und dann versinkt und nichts mehr von sich weiß,

wenn dieses Auge, welches scheinbar ruht,
sich auftut und zusammenschlägt mit Tosen               10
und ihn hineinreißt bis ins rote Blut –:

## L'Ange du Méridien*

Chartres*

WHEN storm assaults the indomitable cathedral,
like the sceptic,* battering with his thinking,
unexpectedly we sense your smile
binding us to you in its tenderer linking:

smiling angel, feeling figure,     5
with mouth created from a hundred mouths,*
are you ever conscious how our hours
slip over to you off the full dial

that holds the day's entire hours in deep
equilibrium, each real in equal     10
degree and as though rich and ripe?

Angel of stone, what do you know of us?
Are you perhaps yet more serene of face
holding your tablet out into the night?

## The Rose Window

INSIDE,* the lazy padding of their paws
dazes you with the silence that it makes,
and when your gaze, straying back and forth
over a great cat, awakes at being taken

and dragged by force into its huge eye—     5
your gaze, as though entoiled, as though it fell
into a whirlpool, swims a short while
and sinks under and loses sense of self—

then the eye that had seemed at rest
opens and roars into your ears and spring-closes,     10
wrenching your gaze into its red blood—:

So griffen einstmals aus dem Dunkelsein
der Kathedralen große Fensterrosen
ein Herz und rissen es in Gott hinein.

## *Gott im Mittelalter*

UND sie hatten Ihn in sich erspart
und sie wollten, daß er sei und richte,
und sie hängten schließlich wie Gewichte
(zu verhindern seine Himmelfahrt)

an ihn ihrer großen Kathedralen                    5
Last und Masse. Und er sollte nur
über seine grenzenlosen Zahlen
zeigend kreisen und wie eine Uhr

Zeichen geben ihrem Tun und Tagwerk.
Aber plötzlich kam er ganz in Gang,               10
und die Leute der entsetzten Stadt

ließen ihn, vor seiner Stimme bang,
weitergehn mit ausgehängtem Schlagwerk
und entflohn vor seinem Zifferblatt.

## *Der Panther*

Im Jardin des Plantes, Paris

SEIN Blick ist vom Vorübergehn der Stäbe
so müd geworden, daß er nichts mehr hält.
Ihm ist, als ob es tausend Stäbe gäbe
und hinter tausend Stäben keine Welt.

Der weiche Gang geschmeidig starker Schritte,      5
der sich im allerkleinsten Kreise dreht,
ist wie ein Tanz von Kraft um eine Mitte,
in der betäubt ein großer Wille steht.

And in this way, in centuries long past
out of the dark, cathedral window-roses
wrenched a heart and tore it up to God.


## *God in the Middle Ages*

AND they had saved Him up inside themselves,
wanting Him to be, to regulate,
then (to slow His ascent) hung on Him
as hindrances of last resort, like weights,*

the massed loading of their great cathedrals'          5
stone burden. And it was for Him,
above His boundless numbers, just to circle
and point and provide signs for them, to guide

clock-like the doings of their working days.
But without warning He was in His stride,               10
and the people of the shocked city,

fearful at His voice, let Him pass*
and saw His heavy clockwork hang free
and fled before the dial of His face.


## *The Panther*

In the Jardin des Plantes,* Paris

HIS eyes have grown so tired with the passing
of bars that their reservoirs can hold
no more. There seem a thousand bars, and in
the drowse beyond a thousand bars no world.

The supple, powerful footfall paces softly               5
in ever-tinier circles, tight-described,
a danced strength, as though about a centre
where a great will stays, stupefied.

Nur manchmal schiebt der Vorhang der Pupille
sich lautlos auf –. Dann geht ein Bild hinein,     10
geht durch der Glieder angespannte Stille –
und hört im Herzen auf zu sein.


## Die Gazelle

*Gazella Dorcas*

VERZAUBERTE: wie kann der Einklang zweier
erwählter Worte je den Reim erreichen,
der in dir kommt und geht, wie auf ein Zeichen.
Aus deiner Stirne steigen Laub und Leier,

und alles Deine geht schon im Vergleich      5
durch Liebeslieder, deren Worte, weich
wie Rosenblätter, dem, der nicht mehr liest,
sich auf die Augen legen, die er schließt:

um dich zu sehen: hingetragen, als
wäre mit Sprüngen jeder Lauf geladen      10
und schösse nur nicht ab, solang der Hals

das Haupt ins Horchen hält: wie wenn beim Baden
im Wald die Badende sich unterbricht:
den Waldsee im gewendeten Gesicht.


## Das Einhorn

DER Heilige hob das Haupt, und das Gebet
fiel wie ein Helm zurück von seinem Haupte:
denn lautlos nahte sich das niegeglaubte,
das weiße Tier, das wie eine geraubte
hülflose Hindin mit den Augen fleht.      5

Der Beine elfenbeinernes Gestell
bewegte sich in leichten Gleichgewichten,

Sometimes the curtain in his eye lifts
inaudibly.* An image enters dully,     10
travels the tautened quiet of the limbs—
and in the heart ceases to be.


## *The Gazelle*

Gazella dorcas*

ENCHANTED creature, how can the twinned tuning
of words I choose ever reach the rhyme
that comes and goes in you, as at a sign?
Your brow produces leaf and lyre, subsumes

all that you are in metaphor: through songs     5
of love* you move, whose words, if one should tire
of reading, settle delicate as rose-
petals onto eyelids that must close

to bring you near: borne on leaps that each
appear spring-loaded in the gun,* only     10
held on the trigger as the neck poises

your head alert: as at a bathing-place
the woodland bather* startles at a noise
and stands, the still pool in her turned face.*


## *The Unicorn**

THE saint raised his head, and prayer fell
helm-like flung back from its citadel,
for noiseless the white beast of disbelief
came to him, like the deer held in the chase,
hind-like and helpless, pleading in its eyes.     5

The ivory-constructed limbs lent
balance to balance as they moved, and sent

ein weißer Glanz glitt selig durch das Fell,
und auf der Tierstirn, auf der stillen, lichten,
stand, wie ein Turm im Mond, das Horn so hell,          10
und jeder Schritt geschah, es aufzurichten.

Das Maul mit seinem rosagrauen Flaum
war leicht gerafft, so daß ein wenig Weiß
(weißer als alles) von den Zähnen glänzte;
die Nüstern nahmen auf und lechzten leis.          15
Doch seine Blicke, die kein Ding begrenzte,
warfen sich Bilder in den Raum
und schlossen einen blauen Sagenkreis.

## Der Schwan

DIESE Mühsal, durch noch Ungetanes
schwer und wie gebunden hinzugehn,
gleicht dem ungeschaffnen Gang des Schwanes.

Und das Sterben, dieses Nichtmehrfassen
jenes Grunds, auf dem wir täglich stehn,          5
seinem ängstlichen Sich-Niederlassen –:

in die Wasser, die ihn sanft empfangen
und die sich, wie glücklich und vergangen,
unter ihm zurückziehn, Flut um Flut;
während er unendlich still und sicher          10
immer mündiger und königlicher
und gelassener zu ziehn geruht.

## Der Dichter

DU entfernst dich von mir, du Stunde.
Wunden schlägt mir dein Flügelschlag.
Allein: was soll ich mit meinem Munde?
mit meiner Nacht? mit meinem Tag?

across its coat a lucent white sheen;
and on its still brow a horn, bright
as if it were a spirelet on the moon,                              10
lifted with each step's distinct intent.

The relaxed muzzle, downy grey and rose,
barely showed the teeth's brief brilliance
(whiter than all known things); the nostrils flared,
testing the air's flavour. But its glance,                         15
unboundaried in Things, threw
images into space* and in them drew
a blue* saga–cycle* to a close.

## The Swan*

ALL this pushing through things not yet done,*
with such weary toil, as if constrained,
is like the clumsy waddling of the swan.

And dying, this no longer keeping hold
of the same ground we stand on every day,                          5
is like the swan as, timidly, he lowers

himself into the waters that receive him
very gently, flow by flow retreating
under him, as if glad to be expiring;
while he begins, endlessly quiet, sure,                            10
increasingly regal, increasingly mature
and ever more serene, to deign to move.

## The Poet

YOU, the hour,* are deserting me,
wounding me with the beat of your wings.
Alone: now what use my mouth?
What are my days and nights to me?

Ich habe keine Geliebte, kein Haus,       5
keine Stelle auf der ich lebe.
Alle Dinge, an die ich mich gebe,
werden reich und geben mich aus.


## Blaue Hortensie

So wie das letzte Grün in Farbentiegeln
sind diese Blätter, trocken, stumpf und rauh,
hinter den Blütendolden, die ein Blau
nicht auf sich tragen, nur von ferne spiegeln.

Sie spiegeln es verweint und ungenau,       5
als wollten sie es wiederum verlieren,
und wie in alten blauen Briefpapieren
ist Gelb in ihnen, Violett und Grau;

Verwaschnes wie an einer Kinderschürze,
Nichtmehrgetragnes, dem nichts mehr geschieht:       10
wie fühlt man eines kleinen Lebens Kürze.

Doch plötzlich scheint das Blau sich zu verneuen
in einer von den Dolden, und man sieht
ein rührend Blaues sich vor Grünem freuen.


## Die Kurtisane

Venedigs Sonne wird in meinem Haar
ein Gold bereiten: aller Alchemie
erlauchten Ausgang. Meine Brauen, die
den Brücken gleichen, siehst du sie

hinführen ob der lautlosen Gefahr       5
der Augen, die ein heimlicher Verkehr
an die Kanäle schließt, so daß das Meer
in ihnen steigt und fällt und wechselt. Wer

I have no sweetheart and no house,   5
nowhere that is my home ground.* All things
into which I give myself
grow in riches and give me out.


## Blue Hydrangea

DULL and rough these leaves, like vestiges
of green paint left in a jar,* grown
dry under flowers whose blue is not their own*
but tint reflected from the distances.

They mirror it through stains of tears, blurred,   5
as though they wished it could be lost from them,
and have the look of old, blue letters, dimmed
to violet, and yellow-tinged, and greyed;

washed out like a child's pinafore,
like things no longer worn, kept for no use,   10
and as affecting as a life soon over.

Then with a start* the blue seems new again
within one umbel,* and before your eyes
a touching blue gladdens beside the green.


## The Courtesan

THE sun in Venice* will prepare here
a gold within my hair: the noble outcome
of all alchemy. My brows compare
to the city's bridges; you can see them

leading away over my silent eyes'   5
danger. An inter-course covertly
joins them to canals, so that the tide
rises and falls in them alternately.

mich einmal sah, beneidet meinen Hund,
weil sich auf ihm oft in zerstreuter Pause      10
die Hand, die nie an keiner Glut verkohlt,

die unverwundbare, geschmückt, erholt – .
Und Knaben, Hoffnungen aus altem Hause,
gehn wie an Gift an meinem Mund zugrund.


### Die Treppe der Orangerie

Versailles

Wie Könige die schließlich nur noch schreiten
fast ohne Ziel, nur um von Zeit zu Zeit
sich den Verneigenden auf beiden Seiten
zu zeigen in des Mantels Einsamkeit – :

so steigt, allein zwischen den Balustraden,      5
die sich verneigen schon seit Anbeginn,
die Treppe: langsam und von Gottes Gnaden
und auf den Himmel zu und nirgends hin;

als ob sie allen Folgenden befal
zurückzubleiben, – so daß sie nicht wagen      10
von ferne nachzugehen; nicht einmal
die schwere Schleppe durfte einer tragen.


### Römische Fontäne

Borghese

Zwei Becken, eins das andre übersteigend
aus einem alten runden Marmorrand,
und aus dem oberen Wasser leis sich neigend
zum Wasser, welches unten wartend stand,

dem leise redenden entgegenschweigend      5
und heimlich, gleichsam in der hohlen Hand,

Eyes that watch me are jealous of my hound,
for often in a moment of distraction                    10
my hand, which no fever ever burned,

just rests on him, invulnerable, adorned—.
And boys with prospects and of good extraction
seem to sink to my mouth as if by poison.*

## The Orangery Steps

Versailles*

LIKE kings who in the end no more than stride,
almost aimless, except from time to time
to show themselves in robes of solitude
to subjects who incline on either side—

set, lone like them, between the balustrades          5
that from the old days make their endless bow,
the steps climb: in God's grace and slow
here and up to heaven and towards no place;*

as though they charge those following to remain
behind, just so that they do not endeavour            10
from such a distance to pursue them further
or even presume to bear the heavy train.

## Roman Fountain

Borghese*

TWO basins, one above the other, rising
from a wide, ancient marble rim,
and water from the higher quietly brims
towards the water held below it, waiting,

its silence lifting to the other's speaking            5
and secretly, as in a hollowed palm,

ihm Himmel hinter Grün und Dunkel zeigend
wie einen unbekannten Gegenstand;

sich selber ruhig in der schönen Schale
verbreitend ohne Heimweh, Kreis aus Kreis,                      10
nur manchmal träumerisch und tropfenweis

sich niederlassend an den Moosbehängen
zum letzten Spiegel, der sein Becken leis
von unten lächeln macht mit Übergängen.


## Das Karussell

Jardin du Luxembourg

MIT einem Dach und seinem Schatten dreht
sich eine kleine Weile der Bestand
von bunten Pferden, alle aus dem Land,
das lange zögert, eh es untergeht.
Zwar manche sind an Wagen angespannt,                           5
doch alle haben Mut in ihren Mienen;
ein böser roter Löwe geht mit ihnen
und dann und wann ein weißer Elefant.

Sogar ein Hirsch ist da, ganz wie im Wald,
nur daß er einen Sattel trägt und drüber                        10
ein kleines blaues Mädchen aufgeschnallt.

Und auf dem Löwen reitet weiß ein Junge
und hält sich mit der kleinen heißen Hand,
dieweil der Löwe Zähne zeigt und Zunge.

Und dann und wann ein weißer Elefant.                           15

Und auf den Pferden kommen sie vorüber,
auch Mädchen, helle, diesem Pferdesprunge
fast schon entwachsen; mitten in dem Schwunge
schauen sie auf, irgendwohin, herüber –

showing it, like some strange object, skies
that lie behind a wash of dark and green;

and expanding in the lovely dish,* at peace,
ring by ring and without grief at leaving,                    10
in droplets, in dreams, only now and then

sliding and trickling down the mossy hangings
into the last mirror, which, serene,
makes its bowl smile with transitions.


## The Merry-go-round

Jardin du Luxembourg*


ALONG with roof and shadow, it rotates
during its brief turn, this platform show
of painted horses, creatures of the land
that before fading out hesitates.
A few of them may have a carriage harnessed,              5
but nonetheless their style is fine and gallant;
a red and angry lion runs with them,
and now and then a white, white elephant.

Even a stag, as real as in the wood,
except that sitting buckled to a saddle                   10
it carries someone small and blue in girlhood.

And on the lion rides a boy, quite young,
in white, holding on with sticky hands,
while the lion bares its teeth and tongue.

And now and then a white, white elephant.                 15

And on the horses, too, rushing over,
bright-headed girls, who almost could have outgrown
leaping horses, mid-flight rather given
to glancing up: anywhere—our direction.

Und dann und wann ein weißer Elefant.         20

Und das geht hin und eilt sich, daß es endet,
und kreist und dreht sich nur und hat kein Ziel.
Ein Rot, ein Grün, ein Grau vorbeigesendet,
ein kleines kaum begonnenes Profil –.
Und manchesmal ein Lächeln, hergewendet,       25
ein seliges, das blendet und verschwendet
an dieses atemlose blinde Spiel . . .


## Spanische Tänzerin

WIE in der Hand ein Schwefelzündholz, weiß,
eh es zur Flamme kommt, nach allen Seiten
zuckende Zungen streckt –: beginnt im Kreis
naher Beschauer hastig, hell und heiß
ihr runder Tanz sich zuckend auszubreiten.       5

Und plötzlich ist er Flamme, ganz und gar.

Mit einem Blick entzündet sie ihr Haar
und dreht auf einmal mit gewagter Kunst
ihr ganzes Kleid in diese Feuersbrunst,
aus welcher sich, wie Schlangen die erschrecken,       10
die nackten Arme wach und klappernd strecken.

Und dann: als würde ihr das Feuer knapp,
nimmt sie es ganz zusamm und wirft es ab
sehr herrisch, mit hochmütiger Gebärde
und schaut: da liegt es rasend auf der Erde       15
und flammt noch immer und ergiebt sich nicht –.
Doch sieghaft, sicher und mit einem süßen
grüßenden Lächeln hebt sie ihr Gesicht
und stampft es aus mit kleinen festen Füßen.

And now and then a white, white elephant.              20

And so it goes, and hastens to its end,
merely a circle spun that has no aim.*
A grey sent past us, and a green, a red,
a small profile scarcely yet begun—
And sometimes there's a smile bent this way,            25
a happy one, that spends and overspends
itself playing this blind and breathless game . . .


## Spanish Dancer*

Like a match struck in the hand, white
before the flames catch, putting out quick
twitching tongues—like this, ringed tight
in onlookers, her hot, hasty, bright
dance begins, twitching and concentric.                   5

And is suddenly flame, wholly fire.

With just a look she ignites her hair,
all at once and with audacious flair
whirling her whole dress into the blaze,
raised from which, like snakes affrighted, fretting,      10
her bare arms start awake, come clacking, stretching.

Then, as if the fire will give no more,
she snatches it, throws it to the floor
gesturing proudly and imperiously
and looks down: it lies there, grounded, furious          15
and still flickering, and won't give in—.
But now vaunting, sure and with a sweet
smile of acknowledgement she lifts her chin
and stamps it out with little beating feet.

## Orpheus. Eurydike. Hermes

DAS war der Seelen wunderliches Bergwerk.
Wie stille Silbererze gingen sie
als Adern durch sein Dunkel. Zwischen Wurzeln
entsprang das Blut, das fortgeht zu den Menschen,
und schwer wie Porphyr sah es aus im Dunkel.     5
Sonst war nichts Rotes.

Felsen waren da
und wesenlose Wälder. Brücken über Leeres
und jener große graue blinde Teich,
der über seinem fernen Grunde hing     10
wie Regenhimmel über einer Landschaft.
Und zwischen Wiesen, sanft und voller Langmut,
erschien des einen Weges blasser Streifen,
wie eine lange Bleiche hingelegt.

Und dieses einen Weges kamen sie.     15

Voran der schlanke Mann im blauen Mantel,
der stumm und ungeduldig vor sich aussah.
Ohne zu kauen fraß sein Schritt den Weg
in großen Bissen; seine Hände hingen
schwer und verschlossen aus dem Fall der Falten     20
und wußten nicht mehr von der leichten Leier,
die in die Linke eingewachsen war
wie Rosenranken in den Ast des Ölbaums.
Und seine Sinne waren wie entzweit:
indes der Blick ihm wie ein Hund vorauslief,     25
umkehrte, kam und immer wieder weit
und wartend an der nächsten Wendung stand, –
blieb sein Gehör wie ein Geruch zurück.
Manchmal erschien es ihm als reichte es
bis an das Gehen jener beiden andern,     30
die folgen sollten diesen ganzen Aufstieg.
Dann wieder wars nur seines Steigens Nachklang
und seines Mantels Wind was hinter ihm war.
Er aber sagte sich, sie kämen doch;

## *Orpheus. Eurydice. Hermes*\*

THAT was the unearthly mine of souls.
Like silent silver-ore in heavy darkness
they moved, like veins. From between the roots
the blood welled that coursed towards mankind,
as dense as porphyry\* in that lack of light.          5
Nothing else was red.

There were rock-faces there
and void forests. Bridges spanning nothing,
and that vast, blind, shade-grey lake\*
that hung over its own distant depth                     10
like raining sky above a landscape. Mild
and filled with patience, meadows spread away
beside the single path laid out between them
like a pale strip of bleaching cloth.

And along this one path they came.                        15

The slender man\* cloaked in blue walked
ahead, dumb, gazing impatiently
in front of him. His stride ate up the path
in great torn-off bites. His closed fists
hung heavily outside the falling folds,                   20
no longer conscious of the light lyre
growing into his left hand like the twined
rose into the branch of the olive tree.
His senses looked as though divided: while
his sight ran on ahead, like a dog,                       25
time and again stopping, coming back,
and waiting far off at the next turn—
his hearing trailed behind him like an odour.
Sometimes it seemed to him to reach as far
behind as the footsteps of those two others              30
who were to follow up the great slope.
And then once more he heard only his climb's
echo behind him, and the wind of his cloak.
And yet, he told himself, there they still were,

sagte es laut und hörte sich verhallen.      35
Sie kämen doch, nur wärens zwei
die furchtbar leise gingen. Dürfte er
sich einmal wenden (wäre das Zurückschaun
nicht die Zersetzung dieses ganzen Werkes,
das erst vollbracht wird), müßte er sie sehen,      40
die beiden Leisen, die ihm schweigend nachgehn:

Den Gott des Ganges und der weiten Botschaft,
die Reisehaube über hellen Augen,
den schlanken Stab hertragend vor dem Leibe
und flügelschlagend an den Fußgelenken;      45
und seiner linken Hand gegeben: *sie*.

Die So-geliebte, daß aus einer Leier
mehr Klage kam als je aus Klagefrauen;
daß eine Welt aus Klage ward, in der
alles noch einmal da war: Wald und Tal      50
und Weg und Ortschaft, Feld und Fluß und Tier;
und daß um diese Klage-Welt, ganz so
wie um die andre Erde, eine Sonne
und ein gestirnter stiller Himmel ging,
ein Klage-Himmel mit entstellten Sternen –:      55
Diese So-geliebte.

Sie aber ging an jenes Gottes Hand,
den Schritt beschränkt von langen Leichenbändern,
unsicher, sanft und ohne Ungeduld.
Sie war in sich, wie Eine hoher Hoffnung,      60
und dachte nicht des Mannes, der voranging,
und nicht des Weges, der ins Leben aufstieg.
Sie war in sich. Und ihr Gestorbensein
erfüllte sie wie Fülle.
Wie eine Frucht von Süßigkeit und Dunkel,      65
so war sie voll von ihrem großen Tode,
der also neu war, daß sie nichts begriff.

Sie war in einem neuen Mädchentum
und unberührbar; ihr Geschlecht war zu

said it aloud, and heard it die away.                    35
There they came, the two of them, if walking
fearfully softly. Should he be allowed
to turn round, once (if looking back were not
to wreck the whole task, not yet quite fulfilled),
he would be bound to see those quiet two                    40
who followed, treading softly and in silence:

the god of despatch* and far messages,
with travel-hood above his brilliant eyes,
his slender staff held out in front of him
and a god's wings beating at his ankles;                    45
and given into his left hand: *her*.

So loved that one lyre sang with more mourning
than any mourning-women; that a world
came into being made of mourning, in which
all things reappeared:* wood and valley                    50
and road and hamlet, field, river and creature;
that round this lamentation-world turned,
just as round the other earth, a sun,
and then a starred heaven, a lamentation-
heaven of silence with disfigured stars.                    55
She was so greatly loved.

But now she walked beside this god, her steps
hampered by the long grave-wrappings,
uncertain, gentle, and without impatience.
Self-absorbed, like someone near her time,                    60
oblivious of the man ahead, her husband,
and of the path that led up into life.
Self-absorbed. And her being-dead
was filling her like fullness.
For like a fruit all of sweetness and dark                    65
she too was full of her immense death,
which was so new she could not take it in.

This was for her a second maidenhood:
she was untouchable; her hymen, like

wie eine junge Blume gegen Abend,                                    70
und ihre Hände waren der Vermählung
so sehr entwöhnt, daß selbst des leichten Gottes
unendlich leise, leitende Berührung
sie kränkte wie zu sehr Vertraulichkeit.

Sie war schon nicht mehr diese blonde Frau,                          75
die in des Dichters Liedern manchmal anklang,
nicht mehr des breiten Bettes Duft und Eiland
und jenes Mannes Eigentum nicht mehr.

Sie war schon aufgelöst wie langes Haar
und hingegeben wie gefallner Regen                                   80
und ausgeteilt wie hundertfacher Vorrat.

Sie war schon Wurzel.

Und als plötzlich jäh
der Gott sie anhielt und mit Schmerz im Ausruf
die Worte sprach: Er hat sich umgewendet –,                          85
begriff sie nichts und sagte leise: *Wer?*

Fern aber, dunkel vor dem klaren Ausgang,
stand irgend jemand, dessen Angesicht
nicht zu erkennen war. Er stand und sah,
wie auf dem Streifen eines Wiesenpfades                              90
mit trauervollem Blick der Gott der Botschaft
sich schweigend wandte, der Gestalt zu folgen,
die schon zurückging dieses selben Weges,
den Schritt beschränkt von langen Leichenbändern,
unsicher, sanft und ohne Ungeduld.                                   95

## Aus: *Der neuen Gedichte anderer Teil*

### *Archaïscher Torso Apollos*

WIR kannten nicht sein unerhörtes Haupt,
darin die Augenäpfel reiften. Aber

the newest flower at dusk, was closed, her hands    70
by now so unused to the hand of marriage
that even, ethereal as he was, the god's
incomparably gentle guiding touch
injured her, like too far an intimacy.

Already she was not the fair-haired girl    75
at times resonant in the poet's songs,
no more the wide couch's scent and island,
and in this man's ownership no longer.

She was already loosed like long hair,
relinquished like the flowing rain, freely    80
shared like an inextinguishable store.

She was already root.

And when the god
stopped her abruptly with the anguished words:
He has turned round—she did not take them in,    85
those words he spoke, and softly asked: *Who?*

Far off, dark before the radiance
beyond the entrance, someone stood, whose face
was indiscernible. He stood and saw
the god of despatch, on a strip of path    90
between the meadows, with a sorrowed look
and not a word turn and follow the figure
already walking back along the path,
its steps hampered by the long grave-wrappings,
uncertain, gentle, and without impatience.    95

# From *New Poems, Second Part*

## *Archaic Torso of Apollo**

UNHEARD*—his unimaginable head,
its apple-pupils ripening. We have not known it.

sein Torso glüht noch wie ein Kandelaber,
in dem sein Schauen, nur zurückgeschraubt,

sich hält und glänzt. Sonst könnte nicht der Bug          5
der Brust dich blenden, und im leisen Drehen
der Lenden könnte nicht ein Lächeln gehen
zu jener Mitte, die die Zeugung trug.

Sonst stünde dieser Stein entstellt und kurz
unter der Schultern durchsichtigem Sturz          10
und flimmerte nicht so wie Raubtierfelle

und bräche nicht aus allen seinen Rändern
aus wie ein Stern: denn da ist keine Stelle,
die dich nicht sieht. Du mußt dein Leben ändern.

## *Leda*

Als ihn der Gott in seiner Not betrat,
erschrak er fast, den Schwan so schön zu finden;
er ließ sich ganz verwirrt in ihm verschwinden.
Schon aber trug ihn sein Betrug zur Tat,

bevor er noch des unerprobten Seins          5
Gefühle prüfte. Und die Aufgetane
erkannte schon den Kommenden im Schwane
und wußte schon: er bat um Eins,

das sie, verwirrt in ihrem Widerstand,
nicht mehr verbergen konnte. Er kam nieder          10
und halsend durch die immer schwächre Hand

ließ sich der Gott in die Geliebte los.
Dann erst empfand er glücklich sein Gefieder
und wurde wirklich Schwan in ihrem Schoß.

But the torso still glows like a candelabrum,
in which his gaze, only screwed back* yet,

just holds and shines. Otherwise the outline                    5
of the breast could not blind you, and that tranquil
turn of the thighs send no curved smile*
to that procreative centre of his line.

This stone would stand disfigured, marred, small
below the shoulders' sheened fall                               10
and would not glimmer, like predatory pelt;*

and would not burst right through its confines, like
a star: for there's no place in it
that does not see you. You must change your life.*


## *Leda**

WHEN he assumed the swan, driven by need,
the god was almost frightened at its beauty
and disappeared, baffled, in its body.
But his deception pressed him towards the deed,

not testing yet the reaches of this being                      5
or trying its feelings. And the waiting one
could see what was approaching in this swan
and knew: he wanted that one thing

that she in her resistance baffled, dazed,
could not withhold. Settling, he came to her, and            10
pushing his neck into her weakening hand,

the god released himself into his lover—
only then, thrilling within his feathers,
becoming real swan in her embrace.

## Die Insel der Sirenen

WENN er denen, die ihm gastlich waren,
spät, nach ihrem Tage noch, da sie
fragten nach den Fahrten und Gefahren,
still berichtete: er wußte nie,

wie sie schrecken und mit welchem jähen          5
Wort sie wenden, daß sie so wie er
in dem blau gestillten Inselmeer
die Vergoldung jener Inseln sähen,

deren Anblick macht, daß die Gefahr
umschlägt; denn nun ist sie nicht im Tosen      10
und im Wüten, wo sie immer war.
Lautlos kommt sie über die Matrosen,

welche wissen, daß es dort auf jenen
goldnen Inseln manchmal singt –,
und sich blindlings in die Ruder lehnen,        15
wie umringt

von der Stille, die die ganze Weite
in sich hat und an die Ohren weht,
so als wäre ihre andre Seite
der Gesang, dem keiner widersteht.              20


## Ein Prophet

AUSGEDEHNT von riesigen Gesichten,
hell vom Feuerschein aus dem Verlauf
der Gerichte, die ihn nie vernichten, –
sind die Augen, schauend unter dichten
Brauen. Und in seinem Innern richten         5
sich schon wieder Worte auf,

nicht die seinen (denn was wären seine
und wie schonend wären sie vertan),

## The Island of Sirens*

ANSWERING, when they sat at evening,
questions from his hosts about his journeys
and their dangers, never could he choose
words abrupt enough to chill the spine

and turn their minds to his, or words that showed          5
images as bright as he had seen them, out there
in that blue stilled island-sea: the slow
sheening of those islands into gold—

only a glimpse of which alters knowledge
of danger, for the old sea-rage and wave-roar          10
no longer holds it as it did. As other,
and in silence, it comes upon the sailors.

They know: in these gold islands sometimes
travellers are aware of singing—
then, blindly, lean into their oars,          15
ringed round,

seemingly, by tranquil stillness* filled
with the expanses and close-fanned against
the ears; as though its obverse side
were that song that no one can resist.          20

## A Prophet*

HIS eyes—wide open to his vast visions,
blazing with fires started by the judgements
that never strike him down—his eyes gaze
under their bushy brows. And in him rise
words, already formed in preparation:          5

not his own words (for to what purpose his,
chosen to spare the hearers, quick to erode),

andre, harte: Eisenstücke, Steine,
die er schmelzen muß wie ein Vulkan,                    10

um sie in dem Ausbruch seines Mundes
auszuwerfen, welcher flucht und flucht;
während seine Stirne, wie des Hundes
Stirne, *das* zu tragen sucht,

was der Herr von seiner Stirne nimmt:             15
Dieser, Dieser, den sie alle fänden,
folgten sie den großen Zeigehänden,
die Ihn weisen wie Er ist: ergrimmt.


### *Eine Sibylle*

EINST, vor Zeiten, nannte man sie alt.
Doch sie blieb und kam dieselbe Straße
täglich. Und man änderte die Maße,
und man zählte sie wie einen Wald

nach Jahrhunderten. Sie aber stand                      5
jeden Abend auf derselben Stelle,
schwarz wie eine alte Citadelle
hoch und hohl und ausgebrannt;

von den Worten, die sich unbewacht
wider ihren Willen in ihr mehrten,                      10
immerfort umschrieen und umflogen,
während die schon wieder heimgekehrten
dunkel unter ihren Augenbogen
saßen, fertig für die Nacht.


### *Die Bettler*

DU wußtest nicht, was den Haufen
ausmacht. Ein Fremder fand

but harder words: stones, iron fragments
that he must heat and melt in lava-flow

and spew volcanic from his gaping mouth                    10
to run in curses and more curses; while yet,
dog-like,* his forehead readies him for bearing
*that* promised thing the Lord shall set

heavily there, lifted from His own:
He, yes, He whom all could realize                    15
if they obeyed the great pointing hands
that mark His ire, showing Him as He is.


## *A Sibyl**

AEONS ago people called her old.
Yet she endured, and came by the same road
daily. And they simply changed her parameters
and counted her—like timber in a wood—

by centuries.* She, however, stood                    5
evening by evening, irremovable,
upstanding like a citadel, but hollow
and black and burnt out to a shell,

incessantly beset with the flown words
that multiplied in her against her will                    10
and wheeled and screamed, catching her off guard;
while words already in full homing flight
winged in, shadow-dark under her brows,
and sat, roosted for the night.


## *The Beggars*

WHAT the heap was, there was no telling.
A stranger approached and found

Bettler darin. Sie verkaufen
das Hohle aus ihrer Hand.

Sie zeigen dem Hergereisten                              5
ihren Mund voll Mist,
und er darf (er kann es sich leisten)
sehn, wie ihr Aussatz frißt.

Es zergeht in ihren zerrührten
Augen sein fremdes Gesicht;                              10
und sie freuen sich des Verführten
und speien, wenn er spricht.


## Leichen-Wäsche

SIE hatten sich an ihn gewöhnt. Doch als
die Küchenlampe kam und unruhig brannte
im dunkeln Luftzug, war der Unbekannte
ganz unbekannt. Sie wuschen seinen Hals,

und da sie nichts von seinem Schicksal wußten,     5
so logen sie ein anderes zusamm,
fortwährend waschend. Eine mußte husten
und ließ solang den schweren Essigschwamm

auf dem Gesicht. Da gab es eine Pause
auch für die zweite. Aus der harten Bürste          10
klopften die Tropfen; während seine grause
gekrampfte Hand dem ganzen Hause
beweisen wollte, daß ihn nicht mehr dürste.

Und er bewies. Sie nahmen wie betreten
eiliger jetzt mit einem kurzen Huster                15
die Arbeit auf, so daß an den Tapeten
ihr krummer Schatten in dem stummen Muster

sich wand und wälzte wie in einem Netze,
bis daß die Waschenden zu Ende kamen.

beggars in there. Not above selling
the hollow of their hand.

The visitor is drawn well in,                          5
gets shown a mouth of muck*
and the leprosy that eats their skin
(he can afford a look).

His stranger's face breaks up within those
eyes that manufacture tears;                           10
that they have caught him they rejoice,
and spew up* when he speaks.


## *Corpse-washing*

BY now they had grown used to him, but when
the kitchen lamp was set down in the dark
draught and burned on restlessly the unknown
man was quite unknown.* They washed his neck,

and not knowing how he met his death                   5
they made it up, pieced untruths together
and kept on washing. A woman with a cough
put the heavy sponge of vinegar*

down on his face for a while. Then they stopped,
and both the women rested. Droplets dripped            10
from stiff bristles, and his cramped
and terrible hand gave to understand
he needed nothing more to drink.

This they accepted. They began again
more hurriedly, and as if embarrassed                  15
cleared their throats; their shadows, strangely bent,
caught in the wallpaper, in its mute pattern,

as though enmeshed in fishing-nets, and waltzed
and twisted in them till they finished.

Die Nacht im vorhanglosen Fensterrahmen      20
war rücksichtslos. Und einer ohne Namen
lag bar und reinlich da und gab Gesetze.


## Der Blinde

*Paris*

SIEH, er geht und unterbricht die Stadt,
die nicht ist auf seiner dunkeln Stelle,
wie ein dunkler Sprung durch eine helle
Tasse geht. Und wie auf einem Blatt

ist auf ihm der Widerschein der Dinge      5
aufgemalt; er nimmt ihn nicht hinein.
Nur sein Fühlen rührt sich, so als finge
es die Welt in kleinen Wellen ein:

eine Stille, einen Widerstand –,
und dann scheint er wartend wen zu wählen:      10
hingegeben hebt er seine Hand,
festlich fast, wie um sich zu vermählen.


## Schlangen-Beschwörung

WENN auf dem Markt, sich wiegend, der Beschwörer
die Kürbisflöte pfeift, die reizt und lullt,
so kann es sein, daß er sich einen Hörer
herüberlockt, der ganz aus dem Tumult

der Buden eintritt in den Kreis der Pfeife,      5
die will und will und will und die erreicht,
daß das Reptil in seinem Korb sich steife
und die das steife schmeichlerisch erweicht,

abwechselnd immer schwindelnder und blinder
mit dem, was schreckt und streckt, und dem, was löst –;      10

The night, standing framed in bare windows,                    20
ignored them.* And a man without a name
lay clean and naked there and made the laws.*

## *The Blind Man**

Paris

WATCH: he walks, a fissure through the city
that is no city in his dark passage—
moving like a dark crack in the light
porcelain of a cup.* And like a page

coloured by the town's reflected things                    5
he does not take them in. Only his touch
stirs, and sense, as though it caught the world
up in it in wavelets. There is such

stillness in him, and resistance—then,
waiting, he seems to choose someone ahead                    10
and almost ceremonially, devotedly,
extends his hand, as if about to wed.

## *Snake-charming*

WHEN the snake-charmer* at the market
sways, tuning his flute's thrills and lulls,
he may perhaps lure a listener over
who leaves the busy tumult of the stalls,

enticed into the circle of the pipe                    5
that wills and wills and wills: to achieve
the reptile's standing rigid* in its basket,
its flattering-down to let the stiffness give,

switching ever blinder, ever dizzier,
from startling, stretching, to its soft release—                    10

und dann genügt ein Blick: so hat der Inder
dir eine Fremde eingeflößt,

in der du stirbst. Es ist als überstürze
glühender Himmel dich. Es geht ein Sprung
durch dein Gesicht. Es legen sich Gewürze                    15
auf deine nordische Erinnerung,

die dir nichts hilft. Dich feien keine Kräfte,
die Sonne gärt, das Fieber fällt und trifft;
von böser Freude steilen sich die Schäfte,
und in den Schlangen glänzt das Gift.                        20


## Schwarze Katze

EIN Gespenst ist noch wie eine Stelle,
dran dein Blick mit einem Klange stößt;
aber da, an diesem schwarzen Felle
wird dein stärkstes Schauen aufgelöst:

wie ein Tobender, wenn er in vollster                        5
Raserei ins Schwarze stampft,
jählings am benehmenden Gepolster
einer Zelle aufhört und verdampft.

Alle Blicke, die sie jemals trafen,
scheint sie also an sich zu verhehlen,                       10
um darüber drohend und verdrossen
zuzuschauern und damit zu schlafen.
Doch auf einmal kehrt sie, wie geweckt,
ihr Gesicht und mitten in das deine:
und da triffst du deinen Blick im geelen                     15
Amber ihrer runden Augensteine
unerwartet wieder: eingeschlossen
wie ein ausgestorbenes Insekt.

and then a look's enough: you sense,
infiltrating you, an Indian strangeness

in which is death.* Descending skies seem
to rush upon you incandescently.
A fault-line runs across your face. Spices          15
layer over your northern memory—

which cannot help you. Strength cannot protect you,
the sun seethes, fever strikes and shakes;
malicious glee readies its lances, watching
the venom* glinting in the snakes.                  20


## Black Cat*

A GHOST persists, something like a locus
where your eyes and a single sound collide,
but here, on this fur of dense black, your deepest
searching look is suddenly annulled:

like a man in the insanest frenzied                 5
stampings into prisoned blackness,
suddenly brought up against the cell's
padded wall, stopped and vaporized.

All the looks that ever reached and touched her
lie in her, it seems, hidden deep,                  10
kept for eyeing there in sullen threat
and taking with her into sleep.
Of a sudden, as if woken, she directs
her face to gaze pinpointingly at yours,
and you meet your look within the yellow*           15
amber* of her round, stone-hard eyeballs,
caught, locked in, unexpected,
amber-bound like an extinct insect.

## Lied vom Meer

### Capri, Piccola Marina

URALTES Wehn vom Meer,
Meerwind bei Nacht:
   du kommst zu keinem her;
wenn einer wacht,
so muß er sehn, wie er          5
dich übersteht:
   uraltes Wehn vom Meer,
welches weht
nur wie für Ur-Gestein,
lauter Raum          10
reißend von weit herein . . .

O wie fühlt dich ein
treibender Feigenbaum
oben im Mondschein.

## Venezianischer Morgen

### Richard Beer-Hofmann zugeeignet

FÜRSTLICH verwöhnte Fenster sehen immer,
was manchesmal uns zu bemühn geruht:
die Stadt, die immer wieder, wo ein Schimmer
von Himmel trifft auf ein Gefühl von Flut,

sich bildet ohne irgendwann zu sein.          5
Ein jeder Morgen muß ihr die Opale
erst zeigen, die sie gestern trug, und Reihn
von Spiegelbildern ziehn aus dem Kanale,
und sie erinnern an die andern Male:
dann giebt sie sich erst zu und fällt sich ein          10

wie eine Nymphe, die den Zeus empfing.
Das Ohrgehäng erklingt an ihrem Ohre;

## Song of the Sea

Capri, Piccola Marina*

AGE-OLD wind, blowing,
sea-wind, by night:
   but not for our sake;
who lies awake
must fathom a way                                    5
to withstand you:*
   old sea-wind, blowing,
you who blow
only for ancient stone,
tearing sheer                                        10
space in from far . . .

Oh how a fig-tree feels
driven* and full of you,
moonlit, up there.*

## Venetian Morning

Dedicated to Richard Beer-Hofmann*

PRINCELY-FASTIDIOUS windows own the scene
that now and then allows itself to haunt us:
this city, imaging herself in myriad
shimmers of sky upon a sense of flux

and left fluid. Every morning newly               5
shows her the opals that were yesterday
strung in her dress, and pictures drift smoothly
in their reflected rows from the canal,
recalling others to her memory;
then at last she yields herself, and falls        10

stiller, like a nymph receiving Zeus;*
and hearing in each ear her droplets ringing

sie aber hebt San Giorgio Maggiore
und lächelt lässig in das schöne Ding.


## Spätherbst in Venedig

NUN treibt die Stadt schon nicht mehr wie ein Köder,
der alle aufgetauchten Tage fängt.
Die gläsernen Paläste klingen spröder
an deinen Blick. Und aus den Gärten hängt


der Sommer wie ein Haufen Marionetten                    5
kopfüber, müde, umgebracht.
Aber vom Grund aus alten Waldskeletten
steigt Willen auf: als sollte über Nacht


der General des Meeres die Galeeren
verdoppeln in dem wachen Arsenal,                        10
um schon die nächste Morgenluft zu teeren


mit einer Flotte, welche ruderschlagend
sich drängt und jäh, mit allen Flaggen tagend,
den großen Wind hat, strahlend und fatal.


## Die Laute

ICH bin die Laute. Willst du meinen Leib
beschreiben, seine schön gewölbten Streifen:
sprich so, als sprächest du von einer reifen
gewölbten Feige. Übertreib


das Dunkel, das du in mir siehst. Es war                 5
Tullias Dunkelheit. In ihrer Scham
war nicht so viel, und ihr erhelltes Haar
war wie ein heller Saal. Zuweilen nahm


sie etwas Klang von meiner Oberfläche
in ihr Gesicht und sang zu mir.                          10

offers up San Giorgio Maggiore,*
smiling lazily at the lovely thing.


### Late Autumn in Venice

THE city now no longer works like bait,
capturing all those newly surfaced mornings.
The glassy palaces that strike your gaze
ring brittler than before. And summer hangs


out of the gardens like heaped marionettes,                    5
broken-necked, tired and snuffed out.
But from the ground's wildwood–skeletons
new will is rising,* as though overnight


the admiral* were doubling up and arming
the galleys of his eager arsenal,*                    10
ready to tar the air of imminent morning


and lead a fleet forging forth, driving
hard on its oars, its flags unfurled, flying
before a great wind, glittering and lethal.


### The Lute

I AM the lute. If you should think to describe
my body's fine, striped, vaulted lines*
speak as though your words defined the ripe
bulging fig. Over-describe


the darkness you can see in me. Tullia's*                    5
own it was. Her shame could not contain
this much dark, and her hair in light
was like a bright hall. And from time to time


she took a layer of sound from my surface
to her mind and sang to me.                    10

Dann spannte ich mich gegen ihre Schwäche,
und endlich war mein Inneres in ihr.


### Das Rosen-Innere

Wo ist zu diesem Innen
ein Außen? Auf welches Weh
legt man solches Linnen?
Welche Himmel spiegeln sich drinnen
in dem Binnensee         5
dieser offenen Rosen,
dieser sorglosen, sieh:
wie sie lose im Losen
liegen, als könnte nie
eine zitternde Hand sie verschütten.       10
Sie können sich selber kaum
halten; viele ließen
sich überfüllen und fließen
über von Innenraum
in die Tage, die immer          15
voller und voller sich schließen,
bis der ganze Sommer ein Zimmer
wird, ein Zimmer in einem Traum.


### Dame vor dem Spiegel

Wie in einem Schlaftrunk Spezerein,
löst sie leise in dem flüssigklaren
Spiegel ihr ermüdetes Gebaren;
und sie tut ihr Lächeln ganz hinein.

Und sie wartet, daß die Flüssigkeit      5
davon steigt; dann gießt sie ihre Haare
in den Spiegel und, die wunderbare
Schulter hebend aus dem Abendkleid,

Then I flexed myself against her frailty
until at last my inwardness was hers.


## Rose Interior

WHERE is the exterior
to this interior?
And on what wound is laid
such linen for healing? Within them
what sky-ceiling                                          5
reflects in the inland lake
of these open roses—carefree,
loosely lying, see,
in the great looseness round them,
as though no trembling hand could shake them.            10
Barely self-containing, many
allow themselves to fill
to overflowing and stream
out from inner spaces*
into the days that close                                 15
fuller and fuller, until
the whole fulfilled summer grows
into a room, a room in a dream.


## Lady at the Mirror*

LIKE spices in a sleeping draught she slips
into the fluid-lucent glass the weariness
loosed from the tense bearing of her body
and lets her smile settle in its depths.

And waits, watching the fluidity                         5
rising to fill the volume of the glass,
and pours in her unfastened hair; then lifts
her amazing shoulders from the evening dress

trinkt sie still aus ihrem Bild. Sie trinkt,
was ein Liebender im Taumel tränke,                    10
prüfend, voller Mißtraun; und sie winkt

erst der Zofe, wenn sie auf dem Grunde
ihres Spiegels Lichter findet, Schränke
und das Trübe einer späten Stunde.


## Die Flamingos

Jardin des Plantes, Paris

IN Spiegelbildern wie von Fragonard
ist doch von ihrem Weiß und ihrer Röte
nicht mehr gegeben, als dir einer böte,
wenn er von seiner Freundin sagt: sie war

noch sanft von Schlaf. Denn steigen sie ins Grüne      5
und stehn, auf rosa Stielen leicht gedreht,
beisammen, blühend, wie in einem Beet,
verführen sie verführender als Phryne

sich selber; bis sie ihres Auges Bleiche
hinhalsend bergen in der eignen Weiche,                10
in welcher Schwarz und Fruchtrot sich versteckt.

Auf einmal kreischt ein Neid durch die Volière;
sie aber haben sich erstaunt gestreckt
und schreiten einzeln ins Imaginäre.


## Rosa Hortensie

WER nahm das Rosa an? Wer wußte auch,
daß es sich sammelte in diesen Dolden?
Wie Dinge unter Gold, die sich entgolden,
enträten sie sich sanft, wie im Gebrauch.

and drinks quietly from an image such
as would transport a lover, but her gaze                    10
searching and mistrustful—only then

summoning her maid to her, when
she catches lights mirror-deep, and cupboards,
and glooming of the late hour's approach.


## The Flamingos

Jardin des Plantes, Paris

IN reflections resembling Fragonard,*
there is in the touches of their red and white
no more than something just as slight
as brings to mind a mistress, in the murmur:

she is still soft with sleep. They rise into green                    5
and stand, turned slightly on pink stems
together, blooming* as in a garden bed,
seducing, more seductively than Phryne*—

self-seducing; and with tensed neck glide
that pallid eye into their own down,                    10
where unlooked-for black and fruit-red hide.

Of a sudden, jealousy shrieks through the aviary;
they have but stretched themselves, surprised,
striding singly into the imaginary.


## Pink Hydrangea

WHO of us guessed this pink?* Who was aware
that it collected in the flower-umbels?
Like gilded things from which the gold rubs
they pale and fade softly, as in use.

Daß sie für solches Rosa nichts verlangen.                    5
Bleibt es für sie und lächelt aus der Luft?
Sind Engel da, es zärtlich zu empfangen,
wenn es vergeht, großmütig wie ein Duft?

Oder vielleicht auch geben sie es preis,
damit es nie erführe vom Verblühn.                            10
Doch unter diesem Rosa hat ein Grün
gehorcht, das jetzt verwelkt und alles weiß.


## Der Ball

Du Runder, der das Warme aus zwei Händen
im Fliegen, oben, fortgiebt, sorglos wie
sein Eigenes; was in den Gegenständen
nicht bleiben kann, zu unbeschwert für sie,

zu wenig Ding und doch noch Ding genug,                       5
um nicht aus allem draußen Aufgereihten
unsichtbar plötzlich in uns einzugleiten:
das glitt in dich, du zwischen Fall und Flug

noch Unentschlossener: der, wenn er steigt,
als hätte er ihn mit hinaufgehoben,                           10
den Wurf entführt und freiläßt –, und sich neigt
und einhält und den Spielenden von oben
auf einmal eine neue Stelle zeigt,
sie ordnend wie zu einer Tanzfigur,

um dann, erwartet und erwünscht von allen,                    15
rasch, einfach, kunstlos, ganz Natur,
dem Becher hoher Hände zuzufallen.


## Der Hund

Da oben wird das Bild von einer Welt
aus Blicken immerfort erneut und gilt.

And for a pink like this they ask nothing.                    5
Does it endure for their sake? Smile from the air?
Do angels wait* tenderly to take it,
profuse as fragrance, as it disappears?

Or, perhaps, even abandon it,
to keep it from awareness of the fading.                      10
And yet beneath the pink a green has listened
and now decays, knowing everything.*


## The Ball

YOU roundness,* high in flight, giving away
both hands' warmth as if it were your own,
carefree; what has not the will to stay
constrained in objects, flying too buoyant for them,

not quite Thing and yet still Thing enough                    5
to have remained, unlooked for and unseen,
beyond us in the organized outside,
slipped, though, into you at the uncertain

fulcrum tilting flight to fall;* climbing
you seem to catch the throw and lift it with you,             10
stealing and freeing it—and now incline,
slide onward, point to the players their new stance,
suddenly from your height ordering them
as though they were a figure of the dance—

until, awaited by them all, wished for,                       15
fast, simple, artless, natural, falling
into the cup of their raised-up hands.


## The Dog*

UP there, the image* is a world of looking,
always renewed, invariably true.

Nur manchmal, heimlich, kommt ein Ding und stellt
sich neben ihn, wenn er durch dieses Bild

sich drängt, ganz unten, anders, wie er ist;                    5
nicht ausgestoßen und nicht eingereiht,
und wie im Zweifel seine Wirklichkeit
weggebend an das Bild, das er vergißt,

um dennoch immer wieder sein Gesicht
hineinzuhalten, fast mit einem Flehen,                          10
beinah begreifend, nah am Einverstehen
und doch verzichtend: denn er wäre nicht.


### Buddha in der Glorie

MITTE aller Mitten, Kern der Kerne,
Mandel, die sich einschließt und versüßt, –
dieses Alles bis an alle Sterne
ist dein Fruchtfleisch: Sei gegrüßt.

Sieh, du fühlst, wie nichts mehr an dir hängt;                  5
im Unendlichen ist deine Schale,
und dort steht der starke Saft und drängt.
Und von außen hilft ihm ein Gestrahle,

denn ganz oben werden deine Sonnen
voll und glühend umgedreht.                                     10
Doch in dir ist schon begonnen,
was die Sonnen übersteht.

At times* a Thing approaches secretly
to stand beside him when he nudges through

the image, even as far beneath and other          5
as he is; not cast out but not let in,
unsure, he offers up his reality
into the image, which he has forgotten,

only to begin to press his face
into it again, almost beseechingly,               10
near to understanding and accepting—
yet desists: for there, he could not *be*.


## Buddha* in Glory

CENTRE of all centres. Core of cores,*
almond,* enclosing, sweetening itself—
all this, reaching up to all the stars,
this your fruit-flesh. And we greet you.

See, you feel how nothing cleaves to you:         5
your peel adheres now to the infinite
and your juice stands, pressing, potent, urgent.
And an exterior radiance fortifies it,

for above, your suns fill and expand, sent
incandescent to their rotation.                   10
Yet, in you, something begun
shall outlast the suns' duration.*

# Gedichte 1912–1922

ACH, da wir Hülfe von Menschen erharrten: stiegen
Engel lautlos mit einem Schritte hinüber
über das liegende Herz


## *Auferweckung des Lazarus*

ALSO, das tat not für den und den,
weil sie Zeichen brauchten, welche schrieen.
Doch er träumte, Marthen und Marieen
müßte es genügen, einzusehn,
daß er *könne*. Aber keiner glaubte,                                  5
alle sprachen: Herr, was kommst du *nun*?
Und da ging er hin, das Unerlaubte
an der ruhigen Natur zu tun.
Zürnender. Die Augen fast geschlossen,
fragte er sie nach dem Grab. Er litt.                                 10
Ihnen schien es, seine Tränen flossen,
und sie drängten voller Neugier mit.
Noch im Gehen wars ihm ungeheuer,
ein entsetzlich spielender Versuch,
aber plötzlich brach ein hohes Feuer                                  15
in ihm aus, ein solcher Widerspruch
gegen alle ihre Unterschiede,
ihr Gestorben-, ihr Lebendigsein,
daß er Feindschaft war in jedem Gliede,
als er heiser angab: Hebt den Stein!                                  20
Eine Stimme rief, daß er schon stinke,
(denn er lag den vierten Tag) – doch Er
stand gestrafft, ganz voll von jenem Winke,
welcher stieg in ihm und schwer, sehr schwer
ihm die Hand hob – (niemals hob sich eine                            25
langsamer als diese Hand und mehr)
bis sie dastand, scheinend in der Luft;

# Uncollected Poems 1912–1922

Ah, as we waited for human help, angels climbed
without a sound and in a stride
over our strewn hearts

## *The Raising of Lazarus**

So, for them all, this was something needed,
since they required signs that cried out.
Yet he dreamed that it would satisfy
Martha and Mary if he had the *power*
to do it. But not one of them believed,                              5
asking: 'Lord, why do you come *now*?'
And he walked on, to work in tranquil Nature
what was forbidden. Growing angrier.
Then with closed eyes he asked them how
to find the grave. For he clearly grieved.                           10
Even it seemed to them his tears flowed,*
and filled with curiosity they pressed forward
tight at his side. As he walked he sensed
enormity: this terrible attempt,
playing with chance. A fire broke out in him,                       15
sudden heat that burned incandescent,
such hot protest at their small distinctions*—
all this being alive and being dead—
that animosity ran through his limbs
as he instructed hoarsely: Raise the stone!                          20
A voice called: that he already stank*
(this was the fourth day he lay there). Yet He
stood there, tense, filling to the brim
with wave, which heavily, so heavily,
raised his hand in greeting (never hand                              25
lifted more gradually), till it stopped,
shining in the air; and there, held up,

und dort oben zog sie sich zur Kralle:
denn ihn graute jetzt, es möchten alle
Toten durch die angesaugte Gruft          30
wiederkommen, wo es sich herauf
raffte, larvig, aus der graden Lage – –
doch dann stand nur Eines schief im Tage,
und man sah: das ungenaue vage
Leben nahm es wieder mit in Kauf.          35


TRÄNEN, Tränen, die aus mir brechen,
Mein Tod, Mohr, Träger
meines Herzens, halte mich schräger,
daß sie abfließen. Ich will sprechen.


Schwarzer, riesiger Herzhalter.          5
Wenn ich auch spräche,
glaubst du denn, daß das Schweigen bräche?


Wiege mich, Alter.


SO, nun wird es doch der Engel sein,
der aus meinen Zügen langsam trinkt
der Gesichte aufgeklärten Wein.
Dürstender, wer hat dich hergewinkt?


Daß du dürstest. Dem der Katarakt          5
Gottes stürzt durch alle Adern. Daß
*du* noch dürstest. Überlaß
dich dem Durst. (Wie hast du mich gepackt.)


Und ich fühle fließend, wie dein Schaun
trocken war, und bin zu deinem Blute          10
so geneigt, daß ich die Augenbraun
dir, die reinen, völlig überflute.

tightened like a claw: for now, the dread
came to him that all the dead might rise
through this sucked vault, where something larval          30
jerked itself out of its rigid bed—
but only one thing leaned into the light,
and as they watched: indistinct
vague life undertook to reaccept it.


TEARS, tears breaking out of me.
Death mine, Moor,* this heart's
bearer, hold me more slantingly,
easing their run-off. I must speak.

Black, gigantic heart-holder.                                    5
And if I spoke,
do you believe the silence would break?

Old man, cradle me.


So it must surely be the angel,* drinking
slowly from my features* the bright wine
clarified by visions. You who thirst,
who was it brought you, waved to you to come?

You, thirsting. Whom the cataracts of God                    5
inundate through every coursing vein.
That *you* should thirst. Submit to it.
(How you enthralled me into your possession.)

And I feel, flowing, how your gaze
droughted. And incline so to your blood                     10
that my filling eyebrows pour
pure to you and wholly overflood.

HINWEG, die ich bat,    endlich mein Lächeln zu kosten
(ob es kein köstliches wäre),
unaufhaltsam genaht    hinter den Sternen im Osten
wartet der Engel, daß ich mich kläre.

Daß ihn kein Spähn, keine Spur    euer beschränke,          5
wenn er die Lichtung betritt;
sei ihm das Leid, das ich litt,    wilde Natur:
er traue der Tränke.

War ich euch grün oder süß,    laßt uns das alles vergessen,
sonst überholt uns die Scham.                               10
Ob ich blüh oder büß,    wird er gelassen ermessen,
den ich nicht lockte, der kam . .


DU im Voraus
verlorne Geliebte, Nimmergekommene,
nicht weiß ich, welche Töne dir lieb sind.
Nicht mehr versuch ich, dich, wenn das Kommende wogt,
zu erkennen. Alle die großen                                5
Bilder in mir, im Fernen erfahrene Landschaft,
Städte und Türme und Brücken und un-
vermutete Wendung der Wege
und das Gewaltige jener von Göttern
einst durchwachsenen Länder:                                10
steigt zur Bedeutung in mir
deiner, Entgehende, an.

Ach, die Gärten bist du,
ach, ich sah sie mit solcher
Hoffnung. Ein offenes Fenster                               15
im Landhaus –, und du tratest beinahe
mir nachdenklich heran. Gassen fand ich, –
du warst sie gerade gegangen,
und die Spiegel manchmal der Läden der Händler
waren noch schwindlich von dir und gaben erschrocken        20
mein zu plötzliches Bild. – Wer weiß, ob derselbe
Vogel nicht hinklang durch uns
gestern, einzeln, im Abend?

OH leave me, you whom I asked    to taste my smile*
(if it were clear in the tasting);
drawn relentlessly nearer    far behind eastern stars
the angel awaits my self-clarifying.

May no peering,    no tracking of yours restrict him          5
when he steps into the clearing;
may my pain be to him    that of the wild;
may he trust the imbibing.

Whatever I was to you, all that:    green, sweet—let us forget,*
or we fall foul of shame.                                      10
Whether I bloom or atone    he will serenely assess,
he, un-lured,* but who came . .


YOU, beloved,
lost in advance,* the never-arrived,
I do not know the notes that would please you.
No longer, in the surge of what approaches,
do I try to discern you. All the immense                       5
images in me, landscapes learned from a distance,
cities and towers and bridges* and un-
expected turns in the ways,
and the full force of those lands that once grew
intertwined with the gods:                                     10
all these rise in me, signifying
you, my eternal eluder.

Gardens you are, beloved;
I have looked on them with such
great hope. An open window                                     15
of the country house here—and you stepped,
pensive, almost up to me. I have found alleys—
knowing you had just walked them,
and the mirror-reflections of shops* were sometimes
still dizzy with you, giving back, shocked, my                 20
too-sudden image.—Who knows if the same bird did not
ring, apart, through both of us
yesterday, at evening?

## *Wendung*

Der Weg von der Innigkeit zur Größe geht durch das Opfer.

Kassner

LANGE errang ers im Anschaun.
Sterne brachen ins Knie
unter dem ringenden Aufblick.
Oder er anschaute knieend,
und seines Instands Duft                                            5
machte ein Göttliches müd,
daß es ihm lächelte schlafend.

Türme schaute er so,
daß sie erschraken:
wieder sie bauend, hinan, plötzlich, in Einem!                     10
Aber wie oft, die vom Tag
überladene Landschaft
ruhete hin in sein stilles Gewahren, abends.

Tiere traten getrost
in den offenen Blick, weidende,                                    15
und die gefangenen Löwen
starrten hinein wie in unbegreifliche Freiheit;
Vögel durchflogen ihn grad,
den gemütigen; Blumen
wiederschauten in ihn                                              20
groß wie in Kinder.

Und das Gerücht, daß ein Schauender sei,
rührte die minder,
fraglicher Sichtbaren,
rührte die Frauen.                                                 25

Schauend wie lang?
Seit wie lange schon innig entbehrend,
flehend im Grunde des Blicks?

Wenn er, ein Wartender, saß in der Fremde; des Gasthofs
zerstreutes, abgewendetes Zimmer                                   30

### Turning*

The path from inwardness to greatness is through sacrifice.
                                                        Kassner*

LONG he had won it through gazing.*
Stars would fall to their knees
under his grappling up-look.
Or he would gaze while kneeling,
and the scent of his urgency would                                5
make a divinity tired,
until it smiled at him, sleeping.

Towers he saw with such force
that they were startled:
building them up again,* suddenly, all in an instant!            10
But yet how often the landscape,
overburdened with day,
rested into his silent awareness by evening.

Animals stepped, undaunted,
into his open gaze, grazing,                                     15
even the captive lions
stared into it,* as into baffling freedom;
birds flew through it directly;
and it felt them; flowers
gazed back into it, large,                                       20
as if into children.*

And the rumour that here was a gazer
moved those more slightly,
doubtfully visible,*
moved the women.                                                 25

Gazing for how long?
How long so deeply renouncing,
beseeching deep down in his gaze?

When, in strange parts, he sat there, waiting; the inn room*
around him distracted and turned                                 30

mürrisch um sich, und im vermiedenen Spiegel
wieder das Zimmer
und später vom quälenden Bett aus
wieder:
da beriets in der Luft,                                                    35
unfaßbar beriet es
über sein fühlbares Herz,
uber sein durch den schmerzhaft verschütteten Körper
dennoch fühlbares Herz
beriet es und richete:                                                     40
daß es der Liebe nicht habe.

(Und verwehrte ihm weitere Weihen.)

Denn des Anschauns, siehe, ist eine Grenze.
Und die geschautere Welt
will in der Liebe gedeihn.                                                  45

Werk des Gesichts ist getan,
tue nun Herz-Werk
an den Bildern in dir, jenen gefangenen; denn du
überwältigtest sie: aber nun kennst du sie nicht.
Siehe, innerer Mann, dein inneres Mädchen,                                 50
dieses errungene aus
tausend Naturen, dieses
erst nur errungene, nie
noch geliebte Geschöpf.


## Klage

WEM willst du klagen, Herz? Immer gemiedener
ringt sich dein Weg durch die unbegreiflichen
Menschen. Mehr noch vergebens vielleicht,
da er die Richtung behält,
Richtung zur Zukunft behält,                                                5
zu der verlorenen.

sullenly from him, and in the avoided mirror
again the room
and later from the torturous bed
again:
then the air did pronounce,                                      35
it unfathomably pronounced
over his tangible heart,
over his heart still nonetheless tangible through
a body consumed with pain
it pronounced and judged:                                        40
that it had nothing of love.

(And forbade him further consecrations.)

For gazing, you see, has a limit.*
And the more gazed upon world
desires to thrive in love.                                       45

Work of seeing is done,
now do heart-work
on the images in you, your captives; for you
overpowered them; but you do not know them now.
See, inner man, your inner young girl,*                          50
she who was won from
a thousand natures, she who was
only just won, this creature,
as yet never loved.

## Plaint

HEART, to whom make plaint?* Ever more shunned:
your path's wrung passage through uncomprehended
mankind. All the more vainly, perhaps,
for that it holds its direction,
holds to a course for the future,                                5
that that is lost.*

Früher. Klagtest? Was wars? Eine gefallene
Beere des Jubels, unreife.
Jetzt aber bricht mir mein Jubel-Baum,
bricht mir im Sturme mein langsamer                                    10
Jubel-Baum.
Schönster in meiner unsichtbaren
Landschaft, der du mich kenntlicher
machtest Engeln, unsichtbaren.


Es winkt zu Fühlung fast aus allen Dingen,
aus jeder Wendung weht es her: Gedenk!
Ein Tag, an dem wir fremd vorübergingen,
entschließt im künftigen sich zum Geschenk.

Wer rechnet unseren Ertrag? Wer trennt                                 5
uns von den alten, den vergangnen Jahren?
Was haben wir seit Angebinn erfahren,
als daß sich eins im anderen erkennt?

Als daß an uns Gleichgültiges erwarmt?
O Haus, o Wiesenhang, o Abendlicht,                                    10
auf einmal bringst du's beinah zum Gesicht
und stehst an uns, umarmend und umarmt.

Durch alle Wesen reicht der *eine* Raum:
Weltinnenraum. Die Vögel fliegen still
durch uns hindurch. O, der ich wachsen will,                          15
ich seh hinaus, und *in* mir wächst der Baum.

Ich sorge mich, und in mir steht das Haus.
Ich hüte mich, und in mir ist die Hut.
Geliebter, der ich wurde: an mir ruht
der schönen Schöpfung Bild und weint sich aus.                        20

Earlier. Your lament—what was it? A fallen
unripe berry of jubilation.
Now but what breaks is my jubilation-tree,
breaks in the gale, my slow                                    10
jubilation-tree.
Loveliest in my invisible
landscape,* you that have made me more closely
known to angels, the invisible.

ALMOST all things beckon us to feeling,
and turnings send wind-messages: Be mindful!*
A day we passed by in estrangement wills
itself as gift to us in future time.

Who tallies what we do? Draws us away                          5
from old abandoned years? In all our learning
what have we seen?—that one thing finds itself
in others. What but this, from the beginning?

Or this: the listless warms itself by us.
O home, slope of the field, evening light,                     10
you summon it almost before our eyes
and stand with us, embracing and embraced.*

The same space spreads through all existences:
world-inner-space.* Through us, tranquilly,
birds* fly unswerving. O, I who would grow                     15
look outward, and *within* me grows the tree.

I am unquiet, and in me stands the house;
am on my guard, and something in me shelters.
And sweetheart that I have become, against me
lovely creation's portrait leans in tears.                     20

AUSGESETZT auf den Bergen des Herzens. Siehe, wie klein dort,
siehe: die letzte Ortschaft der Worte, und höher,
aber wie klein auch, noch ein letztes
Gehöft von Gefühl. Erkennst du's? –
Ausgesetzt auf den Bergen des Herzens. Steingrund                    5
unter den Händen. Hier blüht wohl
einiges auf; aus stummem Absturz
blüht ein unwissendes Kraut singend hervor.
Aber der Wissende? Ach, der zu wissen begann
und schweigt nun, ausgesetzt auf den Bergen des Herzens.             10
Da geht wohl, heilen Bewußtseins,
manches umher, manches gesicherte Bergtier,
wechselt und weilt. Und der große geborgene Vogel
kreist um der Gipfel reine Verweigerung. – Aber
ungeborgen, hier auf den Bergen des Herzens . . . .                  15


### An Hölderlin

VERWEILUNG, auch am Vertrautesten nicht,
ist uns gegeben; aus den erfüllten
Bildern stürzt der Geist zu plötzlich zu füllenden; Seeen
sind erst im Ewigen. Hier ist Fallen
das Tüchtigste. Aus dem gekonnten Gefühl                             5
überfallen hinab ins geahndete, weiter.

Dir, du Herrlicher, war, dir war, du Beschwörer, ein ganzes
Leben das dringende Bild, wenn du es aussprachst,
die Zeile schloß sich wie Schicksal, ein Tod war
selbst in der lindesten, und du betratest ihn; aber                 10
der vorgehende Gott führte dich drüben hervor.

O du wandelnder Geist, du wandelndster! Wie sie doch alle
wohnen im warmen Gedicht, häuslich, und lang
bleiben im schmalen Vergleich. Teilnehmende. Du nur
ziehst wie der Mond. Und unten hellt und verdunkelt            15
deine nächtliche sich, die heilig erschrockene Landschaft,
die du in Abschieden fühlst. Keiner

CAST out, exposed on the mountains of the heart.\* Look,
   how small\* there,
look: the last village of words, and higher,
yet how small it is too, one final
farmstead of feeling. Do you see it?
Cast out, exposed on the mountains of the heart. Hard rock   5
under my hands. Here, true, something
comes into flower; from the mute rock-face
an unknowing weed puts out its flowers, singing.
But the man, knowing? Ah, who began to know,
cast out, silent now, on the mountains of the heart.   10
True, safe in unclouded awareness,
many a mountain creature travels about,
changes and lingers. And the great sheltered bird
circles the pure rejection of peaks.—But
unsheltered here on the mountains of the heart . . . .   15


## *To Hölderlin\**

LINGERING, even with the most intimate,
is not granted; from image fulfilled
the spirit swoops to the image for sudden filling. Lakes
are not, till eternity. Here, falling\*
is best: precipitately from mastered emotion   5
down into the barely conjectured, onwards.

To you, who are so glorious, to you, the adjurer, one whole
life\* was the urgent image; when you pronounced it
the line fell shut, like fate, a death was
even in the gentlest, and you went in; yet   10
the god who walked ahead of you led you out and beyond.

O you wandering spirit, furthest wandering! How the others
settle in warm rooms of poems and stay long,
tied into simile. Taking part. Only you
move like the moon. And below brightens and darkens,   15
shocked into sacred fear, that same, that deep-night landscape,
yours, that you sense in farewells. No–one

gab sie erhabener hin, gab sie ans Ganze
heiler zurück, unbedürftiger. So auch
spieltest du heilig durch nicht mehr gerechnete Jahre          20
mit dem unendlichen Glück, als wär es nicht innen, läge
keinem gehörend im sanften
Rasen der Erde umher, von göttlichen Kindern verlassen.
Ach, was die Höchsten begehren, du legtest es wunschlos
Baustein auf Baustein: es stand. Doch selber sein Umsturz          25
irrte dich nicht.


Was, da ein solcher, Ewiger, war, mißtraun wir
immer dem Irdischen noch? Statt im Vorläufigen ernst
die Gefühle zu lernen für welche
Neigung, künftig im Raum?          30


## Der Tod

DA steht der Tod, ein bläulicher Absud
in einer Tasse ohne Untersatz.
Ein wunderlicher Platz für eine Tasse:
steht auf dem Rücken einer Hand. Ganz gut
erkennt man noch an dem glasierten Schwung          5
den Bruch des Henkels. Staubig. Und: ›*Hoff-nung*‹
an ihrem Bug in aufgebrauchter Schrift.


Das hat der Trinker, den der Trank betrifft,
bei einem fernen Frühstück ab-gelesen.


Was sind denn das für Wesen,          10
die man zuletzt wegschrecken muß mit Gift?


Blieben sie sonst? Sind sie denn hier vernarrt
in dieses Essen voller Hindernis?
Man muß ihnen die harte Gegenwart
ausnehmen, wie ein künstliches Gebiß.          15
Dann lallen sie.    Gelall, Gelall . . . .
. . . . . . . . . . . . . . . . . . . . . . . . . . . . .

gave it out of his hands more sublimely, returned it
more unscathed to the whole, more selflessly. So too
down the uncounted years* you have played devoutly　　20
with endless rapture, as though, no internal thing, it lay there
ownerless in the tender
grass of the earth, abandoned, strewn by celestial children.
Ah, what the greatest covet you laid down, wishless,
stone upon built stone: it stood. Yet even its toppling　　25
left you in calm.


Why, when such a man lived, and is timeless, do we
still mistrust what is earthly? Rather than from the preliminary
carefully learn the feelings for some future
inclination, in space?　　　　30


## Death

Look: here is death, this faintly blue decoction
standing in a cup without a saucer.*
Strange place for a cup, set down like that
on the back of a hand. Still quite clear
to see in the glazed turn the break and scar　　　　5
of the handle. Dusty. And on the curvature
the word '*hope*' in worn lettering.

This was how the drinker it was meant for
read it, at some breakfast in the distance.

What sort of creatures, these, who must　　　　10
be frightened off with poison at the last?

Or they would hang on? Are they not over-fond
of all this breakfasting on bitter hindrance?
We have to take the hard present moment
out of their mouth, like a set of dentures.　　　　15
Then they babble.　 Bibble, bibble babble . . . .
. . . . . . . . . . . . . . . . . . . . . . . . . . . . .

O Sternenfall,
von einer Brücke einmal eingesehn – :
dich nicht vergessen. Stehn!


### *An die Musik*

MUSIK: Atem der Statuen.   Vielleicht:
Stille der Bilder.   Du Sprache wo Sprachen
enden.   Du Zeit,
die senkrecht steht auf der Richtung vergehender Herzen.

Gefühle zu wem? O du der Gefühle                              5
Wandlung in was? – in hörbare Landschaft.
Du Fremde: Musik. Du uns entwachsener
Herzraum. Innigstes unser,
das, uns übersteigend, hinausdrängt, –
heiliger Abschied:                                           10
da uns das Innre umsteht
als geübteste Ferne, als andre
Seite der Luft:
rein,
riesig,                                                      15
nicht mehr bewohnbar.


IN Karnak wars. Wir waren hingeritten,
Hélène und ich, nach eiligem diner.
Der Dragoman hielt an: die Sphinxallee –,
ah! der Pilon: nie war ich so inmitten

mondener Welt! (Ists möglich, du vermehrst                    5
dich in mir, Großheit, damals schon zu viel!)
Ist Reisen – Suchen? Nun, dies war ein Ziel.
Der Wächter an dem Eingang gab uns erst

O star-fall,
once from a bridge intensely visible.*
Not to forget you. And stand!*


## To Music*

MUSIC: breath* of statues.    Perhaps even
silence of pictures.    You language where languages
end.*    You time,
set upright in the grain of hearts' evanescence.*

Feelings for whom? O you, transformation                    5
of feelings to what?—to audible landscape.
You stranger: music. You heart-space
grown out beyond us.* Inmost thing
outstripping us, surging onward—
holy leavetaking;                                          10
when what is inward rings us
as most mastered remoteness, the other
side of the air:*
pure,
towering,                                                  15
now uninhabitable.*



IT was in Karnak.* We had ridden there,
Hélène and I, after a brief meal.
The guide* stopped in the avenue of sphinxes*—
the Pylon*—ah!—I never felt more deeply

moon-world-wrapped!* (Immensity—dost thou              5
extend in me, even then too great?)
Is travel search? No, this was destination.
The keeper at the entrance first to transmit

des Maßes Schreck. Wie stand er niedrig neben
dem unaufhörlichen Sich-überheben       10
des Tors. Und jetzt, für unser ganzes Leben,
die Säule – : jene! War es nicht genug?

Zerstörung gab ihr recht: dem höchsten Dache
war sie zu hoch. Sie überstand und trug
Ägyptens Nacht.
              Der folgende Fellache       15

blieb nun zurück. Wir brauchten eine Zeit,
dies auszuhalten, weil es fast zerstörte,
daß *solches Stehn* dem Dasein angehörte,
in dem wir starben. – Hätt ich einen Sohn,
ich schickt ihn hin, in jenem Wendejahre,       20
da einer sich entringt ums einzig Wahre.
»Dort ist es, Charles, – geh durch den Pilon
und steh und schau . . . «
              *Uns* half es nicht mehr, wie?
Daß wirs ertrugen, war schon viel. Wir Beide:
du Leidende, in deinem Reisekleide,       25
und ich, Hermit in meiner Theorie.

Und doch, die Gnade! Weißt du noch den See,
um den granitne Katzen-Bilder saßen,
Marksteine – wessen? Und man war dermaßen
gebannt ins eingezauberte Carré,       30

daß, wären fünf an einer Seite nicht
gestürzt gewesen (du auch sahst dich um),
sie, wie sie waren, katzig, steinern, stumm,
Gericht gehalten hätten. Voll Gericht

war dieses alles. Hier der Bann am Teich       35
und dort am Rand die Riesen-Skarabäe
und an den Wänden längs die Epopäe
der Könige: Gericht. Und doch zugleich

the shock of height. How small he stood, next to
the unstoppable soaring of the gate.  10
And now, to last us for the rest of life,
that one column*—surely adequate?

Destruction was the making of it. Roofs
it over-stood and outlived, and it carried
Egypt's night.
            The guide who followed us  15

hung behind. For this we needed time,
holding-time, for it almost crushed us
that *such standing* shared the same existence
in which we died.—If I had a son
I'd send him there, in just that year that wrests  20
the young mind towards the sole truth.
'There, Charles: the Pylon. Walk through it
and stand and look . . .'
            No such help for *us*?
It was enough that we endured it, you,
unwell, suffering in your travelling-dress  25
and I wrapped in my theory like a hermit.

And yet its divine aura! The lake, remember,
girded by granite cats—stones of what
boundary? And we, held almost spellbound
in the quadrangular enchanted site,  30

for if, on one side, five of them* had not been
toppled over (you too gazed about you)
they would have made a mute, stone, feline
judgment-seat. For the entire scene

was judgment. Here, the enchanted lake; and there,  35
bordering it, the giant scarab-sculptures,*
and on the walls reliefs of kings; judgment,
and yet the sense of simultaneous

ein Freispruch, ungeheuer. Wie Figur
sich nach Figur mit reinem Mondschein füllte,                    40
war das im klarsten Umriß ausgedüllte
Relief, in seiner muldigen Natur,

so sehr Gefäß – – : und hier war *das* gefaßt,
was nie verborgen war und nie gelesen:
der Welt Geheimnis, *so geheim im Wesen*,              45
daß es in kein Verheimlicht-Werden paßt!

Bücher verblätterns alle: keiner las
so Offenbares je in einem Buche –,
(was hülfts, daß ich nach einem Namen suche):
das Unermeßliche kam in das Maß                    50

der Opferung. – Oh sieh, was ist Besitz,
solang er nicht versteht, sich darzubringen?
Die Dinge gehn vorüber. Hülf den Dingen
in ihrem Gang. Daß nicht aus einem Ritz

dein Leben rinne. Sondern immerzu             55
sei du der Geber. Maultier drängt und Kuh
zur Stelle, wo des Königs Ebenbild,
der Gott, wie ein gestilltes Kind, gestillt

hinnimmt und lächelt. Seinem Heiligtume
geht nie der Atem aus. Er nimmt und nimmt,            60
und doch ist solche Milderung bestimmt,
daß die Prinzessin die Papyros-Blume
oft nur umfaßt, statt sie zu brechen. –
                                                *Hier*
sind alle Opfer-Gänge unterbrochen,
der Sonntag rafft sich auf, die langen Wochen         65
verstehn ihn nicht. Da schleppen Mensch und Tier

abseits Gewinne, die der Gott nicht weiß.
Geschäft, mags schwierig sein, es ist bezwinglich;
man übts und übts, die Erde wird erschwinglich, –
wer aber nur den Preis giebt, der giebt preis.       70

vast acquittal. As the carvings filled
with pure moonlight, figure after figure,          40
the hollowed nature of the frieze-relief
moulded itself in stark bright contour,

so vessel-like—and here, held in them,
the never hidden and the never read,
the world's secret,* *essentially so latent*          45
as to accommodate no more secreting!

Riffling in books has lost it: no book's reader
ever read so manifest a writing—
(what would it help, to try to find a name?):
this is the immeasurable, entering          50

dimensions of the sacrifice.—What is
possession if it cannot give itself?
All things pass away. Help these things
during their passage from us. That your life

may not trickle heedless through the cracks.          55
Lifelong, be the giver. Mule must pass,
and cow, ahead to where the king's image,
the god, like a stilled child, accepts,

stilled, and smiles. His sanctity emits
never a breath. He takes and takes, and yet          60
this easing has its purpose, that the princess
lays no hand on the papyrus-flower
but holds it gently in embrace.—
                              *Here*,
the old sacrifices break off,
Sunday regains its feet and the long weeks          65
fail to understand it. Man and steer

drag off their profits, unknown to the god.
Against all odds it wins, the lure of business;
practise it and gain the earth—but simply
giving the price asked *relinquishes*.          70

WUNDERLICHES Wort: die Zeit vertreiben!
Sie zu *halten*, wäre das Problem.
Denn, wen ängstigts nicht: wo ist ein Bleiben,
wo ein endlich *Sein* in alledem? –

Sieh, der Tag verlangsamt sich, entgegen          5
jenem Raum, der ihn nach Abend nimmt:
Aufstehn wurde Stehn, und Stehn wird Legen,
und das willig Liegende verschwimmt –

Berge ruhn, von Sternen überprächtigt; –
aber auch in ihnen flimmert Zeit.          10
Ach, in meinem wilden Herzen nächtigt
obdachlos die Unvergänglichkeit.

ODD, the words: 'while away the time'.
How to *hold it fast* the harder thing.
Who is not fearful: where is there a staying,*
where in all this is there any *being*?

Look, as the day slows towards the space     5
that draws it into dusk: rising became
upstanding,* standing a laying down, and then
that which accepts its lying blurs to darkness.

Mountains rest, outgloried by the stars—
but even there, time's transition glimmers.     10
Ah, nightly refuged in my wild heart,
roofless, the imperishable lingers.

## Duineser Elegien

Aus dem Besitz der Fürstin
Marie von Thurn und Taxis-Hohenlohe

(1912/1922)

### Die erste Elegie

WER, wenn ich schriee, hörte mich denn aus der Engel
Ordnungen? und gesetzt selbst, es nähme
einer mich plötzlich ans Herz: ich verginge von seinem
stärkeren Dasein. Denn das Schöne ist nichts
als des Schrecklichen Anfang, den wir noch grade ertragen,      5
und wir bewundern es so, weil es gelassen verschmäht,
uns zu zerstören. Ein jeder Engel ist schrecklich.
    Und so verhalt ich mich denn und verschlucke den Lockruf
dunkelen Schluchzens. Ach, wen vermögen
wir denn zu brauchen? Engel nicht, Menschen nicht,      10
und die findigen Tiere merken es schon,
daß wir nicht sehr verläßlich zu Haus sind
in der gedeuteten Welt. Es bleibt uns vielleicht
irgend ein Baum an dem Abhang, daß wir ihn täglich
wiedersähen; es bleibt uns die Straße von gestern      15
und das verzogene Treusein einer Gewohnheit,
der es bei uns gefiel, und so blieb sie und ging nicht.
    O und die Nacht, die Nacht, wenn der Wind voller Weltraum
uns am Angesicht zehrt –, wem bliebe sie nicht, die ersehnte,
sanft enttäuschende, welche dem einzelnen Herzen      20
mühsam bevorsteht. Ist sie den Liebenden leichter?
Ach, sie verdecken sich nur mit einander ihr Los.
    Weißt du's *noch* nicht? Wirf aus den Armen die Leere
zu den Räumen hinzu, die wir atmen; vielleicht daß die Vögel
die erweiterte Luft fühlen mit innigerm Flug.      25

Ja, die Frühlinge brauchten dich wohl. Es muteten manche
Sterne dir zu, daß du sie spürtest. Es hob

# Duino Elegies

From the Castle of Princess
Marie von Thurn und Taxis-Hohenlohe*

(1912/1922)


## The First Elegy

WHO, if I cried out, would hear me among the orders
of Angels?* and even if one should suddenly
hold me to his heart I would fade back, touching
his intenser existence. For beauty is nothing
but the beginning edge of the dread* we may barely endure,      5
object of our awe because it serenely disdains
to annihilate us. Every Angel is dread.
   And so, curbing myself, I choke back the dark
sobbed call to them. Ah, whom to summon
here, to our need? Not Angels, not men; and the animals      10
canny, are well aware we are not reliably
one with the interpreted world.* Perhaps
growing upon the hill there is some tree
left us, so that we see it daily. Perhaps there is
yesterday's street still left us, and the loyalty of habit      15
that, once moved in with us, found our life to its liking
and so stayed on, not leaving again.
   Oh and the night*—the night, where the outer-space-filled
wind gnaws at the face—with whom should it not stay, longed for,
gently disillusioning, painful to meet      20
in the heart's solitude? Is it less so for lovers? Only
covering each other over do they hide their lot.
   You *still* don't know this? Fling your arms' emptiness from you
into the spaces we breathe; and then the birds may perhaps
sense the expanded air with more fervent flight.      25

Yes, the springs of the year have needed you. Numbers of stars
looked for you to perceive them. Towards you a wave flowed,

sich eine Woge heran im Vergangenen, oder
da du vorüberkamst am geöffneten Fenster,
gab eine Geige sich hin. Das alles war Auftrag.　　　　　30
Aber bewältigtest du's? Warst du nicht immer
noch von Erwartung zerstreut, als kündigte alles
eine Geliebte dir an? (Wo willst du sie bergen,
da doch die großen fremden Gedanken bei dir
aus und ein gehn und öfters bleiben bei Nacht.)　　　　　35
Sehnt es dich aber, so singe die Liebenden; lange
noch nicht unsterblich genug ist ihr berühmtes Gefühl.
Jene, du neidest sie fast, Verlassenen, die du
so viel liebender fandst als die Gestillten. Beginn
immer von neuem die nie zu erreichende Preisung;　　　　　40
denk: es erhält sich der Held, selbst der Untergang war ihm
nur ein Vorwand, zu sein: seine letzte Geburt.
Aber die Liebenden nimmt die erschöpfte Natur
in sich zurück, als wären nicht zweimal die Kräfte,
dieses zu leisten. Hast du der Gaspara Stampa　　　　　45
denn genügend gedacht, daß irgend ein Mädchen,
dem der Geliebte entging, am gesteigerten Beispiel
dieser Liebenden fühlt: daß ich würde wie sie?
Sollen nicht endlich uns diese ältesten Schmerzen
fruchtbarer werden? Ist es nicht Zeit, daß wir liebend　　　　　50
uns vom Geliebten befrein und es bebend bestehn:
wie der Pfeil die Sehne besteht, um gesammelt im Absprung
*mehr* zu sein als er selbst. Denn Bleiben ist nirgends.

Stimmen, Stimmen. Höre, mein Herz, wie sonst nur
Heilige hörten: daß sie der riesige Ruf　　　　　55
aufhob vom Boden; sie aber knieten,
Unmögliche, weiter und achtetens nicht:
*So* waren sie hörend. Nicht, daß du *Gottes* ertrügest
die Stimme, bei weitem. Aber das Wehende höre,
die ununterbrochene Nachricht, die aus Stille sich bildet.　　　　　60
Es rauscht jetzt von jenen jungen Toten zu dir.
Wo immer du eintratst, redete nicht in Kirchen
zu Rom und Neapel ruhig ihr Schicksal dich an?
Oder es trug eine Inschrift sich erhaben dir auf,
wie neulich die Tafel in Santa Maria Formosa.　　　　　65

risen in things of the past, or just as you walked
under an open window a violin*
gave itself to your ear. All these were your mission.*    30
But did you accomplish it? Or rather find yourself
side-tracked by expectation, as though all your world
announced a beloved? (Where would you hope to keep her,
with all these large, strange thoughts crowding you,
in and out constantly, and often staying all night.)    35
Yet, if longing takes hold, sing of lovers;* their famed
passion has still not nearly enough in it of the immortal.
Those whom you almost envy, the jilted, finding them
truer lovers by far than lovers requited. Begin
time and again their unattainable praise;    40
consider: the hero's* life goes on, and he counts his failure
no more than pretext for being: ultimate birth.
But Nature, as though exhausted, lacking perhaps
strength for repeated achievement, takes lovers back
into herself. Have you been mindful enough    45
of Gaspara Stampa,* so that perhaps some young girl
jilted in love feels by the high example
of this famed lover: if I might only be like her?
Should not at last even these most ancient of torments
bear fruit? Is it not time that we freed ourselves, loving it    50
still, from the object of love, and trembling survived it:
just as the arrow withstands the string to gather itself
for the leap and be *more* than it is. There is no place for staying.

Voices, voices. Listen, my heart, as formerly
only the saints did, hearing the immense call    55
that levitated them, strangest of beings,
while they yet kneeled and paid no heed to it.
That was the style of their listening. Not by any stretch could you
think to endure *God's* voice. But the long wind's message:
hear it, blowing eternally, forming itself out of silence.    60
A whisper of it approaches from those young dead.*
Whenever you entered a church in Rome or Naples,
has their fate not calmly spoken to you?
Or an inscription read you an exhortation,*
such as the tablet lately in Santa Maria Formosa.*    65

Was sie mir wollen? leise soll ich des Unrechts
Anschein abtun, der ihrer Geister
reine Bewegung manchmal ein wenig behindert.

Freilich ist es seltsam, die Erde nicht mehr zu bewohnen,
kaum erlernte Gebräuche nicht mehr zu üben,                     70
Rosen, und andern eigens versprechenden Dingen
nicht die Bedeutung menschlicher Zukunft zu geben;
das, was man war in unendlich ängstlichen Händen,
nicht mehr zu sein, und selbst den eigenen Namen
wegzulassen wie ein zerbrochenes Spielzeug.                     75
Seltsam, die Wünsche nicht weiterzuwünschen. Seltsam,
alles, was sich bezog, so lose im Raume
flattern zu sehen. Und das Totsein ist mühsam
und voller Nachholn, daß man allmählich ein wenig
Ewigkeit spürt. – Aber Lebendige machen                        80
alle den Fehler, daß sie zu stark unterscheiden.
Engel (sagt man) wüßten oft nicht, ob sie unter
Lebenden gehn oder Toten. Die ewige Strömung
reißt durch beide Bereiche alle Alter
immer mit sich und übertönt sie in beiden.                     85

Schließlich brauchen sie uns nicht mehr, die Früheentrückten,
man entwöhnt sich des Irdischen sanft, wie man den Brüsten
milde der Mutter entwächst. Aber wir, die so große
Geheimnisse brauchen, denen aus Trauer so oft
seliger Fortschritt entspringt – : *könnten* wir sein ohne sie?    90
Ist die Sage umsonst, daß einst in der Klage um Linos
wagende erste Musik dürre Erstarrung durchdrang;
daß erst im erschrocknen Raum, dem ein beinah göttlicher Jüngling
plötzlich für immer enttrat, das Leere in jene
Schwingung geriet, die uns jetzt hinreißt und tröstet und hilft.   95

### Die zweite Elegie

JEDER Engel ist schrecklich. Und dennoch, weh mir,
ansing ich euch, fast tödliche Vögel der Seele,

What do they want of me? That I should gently remove
the guise of injustice that sometimes lightly
hinders the pure movement of their spirits.

Yes, it is strange no longer to live on the earth, practising
customs barely yet learned, no longer imbuing                    70
roses, and other things rich in peculiar promise,
with that meaning accrued from our human future.
No longer to be what one was, held in endlessly
anxious hands; to let go even the use
of one's own name, as if dropping a broken toy.                  75
Strange, to wish no more widening wishes. Strange,
to see all interrelatedness fluttering loose
and disconnected. Being dead is a struggle,
full of the making good that brings us slowly
to feel a touch of eternity.—But the living                      80
err in creating clarity of distinction.
Angels (they say) cannot tell if they walk with the dead
or the living. Through either realm* the eternal river
tears all ages along in its flood, relentless,
drowning out their voice in its thunder.                         85

Ultimately they need us no longer, those who were snatched
too soon, and wean themselves from the earthly as naturally
as from their mother's breast. But we, needing
such vast mysteries, finding so often that grief
puts forth serene growth—*could* we survive without them?       90
Can we ignore the legend that in the lament over Linos*
daring music, the first, pierced that stiffened congealment,
and there, in the startled space that the all but godlike youth
straightforth stepped away from for ever, the void
fell to that pulsing that now transports and comforts and helps us.  95

## The Second Elegy

EVERY Angel is dread. And yet, alas,
knowing you, I sing out to you, all but fatal

wissend um euch. Wohin sind die Tage Tobiae,
da der Strahlendsten einer stand an der einfachen Haustür,
zur Reise ein wenig verkleidet und schon nicht mehr furchtbar;          5
(Jüngling dem Jüngling, wie er neugierig hinaussah).
Träte der Erzengel jetzt, der gefährliche, hinter den Sternen
eines Schrittes nur nieder und herwärts: hochauf-
schlagend erschlüg uns das eigene Herz. Wer seid ihr?

Frühe Geglückte, ihr Verwöhnten der Schöpfung,          10
Höhenzüge, morgenrötliche Grate
aller Erschaffung, – Pollen der blühenden Gottheit,
Gelenke des Lichtes, Gänge, Treppen, Throne,
Räume aus Wesen, Schilde aus Wonne, Tumulte
stürmisch entzückten Gefühls und plötzlich, einzeln,          15
*Spiegel*: die die entströmte eigene Schönheit
wiederschöpfen zurück in das eigene Antlitz.

Denn wir, wo wir fühlen, verflüchtigen; ach wir
atmen uns aus und dahin; von Holzglut zu Holzglut
geben wir schwächern Geruch. Da sagt uns wohl einer:          20
ja, du gehst mir ins Blut, dieses Zimmer, der Frühling
füllt sich mit dir . . . Was hilfts, er kann uns nicht halten,
wir schwinden in ihm und um ihn. Und jene, die schön sind,
o wer hält sie zurück? Unaufhörlich steht Anschein
auf in ihrem Gesicht und geht fort. Wie Tau von dem Frühgras          25
hebt sich das Unsre von uns, wie die Hitze von einem
heißen Gericht. O Lächeln, wohin? O Aufschaun:
neue, warme, entgehende Welle des Herzens – ;
weh mir: wir *sinds* doch. Schmeckt denn der Weltraum,
in den wir uns lösen, nach uns? Fangen die Engel          30
wirklich nur Ihriges auf, ihnen Entströmtes,
oder ist manchmal, wie aus Versehen, ein wenig
unseres Wesens dabei? Sind wir in ihre
Züge so viel nur gemischt wie das Vage in die Gesichter
schwangerer Frauen? Sie merken es nicht in dem Wirbel          35
ihrer Rückkehr zu sich. (Wie sollten sie's merken.)

Liebende könnten, verstünden sie's, in der Nachtluft
wunderlich reden. Denn es scheint, daß uns alles

birds of the soul. Where are the days of Tobias,* when
one of these brightest beings stood at the simple threshold,
in light disguise for the journey, no longer terrible                    5
(merely his fellow, to the young man curious at the window).
At the back of the stars, if an Archangel now, dangerous, took even
one step down to us, our own heart, wound upward,
beating in leaps, would beat us to death. Who *are* you?*

Young fortunates, spoilt favourites of creation,                        10
mountain peaks and ridges, roseate in the glow
of all first making—pollen* from flower of the godhead,
junctures of light, corridors, stairways, thrones,
spheres of essence, shields of ecstasy, tumults
of fiercely enraptured emotion, and suddenly, lone                      15
*mirrors:*  which each scoop up their streamed–out beauty
for pouring back into their own eyes.

We, when heart-stirred, vaporize, breathing ourselves
out and beyond, ember to cooling ember,
waning in fragrance. Though someone may say: you are here                20
in my blood, or this room, or the spring is filled with you . . . can this
change anything? He has no hold on us; in him
and round him we fade. And those who are lovely: who—
oh, who can pause them? Ceaselessly, altered appearance
rises into their faces and vanishes. Like the dew                       25
from the morning grass it lifts from us, all that is ours,
like heat from the dish. Where have our smiles gone? Oh where
the upturned look and the new, warm, swell of the heart,
brief as the tide—alas, but so we *are*.
Does space, dissolving us, taste of us? Do the Angels                   30
really catch only their own, streaming out from them, or,
sometimes, as if by mistake, a trace of our essence
commingled? Are we mixed into their features only
just so much as that familiar vagueness in faces
of pregnant women?* They notice nothing (how could they?)              35
in all the whirl of return into themselves.

Lovers, if they knew how, would speak marvellous words
into the night air. Everything, it would seem,

verheimlicht. Siehe, die Bäume *sind*; die Häuser,
die wir bewohnen, bestehn noch. Wir nur                              40
ziehen allem vorbei wie ein luftiger Austausch.
Und alles ist einig, uns zu verschweigen, halb als
Schande vielleicht und halb als unsägliche Hoffnung.

Liebende, euch, ihr in einander Genügten,
frag ich nach uns. Ihr greift euch. Habt ihr Beweise?          45
Seht, mir geschiehts, daß meine Hände einander
inne werden oder daß mein gebrauchtes
Gesicht in ihnen sich schont. Das giebt mir ein wenig
Empfindung. Doch wer wagte darum schon zu *sein*?
Ihr aber, die ihr im Entzücken des anderen                        50
zunehmt, bis er euch überwältigt
anfleht: nicht *mehr* –; die ihr unter den Händen
euch reichlicher werdet wie Traubenjahre;
die ihr manchmal vergeht, nur weil der andre
ganz überhand nimmt: euch frag ich nach uns. Ich weiß,     55
ihr berührt euch so selig, weil die Liebkosung verhält,
weil die Stelle nicht schwindet, die ihr, Zärtliche,
zudeckt; weil ihr darunter das reine
Dauern verspürt. So versprecht ihr euch Ewigkeit fast
von der Umarmung. Und doch, wenn ihr der ersten               60
Blicke Schrecken besteht und die Sehnsucht am Fenster,
und den ersten gemeinsamen Gang, *ein* Mal durch den Garten:
Liebende, *seid* ihrs dann noch? Wenn ihr einer dem andern
euch an den Mund hebt und ansetzt – : Getränk an Getränk:
o wie entgeht dann der Trinkende seltsam der Handlung.       65

Erstaunte euch nicht auf attischen Stelen die Vorsicht
menschlicher Geste? war nicht Liebe und Abschied
so leicht auf die Schultern gelegt, als wär es aus anderm
Stoffe gemacht als bei uns? Gedenkt euch der Hände,
wie sie drucklos beruhen, obwohl in den Torsen die Kraft steht.   70
Diese Beherrschten wußten damit: so weit sind wirs,
*dieses* ist unser, uns *so* zu berühren; stärker
stemmen die Götter uns an. Doch dies ist Sache der Götter.

hides us. For look, there *are* trees, and the houses we live in
still stand. Only we drift past all things, 40
like some change in the air. And all things conspire
in maintaining silence about us, half from shame,
perhaps, and half from inexpressible hope.

Lovers, sufficing each other: of you I would ask
questions about us. You hold each other. Your proof? 45
Look: sometimes I find that my hands are aware of each other,
or that my worn features take refuge in them,
allowing a faint sensation. Yet who, just for this,
would dare to *be*? You, though, each of you growing
by reciprocal passion until, overwhelmed, 50
you beg: No more!—each of you, by the
other's hands,* in the other's eyes,
becoming rich as the vine in the year of the grape;
or sometimes fading simply because the other
flourishes wildly: I ask about *us*. I know, 55
you touch with such a rapture because a caress is retention,
because that spot you cover, most gentle ones,
does not vanish; beneath it you feel
pure duration.* From the embrace, you promise each other
almost eternity. Yet, when you have survived 60
shock in those first few glances, the window-longing,
walking together that first time, once, through the garden;
lovers: *are* you the people you were? When you each
lift mouth to mouth and your lips meet—drink against drink:
oh, how strangely the drinker escapes from his actions. 65

Surely it struck you, the caution of human gestures
carved upon Attic gravestones?* Their love and farewell
laid so lightly on shoulders, as though fashioned in
substance that is not our own? Remember
the hands, resting weightless, for all the strength in the torso. 70
These disciplined people know: here are our limits,
this is ours, this touching each other so lightly.
The gods bear down on us harder. But that is the gods' affair.

Fänden auch wir ein reines, verhaltenes, schmales
Menschliches, einen unseren Streifen Fruchtlands                    75
zwischen Strom und Gestein. Denn das eigene Herz übersteigt uns
noch immer wie jene. Und wir können ihm nicht mehr
nachschaun in Bilder, die es besänftigen, noch in
göttliche Körper, in denen es größer sich mäßigt.


## *Die dritte Elegie*

EINES ist, die Geliebte zu singen. Ein anderes, wehe,
jenen verborgenen schuldigen Fluß-Gott des Bluts.
Den sie von weitem erkennt, ihren Jüngling, was weiß er
selbst von dem Herren der Lust, der aus dem Einsamen oft,
ehe das Mädchen noch linderte, oft auch als wäre sie nicht,        5
ach, von welchem Unkenntlichen triefend, das Gotthaupt
aufhob, aufrufend die Nacht zu unendlichem Aufruhr.
O des Blutes Neptun, o sein furchtbarer Dreizack.
O der dunkele Wind seiner Brust aus gewundener Muschel.
Horch, wie die Nacht sich muldet und höhlt. Ihr Sterne,           10
stammt nicht von euch des Liebenden Lust zu dem Antlitz
seiner Geliebten? Hat er die innige Einsicht
in ihr reines Gesicht nicht aus dem reinen Gestirn?

Du nicht hast ihm, wehe, nicht seine Mutter
hat ihm die Bogen der Braun so zur Erwartung gespannt.           15
Nicht an dir, ihn fühlendes Mädchen, an dir nicht
bog seine Lippe sich zum fruchtbarern Ausdruck.
Meinst du wirklich, ihn hätte dein leichter Auftritt
also erschüttert, du, die wandelt wie Frühwind?
Zwar du erschrakst ihm das Herz; doch ältere Schrecken           20
stürzten in ihn bei dem berührenden Anstoß.
Ruf ihn . . . du rufst ihn nicht ganz aus dunkelem Umgang.
Freilich, er *will*, er entspringt; erleichtert gewöhnt er
sich in dein heimliches Herz und nimmt und beginnt sich.
Aber begann er sich je?                                          25
Mutter, *du* machtest ihn klein, du warsts, die ihn anfing;
dir war er neu, du beugtest über die neuen

If we too could only find what is pure, constrained,
narrow, human; our own strip of land to bear fruit,                      75
between river and rock.* For our own heart, like theirs, constantly
outpaces us. And our gaze can no longer follow it
into chastening pictures, nor into figures,
godlike, where it achieves a greater control.*


## The Third Elegy

IT is one thing to sing the beloved, but another, alas,
that hidden, guilty river-god of the blood.*
Her young lover even, whom she finds in the distance, what does he
know of the lord of desire, who before her assuaging,
often as though she *were* not, out of the solitude                       5
lifted his god–head,* ah, streaming with the unknowable,
summoning the night into infinite uproar.
O the Neptune* of the blood, O his terrible trident.
O the dark wind from his breast breathed through the wound
   conch.
Listen to how the night rounds itself, hollows. O stars,                  10
surely the lover's desire for the face of his love
originates from you? And his tender insight
into her pure features, that too from the pure constellations?*


You it was not, alas, nor his mother, who shaped the expectant
arc of his eyebrows. Nor was it you for whom,                            15
in your girlish awareness of him, his lips curved
into a sweeter fruitfulness of expression.
Do you believe that your quiet approaching steps
would have shaken him, you who move lightly as morning wind?
Clearly, you alarmed his heart, but more ancient terrors*                 20
burst in upon him with this impact of feeling.
Call him . . . but you cannot quite call him from dark conversations.
Of course, he desires to—escapes—and settles lightly
close in your heart, takes on himself, his beginning.
Did he ever begin himself?                                               25
Mother, you made his pattern; it was you who began him.
He was new for you; over his new eyes

Augen die freundliche Welt und wehrtest der fremden.
Wo, ach, hin sind die Jahre, da du ihm einfach
mit der schlanken Gestalt wallendes Chaos vertratst?          30
Vieles verbargst du ihm so; das nächtlich-verdächtige Zimmer
machtest du harmlos, aus deinem Herzen voll Zuflucht
mischtest du menschlichern Raum seinem Nacht-Raum hinzu.
Nicht in die Finsternis, nein, in dein näheres Dasein
hast du das Nachtlicht gestellt, und es schien wie aus
    Freundschaft.                                              35
Nirgends ein Knistern, das du nicht lächelnd erklärtest,
so als wüßtest du längst, *wann* sich die Diele benimmt . . .
Und er horchte und linderte sich. So vieles vermochte
zärtlich dein Aufstehn; hinter den Schrank trat
hoch im Mantel sein Schicksal, und in die Falten des
    Vorhangs                                                  40
paßte, die leicht sich verschob, seine unruhige Zukunft.


Und er selbst, wie er lag, der Erleichterte, unter
schläfernden Lidern deiner leichten Gestaltung
Süße lösend in den gekosteten Vorschlaf – :
*schien* ein Gehüteter . . . Aber *innen*: wer wehrte,        45
hinderte innen in ihm die Fluten der Herkunft?
Ach, da *war* keine Vorsicht im Schlafenden; schlafend,
aber träumend, aber in Fiebern: wie er sich ein-ließ.
Er, der Neue, Scheuende, wie er verstrickt war,
mit des innern Geschehens weiterschlagenden Ranken            50
schon zu Mustern verschlungen, zu würgendem Wachstum, zu
    tierhaft
jagenden Formen. Wie er sich hingab –. Liebte.
Liebte sein Inneres, seines Inneren Wildnis,
diesen Urwald in ihm, auf dessen stummem Gestürztsein
lichtgrün sein Herz stand. Liebte. Verließ es, ging die       55
eigenen Wurzeln hinaus in gewaltigen Ursprung,
wo seine kleine Geburt schon überlebt war. Liebend
stieg er hinab in das ältere Blut, in die Schluchten,
wo das Furchtbare lag, noch satt von den Vätern. Und jedes
Schreckliche kannte ihn, blinzelte, war wie verständigt.      60
Ja, das Entsetzliche lächelte . . . Selten
hast du so zärtlich gelächelt, Mutter. Wie sollte

bending your motherly world, you held off the hostile.
Ah, where now are the years when your slender figure
simply substituted itself for onrushing chaos?　　　　　　　30
Like this you hid so much from him, rendered harmless his room's
nightly imaginings;* from your heart's refuge mingled
more human space into the space of his nights.
You set down his lamp—no, not so much in the dark
as near, in your presence, and it shone on him like friendship.　35
Never a creak you couldn't explain, smiling
as though you had always known the instant the floorboards
　　would go . . .
And he listened, quieter. Your rising and going to his bedside
achieved so much, for his tall, cloaked fate
stepped back behind the wardrobe, and his uneasy future,
　　subtly　　　　　　　　　　　　　　　　　　　　　40
placing itself beyond, slipped into folds of the curtain.

Lying there, freed, dissolving under drowsy eyelids
the sweetness of your delicate made world,
mingling it into the foretaste of sleep, he *seemed* shielded . . .
inwardly though, who would now hinder in him,　　　　　　45
ward off, divert, the flood-tides of origin?
In the sleeper there *was* no caution; sleeping,
yet through his dreams and fevers how wholly immersed.
New, apprehensive, how intricately he was tangled
in tendril-attacks of inner event that already　　　　　　　50
twisted in patterns, in stranglehold growth, in animal forms
that hunted. How he yielded himself.—Loved.
Loved his inner world, the wilderness in him, this
untouched wildwood* in him, on whose mute fallen floor
his heart stood, light green. Loved. And left it, went through
　　his own roots　　　　　　　　　　　　　　　　　　55
out towards powerful genesis, where already
his little birth was outlived. And loving, climbed down into
older blood, to ravines where Horror lay,
gorged with his fathers still. And the Indescribable
knew him and winked at him, as in a shared conspiracy.　　60
Yes, Ghastliness smiled at him . . . Seldom,
Mother, have you smiled so tenderly. How could he help

er es nicht lieben, da es ihm lächelte. *Vor* dir
hat ers geliebt, denn, da du ihn trugst schon,
war es im Wasser gelöst, das den Keimenden leicht macht. 65

Siehe, wir lieben nicht, wie die Blumen, aus einem
einzigen Jahr; uns steigt, wo wir lieben,
unvordenklicher Saft in die Arme. O Mädchen,
*dies*: daß wir liebten *in* uns, nicht Eines, ein Künftiges, sondern
das zahllos Brauende; nicht ein einzelnes Kind, 70
sondern die Väter, die wie Trümmer Gebirgs
uns im Grunde beruhn; sondern das trockene Flußbett
einstiger Mütter –; sondern die ganze
lautlose Landschaft unter dem wolkigen oder
reinen Verhängnis – : *dies* kam dir, Mädchen, zuvor. 75

Und du selber, was weißt du –, du locktest
Vorzeit empor in dem Liebenden. Welche Gefühle
wühlten herauf aus entwandelten Wesen. Welche
Frauen haßten dich da. Was für finstere Männer
regtest du auf im Geäder des Jünglings? Tote 80
Kinder wollten zu dir . . . O leise, leise,
tu ein liebes vor ihm, ein verläßliches Tagwerk, – führ ihn
nah an den Garten heran, gieb ihm der Nächte
Übergewicht . . . . . .
                    Verhalt ihn . . . . . .


## Die vierte Elegie

O BÄUME Lebens, o wann winterlich?
Wir sind nicht einig. Sind nicht wie die Zug-
vögel verständigt. Überholt und spät,
so drängen wir uns plötzlich Winden auf
und fallen ein auf teilnahmslosen Teich. 5
Blühn und verdorrn ist uns zugleich bewußt.
Und irgendwo gehn Löwen noch und wissen,
solang sie herrlich sind, von keiner Ohnmacht.

Uns aber, wo wir Eines meinen, ganz,

loving it, since it smiled at him. And before
*you* he has loved it, for even as you carried him
it was dissolved in the waters that buoy the embryo.    65

We do not love, you see, like flowers, for a year;
*our* love sends the immemorial sap
mounting into our arms. Dear girl, just this:
that we have loved, in our inmost core, not one, from the future,
but the numberless seething many; not one sole child    70
but the fathers, lying like debris of wrecked mountains
within us, chasm-deep, and the dried-up river beds
of those who were mothers—and also the whole
soundless landscape, under its clouded doom
or bright destiny—all this, my dear girl, preceded you.    75

And you yourself, little knowing—calling up
past aeons in him, your lover. What passions
sought their way out in him from departed beings.
How many women hated you there. What dark-hearted men
you have roused up in his young man's veins. Dead children    80
wanted to come to you . . . gently, oh gently, carry out
this task in his sight, reliably, out of affection for him—
lead him near to the garden, give him what will
outweigh the nights . . . . . .
                    Contain him . . . . . .

## The Fourth Elegy

O TREES of life, when is your winter?* Ours
is not agreed.* Unlike migratory birds
we have no warning. Overtaken, late,
we launch ourselves abruptly on the wind
and plummet over an indifferent pond.    5
Flowering and fading share our consciousness.
And somewhere lions roam, unaware,
in their magnificence, of frailty.

But we, wholly intent on one thing, sense

ist schon des andern Aufwand fühlbar. Feindschaft        10
ist uns das Nächste. Treten Liebende
nicht immerfort an Ränder, eins im andern,
die sich versprachen Weite, Jagd und Heimat.

Da wird für eines Augenblickes Zeichnung
ein Grund von Gegenteil bereitet, mühsam,        15
daß wir sie sähen; denn man ist sehr deutlich
mit uns. Wir kennen den Kontur
des Fühlens nicht: nur, was ihn formt von außen.

Wer saß nicht bang vor seines Herzens Vorhang?
Der schlug sich auf: die Szenerie war Abschied.        20
Leicht zu verstehen. Der bekannte Garten,
und schwankte leise: dann erst kam der Tänzer.
Nicht *der*. Genug! Und wenn er auch so leicht tut,
er ist verkleidet und er wird ein Bürger
und geht durch seine Küche in die Wohnung.        25

Ich will nicht diese halbgefüllten Masken,
lieber die Puppe. Die ist voll. Ich will
den Balg aushalten und den Draht und ihr
Gesicht aus Aussehn. Hier. Ich bin davor.
Wenn auch die Lampen ausgehn, wenn mir auch        30
gesagt wird: Nichts mehr –, wenn auch von der Bühne
das Leere herkommt mit dem grauen Luftzug,
wenn auch von meinen stillen Vorfahrn keiner
mehr mit mir dasitzt, keine Frau, sogar
der Knabe nicht mehr mit dem braunen Schielaug:        35
Ich bleibe dennoch. Es giebt immer Zuschaun.

Hab ich nicht recht? Du, der um mich so bitter
das Leben schmeckte, meines kostend, Vater,
den ersten trüben Aufguß meines Müssens,
da ich heranwuchs, immer wieder kostend        40
und, mit dem Nachgeschmack so fremder Zukunft
beschäftigt, prüftest mein beschlagnes Aufschaun, –
der du, mein Vater, seit du tot bist, oft
in meiner Hoffnung, innen in mir, Angst hast,
und Gleichmut, wie ihn Tote haben, Reiche        45
von Gleichmut, aufgiebst für mein bißchen Schicksal,
hab ich nicht recht? Und ihr, hab ich nicht recht,

the next already intervening. Conflict                              10
is close relation to us. Are not lovers
always reaching boundaries in each other
despite their promised free space, hunting, home?*

   A lightning sketch has its contrasting background
carefully prepared, so that we see                                  15
what they desire to be quite open to us.
And yet we cannot know our feeling's contour
beyond the outer influence that shapes it.

   Who has not sat, nervous, before his heart's
curtain?* It rises. On a scene of parting*                          20
Easy to understand. That garden,* familiar,
a little shaky. Then the dancer's entrance.*
*Him?* No, that's too much! Graceful he may be,
but out of costume really just the bourgeois
type who enters his house by the kitchen door.                      25

   I cannot bear these half-filled masks: give me
the puppet.* It's well stuffed out. Its casing
I can put up with, and its wire, its face
made out of show. Here. I am sitting waiting.
Even if the lights go out, or someone says:                         30
that's all we get—even if emptiness
drifts down from the stage in grey draughts,
and not a single silent forebear still
sits here in company with me, whether a woman,
or even the boy with brown eyes and the squint.*                    35
In spite of that, I'll stay. Plenty to see.


Am I not right? Father, you whose life
was bitter-tasting after sips of mine:
the first cloudy infusion of my will,
as I grew older, always on your tongue;                             40
who searched my misty gaze, pained at the after-
taste of such an alien future—you,
Father, here in my hope still anxious for me
after your death, renouncing for my little
destiny that calm the dead possess,                                 45
entire realms of equanimity—
am I not right to watch? And you too, all

die ihr mich liebtet für den kleinen Anfang
Liebe zu euch, von dem ich immer abkam,
weil mir der Raum in eurem Angesicht,                    50
da ich ihn liebte, überging in Weltraum,
in dem ihr nicht mehr wart . . . . : wenn mir zumut ist,
zu warten vor der Puppenbühne, nein,
so völlig hinzuschaun, daß, um mein Schauen
am Ende aufzuwiegen, dort als Spieler                    55
ein Engel hinmuß, der die Bälge hochreißt.
Engel und Puppe: dann ist endlich Schauspiel.
Dann kommt zusammen, was wir immerfort
entzwein, indem wir da sind. Dann entsteht
aus unsern Jahreszeiten erst der Umkreis                 60
des ganzen Wandelns. Über uns hinüber
spielt dann der Engel. Sieh, die Sterbenden,
sollten sie nicht vermuten, wie voll Vorwand
das alles ist, was wir hier leisten. Alles
ist nicht es selbst. O Stunden in der Kindheit,          65
da hinter den Figuren mehr als nur
Vergangnes war und vor uns nicht die Zukunft.
Wir wuchsen freilich und wir drängten manchmal,
bald groß zu werden, denen halb zulieb,
die andres nicht mehr hatten, als das Großsein.          70
Und waren doch, in unserem Alleingehn,
mit Dauerndem vergnügt und standen da
im Zwischenraume zwischen Welt und Spielzeug,
an einer Stelle, die seit Anbeginn
gegründet war für einen reinen Vorgang.                  75

Wer zeigt ein Kind, so wie es steht? Wer stellt
es ins Gestirn und giebt das Maß des Abstands
ihm in die Hand? Wer macht den Kindertod
aus grauem Brot, das hart wird, – oder läßt
ihn drin im runden Mund, so wie den Gröps                80
von einem schönen Apfel? . . . . . . Mörder sind
leicht einzusehen. Aber dies: den Tod,
den ganzen Tod, noch *vor* dem Leben so
sanft zu enthalten und nicht bös zu sein,
ist unbeschreiblich.                                     85

who loved me for my slight incipient love—
a love for you I always turned away from,
because the space I saw within your faces 50
changed when I loved it into cosmic space,
where you no longer were . . . . am I not right
to want to sit before the puppet-stage—no,
to stare at it, so that as counterweight
to my long gaze an Angel–player must come 55
and jerk the stuffed skins upward in a leap?
Angel and puppet: we have a play at last.
Then what we separate by being here
comes together; out of our short seasons
the cycle of the whole transformation 60
arises. Then, moving past and over us,
the angel plays his part. Look at the dying:
they must suspect how fabricated, here,
all our achievement is. Everything
is absent from itself. O childhood hours: 65
behind whose figures there was more than just
the past, ahead of which we did not see the future.
Slowly we grew, but sometimes urged ourselves
to grow up early, half to please people
for whom to be grown up was all they had. 70
Yet once alone, we found ourselves sustained
by things that lasted, and were in a place
interjacent between world and toy,*
an interval established from the first
as home to the affairs of innocence. 75


Who shows a child in his own light? Sets him
among the stars, puts the measuring-rod
of difference* in his hand? Serves him a death
of grey bread, hardening—or leaves it there
in the round mouth, like the luscious apple's 80
hard–edged core? . . . . . . Murderers are easy
to understand. But death, entire death:
to take it in so meekly, gently, even
before the start of life, and feel no anger,
that is unspeakable. 85

## Die fünfte Elegie

Frau Hertha Koenig zugeeignet

WER aber *sind* sie, sag mir, die Fahrenden, diese ein wenig
Flüchtigern noch als wir selbst, die dringend von früh an
wringt ein *wem, wem* zu Liebe
niemals zufriedener Wille? Sondern er wringt sie,
biegt sie, schlingt sie und schwingt sie,                              5
wirft sie und fängt sie zurück; wie aus geölter,
glatterer Luft kommen sie nieder
auf dem verzehrten, von ihrem ewigen
Aufsprung dünneren Teppich, diesem verlorenen
Teppich im Weltall.                                                    10
Aufgelegt wie ein Pflaster, als hätte der Vorstadt-
Himmel der Erde dort wehe getan.
                              Und kaum dort,
aufrecht, da und gezeigt: des Dastehns
großer Anfangsbuchstab . . ., schon auch, die stärksten
Männer, rollt sie wieder, zum Scherz, der immer               15
kommende Griff, wie August der Starke bei Tisch
einen zinnenen Teller.

Ach und um diese
Mitte, die Rose des Zuschauns:
blüht und entblättert. Um diesen                                       20
Stampfer, den Stempel, den von dem eignen
blühenden Staub getroffnen, zur Scheinfrucht
wieder der Unlust befruchteten, ihrer
niemals bewußten, – glänzend mit dünnster
Oberfläche leicht scheinlächelnden Unlust.                            25

Da: der welke, faltige Stemmer,
der alte, der nur noch trommelt,
eingegangen in seiner gewaltigen Haut, als hätte sie früher
*zwei* Männer enthalten, und einer
läge nun schon auf dem Kirchhof, und er überlebte den andern,  30
taub und manchmal ein wenig
wirr, in der verwitweten Haut.

## The Fifth Elegy

Dedicated to Frau Hertha Koenig*

TELL me, who *are* they, these travelling, transient people,* more so
even than we ourselves, from their earliest youth wrung
in an urgent will (to please *whom?*), a will
not to be satisfied. But instead it wrings them,
bends them, winds them and swings them,                                      5
slings them and catches them back; as out of oiled
slippery air they land on the shredded
mat they have worn, by their perpetual
leaping, thinner and thinner, on what is now a lost
mat in the universe.                                                        10
Laid on the earth like a plaster, as though suburbia's
sky had injured it.
                            Scarce have they landed, and there
revealed is the tall, upright, initial D*
of their standing's Duration . . . and yet, already the toying,
ever-approaching handgrip rolls them, even the strongest,              15
just as Prince August the Strong,* at table,
would roll up a pewter plate.

Ah, and round this
centre the rose of onlookers*
petals and falls. Round this                                          20
stamping piston:* a pistil* dusted
by its own pollen, brought to the spurious
fruiting of absent inertness once more,
sheened in the thinnest surface-glaze of its
delicately, barely half-smiling listlessness.                        25

There the weight-lifter, shrunken, wrinkled
and too old to be anything now but a drummer,
shrivelled inside a skin so prodigious it might once have held
two men, one of them lying
by now in the churchyard, and he himself the survivor,               30
deaf and sometimes a little
befuddled in that widowed skin.*

Aber der junge, der Mann, als wär er der Sohn eines Nackens
und einer Nonne: prall und strammig erfüllt
mit Muskeln und Einfalt.                                    35

Oh ihr,
die ein Leid, das noch klein war,
einst als Spielzeug bekam, in einer seiner
langen Genesungen . . . .

Du, der mit dem Aufschlag,                                  40
wie nur Früchte ihn kennen, unreif,
täglich hundertmal abfällt vom Baum der gemeinsam
erbauten Bewegung (der, rascher als Wasser, in wenig
Minuten Lenz, Sommer und Herbst hat) –
abfällt und anprallt ans Grab:                              45
manchmal, in halber Pause, will dir ein liebes
Antlitz entstehn hinüber zu deiner selten
zärtlichen Mutter; doch an deinen Körper verliert sich,
der es flächig verbraucht, das schüchtern
kaum versuchte Gesicht . . . Und wieder                     50
klatscht der Mann in die Hand zu dem Ansprung, und eh dir
jemals ein Schmerz deutlicher wird in der Nähe des immer
trabenden Herzens, kommt das Brennen der Fußsohln
ihm, seinem Ursprung, zuvor mit ein paar dir
rasch in die Augen gejagten leiblichen Tränen.             55
Und dennoch, blindlings,
das Lächeln . . . . .

Engel! o nimms, pflücks, das kleinblütige Heilkraut.
Schaff eine Vase, verwahrs! Stells unter jene, uns *noch* nicht
offenen Freuden; in lieblicher Urne                         60
rühms mit blumiger schwungiger Aufschrift: ›*Subrisio Saltat.*‹

Du dann, Liebliche,
du, von den reizendsten Freuden
stumm Übersprungne. Vielleicht sind
deine Fransen glücklich für dich –,                         65
oder über den jungen
prallen Brüsten die grüne metallene Seide

But the young one, the man who looks for all the world like the son
of a neck and a nun:* he's filled out taut with muscles
and ingenuousness.                                                    35

You few,
whom a Grief once received
as plaything, during the course of one of its
long convalescences . . . .

You, boy,* falling each day,                                          40
with the thud known only to fruit, unripe,
a hundred times out of the tree of mutually
constructed movement* (which, faster than water, in a few
minutes goes through its spring, summer, autumn)—
landing with a shock on the grave:                                    45
sometimes, in semi-pauses, a loving look
starts in your face, making to reach your rarely
affectionate mother, but loses itself in your body's
planar, consuming forces, the shyly,
barely attempted glance . . . And again                               50
the man's hand-clap to signal your leap, and before
pain at the loss can become a clarity next to your constantly
racing heart, the stinging in the soles of your feet
intercepts its source-pain, chasing
a pair of quick physical tears into your eyes.                        55
And none the less, blindly,
that smile* . . . . .

Angel, oh take it, gather it, that small-flowered heal-wort.
Find some vase to preserve it! Store it among those pleasures
not yet open to us; on its lovely urn                                 60
celebrate it in words, with a flourish: *Subrisio Saltat*.*

Then you, darling one,*
you whom the sweetest diversions
have mutely skipped over. Perhaps
your fringes feel your happiness for you—                             65
or the metallic green silk
over your firm young breasts is aware of being

fühlt sich unendlich verwöhnt und entbehrt nichts.
Du,
immerfort anders auf alle des Gleichgewichts schwankende
    Waagen           70
hingelegte Marktfrucht des Gleichmuts,
öffentlich unter den Schultern.


Wo, o *wo* ist der Ort – ich trag ihn im Herzen –,
wo sie noch lange nicht *konnten*, noch voneinander
abfieln, wie sich bespringende, nicht recht    75
paarige Tiere; –
wo die Gewichte noch schwer sind;
wo noch von ihren vergeblich
wirbelnden Stäben die Teller
torkeln . . . . .    80


Und plötzlich in diesem mühsamen Nirgends, plötzlich
die unsägliche Stelle, wo sich das reine Zuwenig
unbegreiflich verwandelt –, umspringt
in jenes leere Zuviel.
Wo die vielstellige Rechnung    85
zahlenlos aufgeht.


Plätze, o Platz in Paris, unendlicher Schauplatz,
wo die Modistin, *Madame Lamort*,
die ruhlosen Wege der Erde, endlose Bänder,
schlingt und windet und neue aus ihnen    90
Schleifen erfindet, Rüschen, Blumen, Kokarden, künstliche
    Früchte –, alle
unwahr gefärbt, – für die billigen
Winterhüte des Schicksals.
. . . . . . . . . . . . . . . . . . . . . . .


Engel!: Es wäre ein Platz, den wir nicht wissen, und dorten,  95
auf unsäglichem Teppich, zeigten die Liebenden, die's hier
bis zum Können nie bringen, ihre kühnen
hohen Figuren des Herzschwungs,
ihre Türme aus Lust, ihre
längst, wo Boden nie war, nur an einander    100

endlessly indulged and in need of nothing.
You,
poised* market-fruit, set out in constantly varied display          70
on the swaying scales of equilibrium,*
shown off among the shoulders.

Oh *where* is the place—I carry it in my heart—
where they were still very far from able, still
fell off each other, like animals paired                          75
unsatisfactorily—
where the weights still weigh heavy,
where the poles twirl uselessly
still, under plates that wobble
and spin down . . . . .                                            80

And suddenly in this strained void, suddenly
that untellable point, where the pure too-little transforms
inexplicably—and leaps veering
into that empty too-much.*
Where the dense calculation                                        85
resolves, numberless.

Squares—O Parisian square, that infinite showplace
where the milliner *Madame Lamort**
twists and winds the unending ribbons, the unquiet
paths of the earth, creating from them                             90
new bows, ruchings, flowers, cockades, artificial fruits—dyed
all unlikely hues—for the cheap
winter bonnets of fate.

. . . . . . . . . . . . . . . . . . . . . . .

Angel: if there were a square we knew nothing of, where lovers     95
played out on some unimagined carpet what they have never,
     here,
fully been able to master, their daring
high-flung, heart-swinging figures,
their towers of ecstasy, ladders
long since tremblingly leaning just on each other,                 100

lehnenden Leitern, bebend, – und *könntens*,
vor den Zuschauern rings, unzähligen lautlosen Toten:
    Würfen die dann ihre letzten, immer ersparten,
immer verborgenen, die wir nicht kennen, ewig
gültigen Münzen des Glücks vor das endlich                    105
wahrhaft lächelnde Paar auf gestilltem
Teppich?


## Die sechste Elegie

FEIGENBAUM, seit wie lange schon ists mir bedeutend,
wie du die Blüte beinah ganz überschlägst
und hinein in die zeitig entschlossene Frucht,
ungerühmt, drängst dein reines Geheimnis.
Wie der Fontäne Rohr treibt dein gebognes Gezweig              5
abwärts den Saft und hinan: und er springt aus dem Schlaf,
fast nicht erwachend, ins Glück seiner süßesten Leistung.
Sieh: wie der Gott in den Schwan.
                   . . . . . . Wir aber verweilen,
ach, uns rühmt es zu blühn, und ins verspätete Innre
unserer endlichen Frucht gehn wir verraten hinein.           10
Wenigen steigt so stark der Andrang des Handelns,
daß sie schon anstehn und glühn in der Fülle des Herzens,
wenn die Verführung zum Blühn wie gelinderte Nachtluft
ihnen die Jugend des Munds, ihnen die Lider berührt:
Helden vielleicht und den frühe Hinüberbestimmten,            15
denen der gärtnernde Tod anders die Adern verbiegt.
Diese stürzen dahin: dem eigenen Lächeln
sind sie voran, wie das Rossegespann in den milden
muldigen Bildern von Karnak dem siegenden König.


Wunderlich nah ist der Held doch den jugendlich Toten.
    Dauern                                                         20
ficht ihn nicht an. Sein Aufgang ist Dasein; beständig
nimmt er sich fort und tritt ins veränderte Sternbild
seiner steten Gefahr. Dort fänden ihn wenige. Aber,
das uns finster verschweigt, das plötzlich begeisterte Schicksal

where ground never was—and there *found* mastery,            100
ringed by other spectators, the numberless silent dead:
    Would not these dead then scatter their last, ever-hoarded,
ever-hidden, eternally valid, unknown
coins of happiness before that pair,
genuinely smiling at last, on the stilled                     105
carpet?*


## The Sixth Elegy

FIG-TREE,* how long you have held this meaning for me,
in that you almost completely neglect to flower,*
pouring and pressing, uncelebrated, your pure
mystery into the early-determined fruit.
Like the run of pipe in the fountain, your curved boughs      5
drive the sap downwards and on, to spring from sleep,
barely woken, into the bliss of its sweetest achievement.
See, like the god become swan.*
                        . . . . . . But we, alas, linger,*
glorying in our flowering,* and pass into the late-formed
inner core of our eventual fruit—betrayed.                    10
In few does the impulse to action grow so urgent
that they must stand tensed, glowing in fullness of heart,
as the temptation to bloom, like the gentle night air,
touches the youth of their mouth and brushes their eyelids:
heroes perhaps, and those due for early transition,           15
whose veins the gardener Death has trained to a different design.
Precipitately they plunge on, running ahead
of their own smile, like the horses pulling the king-
conqueror's chariot in the bas-reliefs at Karnak.*

The hero* is strangely close to those who die young.
    Permanence                                                20
simply is not his concern. He ascends through existence,
constantly leaving us for the shifting constellation
of his incessant danger. There, few would find him. Fate, though,
sinister, silent about *us*, is entranced on the instant,

singt ihn hinein in den Sturm seiner aufrauschenden Welt.                    25
Hör ich doch keinen wie *ihn*. Auf einmal durchgeht mich
mit der strömenden Luft sein verdunkelter Ton.

Dann, wie verbärg ich mich gern vor der Sehnsucht: O wär ich,
wär ich ein Knabe und dürft es noch werden und säße
in die künftigen Arme gestützt und läse von Simson,                          30
wie seine Mutter erst nichts und dann alles gebar.

War er nicht Held schon in dir, o Mutter, begann nicht
dort schon, in dir, seine herrische Auswahl?
Tausende brauten im Schoß und wollten *er* sein,
aber sieh: er ergriff und ließ aus –, wählte und konnte.                      35
Und wenn er Säulen zerstieß, so wars, da er ausbrach
aus der Welt deines Leibs in die engere Welt, wo er weiter
wählte und konnte. O Mütter der Helden, o Ursprung
reißender Ströme! Ihr Schluchten, in die sich
hoch von dem Herzrand, klagend,                                              40
schon die Mädchen gestürzt, künftig die Opfer dem Sohn.

Denn hinstürmte der Held durch Aufenthalte der Liebe,
jeder hob ihn hinaus, jeder ihn meinende Herzschlag,
abgewendet schon, stand er am Ende der Lächeln, – anders.

## Die siebente Elegie

WERBUNG nicht mehr, nicht Werbung, entwachsene Stimme,
sei deines Schreies Natur; zwar schrieest du rein wie der Vogel,
wenn ihn die Jahreszeit aufhebt, die steigende, beinahe
      vergessend,
daß er ein kümmerndes Tier und nicht nur ein einzelnes Herz sei,
das sie ins Heitere wirft, in die innigen Himmel. Wie er, so            5
würbest du wohl, nicht minder –, daß, noch unsichtbar,
dich die Freundin erführ, die stille, in der eine Antwort
langsam erwacht und über dem Hören sich anwärmt, –
deinem erkühnten Gefühl die erglühte Gefühlin.

singing him onward into the storm of his surging world.          25
I have not heard his like. His voice, darkened,
all at once pierces me, borne in the streaming air.

Then, how gladly I would hide from the longing to enter my
    boyhood:*
once more, boyhood, with its hopes of becoming, and sit
propped on my future elbows reading* of Samson*          30
and of his mother, who was first barren, then bore all.

Mother, as you carried him was he not even then hero,
making, already, imperious choice?
Thousands seethed in your womb and wanted to *be him*,
but watch how he seized and discarded, chose and achieved.          35
And if he overthrew pillars—it was when breaking
out of your body's world* to the narrower world, where again
he chose and achieved. O mothers of heroes,
O sources of river-torrents. You clefts into which,
crying high on the heart's edge,          40
virgins have plunged to their future, sacrificed to the son.*

For seeing the hero storm through the habitations of love,*
hearts that beat for him lifted him up and beyond them;
then, turned from them, he stood at the far end of smiling—other.

## The Seventh Elegy

No more of wooing,* O voice grown beyond it,* no more let
wooing be the soul of your cry, though you cry pure as the bird*
raised up by the rising days, exalted almost to forgetting
that he is a suffering creature and not just a single heart
flung up to gladness and intimate heavens. No less than the bird,          5
you would be wooing—so that your yet unglimpsed
silent lover might sense and learn of you, she in whom answer
slowly awakens and warms with her listening—the burning
counterpart of your own emboldened emotion.

O und der Frühling begriffe –, da ist keine Stelle,                                                  10
die nicht trüge den Ton der Verkündigung. Erst jenen kleinen
fragenden Auflaut, den, mit steigernder Stille,
weithin umschweigt ein reiner, bejahender Tag.
Dann die Stufen hinan, Ruf-Stufen hinan zum geträumten
Tempel der Zukunft –; dann den Triller, Fontäne,                                         15
die zu dem drängenden Strahl schon das Fallen zuvornimmt
im versprechlichen Spiel . . . . Und vor sich, den Sommer.

Nicht nur die Morgen alle des Sommers –, nicht nur
wie sie sich wandeln in Tag und strahlen vor Anfang.
Nicht nur die Tage, die zart sind um Blumen, und oben,                             20
um die gestalteten Bäume, stark und gewaltig.
Nicht nur die Andacht dieser entfalteten Kräfte,
nicht nur die Wege, nicht nur die Wiesen im Abend,
nicht nur, nach spätem Gewitter, das atmende Klarsein,
nicht nur der nahende Schlaf und ein Ahnen, abends . . .                            25
sondern die Nächte! Sondern die hohen, des Sommers,
Nächte, sondern die Sterne, die Sterne der Erde.
O einst tot sein und sie wissen unendlich,
alle die Sterne: denn wie, wie, wie sie vergessen!

Siehe, da rief ich die Liebende. Aber nicht *sie* nur                                      30
käme . . . Es kämen aus schwächlichen Gräbern
Mädchen und ständen . . . Denn, wie beschränk ich,
wie, den gerufenen Ruf? Die Versunkenen suchen
immer noch Erde. – Ihr Kinder, ein hiesig
einmal ergriffenes Ding gälte für viele.                                                              35
Glaubt nicht, Schicksal sei mehr, als das Dichte der
     Kindheit;
wie überholtet ihr oft den Geliebten, atmend,
atmend nach seligem Lauf, auf nichts zu, ins Freie.

Hiersein ist herrlich. Ihr wußtet es, Mädchen, *ihr* auch,
die ihr scheinbar entbehrtet, versank –, ihr, in den ärgsten                         40
Gassen der Städte, Schwärende, oder dem Abfall
Offene. Denn eine Stunde war jeder, vielleicht nicht
ganz eine Stunde, ein mit den Maßen der Zeit kaum

Oh, and the spring would hear and absorb—not a space in it          10
that would not ring with annunciation. First the tiny
questioning grace-note which pure affirmative day
widely wraps with intensifying silence.
Then the steps upward,* the calling flights up to the dreamed
temple that is the future; the trill, fountain-                     15
play of promise that has in its jetted brilliance
already its pre-known falling . . . . And ahead, summer.

Not only all summer's mornings—not only the way
they modulate into day, and shine with beginning.
Not only days, lying softly round flowers, and above them           20
canopied patterns of trees, massed in their strength.
Not only reverence in these unfolding forces,
not only paths and ways, the meadows at dusk,
and freshness sighing behind an evening storm,
not only oncoming sleep and a premonition . . .                     25
but nights!* But above all the huge high-summer
nights, and the stars, stars of the earth.
Oh to be dead at last and know them endlessly,
all the stars; for how, how, how to forget them!

See, I have called my love. But not only she*                       30
would come . . . From unsettled graves would come girls,
    other girls
standing there . . . For how limit the call,
how, since I called it? And the interred are always
seeking our earth.—Children: one thing
solidly grasped, even once, would serve for many.                   35
Don't think your fated lost years of more value than childhood;*
how often you outran your lover, breathing, deep-breathing
after the ecstatic chase, into the void, into freedom.

Being here is glorious. And even you knew it, you young girls
deeply deprived, so it seemed, submerged beyond trace in the
    foulest                                                         40
alleys of cities, festering, laying yourselves open
to filth. For each of you had, for an hour or perhaps even
less, for a time immeasurably short between

Meßliches zwischen zwei Weilen –, da sie ein Dasein
hatte. Alles. Die Adern voll Dasein.     45
Nur, wir vergessen so leicht, was der lachende Nachbar
uns nicht bestätigt oder beneidet. Sichtbar
wollen wirs heben, wo doch das sichtbarste Glück uns
erst zu erkennen sich giebt, wenn wir es innen verwandeln.

Nirgends, Geliebte, wird Welt sein, als innen. Unser     50
Leben geht hin mit Verwandlung. Und immer geringer
schwindet das Außen. Wo einmal ein dauerndes Haus war,
schlägt sich erdachtes Gebild vor, quer, zu Erdenklichem
völlig gehörig, als ständ es noch ganz im Gehirne.
Weite Speicher der Kraft schafft sich der Zeitgeist, gestaltlos     55
wie der spannende Drang, den er aus allem gewinnt.
Tempel kennt er nicht mehr. Diese, des Herzens, Verschwendung
sparen wir heimlicher ein. Ja, wo noch eins übersteht,
ein einst gebetetes Ding, ein gedientes, gekniees –,
hält es sich, so wie es ist, schon ins Unsichtbare hin.     60
Viele gewahrens nicht mehr, doch ohne den Vorteil,
daß sie's nun *innerlich* baun, mit Pfeilern und Statuen, größer!

Jede dumpfe Umkehr der Welt hat solche Enterbte,
denen das Frühere nicht und noch nicht das Nächste gehört.
Denn auch das Nächste ist weit für die Menschen. *Uns* soll     65
dies nicht verwirren; es stärke in uns die Bewahrung
der noch erkannten Gestalt. – Dies *stand* einmal unter Menschen,
mitten im Schicksal stands, im vernichtenden, mitten
im Nichtwissen-Wohin stand es, wie seiend, und bog
Sterne zu sich aus gesicherten Himmeln. Engel,     70
*dir* noch zeig ich es, *da!* in deinem Anschaun
steh es gerettet zuletzt, nun endlich aufrecht.
Säulen, Pylone, der Sphinx, das strebende Stemmen,
grau aus vergehender Stadt oder aus fremder, des Doms.

War es nicht Wunder? O staune, Engel, denn *wir* sinds,     75
wir, o du Großer, erzähls, daß wir solches vermochten, mein Atem
reicht für die Rühmung nicht aus. So haben wir dennoch
nicht die Räume versäumt, diese gewährenden, diese
*unseren* Räume. (Was müssen sie fürchterlich groß sein,

two durations, your own being. Everything.
Arteries running with being. Only—                                     45
we can so lightly forget what our laughing neighbour
neither confirms nor envies. We want to lift it,
show it, yet the most evident happiness submits
to our recognition only if we transform it within us.*

Nowhere, beloved, can world be but within us. Our life          50
passes in transformation. And the external
dwindles away. Where a house stood and endured,
now it will move across consciousness as image,*
wholly concept, as though still there—in the brain.
Vast reserves of power* are born of the Zeitgeist: intangible,    55
like that charge of energy it draws from the physical world.
Knowledge of temples has left it. Such luxuries of the heart
are ours to put by in secret. Where one survives still, Thing
worshipped once, prayed to, attended—just as it is
it offers itself already to the invisible. Many              60
no longer recognize it, or the advantage
of temples constructed *within*, with pillars and statues: greater!

Each new lumbering turn of the world has its own disinherited,
those to whom neither the past belongs nor what meets them next.
For even that next is far for mankind. It must not     65
lead us into confusion but safeguard in us
form we still recognize.—This once *stood* among people,
in the midst of Fate, the annihilator, in the midst
of our Not-Knowing-Where-Next, like an existence, and curved
stars down to it out of their sure heavens. Angel,     70
*there!* To you I can show it still: in your vision
let it at last stand, saved, now at last upright. Columns,
pylons,* the Sphinx, and looming out of a strange
or passing city the grey soar of the cathedral.*

Marvel at this, Angel, this miracle. For it is we—     75
tell it, O Great One—we who achieved such a thing; my breath
cannot last for such praise. So, after all, we have not
left these generous spaces unused, these *our* spaces.
Fearfully great they must be, if millennia

da sie Jahrtausende nicht unseres Fühlns überfülln.) 80
Aber ein Turm war groß, nicht wahr? O Engel, er war es, –
groß, auch noch neben dir? Chartres war groß –, und Musik
reichte noch weiter hinan und überstieg uns. Doch selbst nur
eine Liebende –, oh, allein am nächtlichen Fenster . . . .
reichte sie dir nicht ans Knie –?

                         Glaub *nicht*, daß ich werbe. 85
Engel, und würb ich dich auch! Du kommst nicht. Denn mein
Anruf ist immer voll Hinweg; wider so starke
Strömung kannst du nicht schreiten. Wie ein gestreckter
Arm ist mein Rufen. Und seine zum Greifen
oben offene Hand bleibt vor dir 90
offen, wie Abwehr und Warnung,
Unfaßlicher, weitauf.

## Die achte Elegie

### Rudolf Kassner zugeeignet

MIT allen Augen sieht die Kreatur
das Offene. Nur unsre Augen sind
wie umgekehrt und ganz um sie gestellt
als Fallen, rings um ihren freien Ausgang.
Was draußen *ist*, wir wissens aus des Tiers 5
Antlitz allein; denn schon das frühe Kind
wenden wir um und zwingens, daß es rückwärts
Gestaltung sehe, nicht das Offne, das
im Tiergesicht so tief ist. Frei von Tod.
*Ihn* sehen wir allein; das freie Tier 10
hat seinen Untergang stets hinter sich
und vor sich Gott, und wenn es geht, so gehts
in Ewigkeit, so wie die Brunnen gehen.
    *Wir* haben nie, nicht einen einzigen Tag,
den reinen Raum vor uns, in den die Blumen 15
unendlich aufgehn. Immer ist es Welt
und niemals Nirgends ohne Nicht: das Reine,
Unüberwachte, das man atmet und

of filling them with our feelings have not overflowed them. 80
But a tower was great too, surely? O Angel, it *was*—
still great, set next to you? Chartres was great—and music
  reached up
higher again and transcended us. But even a woman,
in love—oh, alone at night by her window* . . . .
did she not reach to your knee?

                        Do not take this to be wooing, 85
Angel, even if it were! You would not come. For my
call is full of my leaving;* against this strong
current you cannot move forward. It is like an outstretched
arm, my call. And its open hand, ready
to grasp, remains there before you, open 90
like a defence and a warning,
you high Ungraspable.

## *The Eighth Elegy*

### Dedicated to Rudolf Kassner*

WITH all its eyes the natural world looks far
into the Open.* Only *our* eyes look back,
set like traps about all living things,
encircled round their free, outward path.
What *is*, in that outside, we learn only 5
by looking in their faces; for we force
even the youngest child to turn and look
backwards into design, not at the Open
deep in animals' eyes. Free of death.
That, only we can see. The free animal* 10
has its decline perpetually behind it
and God before, and in its movement moves
within eternity,* like the welling springs.

    Never, for a day, do *we* have
pure space before us for the opening 15
of endless flowers. Always there is World,
never the negativeless Nowhere: that pure,
unoverlooked, breathed element we know

unendlich *weiß* und nicht begehrt. Als Kind
verliert sich eins im Stilln an dies und wird
gerüttelt. Oder jener stirbt und *ists*.　　　　　　　20
Denn nah am Tod sieht man den Tod nicht mehr
und starrt *hinaus*, vielleicht mit großem Tierblick.
Liebende, wäre nicht der andre, der
die Sicht verstellt, sind nah daran und staunen . . .　25
Wie aus Versehn ist ihnen aufgetan
hinter dem andern . . . Aber über ihn
kommt keiner fort, und wieder wird ihm Welt.
Der Schöpfung immer zugewendet, sehn
wir nur auf ihr die Spiegelung des Frein,　　　　　30
von uns verdunkelt. Oder daß ein Tier,
ein stummes, aufschaut, ruhig durch uns durch.
Dieses heißt Schicksal: gegenüber sein
und nichts als das und immer gegenüber.

Wäre Bewußtheit unsrer Art in dem　　　　　　35
sicheren Tier, das uns entgegenzieht
in anderer Richtung –, riß es uns herum
mit seinem Wandel. Doch sein Sein ist ihm
unendlich, ungefaßt und ohne Blick
auf seinen Zustand, rein, so wie sein Ausblick.　40
Und wo wir Zukunft sehn, dort sieht es Alles
und sich in Allem und geheilt für immer.

Und doch ist in dem wachsam warmen Tier
Gewicht und Sorge einer großen Schwermut.
Denn ihm auch haftet immer an, was uns　　　45
oft überwältigt, – die Erinnerung,
als sei schon einmal das, wonach man drängt,
näher gewesen, treuer und sein Anschluß
unendlich zärtlich. Hier ist alles Abstand,
und dort wars Atem. Nach der ersten Heimat　50
ist ihm die zweite zwitterig und windig.
　O Seligkeit der *kleinen* Kreatur,
die immer *bleibt* im Schoße, der sie austrug;
o Glück der Mücke, die noch *innen* hüpft,
selbst wenn sie Hochzeit hat: denn Schoß ist Alles.　55

endlessly, without desire. A child,
if left in stillness,* can be lost in it                                      20
till shaken out. Or we may die: may *be* it.
For nearing death one loses sight of death
and stares out, vastly perhaps, like animals.
Lovers, if the other were not standing
in the light,* approach, marvelling . . .                                    25
An inadvertent view appears to open
behind the other . . . neither can pass
the other, and is in the World again.
Turned back to face creation's face, we see
the mere reflection of the free reaches,                                     30
which we have darkened. Or an animal
mutely, serenely, looks us through and through.
We call this fate: always to be opposed
and nothing else, opposite,* for ever.

Were the animal that moves towards us                                        35
in its assured direction to possess
consciousness such as ours—it would wrench us
round in its steps. But it feels itself
inexhaustible, unapprehended, unaware
of its condition, pure, like its regard.                                     40
And where we see the future it sees all,
and, in the all, itself, healed, for ever.

And yet the animal, alert and warm, goes
weighed by the shadow of a sad heart,
like us laden with what overwhelms                                           45
so often—the memory that what we strive for
was perhaps nearer once, truer to us,
bonded to us with ties infinitely
tender. Here all is set apart; there
it was breath, close. After the first home,*                                 50
the second seems ambivalent and wind-blown.
    Oh bliss of the least creature that has stayed
*inside* the womb that carried it to birth;*
joy of the gnat that leaps *within*, even
at its nuptial dances. For the womb is all things.                           55

Und sieh die halbe Sicherheit des Vogels,
der beinah beides weiß aus seinem Ursprung,
als wär er eine Seele der Etrusker,
aus einem Toten, den ein Raum empfing,
doch mit der ruhenden Figur als Deckel.            60
Und wie bestürzt ist eins, das fliegen muß
und stammt aus einem Schoß. Wie vor sich selbst
erschreckt, durchzuckts die Luft, wie wenn ein Sprung
durch eine Tasse geht. So reißt die Spur
der Fledermaus durchs Porzellan des Abends.        65

Und wir: Zuschauer, immer, überall,
dem allen zugewandt und nie hinaus!
Uns überfüllts. Wir ordnens. Es zerfällt.
Wir ordnens wieder und zerfallen selbst.

Wer hat uns also umgedreht, daß wir,               70
was wir auch tun, in jener Haltung sind
von einem, welcher fortgeht? Wie er auf
dem letzten Hügel, der ihm ganz sein Tal
noch einmal zeigt, sich wendet, anhält, weilt –,
so leben wir und nehmen immer Abschied.            75

## Die neunte Elegie

WARUM, wenn es angeht, also die Frist des Daseins
hinzubringen, als Lorbeer, ein wenig dunkler als alles
andere Grün, mit kleinen Wellen an jedem
Blattrand (wie eines Windes Lächeln) –: warum dann
Menschliches müssen – und, Schicksal vermeidend,     5
sich sehnen nach Schicksal? . . .

        Oh, *nicht*, weil Glück *ist*,
dieser voreilige Vorteil eines nahen Verlusts.
Nicht aus Neugier, oder zur Übung des Herzens,
das auch im Lorbeer *wäre* . . . . .

Look at the half-confidence of the bird:
its twin awareness of its origins,
as though it were the soul of an Etruscan
received at death into a space but yet
lidded* with his reclining effigy.                          60
And how perplexed a creature from the womb,
if it must fly. As though self-terrified,
it jerks across the air, like a crack
running through a cup. The bat,* like this,
flickers across the porcelain of evening.                   65

And we: onlookers, always, everywhere,
face a world of Things, and never outwards.
We brim with it. Arrange it. It fragments.
We rearrange it and we too fragment.

Who swivelled us like this, so that whatever           70
course we take we have the air of someone
who is departing? On the last hill,
which shows him one more time his whole valley,
like him as he turns, and stops, and lingers—
so we live, for ever in farewell.*                          75


## *The Ninth Elegy*

WHY, when we could live out our span of existence
adequately in the form of laurel:* a little darker than
all other green, with miniature waves round the edges
of every leaf (like a wind, smiling*)—why, then,
*have* to be human—and, bent on avoiding destiny,        5
long for its presence? . . .

                        Oh, not because pleasure* *is*,
that over-precipitate gain before oncoming loss.
Not from curiosity, nor as heart-beat practice
for the heart that *may* live in the laurel . . . . .

Aber weil Hiersein viel ist, und weil uns scheinbar          10
alles das Hiesige braucht, dieses Schwindende, das
seltsam uns angeht. Uns, die Schwindendsten. *Ein* Mal
jedes, nur *ein* Mal. *Ein* Mal und nichtmehr. Und wir auch
*ein* Mal. Nie wieder. Aber dieses
*ein* Mal gewesen zu sein, wenn auch nur *ein* Mal:          15
*irdisch* gewesen zu sein, scheint nicht widerrufbar.

Und so drängen wir uns und wollen es leisten,
wollens enthalten in unsern einfachen Händen,
im überfüllteren Blick und im sprachlosen Herzen.
Wollen es werden. – Wem es geben? Am liebsten          20
alles behalten für immer . . . Ach, in den andern Bezug,
wehe, was nimmt man hinüber? Nicht das Anschaun, das hier
langsam erlernte, und kein hier Ereignetes. Keins.
Also die Schmerzen. Also vor allem das Schwersein,
also der Liebe lange Erfahrung, – also          25
lauter Unsägliches. Aber später,
unter den Sternen, was solls: *die* sind *besser* unsäglich.
Bringt doch der Wanderer auch vom Hange des Bergrands
nicht eine Hand voll Erde ins Tal, die Allen unsägliche, sondern
ein erworbenes Wort, reines, den gelben und blaun          30
Enzian. Sind wir vielleicht *hier*, um zu sagen: Haus,
Brücke, Brunnen, Tor, Krug, Obstbaum, Fenster, –
höchstens: Säule, Turm . . . aber zu *sagen*, verstehs,
oh zu sagen *so*, wie selber die Dinge niemals
innig meinten zu sein. Ist nicht die heimliche List          35
dieser verschwiegenen Erde, wenn sie die Liebenden drängt,
daß sich in ihrem Gefühl jedes und jedes entzückt?
Schwelle: was ists für zwei
Liebende, daß sie die eigne ältere Schwelle der Tür
ein wenig verbrauchen, auch sie, nach den vielen vorher          40
und vor den Künftigen . . . ., leicht.

*Hier* ist des *Säglichen* Zeit, *hier* seine Heimat.
Sprich und bekenn. Mehr als je
fallen die Dinge dahin, die erlebbaren, denn,
was sie verdrängend ersetzt, ist ein Tun ohne Bild.          45
Tun unter Krusten, die willig zerspringen, sobald

But because life here is much,* because seemingly*       10
everything in this fleeting world of ours needs us,
strangely concerns us. Us, the most fleeting of all.
Everything, just once. Once and no more. And we too
once. And then not again. However,
that we have *been*, even though only once:       15
that we have been *of the earth* seems irreversible.

And so we press onward in our attempt to achieve it,
wanting to hold it contained in our simple hands,
in our overladen eyes, in our mute heart.
We want to become it.—To whom could we give it? Rather       20
keep it, all of it, always . . . Alas, but what should we take
with us to the other dimension?* Not our looking,*
learned here so slowly, and nothing that happened here. Nothing.
Suffering, then. And above all heavy-heartedness,
love's extended experience, then—the sheer       25
leftover sum of what cannot be told. But later,
among the stars, what is the good? For *they* are *better* unsayable.
The traveller brings from the mountain slope to the valley
no handful of earth, which cannot be said to the world, but instead
a word he has won, a pure word, the yellow and blue       30
gentian.* Are we perhaps *here* for the saying of: house,
bridge, spring of water, gate, pitcher, fruit-tree, window—
at the utmost: column, tower* . . . but to *speak* them, you understand,
oh, to speak them in forms these Things themselves in their heart
never believed they would be. When this secretive earth impels       35
lovers into union, her hidden intent is surely
that in their passion each Thing—each—is enraptured.
Threshold: small matter for two
lovers to wear away their own worn threshold a little,
they too, after so many before them, and followed       40
by those still to come . . . . so lightly.

Here is the time of the sayable, *here* its homeland.
Speak and bear witness. More than ever,
Things we might experience are falling away,
for what forcefully take their place are acts without symbol,       45
crusted acts,* whose casing soon breaks open,

innen das Handeln entwächst und sich anders begrenzt.
Zwischen den Hämmern besteht
unser Herz, wie die Zunge
zwischen den Zähnen, die doch,                                    50
dennoch, die preisende bleibt.


Preise dem Engel die Welt, nicht die unsägliche, *ihm*
kannst du nicht großtun mit herrlich Erfühltem; im Weltall,
wo er fühlender fühlt, bist du ein Neuling. Drum zeig
ihm das Einfache, das von Geschlecht zu Geschlechtern
      gestaltet,                                                    55
als ein Unsriges lebt, neben der Hand und im Blick.
Sag ihm die Dinge. Er wird staunender stehn; wie du standest
bei dem Seiler in Rom, oder beim Töpfer am Nil.
Zeig ihm, wie glücklich ein Ding sein kann, wie schuldlos
      und unser,
wie selbst das klagende Leid rein zur Gestalt sich entschließt, 60
dient als ein Ding, oder stirbt in ein Ding –, und jenseits
selig der Geige entgeht. – Und diese, von Hingang
lebenden Dinge verstehn, daß du sie rühmst; vergänglich,
traun sie ein Rettendes uns, den Vergänglichsten, zu.
Wollen, wir sollen sie ganz im unsichtbarn Herzen
      verwandeln                                                   65
in – o unendlich – in uns! Wer wir am Ende auch seien.


Erde, ist es nicht dies, was du willst: *unsichtbar*
in uns erstehn? – Ist es dein Traum nicht,
einmal unsichtbar zu sein? – Erde! unsichtbar!
Was, wenn Verwandlung nicht, ist dein drängender Auftrag?  70
Erde, du liebe, ich will. Oh glaub, es bedürfte
nicht deiner Frühlinge mehr, mich dir zu gewinnen –, *einer*,
ach, ein einziger ist schon dem Blute zu viel.
Namenlos bin ich zu dir entschlossen, von weit her.
Immer warst du im Recht, und dein heiliger Einfall            75
ist der vertrauliche Tod.


Siehe, ich lebe. Woraus? Weder Kindheit noch Zukunft
werden weniger . . . . . Überzähliges Dasein
entspringt mir im Herzen.

outgrown by the working inside that explores new limits.
Constrained between hammers, the heart
lives on, like our tongue,
pent between teeth but for all that                                50
still the glad speaker of praise.


Praise *this* world, not the untold world, to the Angel: bragging
    our
glorious emotions will not affect *him*; in the cosmos,
where he feels the more feelingly, you are a novice. So show him
that which is simple,* shaped over generations, at home here,     55
truly our own, near at hand, in our range of vision.
Tell him Things. He will stand in amazement, as you did
by the Roman rope-maker, or the potter* who worked by the
    Nile.
Show him how happy the Thing can be, ours, innocent,
how even grief's lament decides, pure, to take form,             60
serves as a Thing, or dies into a Thing—serenely,
slipping far past the violin. And these Things,
living by passing from life, understand that you praise them.
    Transient,
they trust us to rescue them, us, the most transient of all.
Wish us to change them, utterly, in our invisible heart—         65
oh, endlessly!—here, within us! Whoever, in the end, we may be.


Earth, is not this your desire: to arise within us,
invisible? And not your dream: that of being,
some day, invisible? O Earth! no longer visible!
What, if not to transform, is your urgent command?               70
Earth, my dearest, *I will*.* Believe me, there would be
no more need of your springs to win you my love: one of them,
ah, one spring, is already too much for the blood.
From the beginning I have been yours, inexpressibly.
Always you were in the right, and your holy idea,               75
Death, is our friend and companion.


Look, I live. But on what? Neither childhood nor future,
for neither diminishes . . . . . Superabundant being
wells up in my heart.

## Die zehnte Elegie

Dass ich dereinst, an dem Ausgang der grimmigen Einsicht,
Jubel und Ruhm aufsinge zustimmenden Engeln.
Daß von den klar geschlagenen Hämmern des Herzens
keiner versage an weichen, zweifelnden oder
reißenden Saiten. Daß mich mein strömendes Antlitz                    5
glänzender mache; daß das unscheinbare Weinen
blühe. O wie werdet ihr dann, Nächte, mir lieb sein,
gehärmte. Daß ich euch knieender nicht, untröstliche Schwestern,
hinnahm, nicht in euer gelöstes
Haar mich gelöster ergab. Wir, Vergeuder der Schmerzen.           10
Wie wir sie absehn voraus, in die traurige Dauer,
ob sie nicht enden vielleicht. Sie aber sind ja
unser winterwähriges Laub, unser dunkeles Sinngrün,
*eine* der Zeiten des heimlichen Jahres –, nicht nur
Zeit –, sind Stelle, Siedelung, Lager, Boden, Wohnort.           15

Freilich, wehe, wie fremd sind die Gassen der Leid-Stadt,
wo in der falschen, aus Übertönung gemachten
Stille, stark, aus der Gußform des Leeren der Ausguß
prahlt: der vergoldete Lärm, das platzende Denkmal.
O, wie spurlos zerträte ein Engel ihnen den Trostmarkt,           20
den die Kirche begrenzt, ihre fertig gekaufte:
reinlich und zu und enttäuscht wie ein Postamt am Sonntag.
Draußen aber kräuseln sich immer die Ränder von Jahrmarkt.
Schaukeln der Freiheit! Taucher und Gaukler des Eifers!
Und des behübschten Glücks figürliche Schießstatt,           25
wo es zappelt von Ziel und sich blechern benimmt,
wenn ein Geschickterer trifft. Von Beifall zu Zufall
taumelt er weiter; denn Buden jeglicher Neugier
werben, trommeln und plärrn. Für Erwachsene aber
ist noch besonders zu sehn, wie das Geld sich vermehrt,
      anatomisch,                                                 30
nicht zur Belustigung nur: der Geschlechtsteil des Gelds,
alles, das Ganze, der Vorgang –, das unterrichtet und macht
fruchtbar . . . . . . . .
. . . . Oh aber gleich darüber hinaus,

## The Tenth Elegy

SOME day, when I emerge from the fiercest of insights,
let me sing out in paeans of rejoicing* to assenting
Angels. Let not a single clear-struck hammer's beat
of my heart fail, finding a string* that is slack or weak
or about to break. May the tears of my streaming face                5
illumine me, and my latent weeping flower.
Oh, then how dear you will be to me, grief-wracked nights. If only,
inconsolable sisters, accepting you, I had knelt deeper,
lost myself and surrendered myself
into your loosed hair. We are squanderers of our sorrows.            10
How we predict them, into the sad long term,
to tell if perhaps they may end. But they are our dark, lasting,
winter-green leaves of the mind,* *one* of the seasons
of our interior year—and not just time:
place and settlement to us, site and foundation and hearth.         15

Alas, but how alien the streets of Mourning's capital.*
There, in the false lull left by an uproar, sheer
excess poured from the mould of emptiness swaggers
brawnily: gilded blare and the cracked memorial.
Oh, an Angel would utterly trample their marketed comforts,*        20
ready-made and restricted by a Church
tidy, shut down and diminished as the Post on Sundays.
Further out, though, the edge of the town is a-ripple with
    fairgrounds.
Swing-boats of freedom! Divers and jugglers* of thrill!
And the shooting-gallery's prettified lucky figures,               25
twitching targets that flip tinnily, hit
by a good shot—who stumbles from cheering to chancing,
for booths that suit all curiosities woo and drum and
clamour. There is something special to see for adults only:
how money reproduces—here, in the flesh! More than just            30
fun, this: money, down to the genitalia!
Roll up for the whole works!—educational! guaranteed potency-
boosting . . . . . . . . .!
. . . . Oh, and a little way further on,

hinter der letzten Planke, beklebt mit Plakaten des ›Todlos‹,        35
jenes bitteren Biers, das den Trinkenden süß scheint,
wenn sie immer dazu frische Zerstreuungen kaun . . .,
gleich im Rücken der Planke, gleich dahinter, ists *wirklich*.
Kinder spielen, und Liebende halten einander, – abseits,
ernst, im ärmlichen Gras, und Hunde haben Natur.        40
Weiter noch zieht es den Jüngling; vielleicht, daß er eine junge
Klage liebt . . . . . Hinter ihr her kommt er in Wiesen. Sie sagt:
– Weit. Wir wohnen dort draußen . . . .

                                        Wo? Und der Jüngling
folgt. Ihn rührt ihre Haltung. Die Schulter, der Hals –,
   vielleicht
ist sie von herrlicher Herkunft. Aber er läßt sie, kehrt um,        45
wendet sich, winkt . . . Was solls? Sie ist eine Klage.

Nur die jungen Toten, im ersten Zustand
zeitlosen Gleichmuts, dem der Entwöhnung,
folgen ihr liebend. Mädchen
wartet sie ab und befreundet sie. Zeigt ihnen leise,        50
was sie an sich hat. Perlen des Leids und die feinen
Schleier der Duldung. – Mit Jünglingen geht sie
schweigend.

Aber dort, wo sie wohnen, im Tal, der Älteren eine, der
   Klagen,
nimmt sich des Jünglinges an, wenn er fragt; – Wir waren,        55
sagt sie, ein Großes Geschlecht, einmal, wir Klagen. Die Väter
trieben den Bergbau dort in dem großen Gebirg; bei Menschen
findest du manchmal ein Stück geschliffenes Ur-Leid
oder, aus altem Vulkan, schlackig versteinerten Zorn.
Ja, das stammte von dort. Einst waren wir reich. –        60

Und sie leitet ihn leicht durch die weite Landschaft der
   Klagen,
zeigt ihm die Säulen der Tempel oder die Trümmer
jener Burgen, von wo Klage-Fürsten das Land
einstens weise beherrscht. Zeigt ihm die hohen

when you have passed the last hoarding, covered with posters
     for 'Deathless',                                      35
that bitter beer that tastes sweet enough to drinkers
so long as they munch new distractions with it . . . just here,
     behind,
just at the back of the hoarding, it all becomes real!
Children are playing, lovers are holding each other—apart,
solemn in threadbare grass, and dogs are doing what they do.   40
The young man is drawn further on; perhaps he has fallen lovesick
for a young Grief . . . . . In her footsteps,* he reaches meadows.
     She says:
—Some distance. We live out that way . . . .

                                        Where? And the young man
follows. He is moved by her bearing. The shoulder, the neck—
     perhaps
she is of noble descent. But he leaves her, turns round again,   45
looks back and waves . . . but what use? She is one of the Grieving.

Only the young dead, first experiencing
timeless serenity as withdrawal,
follow her, loving her. Girls
she awaits and befriends. Gently, she shows them      50
what she is wearing. Pearls of pain and the fine-spun
veils of endurance.—With young men she walks
silent.

But there, in the valley where they live, one of the elder Grieving
turns to a questioning youth:* In our day                55
we were a powerful race, she explains. Our ancestors
worked the mines over there in the mountains. You occasionally
     find,
among men, lumps of polished original Grief-stone,
or anger-glass from the slag of the old volcano.
Yes, that's where it came from. In those days we were rich.—   60

Lightly she leads him across the open landscape of Grieving,
showing him columns of temples and the ruins
of castles from former times where the princes of Grieving
wisely governed the land. Shows him the lofty

Tränenbäume und Felder blühender Wehmut,                                      65
(Lebendige kennen sie nur als sanftes Blattwerk);
zeigt ihm die Tiere der Trauer, weidend, – und manchmal
schreckt ein Vogel und zieht, flach ihnen fliegend durchs
    Aufschaun,
weithin das schriftliche Bild seines vereinsamten Schreis. –
Abends führt sie ihn hin zu den Gräbern der Alten                            70
aus dem Klage-Geschlecht, den Sibyllen und Warn-Herrn.
Naht aber Nacht, so wandeln sie leiser, und bald
mondets empor, das über Alles
wachende Grab-Mal. Brüderlich jenem am Nil,
der erhabene Sphinx –: der verschwiegenen Kammer                             75
Antlitz.
Und sie staunen dem krönlichen Haupt, das für immer,
schweigend, der Menschen Gesicht
auf die Waage der Sterne gelegt.

Nicht erfaßt es sein Blick, im Frühtod                                        80
schwindelnd. Aber ihr Schaun,
hinter dem Pschent-Rand hervor, scheucht es die Eule. Und sie,
streifend im langsamen Abstrich die Wange entlang,
jene der reifesten Rundung,
zeichnet weich in das neue                                                    85
Totengehör, über ein doppelt
aufgeschlagenes Blatt, den unbeschreiblichen Umriß.

Und höher, die Sterne. Neue. Die Sterne des Leidlands.
Langsam nennt sie die Klage; – Hier,
siehe: den *Reiter*, den *Stab*, und das vollere Sternbild                    90
nennen sie: *Fruchtkranz*. Dann, weiter, dem Pol zu:
*Wiege*; *Weg*; *Das Brennende Buch*; *Puppe*; *Fenster*.
Aber im südlichen Himmel, rein wie im Innern
einer gesegneten Hand, das klar erglänzende ›*M*‹,
das die Mütter bedeutet . . . . . . –                                        95

Doch der Tote muß fort, und schweigend bringt ihn die ältere
Klage bis an die Talschlucht,
wo es schimmert im Mondschein:
die Quelle der Freude. In Ehrfurcht

trees-of-tears and the flowering melancholia fields 65
(known to the living only in soft, new leaf).
Shows him the grazing sorrow-cattle—and now and then,
as they look up, a far bird startles into their vision,
scoring across it the level scrawl of its lonely cry.—
At evening she leads him out to the graves of the elders 70
among the race of the Grieving, sibyls* and seers.*
Night draws on, and they move more softly; soon,
watcher of all things, the sepulchre
moon-rises upwards. Brother to that by the Nile:
Sphinx,* the majestic—the still inner chamber's 75
countenance.
And they stare awed at the regal head
that has laid the face of mankind for all time
in the balancing-pans of the stars.

Dizzied in early death, his sight 80
fails to grasp it. Her eyes
frighten an owl* from behind the rim of the crown.* And
    the bird's
slow downstroke brushes along the fully
ripened rounded cheek,
and writes lightly into 85
death's young hearing, as on a double-
page spread, lying open, the indescribable outline.

And higher, the stars. New stars, of the land of sorrow.
Slowly the elder names them: There—
look—the *Rider*,* the *Staff*, and that starrier constellation 90
they call the *Garland of Fruit*. Then, further, towards the Pole,
*Cradle*,* *Path*,* *The Burning Book*,* *Puppet*, *Window*.*
But to the south, pure as the lines inscribed
in the palm of a hand that is blessed, the lucent, brilliant *M*\*
that stands for mothers . . . . . . 95

Yet the dead youth must go on, and in silence the elder Grief
brings him as far as the gorge,
where, moonlit and shimmering,
the joy-spring rises. Reverently

nennt sie sie, sagt; – Bei den Menschen                    100
ist sie ein tragender Strom. –

Stehn am Fuß des Gebirgs.
Und da umarmt sie ihn, weinend.

Einsam steigt er dahin, in die Berge des Ur-Leids.
Und nicht einmal sein Schritt klingt aus dem tonlosen Los.    105

\*

Aber erweckten sie uns, die unendlich Toten, ein Gleichnis,
siehe, sie zeigten vielleicht auf die Kätzchen der leeren
Hasel, die hängenden, oder
meinten den Regen, der fällt auf dunkles Erdreich im Frühjahr. –

Und wir, die an *steigendes* Glück                         110
denken, empfänden die Rührung,
die uns beinah bestürzt,
wenn ein Glückliches *fällt*.

she names it, and says: Among men                        100
this is a stream of great power.—

At the foot of the great peaks they stop.
There she embraces him, weeping.

Alone, he climbs on, into the peaks of Original Grief.
And not an echo rings from his step on the soundless path.    105

*

But were the eternally dead to prompt us to find a symbol,
consider: they might well point us towards the catkins
that hang in the bare hazel,*
or might suggest the rain that falls* on the dark spring earth.—

And we, thinking of happiness                            110
*rising*, would find our emotion
almost bewildering us,
seeing a happiness *fall*.

## Die Sonette an Orpheus

Geschrieben als ein Grab-Mal
für Wera Ouckama Knoop

Château de Muzot im Februar 1922

ERSTER TEIL

### I

DA stieg ein Baum. O reine Übersteigung!
O Orpheus singt! O hoher Baum im Ohr!
Und alles schwieg. Doch selbst in der Verschweigung
ging neuer Anfang, Wink und Wandlung vor.

Tiere aus Stille     drangen aus dem klaren          5
gelösten Wald     von Lager und Genist;
und da ergab sich, daß sie nicht aus List
und nicht aus Angst in sich so leise waren,

sondern aus Hören. Brüllen, Schrei, Geröhr
schien klein in ihren Herzen. Und wo eben          10
kaum eine Hütte war, dies zu empfangen,

ein Unterschlupf aus dunkelstem Verlangen
mit einem Zugang, dessen Pfosten beben, –
da schufst du ihnen Tempel im Gehör.

### II

UND fast ein Mädchen wars und ging hervor
aus diesem einigen Glück von Sang und Leier
und glänzte klar durch ihre Frühlingsschleier
und machte sich ein Bett in meinem Ohr.

Und schlief in mir. Und alles war ihr Schlaf.          5
Die Bäume, die ich je bewundert, diese

## *The Sonnets to Orpheus**

Written as a memorial
for Wera Ouckama Knoop*

Château de Muzot, February 1922

### PART ONE

### I

A SUDDEN tree soars.* O sheer exceeding!
O Orpheus is singing! O high tree in the ear!
And all fell still. But even in this silence
came transformation, new signs, and beginning.

Beasts of quiet    advanced out of the clear          5
loosened forest    from their lair and nest;
and it happened they did not arrive hushed
within themselves in cunning or in fear

but in listening. Shrieking, roaring, braying
seemed dwindled in their hearts. And where a shelter,      10
no more than the slightest, could receive this,

dwelling hollowed lightly out of darkest
desires, its entrance pillars set in tremor—
there you made them temples in their hearing.*

### II

AND she was almost a girl,* appearing out of
song and lyre's twinned, delighted play,
and she gleamed lucent through her spring veil*
and made herself a bed inside my ear.

And slept in me. And all was in her sleep.          5
All the trees I had admired, the tangible

fühlbare Ferne, die gefühlte Wiese
und jedes Staunen, das mich selbst betraf.

Sie schlief die Welt. Singender Gott, wie hast
du sie vollendet, daß sie nicht begehrte,                    10
erst wach zu sein? Sieh, sie erstand und schlief.

Wo ist ihr Tod? O, wirst du dies Motiv
erfinden noch, eh sich dein Lied verzehrte? –
Wo sinkt sie hin aus mir? . . . Ein Mädchen fast . . . .

### III

EIN Gott vermags. Wie aber, sag mir, soll
ein Mann ihm folgen durch die schmale Leier?
Sein Sinn ist Zwiespalt. An der Kreuzung zweier
Herzwege steht kein Tempel für Apoll.

Gesang, wie du ihn lehrst, ist nicht Begehr,                 5
nicht Werbung um ein endlich noch Erreichtes;
Gesang ist Dasein. Für den Gott ein Leichtes.
Wann aber *sind* wir? Und wann wendet *er*

an unser Sein die Erde und die Sterne?
Dies *ists* nicht, Jüngling, daß du liebst, wenn auch         10
die Stimme dann den Mund dir aufstößt, – lerne

vergessen, daß du aufsangst. Das verrinnt.
In Wahrheit singen, ist ein andrer Hauch.
Ein Hauch um nichts. Ein Wehn im Gott. Ein Wind.

### IV

O IHR Zärtlichen, tretet zuweilen
in den Atem, der euch nicht meint,
laßt ihn an eueren Wangen sich teilen,
hinter euch zittert er, wieder vereint.

distances, the meadow I knew and felt
and all the awe that ever overwhelmed me.

She slept the world. Singing god, how did you deeply
perfect her that she did not feel desire                        10
ever to wake? See, she arose and slept.

Where is her death? Oh, will you invent it,
this last motif before your song expires?—
She is sinking out of me—to where? . . . An almost-girl . . . .

## III

A GOD can do it. But how may a man follow
after him, tell me, through the narrow lyre?*
His mind is riven. The crossing* of two hearts'
paths raises no temple for Apollo.*

Singing as you teach it is not desire,                          5
does not seek to possess, does not pay court;*
singing is being. And easy for a god.
But when are we actual? And when his thought

to turn the earth and stars towards our being?
Young man, that you should love is not enough,                  10
and though your voice may gape your mouth wide—learn

to forget you sang it out. It is soon spent.
To sing in truth is drawing a different breath.
A breath about nothing. A blowing in the god. A wind.

## IV

O YOU tender ones, step now and then
into the breath breathed not for you;*
let it divide as your cheek meets it,
rejoin trembling as you pass through.

O ihr Seligen, o ihr Heilen,                                    5
die ihr der Anfang der Herzen scheint.
Bogen der Pfeile und Ziele von Pfeilen,
ewiger glänzt euer Lächeln verweint.

Fürchtet euch nicht zu leiden, die Schwere,
gebt sie zurück an der Erde Gewicht;                            10
schwer sind die Berge, schwer sind die Meere.

Selbst die als Kinder ihr pflanztet, die Bäume,
wurden zu schwer längst; ihr trüget sie nicht.
Aber die Lüfte . . . aber die Räume . . . .


# V

ERRICHTET keinen Denkstein. Laßt die Rose
nur jedes Jahr zu seinen Gunsten blühn.
Denn Orpheus ists. Seine Metamorphose
in dem und dem. Wir sollen uns nicht mühn

um andre Namen. Ein für alle Male                               5
ists Orpheus, wenn es singt. Er kommt und geht.
Ists nicht schon viel, wenn er die Rosenschale
um ein paar Tage manchmal übersteht?

O wie er schwinden muß, daß ihrs begrifft!
Und wenn ihm selbst auch bangte, daß er schwände.              10
Indem sein Wort das Hiersein übertrifft,

ist er schon dort, wohin ihrs nicht begleitet.
Der Leier Gitter zwängt ihm nicht die Hände.
Und er gehorcht, indem er überschreitet.

O you are blest, you are whole, each the heart's
apparent beginning and bow to the arrow*                5
and arrow's arriving, your smile more enduring
when it illuminates your sorrow.

Do not fear pain but offer its burden
back to the earth's weighted places—                    10
mass of the mountains, ballast of seas.

Even your childhood's child-set trees
weigh well past the grown strength of your arm.
But the light airs . . . but the light spaces . . . .

# V

MAKE no memorial.* Simply let the roses
come into flower each year for his sake.
For it is Orpheus. His metamorphosis*
in this, and that. We should not try to make

for him any other names. It is Orpheus,                  5
of course, when there is singing. He comes and goes.
Does he not grant us much, when he outlives
sometimes, by a few days, the rose-bowl?

Though he might be afraid to disappear,
he has to vanish: can you understand?                    10
Because his word exceeds all being-here,

he is where you may not accompany.
The latticed lyre does not constrain his hands.
And in his passing over he obeys.

## VI

Ist er ein Hiesiger? Nein, aus beiden
Reichen erwuchs seine weite Natur.
Kundiger böge die Zweige der Weiden,
wer die Wurzeln der Weiden erfuhr.

Geht ihr zu Bette, so laßt auf dem Tische                    5
Brot nicht und Milch nicht; die Toten ziehts –.
Aber er, der Beschwörende, mische
unter der Milde des Augenlids

ihre Erscheinung in alles Geschaute;
und der Zauber von Erdrauch und Raute                       10
sei ihm so wahr wie der klarste Bezug.

Nichts kann das gültige Bild ihm verschlimmern;
sei es aus Gräbern, sei es aus Zimmern,
rühme er Fingerring, Spange und Krug.

## VII

Rühmen, das ists! Ein zum Rühmen Bestellter,
ging er hervor wie das Erz aus des Steins
Schweigen. Sein Herz, o vergängliche Kelter
eines den Menschen unendlichen Weins.

Nie versagt ihm die Stimme am Staube,                       5
wenn ihn das göttliche Beispiel ergreift.
Alles wird Weinberg, alles wird Traube,
in seinem fühlenden Süden gereift.

Nicht in den Grüften der Könige Moder
straft ihm die Rühmung lügen, oder                          10
daß von den Göttern ein Schatten fällt.

## VI

Is he from here? No, for his full
nature accrued from both these realms.*
He who knows the roots of the willows*
grows the most skilled at flexing their stems.

Going to bed, do not leave on the table                    5
bread and milk*—it draws the dead—
But let him conjure them under the mild
incline of the eyelids, let him combine

their spectral guise with what lies in our view;
and the magic of fumitory* and rue*                       10
be as true to him as the clearest relation.

Nothing impairs the image he sings;
be they from graves or be they from chambers,
may he praise pitchers, brooches and rings.*


## VII

PRAISING* is everything! Appointed to praise,
he rose up from the silence of stone
like an ore. His heart O transient press
of an endless wine* for the human soul.

When he sings over dust, his voice never fails,            5
for the divine possesses his mouth.
All becomes vineyard, all becomes grape,
grown ripe in his tender and sensuous South.*

When he sees in tombs the kings in decay,
this cannot give the lie to his praise,                    10
nor yet can a shadow the gods have sent.

Er ist einer der bleibenden Boten,
der noch weit in die Türen der Toten
Schalen mit rühmlichen Früchten hält.


# VIII

Nur im Raum der Rühmung darf die Klage
gehn, die Nymphe des geweinten Quells,
wachend über unserm Niederschlage,
daß er klar sei    an demselben Fels,

der die Tore trägt und die Altäre. –                    5
Sieh, um ihre stillen Schultern früht
das Gefühl, daß sie die jüngste wäre
unter den Geschwistern im Gemüt.

Jubel *weiß*, und Sehnsucht ist geständig, –
nur die Klage lernt noch; mädchenhändig               10
zählt sie nächtelang das alte Schlimme.

Aber plötzlich, schräg und ungeübt,
hält sie doch ein Sternbild unsrer Stimme
in den Himmel, den ihr Hauch nicht trübt.


# IX

Nur wer die Leier schon hob
auch unter Schatten,
darf das unendliche Lob
ahnend erstatten.

Nur wer mit Toten vom Mohn                            5
aß, von dem ihren,
wird nicht den leisesten Ton
wieder verlieren.

He is abiding, a herald who stays
and holds out his bowls of laudable fruits
far into the doors of the dead.

## VIII

ONLY in the realm of praise* may Grief
walk, nymph of the spring* our tears have fed,
watching over our precipitation
that it run clear    in the same rock–bed

as carries gateways and the weight of altars.—      5
Contemplate her as she walks calm-shouldered,
wrapped in the thought's dawning that she might be
youngest of the mind's sisterhood.

Jubilation *knows*; Longing avows;
only Grief* still learns, night after night      10
with girl's fingers figuring ancient sorrows.

All at once, slanting it, unadept,
she holds a constellation of our voices
up to a heaven unmisted by her breath.

## IX

ONLY he raising the lyre
even among shades
may in his song of surmise
endlessly praise.

Only he eating their seeds,      5
poppy-seeds,* with the dead,
lets not the least sound recede
lost or unheeded.

Mag auch die Spieglung im Teich
oft uns verschwimmen:                                        10
*Wisse das Bild.*

Erst in dem Doppelbereich
werden die Stimmen
ewig und mild.

## X

EUCH, die ihr nie mein Gefühl verließt,
grüß ich, antikische Sarkophage,
die das fröhliche Wasser römischer Tage
als ein wandelndes Lied durchfließt.

Oder jene so offenen, wie das Aug                           5
eines frohen erwachenden Hirten,
– innen voll Stille und Bienensaug –
denen entzückte Falter entschwirrten;

alle, die man dem Zweifel entreißt,
grüß ich, die wiedergeöffneten Munde,                       10
die schon wußten, was schweigen heißt.

Wissen wirs, Freunde, wissen wirs nicht?
Beides bildet die zögernde Stunde
in dem menschlichen Angesicht.

## XI

SIEH den Himmel. Heißt kein Sternbild ›Reiter‹?
Denn dies ist uns seltsam eingeprägt:
dieser Stolz aus Erde. Und ein Zweiter,
der ihn treibt und hält und den er trägt.

Though pool-reflections may swim
blurred from the surface,                                        10
*know the image.*

Only the great double-realm
renders our voices
gentle and ageless.

## X

GREETINGS I bear you, who endure in my feeling,
antiquity's sarcophagi*
through whom the glad water of Roman times
courses like transformative* singing.

Or those lying open,* like the pupil                            5
of some glad, awakening herdsman
—within full of stillness and bee nettle—
as rapt butterflies flicker over them.

All who are wrenched from uncertainty
here I greet, the re-opened mouths,                             10
who have long known what silence means.

Friends, do we know this—or not know this?
Both these etch the hesitant hour
into the human countenance.

## XI

LOOK among the stars. Is there no 'Rider'*?
For this is impressed upon us strangely:
steed, all pride, all earth. And a second,
spurring and reining him, and whom he carries.

Ist nicht so, gejagt und dann gebändigt,                    5
diese sehnige Natur des Seins?
Weg und Wendung. Doch ein Druck verständigt.
Neue Weite. Und die zwei sind eins.

Aber *sind* sie's? Oder meinen beide
nicht den Weg, den sie zusammen tun?           10
Namenlos schon trennt sie Tisch und Weide.

Auch die sternische Verbindung trügt.
Doch uns freue eine Weile nun
der Figur zu glauben. Das genügt.


## XII

HEIL dem Geist, der uns verbinden mag;
denn wir leben wahrhaft in Figuren.
Und mit kleinen Schritten gehn die Uhren
neben unserm eigentlichen Tag.

Ohne unsern wahren Platz zu kennen,           5
handeln wir aus wirklichem Bezug.
Die Antennen fühlen die Antennen,
und die leere Ferne trug . . .

Reine Spannung. O Musik der Kräfte!
Ist nicht durch die läßlichen Geschäfte       10
jede Störung von dir abgelenkt?

Selbst wenn sich der Bauer sorgt und handelt,
wo die Saat in Sommer sich verwandelt,
reicht er niemals hin. Die Erde *schenkt*.


## XIII

VOLLER Apfel, Birne und Banane,
Stachelbeere . . . Alles dieses spricht

Spurring and restraint: is it not like  5
this longing of our natural condition?
Road and turning. Pressure communicates.
New-found extents. And the two are one.

Or are they not one? Do they not intend
travelling the road they take together,  10
parted, wordless, by dish and pasture?

Even the stellar reference deceives.
Meanwhile may it rejoice us to believe
this figure. Which suffices in the end.

# XII

To that spirit* who seeks our reference, hail;
truly we live lives in figure-spaces.*
And our clocks move on with petty paces
adjacent to our inner day.

We do not know where our true place should be,  5
yet we act in reference that is real.
Antennae* feel outwards to antennae,
and the empty distance yields . . .

Pure tension. O music of energies!
Do not your trivial activities  10
serve to deflect all sense of perturbation?

However much the farmer toils and sows,
never will he reach the transformation
of the seed into summer. Earth *bestows*.

# XIII

FULL-RIPE fruit: apple, banana, pear,
gooseberry . . .* All that this is says

Tod und Leben in den Mund . . . Ich ahne . . .
Lest es einem Kind vom Angesicht,

wenn es sie erschmeckt. Dies kommt von weit.　　5
Wird euch langsam namenlos im Munde?
Wo sonst Worte waren, fließen Funde,
aus dem Fruchtfleisch überrascht befreit.

Wagt zu sagen, was ihr Apfel nennt.
Diese Süße, die sich erst verdichtet,　　10
um, im Schmecken leise aufgerichtet,

klar zu werden, wach und transparent,
doppeldeutig, sonnig, erdig, hiesig – :
O Erfahrung, Fühlung, Freude –, riesig!


## XIV

WIR gehen um mit Blume, Weinblatt, Frucht.
Sie sprechen nicht die Sprache nur des Jahres.
Aus Dunkel steigt ein buntes Offenbares
und hat vielleicht den Glanz der Eifersucht

der Toten an sich, die die Erde stärken.　　5
Was wissen wir von ihrem Teil an dem?
Es ist seit lange ihre Art, den Lehm
mit ihrem freien Marke zu durchmärken.

Nun fragt sich nur: tun sie es gern? . . .
Drängt diese Frucht, ein Werk von schweren Sklaven,　　10
geballt zu uns empor, zu ihren Herrn?

Sind *sie* die Herrn, die bei den Wurzeln schlafen,
und gönnen uns aus ihren Überflüssen
dies Zwischending aus stummer Kraft und Küssen?

death and life into mouths . . . I am aware . . .
You can read it in a child's face*

as he tastes them. This has covered miles.                    5
In your mouth, is there a namelessness?*
Where there once were words, there now flow findings
freed, surprised, out of the fruit's flesh.

Dare to say just what you mean by apple.
Speak the sweetness that intensifies                          10
only to rise in taste and clarify

tranquilly, awake, transparent,
ambiguously sunny, earthy, present—
O feeling, joy, experience—immense!


## XIV

WE handle flower and fruit, and the vine leaf.
They do not speak the mere language of the year.
From darkness something colourful comes forth,
perhaps with the gleam that is the envious glare

of the dead, invigorators of the earth.                       5
What do we know of the part in this they play?
This long time their role has been to disperse
and feed their open marrow to the clay.

But do they do this without any gall?
Or does this work of surly slaves, this fruit,                10
come clenched and pressing upwards to its lords?

Are *they* the lords,* who sleep there with the roots,*
granting us from their abundances
a hybrid-thing of dumb strength and of kisses?

## XV

WARTET . . ., das schmeckt . . . Schon ists auf der Flucht.
. . . . Wenig Musik nur, ein Stampfen, ein Summen –:
Mädchen, ihr warmen, Mädchen, ihr stummen,
tanzt den Geschmack der erfahrenen Frucht!

Tanzt die Orange. Wer kann sie vergessen,　　　　　　　　5
wie sie, ertrinkend in sich, sich wehrt
wider ihr Süßsein. Ihr habt sie besessen.
Sie hat sich köstlich zu euch bekehrt.

Tanzt die Orange. Die wärmere Landschaft,
werft sie aus euch, daß die reife erstrahle　　　　　　　　10
in Lüften der Heimat! Erglühte, enthüllt

Düfte um Düfte. Schafft die Verwandtschaft
mit der reinen, sich weigernden Schale,
mit dem Saft, der die Glückliche füllt!

## XVI

DU, mein Freund, bist einsam, weil . . . .
*Wir* machen mit Worten und Fingerzeigen
uns allmählich die Welt zu eigen,
vielleicht ihren schwächsten, gefährlichsten Teil.

Wer zeigt mit Fingern auf einen Geruch? –　　　　　　　5
Doch von den Kräften, die uns bedrohten,
fühlst du viele . . . Du kennst die Toten,
und du erschrickst vor dem Zauberspruch.

Sieh, nun heißt es zusammen ertragen
Stückwerk und Teile, als sei es das Ganze.　　　　　　　10
Dir helfen, wird schwer sein. Vor allem: pflanze

## XV

WAIT . . . that tastes good . . . and is on the move.
. . . . Just a slight music, a stamping, a hum—
Girls, for you are so wordless and warm,
dance the taste discovered in fruit!

Dance* the orange. Who can forget                                    5
how it drowns in itself as it tries to resist
its own sure sweetness. You have possessed it.
It made itself over* to you, delicious.

Dance the orange. Thrust warmer landscape
out of yourselves, that it may gleam                                 10
ripe in home breezes! Ardent, unwrap

scents upon scents. Begin to relate
yourself to its pure, refusing peel,
yourself to its full and gladdening sap!

## XVI

YOU* my friend are lonely, because . . . .
*we* make the world our own, with words
and our pointing fingers, perhaps by the pieces
frailest and most dangerous to us.

Who can point fingers to a smell?—                                   5
Yet of the forces that we dread
you feel so many . . . you know the dead,
you are afraid of the magic spell.

See, now together we must bear,
as if the whole, these fragments and parts.                          10
To help you is hard. Above all, do not plant

mich nicht in dein Herz. Ich wüchse zu schnell.
Doch *meines* Herrn Hand will ich führen und sagen:
Hier. Das ist Esau in seinem Fell.


# XVII

Zu unterst der Alte, verworrn,
all der Erbauten
Wurzel, verborgener Born,
den sie nie schauen.

Sturmhelm und Jägerhorn,                                    5
Spruch von Ergrauten,
Männer im Bruderzorn,
Frauen wie Lauten . . .

Drängender Zweig an Zweig,
nirgends ein freier . . . .                                 10
Einer!   O steig . . . o steig . . .

Aber sie brechen noch.
Dieser erst oben doch
biegt sich zur Leier.


# XVIII

Hörst du das Neue, Herr,
dröhnen und beben?
Kommen Verkündiger,
die es erheben.

Zwar ist kein Hören heil                                    5
in dem Durchtobtsein,
doch der Maschinenteil
will jetzt gelobt sein.

me in your heart. I would grow too fast.
Yet, I will guide my own master's hand and swear:
Here. This is Esau,* here in his pelt.

## XVII

THE ancient,* the undermost, ravelled
root of the built,
hidden spring, always concealed,
never beheld.

Helmet and hunter's horn,*                                    5
grey-haired men's truths,
brothers locked deep in scorn,
women like lutes . . .

Branch on branch, surgingly,
no branch is free . . . .                                     10
But one!   O climb . . . higher . . .

But they are breaking now.
Up there the highest bough
curves to a lyre.*

## XVIII

LORD,* have you heard the New,*
droning and jolting?
Heralds will come soon,
uplifting it, lauding.

Nowhere can ears hear                                         5
in this commotion,
yet the machine-part*
seeks acclamation.*

Sieh, die Maschine:
wie sie sich wälzt und rächt                    10
und uns entstellt und schwächt.

Hat sie aus uns auch Kraft,
sie, ohne Leidenschaft,
treibe und diene.


## XIX

WANDELT sich rasch auch die Welt
wie Wolkengestalten,
alles Vollendete fällt
heim zum Uralten.

Über dem Wandel und Gang,                       5
weiter und freier,
währt noch dein Vor-Gesang,
Gott mit der Leier.

Nicht sind die Leiden erkannt,
nicht ist die Liebe gelernt,                    10
und was im Tod uns entfernt,

ist nicht entschleiert.
Einzig das Lied überm Land
heiligt und feiert.


## XX

DIR aber, Herr, o was weih ich dir, sag,
der das Ohr den Geschöpfen gelehrt? –
Mein Erinnern an einen Frühlingstag,
seinen Abend, in Rußland –, ein Pferd . . .

See the machine roll,
wreak its revenge, maul,                              10
warp and distort us.

Even as we grant it power,
may it now labour
and passionless serve us.


## XIX

THOUGH the world changes* fast
like the cloud–firmament,
all that's completed falls
back to the ancient.

Over all shift and change,                            5
further and freer,
still your prime song* remains,
god with the lyre.

Not yet* is pain understood,
nor have we yet learned to love,                      10
and what removes us in death

lies undisclosed.
Only the song over Earth
praises and hallows.


## XX

WHAT shall I dedicate to you, Lord?
You who taught the creatures their hearing?—
My memory of a day in spring
and of its evening, in Russia*—a horse . . .

Herüber vom Dorf kam der Schimmel allein,                    5
an der vorderen Fessel den Pflock,
um die Nacht auf den Wiesen allein zu sein;
wie schlug seiner Mähne Gelock

an den Hals im Takte des Übermuts,
bei dem grob gehemmten Galopp.                                10
Wie sprangen die Quellen des Rossebluts!

Der fühlte die Weiten, und ob!
Der sang und der hörte –, dein Sagenkreis
war *in* ihm geschlossen.
                              Sein Bild: ich weih's.


## XXI

FRÜHLING ist wiedergekommen. Die Erde
ist wie ein Kind, das Gedichte weiß;
viele, o viele . . . . . Für die Beschwerde
langen Lernens bekommt sie den Preis.

Streng war ihr Lehrer. Wir mochten das Weiße             5
an dem Barte des alten Manns.
Nun, wie das Grüne, das Blaue heiße,
dürfen wir fragen: sie kanns, sie kanns!

Erde, die frei hat, du glückliche, spiele
nun mit den Kindern. Wir wollen dich fangen,             10
fröhliche Erde. Dem Frohsten gelingts.

O, was der Lehrer sie lehrte, das Viele,
und was gedruckt steht in Wurzeln und langen
schwierigen Stämmen: sie singts, sie singts!

He came across from the village alone,                    5
his left fetlock trailing a stake,*
for a night in the meadow on his own;
how his mane danced on his neck,

beating the beat of high spirits freed,
no matter his gallop hampered and crude.            10
How it leapt, the springing blood of the steed!

How he felt land speeding away!
He sang—and listened*—your cycle of legend*
closed round *within* him.

His image I dedicate.


# XXI

SPRING* has come round again, and the Earth
is like a child who is brimming with poems;
many, so many . . . . And for the burden
of learning's long labour receives her rewards.

Hard her teacher. We cherished that whiteness     5
thick in the beard of the strict old man.
What are this green and this blue, we now ask:
Earth can do it, she can do it, she can!

Earth, now set free* and rapturous, please
play with the children.* We would love to catch you,     10
jubilant Earth. The happiest wins.

All the learning she has received,
profuse, imprinted in stems and roots,*
elaborate, long: Earth sings it, she sings!

## XXII

WIR sind die Treibenden.
Aber den Schritt der Zeit,
nehmt ihn als Kleinigkeit
im immer Bleibenden.

Alles das Eilende                                    5
wird schon vorüber sein;
denn das Verweilende
erst weiht uns ein.

Knaben, o werft den Mut
nicht in die Schnelligkeit,                          10
nicht in den Flugversuch.

Alles ist ausgeruht:
Dunkel und Helligkeit,
Blume und Buch.

## XXIII

O ERST *dann*, wenn der Flug
nicht mehr um seinetwillen
wird in die Himmelstillen
steigen, sich selber genug,

um in lichten Profilen,                              5
als das Gerät, das gelang,
Liebling der Winde zu spielen,
sicher, schwenkend und schlank, –

erst, wenn ein reines Wohin
wachsender Apparate                                  10
Knabenstolz überwiegt,

wird, überstürzt von Gewinn,
jener den Fernen Genahte
*sein*, was er einsam erfliegt.

## XXII

We are the transient* ones.
Yet, take the march of time
as but the least of things
in what remains.

All that is hastening                                    5
will soon be gone;
that for our hallowing,
only, lives on.

Boys, do not throw your souls
into endeavours                                          10
of flight or momentum.

All this is in repose:
darkness and luminance,
book and bloom.


## XXIII

O only *then* when this flight
not for its own sake climbs
into sky-stillnesses,
self-satisfied in bright

profiles, machine for succeeding,                        5
tool with the aim of becoming
plaything and high winds' darling,
sure, slender, wheeling—

only when pure search is riding
in the advancing machines                                10
outweighing youthful pride,*

then, with the far near him, overcome,
winning, the flier will *be*
that which he flies, alone.

## XXIV

SOLLEN wir unsere uralte Freundschaft, die großen
niemals werbenden Götter, weil sie der harte
Stahl, den wir streng erzogen, nicht kennt, verstoßen
oder sie plötzlich suchen auf einer Karte?

Diese gewaltigen Freunde, die uns die Toten                    5
nehmen, rühren nirgends an unsere Räder.
Unsere Gastmähler haben wir weit –, unsere Bäder,
fortgerückt, und ihre uns lang schon zu langsamen Boten

überholen wir immer. Einsamer nun auf einander
ganz angewiesen, ohne einander zu kennen,                      10
führen wir nicht mehr die Pfade als schöne Mäander,

sondern als Grade. Nur noch in Dampfkesseln brennen
die einstigen Feuer und heben die Hämmer, die immer
größern. Wir aber nehmen an Kraft ab, wie Schwimmer.

## XXV

DICH aber will ich nun, *Dich*, die ich kannte
wie eine Blume, von der ich den Namen nicht weiß,
noch *ein* Mal erinnern und ihnen zeigen, Entwandte,
schöne Gespielin des unüberwindlichen Schrei's.

Tänzerin erst, die plötzlich, den Körper voll Zögern,         5
anhielt, als göß man ihr Jungsein in Erz;
trauernd und lauschend –. Da, von den hohen Vermögern
fiel ihr Musik in das veränderte Herz.

Nah war die Krankheit. Schon von den Schatten bemächtigt,
drängte verdunkelt das Blut, doch, wie flüchtig verdächtigt,  10
trieb es in seinen natürlichen Frühling hervor.

Wieder und wieder, von Dunkel und Sturz unterbrochen,
glänzte es irdisch. Bis es nach schrecklichem Pochen
trat in das trostlos offene Tor.

## XXIV

SHOULD we be breaking our ancient bond with the great
gods who have ceased to recruit us—our new hard steel*
bred too austere to recognize them as real—
or should we be trying to plot them now on charts?

These mighty friends, the gods, who take the dead from us,          5
never approach us so close as to touch our wheels.
Far ahead of them are our baths, our feasts;
even their messengers, now long since too slow for us,

overtaken. Lonelier, thrown back on each other
wholly, yet still so mutually unknown,          10
no more do we build roads that gently meander

but build them straight. Only in boilers burn
the ancient flames,* raising ever heavier hammers.
We, on the contrary, find our strength ebbing, like swimmers.

## XXV

I WILL remember you* now one last time,
you whom I knew like an unfamiliar flower.
Bring you to all their minds, you who were taken,
sweet playmate crying the insurmountable cry.

At first a dancer whose unwilling body suddenly          5
stopped as though her youth were cast into ore;*
mourning, listening.—Then from some higher faculty
came a music that entered your altered heart.

The illness was near. While shadows* already possessed it
your blood welled, obscure, and yet, as we briefly expected,          10
drove itself on in its natural spring of the year.

Again and again, interrupted by darkness and falling,
it shimmered* as earth-ore.* Then after terrible throbbing
it stepped through the open, comfortless door.

## XXVI

Du aber, Göttlicher, du, bis zuletzt noch Ertöner,
da ihn der Schwarm der verschmähten Mänaden befiel,
hast ihr Geschrei übertönt mit Ordnung, du Schöner,
aus den Zerstörenden stieg dein erbauendes Spiel.

Keine war da, daß sie Haupt dir und Leier zerstör.          5
Wie sie auch rangen und rasten, und alle die scharfen
Steine, die sie nach deinem Herzen warfen,
wurden zu Sanftem an dir und begabt mit Gehör.

Schließlich zerschlugen sie dich, von der Rache gehetzt,
während dein Klang noch in Löwen und Felsen verweilte   10
und in den Bäumen und Vögeln. Dort singst du noch jetzt.

O du verlorener Gott! Du unendliche Spur!
Nur weil dich reißend zuletzt die Feindschaft verteilte,
sind wir die Hörenden jetzt und ein Mund der Natur.

### ZWEITER TEIL

### I

Atmen, du unsichtbares Gedicht!
Immerfort um das eigne
Sein rein eingetauschter Weltraum. Gegengewicht,
in dem ich mich rhythmisch ereigne.

Einzige Welle, deren                                         5
allmähliches Meer ich bin;
sparsamstes du von allen möglichen Meeren, –
Raumgewinn.

Wieviele von diesen Stellen der Räume waren schon
innen in mir. Manche Winde                                  10
sind wie mein Sohn.

## XXVI

BUT you, divine being,* you who sang to the end,
when the maenads you spurned set upon you in their throng
you drowned out their shrieks with your order,* you beautiful god,
and then from their ravages rose your uplifting song.

Not one of them could wound your head or your harp,          5
no matter how they wrestled you in their raving
and fury, and each sharp stone they cast at your heart
softened on touching you and was gifted with hearing.*

At last they dragged you down in a vengeful kill,
but your sound lingered on in the lions and in the rock face          10
and in the trees and the birds. You are singing there still.

O you great god who are lost to us! Infinite trace!
Only since enmity finally tore and dispersed you
are *we* now at last the hearers, a mouth of nature.

### PART TWO

### I

BREATHING, you invisible poem!*
Outermost space exchanged
purely, enduringly round your own being. Counter-pole,
where I rhythmically take place.

To you I belong; your gradual          5
sea-swell I am, single wave:
you, most sparing of all the seas possible—
gaining of space.

These portions of spaces were in me before, so deep
and in scores. Many winds          10
are like my seed.

Erkennst du mich, Luft, du, voll noch einst meiniger Orte?
Du, einmal glatte Rinde,
Rundung und Blatt meiner Worte.

## II

So wie dem Meister manchmal das eilig
nähere Blatt den *wirklichen* Strich
abnimmt: so nehmen oft Spiegel das heilig
einzige Lächeln der Mädchen in sich,

wenn sie den Morgen erproben, allein, –          5
oder im Glanze der dienenden Lichter.
Und in das Atmen der echten Gesichter,
später, fällt nur ein Widerschein.

*Was* haben Augen einst ins umrußte
lange Verglühn der Kamine geschaut:          10
Blicke des Lebens, für immer verlorne.

Ach, der Erde, wer kennt die Verluste?
Nur, wer mit dennoch preisendem Laut
sänge das Herz, das ins Ganze geborne.

## III

Spiegel: noch nie hat man wissend beschrieben,
was ihr in euerem Wesen seid.
Ihr, wie mit lauter Löchern von Sieben
erfüllten Zwischenräume der Zeit.

Ihr, noch des leeren Saales Verschwender –,          5
wenn es dämmert, wie Wälder weit . . .
Und der Lüster geht wie ein Sechzehn-Ender
durch eure Unbetretbarkeit.

Do you know me, air, still full of the places I owned?
You, once smooth tree-skin,
curving and leaf of my words.

## II

JUST as a quick sheet of paper sometimes
picks up the master's first, most truthful
pen-stroke,* mirrors take into themselves
girls' smiles, sacredly quintessential,

when they are alone and trying the morning          5
or in the candle-light serving them.
Later in day-time, real and breathing
faces take on a false reflection.*

How many eyes have watched sooty ashes
left in the hearth burn slowly cold:                10
glimpses of life forever gone.

Oh who understands the earth's losses?
Only he praising with undeterred song
who would sing the heart born into the Whole.

## III

MIRRORS: no one has consciously told
the very essence that is your own.
You are the interstices of time,
filled as though wholly with sieve holes.*

You, still wasting the empty hall—                  5
at twilight, vast as forestry . . .
and the lustres* pass like sixteen-pointers*
through your inaccessibility.

Manchmal seid ihr voll Malerei.
Einige scheinen *in* euch gegangen –,                                    10
andere schicktet ihr scheu vorbei.

Aber die Schönste wird bleiben –, bis
drüben in ihre enthaltenen Wangen
eindrang der klare gelöste Narziß.


## IV

O DIESES ist das Tier, das es nicht giebt.
Sie wußtens nicht und habens jeden Falls
– sein Wandeln, seine Haltung, seinen Hals,
bis in des stillen Blickes Licht – geliebt.

Zwar *war* es nicht. Doch weil sie's liebten, ward          5
ein reines Tier. Sie ließen immer Raum.
Und in dem Raume, klar und ausgespart,
erhob es leicht sein Haupt und brauchte kaum

zu sein. Sie nährten es mit keinem Korn,
nur immer mit der Möglichkeit, es sei.                              10
Und die gab solche Stärke an das Tier,

daß es aus sich ein Stirnhorn trieb. Ein Horn.
Zu einer Jungfrau kam es weiß herbei –
und war im Silber-Spiegel und in ihr.


## V

BLUMENMUSKEL, der der Anemone
Wiesenmorgen nach und nach erschließt,
bis in ihren Schoß das polyphone
Licht der lauten Himmel sich ergießt,

in den stillen Blütenstern gespannter                              5
Muskel des unendlichen Empfangs,

Sometimes you are full of paintings.
Some, it seems, have passed into you—                                10
others you sent by, hesitating.

The loveliest, though, will remain, till Narcissus,*
released, clear, presses beyond into
soft cheeks withheld in the mirror-recesses.


## IV

THIS beast does not exist. They did not know
and none the less, watching it as it moved
and taking in its stance, and neck, and step—
deep to the still light of the eyes—loved.

It was not there. Yet in that love it grew                            5
to pure creature. Always they left it space,
and clear and free to take the given room
lightly it raised its head and needed scarce

to come to *be*. They fed it not with grain,
merely with possibility of being.                                     10
And in the new strength of this resource

its brow gave forth a horn. Unicorn.*
It passed—white—along a maid's* way
and was: in her, and in her silver glass.


## V

FLOWER-MUSCLE of the anemone,*
opening slowly out to meadow-sunrise,
until a light pours polyphonically
into its womb from the resounding skies,

into the silent petal-star of muscles                                 5
held tense in an infinite reception,

manchmal *so* von Fülle übermannter,
daß der Ruhewink des Untergangs

kaum vermag die weitzurückgeschnellten
Blätterränder dir zurückzugeben:          10
du, Entschluß und Kraft von *wie*viel Welten!

Wir, Gewaltsamen, wir währen länger.
Aber *wann*, in welchem aller Leben,
sind wir endlich offen und Empfänger?


# VI

ROSE, du thronende, denen im Altertume
warst du ein Kelch mit einfachem Rand.
*Uns* aber bist du die volle zahllose Blume,
der unerschöpfliche Gegenstand.

In deinem Reichtum scheinst du wie Kleidung um Kleidung   5
um einen Leib aus nichts als Glanz;
aber dein einzelnes Blatt ist zugleich die Vermeidung
und die Verleugnung jedes Gewands.

Seit Jahrhunderten ruft uns dein Duft
seine süßesten Namen herüber;                              10
plötzlich liegt er wie Ruhm in der Luft.

Dennoch, wir wissen ihn nicht zu nennen, wir raten . . .
Und Erinnerung geht zu ihm über,
die wir von rufbaren Stunden erbaten.


# VII

BLUMEN, ihr schließlich den ordnenden Händen verwandte,
(Händen der Mädchen von einst und jetzt),

so overcome at times by the profusion
that the sun's departing gesture scarce

finds it can turn the margins of the petals,
far-reflexed, as it would, back to your centre:　　10
you, who have so many worlds' will and vigour.

We live the longer,* we who are more forceful.
But in our many lives, in which of these—
and when—shall we be open to receive?

## VI

ROSE enthroned, to the Ancients* you were simply
a cup, plain to the rim, unadorned—
but to us what flower of fullness,* inexhaustible
object multiple-petal-brimmed.

Your richness enwraps and rewraps this immaterial　　5
body of little but lustrousness—
but your every petal is the denial
and renunciation of all dress.

Centuries long your scent has called us,
bringing its names* with it, those sweetest,　　10
and hanging like glory* in the air.

And yet we cannot give it a name, but have guessed . . .
And memory mingles in the flower,
called from evocable hours of the past.

## VII

YOU flowers, akin, after all, to hands that bring order
(hands of the girls of now and of then),

die auf dem Gartentisch oft von Kante zu Kante
lagen, ermattet und sanft verletzt,

wartend des Wassers, das sie noch einmal erhole          5
aus dem begonnenen Tod –, und nun
wieder erhobene zwischen die strömenden Pole
fühlender Finger, die wohlzutun

mehr noch vermögen, als ihr ahnet, ihr leichten,
wenn ihr euch wiederfandet im Krug,                      10
langsam erkühlend und Warmes der Mädchen, wie Beichten,

von euch gebend, wie trübe ermüdende Sünden,
die das Gepflücktsein beging, als Bezug
wieder zu ihnen, die sich euch blühend verbünden.


## VIII

WENIGE ihr, der einstigen Kindheit Gespielen
in den zerstreuten Gärten der Stadt:
wie wir uns fanden und uns zögernd gefielen
und, wie das Lamm mit dem redenden Blatt,

sprachen als Schweigende. Wenn wir uns einmal freuten,   5
keinem gehörte es. Wessen wars?
Und wie zergings unter allen den gehenden Leuten
und im Bangen des langen Jahrs.

Wagen umrollten uns fremd, vorübergezogen,
Häuser umstanden uns stark, aber unwahr, – und keines    10
kannte uns je. *Was* war wirklich im All?

Nichts. Nur die Bälle. Ihre herrlichen Bogen.
Auch nicht die Kinder ...   Aber manchmal trat eines,
ach ein vergehendes, unter den fallenden Ball.

*(In memoriam Egon von Rilke)*

laid on the garden table, perhaps corner to corner,
mildly wounded, wilted, spent,

waiting for water to bring you back and revive you     5
from the death already begun—
feelingly raised to your height between
these streaming finger-poles that are able to do

far more than you could guess, you who are frail,
as you recovered in the vase,     10
cooling, and giving out the warmth of the girls*

as though you confessed the sad and weary transgressions
of being picked, reimbursing those
who in their blooming would bind to you in relation.

# VIII

You few playmates of a bygone childhood
in the scattered gardens of town:
how timidly we found and liked each other,
and as by the banner of the lamb*

spoke through our silence. Whenever we were gleeful     5
no one owned this. To whom did it belong?
And how it dissolved among moving throngs of people
and in the year's anxiety, so long.

Carriages wound round and passed us, strangers,
houses stood round us, solid but false—not one     10
ever did know us. What in the cosmos was real?

Nothing. Only the balls. Their arcing splendour.
Not even the children . . .   But sometimes there came one,
dying, stepping under the falling ball.*

(*In memoriam Egon von Rilke*)

## IX

Rühmt euch, ihr Richtenden, nicht der entbehrlichen Folter
und daß das Eisen nicht länger an Hälsen sperrt.
Keins ist gesteigert, kein Herz –, weil ein gewollter
Krampf der Milde euch zarter verzerrt.

Was es durch Zeiten bekam, das schenkt das Schafott          5
wieder zurück, wie Kinder ihr Spielzeug vom vorig
alten Geburtstag. Ins reine, ins hohe, ins torig
offene Herz träte er anders, der Gott

wirklicher Milde. Er käme gewaltig und griffe
strahlender um sich, wie Göttliche sind.                     10
*Mehr* als ein Wind für die großen gesicherten Schiffe.

Weniger nicht, als die heimliche leise Gewahrung,
die uns im Innern schweigend gewinnt
wie ein still spielendes Kind aus unendlicher Paarung.


## X

Alles Erworbne bedroht die Maschine, solange
sie sich erdreistet, im Geist, statt im Gehorchen, zu sein.
Daß nicht der herrlichen Hand schöneres Zögern mehr prange,
zu dem entschlossenern Bau schneidet sie steifer den Stein.

Nirgends bleibt sie zurück, daß wir ihr *ein* Mal entrönnen   5
und sie in stiller Fabrik ölend sich selber gehört.
Sie ist das Leben, – sie meint es am besten zu können,
die mit dem gleichen Entschluß ordnet und schafft und zerstört.

Aber noch ist uns das Dasein verzaubert; an hundert
Stellen ist es noch Ursprung. Ein Spielen von reinen         10
Kräften, die keiner berührt, der nicht kniet und bewundert.

Worte gehen noch zart am Unsäglichen aus . . .
Und die Musik, immer neu, aus den bebendsten Steinen,
baut im unbrauchbaren Raum ihr vergöttlichtes Haus.

## IX

Do not boast, judges, that you dispense with torture,
that irons are no longer taken to throats* and clamped.
No heart is uplifted when mercy is forced like a spasm,
yielding a tenderness strained and distorted.*

The scaffold gives back what it has taken throughout        5
the ages, like children giving their toys away
from last year's birthday. How different the god of true mercy,
were he entering the gates of the lofty, pure, open heart.

He would come in his fullest power, with talons of radiance
shining in his circumference, as is divine.                 10
So much more than a wind* for bold, confident sailing.

Nothing less than a silent and secret awareness
winning us quietly from within,
like a child playing peacefully, born of an infinite pairing.*


## X

All we have won the machine* imperils, by
daring to enter our minds rather than simply obeying.
Taking the place of the master's hand of lovely delay,
with less show, stiffly, it slices stone* for more resolute building.

Nowhere does it hold back, that we may overtake it;          5
self-oiling, self-owning, even, in factories stilled of their noise.
Life is machine that believes it delivers the best
when one and the same decision orders, creates and destroys.

Yet our existence enthrals us* still by its store
of hundredfold origins. Pure forces playing loose,          10
untouched by those of us who are not kneeling in awe.

Words turn frail still, dispersing at the unsayable . . .
And music,* arising anew out of trembling stones,
builds in unfeasible space* its deified house.*

## XI

MANCHE, des Todes, entstand ruhig geordnete Regel,
weiterbezwingender Mensch, seit du im Jagen beharrst;
mehr doch als Falle und Netz, weiß ich dich, Streifen von Segel,
den man hinuntergehängt in den höhligen Karst.

Leise ließ man dich ein, als wärst du ein Zeichen,                        5
Frieden zu feiern. Doch dann: rang dich am Rande der Knecht,
– und, aus den Höhlen, die Nacht warf eine Handvoll von
   bleichen
taumelnden Tauben ins Licht . . . Aber auch *das* ist im Recht.

Fern von dem Schauenden sei jeglicher Hauch des Bedauerns,
nicht nur vom Jäger allein, der, was sich zeitig erweist,              10
wachsam und handelnd vollzieht.

*Töten ist eine Gestalt unseres wandernden Trauerns . . .*
Rein ist im heiteren Geist,
was an uns selber geschieht.


## XII

WOLLE die Wandlung. O sei für die Flamme begeistert,
drin sich ein Ding dir entzieht, das mit Verwandlungen prunkt;
jener entwerfende Geist, welcher das Irdische meistert,
liebt in dem Schwung der Figur nichts wie den wendenden
   Punkt.

Was sich ins Bleiben verschließt, schon *ists* das Erstarrte;          5
wähnt es sich sicher im Schutz des unscheinbaren Grau's?
Warte, ein Härtestes warnt aus der Ferne das Harte.
Wehe –: abwesender Hammer holt aus!

Wer sich als Quelle ergießt, den erkennt die Erkennung;
und sie führt ihn entzückt durch das heiter Geschaffne,             10
das mit Anfang oft schließt und mit Ende beginnt.

## XI

MAN, you resolved to hunt, striving to subjugate,
and from this there have ensued death's quiet and orderly
    standards;
but better than snare and net I grasp you, thin strip of sail
let down deep in the Karst's darkest limestone caverns.

Gently they lowered you down as though you were signal       5
for honouring peace. But then: a young lad shook out your margins
—and night sent out from the caves doves in a tumbling handful,
pale, straight into light . . . But even *this* has its permitting.*

May it be far from the onlooker, any slight breath of regretting;
not just from the watchful hunter, seizing his timely chances,     10
ready to actualize.

*Killing is only one aspect of our wandering grieving . . .*
Whatever is enacted upon us
in spirit is pure and blithe.

## XII

DESIRE to be changed.* O be alive for the flame
when in it a thing leaves your reach,* flaunting its transformations;
every creative mind that masters the Earthly's state
loves most in the verve of the figure the brilliant point of the turn.*

Whatever is set upon staying has died at the start;       5
does it think itself safe in the shelter of background greys?
Wait, for hardness is warning of hard from afar.
Alas—an absent hammer is raised!

Knowledge well knows him who pours himself out like a
    wellspring;*
it leads him enraptured through all of this lively creation,     10
where beginning is often closing and ending begins.

Jeder glückliche Raum ist Kind oder Enkel von Trennung,
den sie staunend durchgehn. Und die verwandelte Daphne
will, seit sie lorbeern fühlt, daß du dich wandelst in Wind.


# XIII

Sei allem Abschied voran, als wäre er hinter
dir, wie der Winter, der eben geht.
Denn unter Wintern ist einer so endlos Winter,
daß, überwinternd, dein Herz überhaupt übersteht.

Sei immer tot in Eurydike –, singender steige,                    5
preisender steige zurück in den reinen Bezug.
Hier, unter Schwindenden, sei, im Reiche der Neige,
sei ein klingendes Glas, das sich im Klang schon zerschlug.

Sei – und wisse zugleich des Nicht-Seins Bedingung,
den unendlichen Grund deiner innigen Schwingung,                  10
daß du sie völlig vollziehst dieses einzige Mal.

Zu dem gebrauchten sowohl, wie zum dumpfen und stummen
Vorrat der vollen Natur, den unsäglichen Summen,
zähle dich jubelnd hinzu und vernichte die Zahl.


# XIV

Siehe die Blumen, diese dem Irdischen treuen,
denen wir Schicksal vom Rande des Schicksals leihn, –
aber wer weiß es! Wenn sie ihr Welken bereuen,
ist es an uns, ihre Reue zu sein.

Alles will schweben. Da gehn wir umher wie Beschwerer,           5
legen auf alles uns selbst, vom Gewichte entzückt;
o was sind wir den Dingen für zehrende Lehrer,
weil ihnen ewige Kindheit glückt.

Each happy space is the child or the grandchild of parting;
they explore it in awe. And Daphne, in transformation,
since feeling such laurelling,* wants you to turn into wind.

## XIII

Be ahead of all parting as though you found it behind
you, like this winter whose passing begins.
For among winters one is so endlessly winter
that overwintering it the heart also lives.

Be ever dead in Eurydice*—climb with more singing,          5
climb with more praising back into pure relation.
Here, among dwindling, *be*: in the realm of declining
be a ringing glass shattered in air's oscillation.

Be—and know also non-being: its one condition,
the infinite cause of your inner vibration,                10
so that this time* you fulfil it, and it is content.

To nature's reserves of the functional, to the dumb
and to the dull, to the whole unspeakable sum,
add yourself, jubilant, and then annul the amount.*

## XIV

Look at the flowers, these living things loyal to the earth,
whom, from the margins of fate, we provide with a fate—
but who can be sure! When they bewail their decay
it is our duty to be their regret.*

All things would float. But we go about our burdening,      5
laying ourselves on everything, proud of our weight;
oh, what exhausting teachers* we are to the things
who delight in their infinite childish state.

Nähme sie einer ins innige Schlafen und schliefe
tief mit den Dingen –: o wie käme er leicht,                    10
anders zum anderen Tag, aus der gemeinsamen Tiefe.

Oder er bliebe vielleicht; und sie blühten und priesen
ihn, den Bekehrten, der nun den Ihrigen gleicht,
allen den stillen Geschwistern im Winde der Wiesen.

## XV

O Brunnen-Mund, du gebender, du Mund,
der unerschöpflich Eines, Reines, spricht, –
du, vor des Wassers fließendem Gesicht,
marmorne Maske. Und im Hintergrund

der Aquädukte Herkunft. Weither an                              5
Gräbern vorbei, vom Hang des Apennins
tragen sie dir dein Sagen zu, das dann
am schwarzen Altern deines Kinns

vorüberfällt in das Gefäß davor.
Dies ist das schlafend hingelegte Ohr,                         10
das Marmorohr, in das du immer sprichst.

Ein Ohr der Erde. Nur mit sich allein
redet sie also. Schiebt ein Krug sich ein,
so scheint es ihr, daß du sie unterbrichst.

## XVI

Immer wieder von uns aufgerissen,
ist der Gott die Stelle, welche heilt.
Wir sind Scharfe, denn wir wollen wissen,
aber er ist heiter und verteilt.

If somebody drew them into intimate sleep, slept
deep with those things—how light he would be, and different,  10
coming to the new day from this mutual depth.

Or, if he stayed with them, they would blossom and praise
him, now as one of them and converted to them,
these silent siblings blown in the meadow breeze.

# XV

O FOUNTAIN-MOUTH,* you giving* one, you mouth
speaking unquenchably of one thing, one pure
thing—you mask of marble, set before
the flowing face of water. In the background

the arriving of the aqueducts. Past far graves,  5
from foothills of the Apennines, they bring
the words to you that flow in what you say
over the blackness of your chin's

ageing into the basin curved below.
This is the ear laid to the ground and sleeping,  10
the marble ear to which you always speak.

The Earth's ear. So she must talk alone
for her own hearing. A held jug will make
it seem to her that you are interrupting.*

# XVI

TORN open by our fingers, over and over,
then still torn: the god who is the place
that heals. We are the sharp,* who ask to know.
He, parted and dispersed,* is bright of face.

Selbst die reine, die geweihte Spende                    5
nimmt er anders nicht in seine Welt,
als indem er sich dem freien Ende
unbewegt entgegenstellt.

Nur der Tote trinkt
aus der hier von uns *gehörten* Quelle,                   10
wenn der Gott ihm schweigend winkt, dem Toten.

*Uns* wird nur das Lärmen angeboten.
Und das Lamm erbittet seine Schelle
aus dem stilleren Instinkt.


# XVII

Wo, in welchen immer selig bewässerten Gärten, an welchen
Bäumen, aus welchen zärtlich entblätterten Blüten-Kelchen
reifen die fremdartigen Früchte der Tröstung? Diese
köstlichen, deren du eine vielleicht in der zertretenen Wiese

deiner Armut findest. Von einem zum anderen Male             5
wunderst du dich über die Größe der Frucht,
über ihr Heilsein, über die Sanftheit der Schale,
und daß sie der Leichtsinn des Vogels dir nicht vorwegnahm und
    nicht die Eifersucht

unten des Wurms. Giebt es denn Bäume, von Engeln beflogen,
und von verborgenen langsamen Gärtnern so seltsam gezogen,    10
daß sie uns tragen, ohne uns zu gehören?

Haben wir niemals vermocht, wir Schatten und Schemen,
durch unser voreilig reifes und wieder welkes Benehmen
jener gelassenen Sommer Gleichmut zu stören?


# XVIII

TÄNZERIN: o du Verlegung
alles Vergehens in Gang: wie brachtest du's dar.

Even the pure, the consecrated offering     5
he does not take from us into his world
unless he stands at the uncertain ending
sure, unmoved and undeterred.

Only shall the dead drink
from that well we hear, the *audible*,     10
once the god quietly beckons them.

*We* are offered only noise's mayhem.
And the lamb requests its little bell
with an other, quieter instinct.

## XVII

WHERE and in which ever happily watered gardens, on which
trees, developed from which petal cups tenderly peeled,
do consolation's strange fruits ripen? These, the delicious,
of which you might just find one in the downtrodden field

of your poverty. You are astounded time and again     5
by the fruit's size, its wholesomeness, softness of skin,
and that you are not outdone above by the careless bird
or outdone below by the jealousy of the worm.

Are there then trees in the gardens, thronged instead by
    angels,
tended by hidden gardeners slowly and so strangely     10
that they bear for us though we are not their owners?

Have we never been able, we shades and shadowy figures,
as we prematurely mature and then again wither,
to disturb the calm serenity of those summers?

## XVIII

DANCER,* O you translation
of all transience into movement: how you offered it here!

Und der Wirbel am Schluß, dieser Baum aus Bewegung,
nahm er nicht ganz in Besitz das erschwungene Jahr?

Blühte nicht, daß ihn dein Schwingen von vorhin umschwärme,    5
plötzlich sein Wipfel von Stille? Und über ihr,
war sie nicht Sonne, war sie nicht Sommer, die Wärme,
diese unzählige Wärme aus dir?

Aber er trug auch, er trug, dein Baum der Ekstase.
Sind sie nicht seine ruhigen Früchte: der Krug,                10
reifend gestreift, und die gereiftere Vase?

Und in den Bildern: ist nicht die Zeichnung geblieben,
die deiner Braue dunkler Zug
rasch an die Wandung der eigenen Wendung geschrieben?


# XIX

IRGENDWO wohnt das Gold in der verwöhnenden Bank
und mit Tausenden tut es vertraulich. Doch jener
Blinde, der Bettler, ist selbst dem kupfernen Zehner
wie ein verlorener Ort, wie das staubige Eck unterm Schrank.

In den Geschäften entlang ist das Geld wie zuhause           5
und verkleidet sich scheinbar in Seide, Nelken und Pelz.
Er, der Schweigende, steht in der Atempause
alles des wach oder schlafend atmenden Gelds.

O wie mag sie sich schließen bei Nacht, diese immer offene Hand.
Morgen holt sie das Schicksal wieder, und täglich               10
hält es sie hin: hell, elend, unendlich zerstörbar.

Daß doch einer, ein Schauender, endlich ihren langen Bestand
staunend begriffe und rühmte. Nur dem Aufsingenden säglich.
Nur dem Göttlichen hörbar.

And the whirl at the end,* this tree grown of motion,
did it not wholly take in the hard-won year?

Then did its crown of silence not suddenly blossom,                    5
so that, circling it, your swaying should swarm?
And above it, was it not sun, was it not summer,
this warmth of yours, this endless warmth?

But it also bore: it bore fruit,* your tree of delight.
Are these not its quiet fruits: the jug                               10
striped with ripening, the vase roundedly ripe?

In your scribed figures does not the pen-line remain,
that of your eyebrows' dark stroke,
sketched on the wall of their own remembering turn?

## XIX

SOMEWHERE deep in the bank is the indulgent home of gold,*
intimate, surely, with thousands. But that blind beggar*
is still for the least copper penny too humble to know,
like a lost place, or a dust patch under the cupboard's far corner.

The lines of shops show money* at home in its world,                   5
clad in silk, it seems, in carnations and furs.
While money breathes, be it asleep or awake,
silent between its breaths he stands and waits.

O how, by night, may this hand, unfailingly open, close?*
Fate will bring it tomorrow, again and daily                          10
holding it out: bright and wretched and endlessly frail.

If only someone watching would finally grasp and praise
in amazement this long persistence. Sayable only in song,
audible only to the god.

## XX

ZWISCHEN den Sternen, wie weit; und doch, um wievieles noch
   weiter,
was man am Hiesigen lernt.
Einer, zum Beispiel, ein Kind . . . und ein Nächster, ein Zweiter –,
o wie unfaßlich entfernt.

Schicksal, es mißt uns vielleicht mit des Seienden Spanne,    5
daß es uns fremd erscheint;
denk, wieviel Spannen allein vom Mädchen zum Manne,
wenn es ihn meidet und meint.

Alles ist weit –, und nirgends schließt sich der Kreis.
Sieh in der Schüssel, auf heiter bereitetem Tische,    10
seltsam der Fische Gesicht.

Fische sind stumm . . ., meinte man einmal. Wer weiß?
Aber ist nicht am Ende ein Ort, wo man das, was der Fische
Sprache wäre, *ohne* sie spricht?

## XXI

SINGE die Gärten, mein Herz, die du nicht kennst; wie in Glas
eingegossene Gärten, klar, unerreichbar,
Wasser und Rosen von Ispahan oder Schiras,
singe sie selig, preise sie, keinem vergleichbar.

Zeige, mein Herz, daß du sie niemals entbehrst.    5
Daß sie dich meinen, ihre reifenden Feigen.
Daß du mit ihren, zwischen den blühenden Zweigen
wie zum Gesicht gesteigerten Lüften verkehrst.

Meide den Irrtum, daß es Entbehrungen gebe
für den geschehnen Entschluß, diesen: zu sein!    10
Seidener Faden, kamst du hinein ins Gewebe.

## XX

How far the stars are apart; and yet how much further
we learn from what is here.
Someone, for instance, a child . . . and a second, another—
O how unthinkably far.*

Fate* perhaps measures us with Being's span,                    5
and it seems to us strangely;
think: how many spans there are merely from girl to man
as she evades and craves him.

All is remote—nowhere does the circle close.
See, on the festive table, inside the dish:                     10
strange, the fishes' faces.

Fish cannot speak . . . we used to think. Who knows?
In the end, whatever it is, the language of fish . . .
can it be spoken *without* them,* and in what places?

## XXI

Sing, my heart, the gardens you have never known;*
poured as if into glass, clear, unattainable.
Waters and roses of Shiraz and of Isfahan,*
sing and praise them* in bliss, the incomparable.

Show them you cannot live without them, my heart.               5
That they may ripen for you, those ripening figs.
That you commune with the airs between flowering boughs,
airs that enhance almost as if into visions.

Do not be tempted to think that there are privations
once you determine this: to *become alive*!                     10
Into the textile, silken thread, you are woven.

Welchem der Bilder du auch im Innern geeint bist
(sei es selbst ein Moment aus dem Leben der Pein),
fühl, daß der ganze, der rühmliche Teppich gemeint ist.


## XXII

O TROTZ Schicksal: die herrlichen Überflüsse
unseres Daseins, in Parken übergeschäumt, –
oder als steinerne Männer neben die Schlüsse
hoher Portale, unter Balkone gebäumt!

O die eherne Glocke, die ihre Keule                    5
täglich wider den stumpfen Alltag hebt.
Oder die *eine*, in Karnak, die Säule, die Säule,
die fast ewige Tempel überlebt.

Heute stürzen die Überschüsse, dieselben,
nur noch als Eile vorbei, aus dem waagrechten gelben    10
Tag in die blendend mit Licht übertriebene Nacht.

Aber das Rasen zergeht und läßt keine Spuren.
Kurven des Flugs durch die Luft und die, die sie fuhren,
keine vielleicht ist umsonst. Doch nur wie gedacht.


## XXIII

RUFE mich zu jener deiner Stunden,
die dir unaufhörlich widersteht:
flehend nah wie das Gesicht von Hunden,
aber immer wieder weggedreht,

wenn du meinst, sie endlich zu erfassen.                5
So Entzognes ist am meisten dein.
Wir sind frei. Wir wurden dort entlassen,
wo wir meinten, erst begrüßt zu sein.

No matter which part is most inwardly yours in the pattern
(even a moment within an anguished life),
feel the whole carpet* one glorious intimation.


# XXII

O OUR existence's wondrous abundances,*
foaming over in parks, in spite of Fate—
or rising up under balconies as stone figures
next to the keystones of these high doorways!

O the brazen bell, raising each day a cudgel                    5
against all dull, everyday banality.
Or the one column in Karnak,* one sole column,
outliving temples so nearly built for eternity.

Nowadays these surpluses* merely speed
past us from yellow and horizontal days                         10
into blinding, heavily over-lit nights.*

Yet this racing disperses, leaving no trace.
Vapour trails and pilots high in the sky,
none are in vain. And yet they are never quite real.


# XXIII

SUMMON me* to that hour of all your hours
endlessly revealing its resistance,
close, imploringly, like dogs' faces,
but turned away to look into the distance

when so often you have thought you grasped it.              5
Such a thing, withdrawn, is more your own.
We are free.* For we were dismissed
just where we believed ourselves welcomed.

Bang verlangen wir nach einem Halte,
wir zu Jungen manchmal für das Alte                        10
und zu alt für das, was niemals war.

Wir, gerecht nur, wo wir dennoch preisen,
weil wir, ach, der Ast sind und das Eisen
und das Süße reifender Gefahr.


## XXIV

O DIESE Lust, immer neu, aus gelockertem Lehm!
Niemand beinah hat den frühesten Wagern geholfen.
Städte entstanden trotzdem an beseligten Golfen,
Wasser und Öl füllten die Krüge trotzdem.

Götter, wir planen sie erst in erkühnten Entwürfen,        5
die uns das mürrische Schicksal wieder zerstört.
Aber sie sind die Unsterblichen. Sehet, wir dürfen
jenen erhorchen, der uns am Ende erhört.

Wir, ein Geschlecht durch Jahrtausende: Mütter und Väter,
immer erfüllter von dem künftigen Kind,                    10
daß es uns einst, übersteigend, erschüttere, später.

Wir, wir unendlich Gewagten, was haben wir Zeit!
Und nur der schweigsame Tod, der weiß, was wir sind
und was er immer gewinnt, wenn er uns leiht.


## XXV

SCHON, horch, hörst du der ersten Harken
Arbeit; wieder den menschlichen Takt
in der verhaltenen Stille der starken
Vorfrühlingserde.   Unabgeschmackt

Anxiously we crave a firm foothold,
we who are too young for what is old                          10
and too old for what has not existed,

and just, but only if despite all ill we praise—
for, alas, we are both bough and blade,*
and the sweetness of a ripening hazard.


## XXIV

O this renewing joy of our loosened clay!
So little help they had,* the earliest venturers.
But cities still grew round the exultant bays,
water and oil still filled full the pitchers.

We* try to plan the gods through the bold designs          5
saturnine Fate destroys time and again.
They, though, are the immortals. See, we should listen
to him who will hear us as we near our end.

We are a race for millennia: fathers, mothers,
ever fuller with future offspring, and know,               10
later it will surpass and shatter* us.

We the eternally dauntless, who have so much time!
Only Death in his silence knows what we are
and what he continually wins when he lends us to life.


## XXV

LISTEN, already you can make out the first
rakings of work; human rhythm* again
heard in the vigorous early spring earth,
its cautious silence.   And what is to come

scheint dir das Kommende. Jenes so oft                    5
dir schon Gekommene scheint dir zu kommen
wieder wie Neues. Immer erhofft,
nahmst du es niemals. Es hat dich genommen.

Selbst die Blätter durchwinterter Eichen
scheinen im Abend ein künftiges Braun.                   10
Manchmal geben sich Lüfte ein Zeichen.

Schwarz sind die Sträucher. Doch Haufen von Dünger
lagern als satteres Schwarz in den Aun.
Jede Stunde, die hingeht, wird jünger.


# XXVI

WIE ergreift uns der Vogelschrei . . .
Irgend ein einmal erschaffenes Schreien.
Aber die Kinder schon, spielend im Freien,
schreien an wirklichen Schreien vorbei.

Schreien den Zufall.    In Zwischenräume               5
dieses, des Weltraums, (in welchen der heile
Vogelschrei eingeht, wie Menschen in Träume –)
treiben sie ihre, des Kreischens, Keile.

Wehe, wo sind wir? Immer noch freier,
wie die losgerissenen Drachen                           10
jagen wir halbhoch, mit Rändern von Lachen,

windig zerfetzten. – Ordne die Schreier,
singender Gott! daß sie rauschend erwachen,
tragend als Strömung das Haupt und die Leier.


# XXVII

GIEBT es wirklich die Zeit, die zerstörende?
Wann, auf dem ruhenden Berg, zerbricht sie die Burg?

seems reflavoured. What has before        5
so often come to you seems like the new,
returning. Hoped for always, but never
held in your grasp. It has grasped *you*.

Even the wintered oak trees' leaves
glow an imminent brown in the evening.        10
Sometimes signs are exchanged in the breeze.

Black, the bushes. But heaps of dung,
lusciously black, collect in the fields.
Every hour that passes grows young.*

## XXVI

How we are seized by the bird's cry* . . .
Any newly created crying.
But the children, already, playing outside,
wander and cry *past* real cries.

Chance they cry.*    Into the spaces        5
parting the ether they drive their screams
like wedges (ether that bird-cry enters
smoothly as human beings into dreams).

Alas, where are we? Ever less fettered,
dashing about like kites escaped        10
half-sky-high and with such wind-tattered

edges of laughter.—Order the criers,*
singing god,* to resound as they wake,
river-like, bringing the head and the lyre.

## XXVII

Does time truly exist? And annihilate?
When on the tranquil mount does it shatter the castle?

Dieses Herz, das unendlich den Göttern gehörende,
wann vergewaltigts der Demiurg?

Sind wir wirklich so ängstlich Zerbrechliche,                    5
wie das Schicksal uns wahr machen will?
Ist die Kindheit, die tiefe, versprechliche,
in den Wurzeln – später – still?

Ach, das Gespenst des Vergänglichen,
durch den arglos Empfänglichen                                   10
geht es, als wär es ein Rauch.

Als die, die wir sind, als die Treibenden,
gelten wir doch bei bleibenden
Kräften als göttlicher Brauch.


## XXVIII

O komm und geh. Du, fast noch Kind, ergänze
für einen Augenblick die Tanzfigur
zum reinen Sternbild einer jener Tänze,
darin wir die dumpf ordnende Natur

vergänglich übertreffen. Denn sie regte                          5
sich völlig hörend nur, da Orpheus sang.
Du warst noch die von damals her Bewegte
und leicht befremdet, wenn ein Baum sich lang

besann, mit dir nach dem Gehör zu gehn.
Du wußtest noch die Stelle, wo die Leier                         10
sich tönend hob –; die unerhörte Mitte.

Für sie versuchtest du die schönen Schritte
und hofftest, einmal zu der heilen Feier
des Freundes Gang und Antlitz hinzudrehn.

When will the demiurge* seek to violate
this heart that belongs to the gods for ever?

Are we really as fragile and anxious                                    5
as Fate attempts to make us feel?
Is childhood, deep and full of promise,
in the roots—later—so still?

Alas, the ghost of evanescence,
received into our innocence,                                            10
moves like smoke among us.

Yet though we drift in a transient course,*
we, in the eyes of eternal forces,
have our divine use.


## XXVIII

OH come and go.* You, all but child, augment
for a brief space the figure of the dance
to pure constellation, such a dance
in which we can surpass, though transient,

the dull commands of nature. For she stirred                            5
only as Orpheus sang, hearing then fully.
You were the one the ancient influence moved,
amazed when hesitatingly a tree

thought to follow the heard rhythms with you.
As the lyre raised its voice you knew                                   10
the place—the centre still unheard* by then.

For it you tried steps of the loveliest,
and hoped the pure festivity, at last,
would draw the eye and footstep of your friend.*

## XXIX

STILLER Freund der vielen Fernen, fühle,
wie dein Atem noch den Raum vermehrt.
Im Gebälk der finstern Glockenstühle
laß dich läuten. Das, was an dir zehrt,

wird ein Starkes über dieser Nahrung.                    5
Geh in der Verwandlung aus und ein.
Was ist deine leidendste Erfahrung?
Ist dir Trinken bitter, werde Wein.

Sei in dieser Nacht aus Übermaß
Zauberkraft am Kreuzweg deiner Sinne,                    10
ihrer seltsamen Begegnung Sinn.

Und wenn dich das Irdische vergaß,
zu der stillen Erde sag: Ich rinne.
Zu dem raschen Wasser sprich: Ich bin.

## XXIX

STILL friend of places too far-flung to number,
feel your breath* increase the space.
Bell–like, let them ring you through the sombre
belfries. What abrades you grows apace

and comes to final strength by this nutrition.     5
Move, then, in and out of transformation.*
What is your most biting pain?
If to drink is bitter, become wine.

Be in this night of all our overmeasure
the magic force within your senses' junction,     10
the sense in their mysterious overlap.

And if the earthly should forget you,
to the still earth answer: I am running.
To the rapid water say: I am.*

# Gedichte 1922–1926

## *Odette R . . . .*

TRÄNEN, die innigsten, *steigen*!

O wenn ein Leben
völlig stieg und aus Wolken des eigenen Herzleids
niederfällt: so nennen wir Tod diesen Regen.

Aber fühlbarer wird darüber, uns Armen, das dunkle –,    5
köstlicher wird, uns Reichen, darüber das seltsame Erdreich.


## *Zueignung an M . . . .*

geschrieben am 6. und 8. November 1923
(als Arbeits-Anfang eines neuen Winters auf Muzot)


SCHAUKEL des Herzens. O sichere, an welchem unsichtbaren
Aste befestigt. Wer, wer gab dir den Stoß,
daß du mit mir bis ins Laub schwangst.
Wie nahe war ich den Früchten, köstlichen. Aber nicht Bleiben
ist im Schwunge der Sinn. Nur das Nahesein, nur    5
am immer zu Hohen plötzlich das mögliche
Nahsein. Nachbarschaften und dann
von unaufhaltsam erschwungener Stelle
– wieder verlorener schon – der neue, der Ausblick.
Und jetzt: die befohlene Umkehr    10
zurück und hinüber hinaus in des Gleichgewichts Arme.
Unten, dazwischen, das Zögern, der irdische Zwang, der
    Durchgang
durch die Wende der Schwere –, vorbei: und es spannt sich die
    Schleuder,
von der Neugier des Herzens beschwert,
in das andere Gegenteil aufwärts.    15
Wieder wie anders, wie neu! Wie sie sich beide beneiden
an den Enden des Seils, diese Hälften der Lust.

# Uncollected Poems 1922–1926

## Odette R . . . .

TEARS, the tenderest, *rise*!

O when a life
once fully risen descends* from clouds of its heart's
own hurt, then we describe it as death, this raining.

Yet we poor find all the more tangible for it the dark tilth—          5
  all the more precious for it, we rich, the unfathomed earth.

## Dedicated to M . . . .

Written on 6 and 8 November 1923
(as the start of a new winter's work at Muzot)

HEART'S swing. O safe swinging, from what invisible bough
and sure fastening. Who, who has propelled you,
taking me up into foliage?
So near I was to the fruit, O delectable. Physical stay, though,
has no place in swinging. Only the closeness, only          5
the possible, sudden closeness to constantly
too high things. Proximities; then,
from the relentlessly swung viewpoint—
lost again in an instant—the new-found vista.
And now: the prescribed return          10
down and across to equilibrium's arms.
Between them, the hesitation, the earth-tow at nadir, the
    traversed
turning-point of gravity*—passed—and the loaded sling,
heavy with heart's curiosity, tautens
upward into the opposite.          15
Different again: how new!* How they each envy the other,
at the far ends of the rope, these two half-measures of joy.

Oder: wag ich es: Viertel? – Und rechne, weil er sich weigert,
jenen, den Halbkreis hinzu, der die Schaukel verstößt?
Nicht ertäusch ich mir ihn, als meiner hiesigen Schwünge        20
Spiegel. Errat nichts. Er sei
einmal neuer. Aber von Endpunkt zu Endpunkt
meines gewagtesten Schwungs nehm ich ihn schon in Besitz:
Überflüsse aus mir stürzen dorthin und erfülln ihn,
spannen ihn fast. Und mein eigener Abschied,        25
wenn die werfende Kraft an ihm abbricht,
macht ihn mir eigens vertraut.


### *Für* Nike

Weihnachten 1923

ALLE die Stimmen der Bäche,
jeden Tropfen der Grotte,
bebend mit Armen voll Schwäche
geb ich sie wieder dem Gotte

und wir feiern den Kreis.        5

Jede Wendung der Winde
war mir Wink oder Schrecken;
jedes tiefe Entdecken
machte mich wieder zum Kinde –,

und ich fühlte: ich weiß.        10

Oh, ich weiß, ich begreife
Wesen und Wandel der Namen;
in dem Innern der Reife
ruht der ursprüngliche Samen,

nur unendlich vermehrt.        15

Daß es ein Göttliches binde,
hebt sich das Wort zu Beschwörung,

Or, dare I say it: quarters?—If I add in that reluctant
second semi–circle* that repulses the swing?
It is no delusion of mine, mirror of my swung arcs                    20
of the present. So guess not. Let it
simply differ. But swung at my greatest daring
endpoint to endpoint, already I find it in my possession:
superabundances plunge out of me towards it, filling it,
straining it almost; and when this propelling force meets it          25
and cuts off, my departure* will make it
my sole intimacy.


## *For* Nike

### Christmas 1923

EVERY voice of the streamlet,
grottoes' running drops—
shaken and slack-limbed, all these
I return back to the god:*


and we hail the circle of flow.                                       5


Each wind's turn was a sign, or it
set me in terror of bane;
each new deep discovery
made me a child again—


and I have felt that I know.                                          10


Oh, I know, understand
essence and shifting name;
in the mature the initial
inner seed of the strain


endlessly re-made.                                                    15


That it shall bind the divine,
the word soars to the conjuring,*

aber, statt daß es schwinde,
steht es im Glühn der Erhörung

singend und unversehrt.                                            20


## Der Magier

ER ruft es an. Es schrickt zusamm und steht.
Was steht? Das Andre; alles, was nicht er ist,
wird Wesen. Und das ganze Wesen dreht
ein raschgemachtes Antlitz her, das mehr ist.

O Magier, halt aus, halt aus, halt aus!                            5
Schaff Gleichgewicht. Steh ruhig auf der Waage,
damit sie einerseits dich und das Haus
und drüben jenes Angewachsne trage.

Entscheidung fällt. Die Bindung stellt sich her.
Er weiß, der Anruf überwog das Weigern.                            10
Doch sein Gesicht, wie mit gedeckten Zeigern,
hat Mitternacht. Gebunden ist auch er.


## Eros

MASKEN! Masken! Daß man Eros blende.
Wer erträgt sein strahlendes Gesicht,
wenn er wie die Sommersonnenwende
frühlingliches Vorspiel unterbricht.

Wie es unversehens im Geplauder                                    5
anders wird und ernsthaft . . . Etwas schrie . . .
Und er wirft den namenlosen Schauder
wie ein Tempelinnres über sie.

and does not fade but instead
stands in the glow of the hearing,

singing and unscathed.                              20


## The Magician*

HE calls to it. It startles, halts and stands.
What stands? All that *he* is not; the Other*
emerges into being. Whole, swivelling
an instantaneous visage that is More.

Magician, oh hold out, hold out! Create          5
equilibrium. In the scales, stand still
so that they carry, this side, house and self
and over there that growth inseparable.

Decision's hour comes. The knot is fastened.
He knows: the call outweighed the will to shun.   10
Yet his face, like a covered dial,
registers midnight.* Even he is bound.


## Eros*

MASKS!* Bring masks! For we must shade his gaze.
Who endures the rays of Eros' face
as he interrupts our vernal foreplay,
all the summer's solstice in his eyes.

Unexpectedly, in conversation                     5
there is change—gravity—a cry . . .
And he flings, inner-temple-like
over her, the shuddered mystery.

Oh verloren, plötzlich, oh verloren!
Göttliche umarmen schnell.               10
Leben wand sich, Schicksal ward geboren.
Und im Innern weint ein Quell.

## *Vergänglichkeit*

FLUGSAND der Stunden. Leise fortwährende Schwindung
auch noch des glücklich gesegneten Baus.
Leben weht immer. Schon ragen ohne Verbindung
die nicht mehr tragenden Säulen heraus.

Aber Verfall: ist er trauriger als der Fontäne        5
Rückkehr zum Spiegel, den sie mit Schimmer bestaubt?
Halten wir uns dem Wandel zwischen die Zähne,
daß er uns völlig begreift in sein schauendes Haupt.

WEISST du noch: fallende Sterne, die
quer wie Pferde durch die Himmel sprangen
über plötzlich hingehaltne Stangen
unsrer Wünsche – hatten wir so viele? –
denn es sprangen Sterne, ungezählt;        5
fast ein jeder Aufblick war vermählt
mit dem raschen Wagnis ihrer Spiele,
und das Herz empfand sich als ein Ganzes
unter diesen Trümmern ihres Glanzes
und war heil, als überstünd es sie!        10

## *Wilder Rosenbusch*

WIE steht er da vor den Verdunkelungen
des Regenabends, jung und rein;
in seinen Ranken schenkend ausgeschwungen
und doch versunken in sein Rose-sein;

Oh, she is lost, all at once, lost!
Quick to embrace, the deities.                    10
Life swerved off; destiny* was born.
And within, a well of sorrow weeps.


## Transience

SAND-SHIFT of hours.* Persistent, quiet dissolution
even of a building blessed in fortune.
Life blows on. Already columns jut,*
no longer bearing their connection.

Yet is decay any sadder than the fountain's          5
return to the mirror, strewing shimmer-dust?
Let us hold on to change,* even here, in its teeth,
so that its seeing head* surely grasps us.


DO you remember: falling stars* that leapt
slanted through the sky like horses, clear
over the poles we held out suddenly
of tendered wishes—did we have so many?—
for the stars sprang about countless;              5
wedlocked, almost all our upturned glances,
in the quick-spark daring of their game,
and the heart knew itself whole
under these shards of wrecked radiances,
whole and healed, as though surviving them!         10


## Wild Rose*

LOOK how it stands, against the darkening glooms
of evening rain: pure, young,
fountaining out its leaf-tips in bestowal
and yet submerged into its rose-being;

die flachen Blüten, da und dort schon offen,         5
jegliche ungewollt und ungepflegt:
so, von sich selbst unendlich übertroffen
und unbeschreiblich aus sich selbst erregt,

ruft er den Wandrer, der in abendlicher
Nachdenklichkeit den Weg vorüberkommt:         10
Oh sieh mich stehn, sieh her, was bin ich sicher
und unbeschützt und habe was mir frommt.


WELT war in dem Antlitz der Geliebten –,
aber plötzlich ist sie ausgegossen:
Welt ist draußen, Welt ist nicht zu fassen.

Warum trank ich nicht, da ich es aufhob,
aus dem vollen, dem geliebten Antlitz         5
Welt, die nah war, duftend meinem Munde?

Ach, ich trank. Wie trank ich unerschöpflich.
Doch auch ich war angefüllt mit zuviel
Welt, und trinkend ging ich selber über.


NICHT um-stoßen, was steht!
Aber das Stehende stehender,
aber das Wehende wehender
zuzugeben, – gedreht

zu der Mitte des Schauenden,         5
der es im Schauen preist,
daß es sich am Vertrauenden
jener Schwere entreißt,

drin die Dinge, verlorener
und gebundener, fliehn –,         10
bis sie, durch uns, geborener,
sich in die Spannung beziehn.

its flat blooms here and there open                         5
involuntarily, as if neglectedly;
so, with a never-ending self-excelling,
quickening outwards indescribably,

it calls to the reflective passer-by
walking the paths at evening to pay heed:                  10
look at me,* for I stand here, safe, unguarded,
sure in myself, and owning all I need.


WORLD was there in my beloved's face—
then in an instant it had poured and emptied:*
world on the outside, world not now for grasping.

Why, tilting them up, did I not drink it
out of the brimming and beloved features,                   5
world, near, lifted fragrant to my mouth?

Ah, I drank. And how unquenched I drank.
Yet, like her, I was filled up with too much
world: drinking and running over.*


OVERTURN nothing that stands!
Grant it to stand more sturdily,
drift, if it will, more driftingly—
so that it may, turned round

full to the onlooker's core                                 5
who in the looking lauds it—
trusting, wrest itself free
of the gravity-pull of the orbit

in which, more lost, more helpless and
bound, things flee, until                                  10
born through us more* they tense
into resilience.

GESTIRNE der Nacht, die ich erwachter gewahre,
überspannen sie nur das heutige, meine Gesicht,
oder zugleich das ganze Gesicht meiner Jahre,
diese Brücken, die ruhen auf Pfeilern von Licht?

Wer will dort wandeln? Für wen bin ich Abgrund und Bachbett, 5
daß er mich so im weitesten Kreis übergeht –,
mich überspringt und mich nimmt wie den Läufer im Schachbrett
und auf seinem Siege besteht?

## *Handinneres*

INNRES der Hand. Sohle, die nicht mehr geht
als auf Gefühl. Die sich nach oben hält
und im Spiegel
himmlische Straßen empfängt, die selber
wandelnden.                                                            5
Die gelernt hat, auf Wasser zu gehn,
wenn sie schöpft,
die auf den Brunnen geht,
aller Wege Verwandlerin.
Die auftritt in anderen Händen,                                        10
die ihresgleichen
zur Landschaft macht:
wandert und ankommt in ihnen,
sie anfüllt mit Ankunft.

NACHT. Oh du in Tiefe gelöstes
Gesicht an meinem Gesicht.
Du, meines staunenden Anschauns größtes
Übergewicht.

Nacht in meinem Blicke erschauernd,                                    5
aber in sich so fest;
unerschöpfliche Schöpfung, dauernd
über dem Erdenrest;

NIGHT's constellations, here in my woken awareness:
is it my face that they span, as today knows it,
or with it the whole countenance of my years,
these bridges supported on balusters of light?

Who strolls up there? For whom am I stream-bed, chasm,   5
that he should walk in so wide an arc above me—
overleap,* take me like the bishop* that runs on the chessboard,
and with that declare his win?

## Palm of the Hand*

HAND's interior. Sole that walks the surface
only of feeling. Holds itself upward-facing,
mirror receiving
heavenly streets, themselves those
wanderers.*                                              5
Who has learned the art of walking on water,
scooping,
who is a walker on wells
and alterer* of every way.
Who steps into other hands,                              10
who can transform
hands like it to landscape:
wanders, arrives in them, fills them
full with arrival.

NIGHT.* O you so deeply freed
face up against my face.
You, in my awed gaze greatest
preponderance.

Night, shuddering in my look,                            5
shakeless in yourself;
inexhaustible creation, enduring
over relict earth;

voll von jungen Gestirnen, die Feuer
aus der Flucht ihres Saums                                    10
schleudern ins lautlose Abenteuer
des Zwischenraums:


wie, durch dein bloßes Dasein erschein ich,
Übertrefferin, klein – ;
doch, mit der dunkelen Erde einig,                            15
wag ich es, in dir zu sein.


### Schwerkraft

MITTE, wie du aus allen
dich ziehst, auch noch aus Fliegenden dich
wiedergewinnst, Mitte, du Stärkste.


Stehender: wie ein Trank den Durst
durchstürzt ihn die Schwerkraft.                               5


Doch aus dem Schlafenden fällt,
wie aus lagernder Wolke,
reichlicher Regen der Schwere.


### Mausoleum

KÖNIGSHERZ. Kern eines hohen
Herrscherbaums. Balsamfrucht.
Goldene Herznuß. Urnen-Mohn
mitten im Mittelbau,
(wo der Widerhall abspringt,                                   5
wie ein Splitter der Stille,
wenn du dich rührst,
weil es dir scheint,
daß deine vorige
Haltung zu laut war . . .)                                     10

dense with young star-clusters, fire-
hurling from their fleeing                           10
hems into the soundless fling
of space between;

simply because you are, transcender:
small—how small I seem;
yet,* at one with the dark earth,                    15
in you dare to have my being.


## Gravity

CENTRE-CORE, how you draw yourself
out of all things, even from the flying
win yourself back, centre, all-forceful.

Through the standing, like water through thirst,
gravity* plunges.                                     5

But from the sleeping,* let as from
lowering clouds, falls full
gravitational rain.


## Mausoleum*

KING'S heart. Core of a high
ruling tree. Balsam fruit.*
Golden heartnut.* Poppy-head urn*
mid-placed mid-building
(jumping-off point for the echoes                     5
split off from silence
if you should stir,
seeming to find
your previous stance
loud, all too loud . . .);                            10

Völkern entzogenes,
sterngesinnt,
im unsichtbaren Kreisen
kreisendes Königsherz.


Wo ist, wohin,                                    15
jenes der leichten
Lieblingin?
: Lächeln, von außen,
auf die zögernde Rundung
heiterer Früchte gelegt;                          20
oder der Motte, vielleicht,
Kostbarkeit, Florflügel, Fühler . . .


Wo aber, wo, das sie sang,
das sie in Eins sang,
das Dichterherz?                                  25
: Wind,
unsichtbar,
Windinnres.



WASSER, die stürzen und eilende . . .
heiter vereinte, heiter sich teilende
Wasser . . . Landschaft voll Gang.
Wasser zu Wassern sich drängende
und die in Klängen hängende                       5
Stille am Wiesenhang.


Ist in ihnen die Zeit gelöst,
die sich staut und sich weiterstößt,
vorbei am vergeßlichen Ohr?
Geht indessen aus jedem Hang                      10
in den himmlischen Übergang
irdischer Raum hervor?

heart withdrawn
from its peoples, star-bent,
in the invisible circling
of orbiting king's heart.

Where, where gone                           15
that of the gentle
girl,* his love?
: smile, from outside,
laid on the hesitant, tranquil
roundness of fruit, or perhaps              20
on the costliness of the moth,
its wing-velvet,* feelers . . .

Where, though, that which sang them,
sang them to oneness,*
the poet's heart?                           25
Wind,
invisible,
wind's within-ness.*


WATERS that plunge and the quick-sliding . . .
gaily* mingled and gaily dividing*
waters . . . Landscape in spate.
Waters to waters cascading
and all the hanging, ringing                 5
stillness of meadow-slope.

Time: is it loosed to them and released,
so fast dammed up, eddied and forced
on past the ear's forgetting?
In that time, does earthly space spill       10
out from the meadowed hill, into
heavenly over-stepping?

IRGENDWO blüht die Blume des Abschieds und streut
immerfort Blütenstaub, den wir atmen, herüber;
auch noch im kommendsten Wind atmen wir Abschied.


URNE, Fruchtknoten des Mohns –,
oh und die leichten, die roten
Blätter, die ihr unwissender Wind entriß . . .
Wie schon die Söhne des Sohns!
Alle sooft überboten,                                        5
jeder einzelne ungewiß.

Und da stürzt sich die Zeit weiter mit ihnen ins Tiefe;
was von den Stürzenden bleibt?
Ein verblichenes Bild und vergilbende Briefe
und in dem, der noch lebt, das was keiner beschreibt.       10

Jenes Unsägliche, das wir unendlich beweinen . . .
Nicht wie Gazelle und Reh,
die in dem künftigen Tier heiter wiedererscheinen,
so verläßlich wie eh.

Unser Besitz ist Verlust. Je kühner, je reiner             15
wir verlieren, je mehr


## Herbst

OH hoher Baum des Schauns, der sich entlaubt:
nun heißts gewachsen sein dem Übermaße
von Himmel, das durch seine Äste bricht.
Erfüllt vom Sommer, schien er tief und dicht,
uns beinah denkend, ein vertrautes Haupt.                   5
Nun wird sein ganzes Innere zur Straße
des Himmels. Und der Himmel kennt uns nicht.

SOMEWHERE the flower of farewell blooms, and scatters
perpetual pollen towards us, and we breathe it;
even in approach-blown winds we breathe farewell.


URN, opium-poppy* ovary—
oh, and the drift of the red
petals the unwitting wind has torn away . . .
Like the sons of the son!
All so fast overtaken;                                          5
individually uncertain.

Time throws itself with them onward down the abyss.
What is left us, of those who are falling?
Only yellowing letters and a faded likeness
and, in those still living, what is on no one's lips.           10

That which we cannot express, that we endlessly mourn . . .
Unlike gazelle and deer,
given to re-appear, serene, in the future animal,
reliably as before.

Our possession is loss. The more boldly, purely                15
we lose, the more


### Autumn

O HIGH tree of looking, now in leaf-fall;
we find we must be grown to meet excess
of sky that breaks in through its branches. Summer
had seemed to fill it with a depth and thickness,
*thinking* us, as it were: a friend-like head.                 5
Now it converts its whole inwardness
to pavement for the sky—which does not know us.*

Ein Äußerstes: daß wir wie Vogelflug
uns werfen durch das neue Aufgetane,
das uns verleugnet mit dem Recht des Raums,     10
der nur mit Welten umgeht. Unsres Saums
Wellen-Gefühle suchen nach Bezug
und trösten sich im Offenen als Fahne –

. . . . . . . . . . . . . . . . . . . . . . . . . . . . . .


Aber ein Heimweh meint das Haupt des Baums.


      ROSE, oh reiner Widerspruch, Lust,
      Niemandes Schlaf zu sein unter soviel
      Lidern.


### *Idol*

GOTT oder Göttin des Katzenschlafs,
kostende Gottheit, die in dem dunkeln
Mund reife Augen-Beeren zerdrückt,
süßgewordnen Schauns Traubensaft,
ewiges Licht in der Krypta des Gaumens.     5
Schlaf-Lied nicht, – Gong! Gong!
Was die anderen Götter beschwört,
entläßt diesen verlisteten Gott
an seine einwärts fallende Macht.


### *Gong*

      KLANG, nichtmehr mit Gehör
      meßbar. Als wäre der Ton,
      der uns rings übertrifft,
      eine Reife des Raums.

A last resort: to hurl ourselves like bird-flight
upwards through the new flung-openness
that will, with all of space's right, deny us,                    10
for only worlds consort with space. Our margin's
wave-wash feelings search for reference*
and in the Open, flag-like, find relief—

. . . . . . . . . . . . . . . . . . . . . . . . . . . . . . . .

But it was home, the head that was the tree.

 

 

ROSE,* oh* pure contradiction, delight
in being no one's sleep under so many
eyelids.*

 

 

## Idol

GOD or goddess of cats'* sleep,
savouring deity, crushing ripe
eye-berries* in the dark mouth,
juice of the grape of seeing,* grown sweet,
eternal light of the palate's crypt.                              5
Lullaby, no—gong! gong!*
What would conjure the other gods
releases this god of wiles* to the falling-
inward of its old might.

 

 

## Gong

SOUND, no more in our ears'
measuring. As though the tone
overwhelming us in the round
were space maturing.

## *Gong* (II)

NICHT mehr für Ohren . . . : Klang,
der, wie ein tieferes Ohr,
uns, scheinbar Hörende, hört.
Umkehr der Räume. Entwurf
innerer Welten im Frein . . .,          5
Tempel vor ihrer Geburt,
Lösung, gesättigt mit schwer
löslichen Göttern . . . : Gong!

Summe des Schweigenden, das
sich zu sich selber bekennt,          10
brausende Einkehr in sich
dessen, das an sich verstummt,
Dauer, aus Ablauf gepreßt,
um-gegossener Stern . . . : Gong!

Du, die man niemals vergißt,          15
die sich gebar im Verlust,
nichtmehr begriffenes Fest,
Wein an unsichtbarem Mund,
Sturm in der Säule, die trägt,
Wanderers Sturz in den Weg,          20
unser, an Alles, Verrat . . . : Gong!

## *Eine Folge zur ›Rosenschale‹*

Geschrieben für Mme Riccard

REICH war von ihnen der Raum, immer voller und sätter.
Rosen, verweilende: plötzlich streun sie sich aus.
Abends vielleicht. Der entschlossene Abfall der Blätter
klingt an den Rand des Kamins, wie ein leiser Applaus.

Geben sie Beifall der Zeit, die sie so zärtlich getötet?     5
Währten sie selbst sich genug, die uns zu frühe entgehn?

## *Gong* (II)

No more for our ears . . . : sound*
tuned like a deeper ear
to hear us, who seem the hearers.*
Space's reversal. Design
for inner worlds laid in the open* . . .,　　　5
temple before their birth,
solution clogged with gods
all but insoluble . . . . : gong!*

Sum of the silent, of things
self-confessing to self;　　　10
effervescent self-communing
of what, apart, grows mute;
duration, squeezed from rundown;
newly re-poured star* . . . : gong!

You, whom we never forget,　　　15
giving birth to yourself in loss,
festival past grasping,
wine at invisible lips,
storm in the bearing column,*
traveller's fall to the path,　　　20
our betrayal of all things* . . . : gong!


## *A Sequel to the 'Bowl of Roses'**

Written for Mme Riccard

RICHLY they drenched the room, hourly fuller and stronger.
Roses, lingering; then in a moment fallen.
Maybe at evening. The resolute petal-drop
flutters against the fireplace, like a rippled applause.

Are they honouring time for being so tender a killer?*　　　5
Did they neglect their defence, that they have fled so soon?

Siehe, die rötesten sind bis ans Schwarze verrötet
und den bleicheren ist jegliche Blässe geschehn.

Nun: ihr Jenseits beginnt zwischen den Seiten der Bücher;
unbezwinglicher Duft wohnt in der Lade, im Schrank,          10
drängt in ein Ding, das uns dient, schmiegt in gefaltete Tücher
was uns aus Rosen ergriff und was in Rosen versank.


## *Ankunft*

IN einer Rose steht dein Bett, Geliebte. Dich selber
(oh ich Schwimmer wider die Strömung des Dufts)
hab ich verloren. So wie dem Leben zuvor
diese (von außen nicht meßbar) dreimal drei Monate sind,
so, nach innen geschlagen, werd ich erst *sein*. Auf einmal,          5
zwei Jahrtausende vor jenem neuen Geschöpf,
das wir genießen, wenn die Berührung beginnt,
plötzlich: gegen dir über, werd ich im Auge geboren.


## *Geschrieben für Karl Grafen Lanckoroński*

»NICHT *Geist, nicht Inbrunst wollen wir entbehren*«:
eins durch das andre lebend zu vermehren,
sind wir bestimmt; und manche sind erwählt,
in diesem Streit ein Reinstes zu erreichen,
wach und geübt, erkennen sie die Zeichen,          5
die Hand ist leicht, das Werkzeug ist gestählt.

Das Leiseste darf ihnen nicht entgehen,
sie müssen jenen Ausschlagswinkel sehen,
zu dem der Zeiger sich kaum merklich rührt,
und müssen gleichsam mit den Augenlidern          10
des leichten Falters Flügelschlag erwidern,
und müssen spüren, was die Blume spürt.

Look: the intensest have darkened to black, and varying
pallors have happened upon the paler petal-bloom.

Now their hereafter begins, slipped between pages of books;
irreducible scent inhabits drawers and wardrobes—                    10
pressed through things that serve us, clinging in folded linen—
once that captured us out of roses and sank in roses.


## Arrival*

INSIDE a rose your bed,* beloved. You yourself
(oh, I swim against flood tides of the fragrance),
you I have lost. Just as to earlier life
those (from the outside incalculable) three times three months are,
so, impelled inward, then only shall I *be*.* In an instant,          5
two millennia* before that new creation
whom we delight in when contact of touch begins,
suddenly, facing you:* in the eye I am brought to birth.


## Written for Count Karl Lanckoroński*

'SPIRIT *and fervour: these we would not lose.*'*
For we are meant to use them, to combine
each in the other's increase. Many are chosen
to struggle, to achieve the purest end,
alert, practised, following the signs,                                5
the hand light, holding the steeled tool.

Nor must they miss the very gentlest things,
must note the angle of the swung needle,
touched almost unseen; as delicately
answer the moth's lightly-fluttered wings                            10
with human eyelids' whispering;
and what the flower feels, they must feel.

Zerstörbar sind sie wie die andern Wesen
und müssen doch (sie wären nicht erlesen!)
Gewaltigstem zugleich gewachsen sein.                        15
Und wo die andern wirr und wimmernd klagen,
da müssen sie der Schläge Rhythmen sagen,
und in sich selbst erfahren sie den Stein.


Sie müssen dastehn wie der Hirt, der dauert;
von ferne kann es scheinen, daß er trauert,                  20
im Näherkommen fühlt man wie er wacht.
Und wie für ihn der Gang der Sterne laut ist,
muß ihnen nah sein, wie es ihm vertraut ist,
was schweigend steigt und wandelt in der Nacht.


Im Schlafe selbst noch bleiben sie die Wächter:             25
aus Traum und Sein, aus Schluchzen und Gelächter
fügt sich ein Sinn . . . . Und überwältigt sie's,
und stürzen sie ins Knien vor Tod und Leben,
so ist der Welt ein neues Maß gegeben
mit diesem rechten Winkel ihres Knie's!                      30


## Für Erika

### zum Feste der Rühmung

Taube, die draußen blieb,    außer dem Taubenschlag,
wieder in Kreis und Haus,    einig der Nacht, dem Tag,
weiß sie die Heimlichkeit,    wenn sich der Einbezug
fremdester Schrecken schmiegt    in den gefühlten Flug.


Unter den Tauben, die    allergeschonteste,                  5
niemals gefährdetste,    kennt nicht die Zärtlichkeit;
wiedererholtes Herz    ist das bewohnteste:
freier durch Widerruf    freut sich die Fähigkeit.


Über dem Nirgendssein    spannt sich das Überall!
Ach der geworfene,    ach der gewagte Ball,                  10

Destructible as any other being,
yet they must be (were they to be chosen!)
grown so in strength to match the starkest force.     15
And where, bewildered, others wail and whimper,
they must tell the rhythms of the blows
and in the self experience the stone.

Must stand there like the shepherd,* who endures;
distantly, you seem to see him mourn,     20
but nearing him you notice how he watches.
And as the stars drift loudly in his ears,
must like him be familiar with what rises,
silent, to wander through the night hours.

Still in their sleep they shall remain the watchers:     25
for out of dream and being, the sob, the laughter,
meaning flows . . . . and should it overwhelm them,
should death plunge them to their knees in awe,
or life*—so shall the world be newly measured
here, in the angle of the bent knee!*     30


## *For Erika**

### In celebration of praise*

DOVE, so long gone from us,     under no dovecote roof,
now, back in place, at home,     at one with day and night,
well knows the secrecy     in which the furthest fears
press for inclusion and cling     fast to her feeling flight.

The dove of all doves best     sheltered,* of all doves least     5
open to danger, knows     least, too, of tenderness;
heart that has convalesced     makes the most lived-in home;
strength returned knows delight     all the more boundless.

High over nowhere-life     arches the everywhere!
Ah, the thrown ball* that is     risked in the upward soar,     10

Füllt er die Hände nicht    anders mit Wiederkehr:
rein um sein Heimgewicht    ist er mehr.

Ragaz, am 24. August 1926


KOMM du, du letzter, den ich anerkenne,
heilloser Schmerz im leiblichen Geweb:
wie ich im Geiste brannte, sieh, ich brenne
in dir; das Holz hat lange widerstrebt,
der Flamme, die du loderst, zuzustimmen,                5
nun aber nähr' ich dich und brenn in dir.
Mein hiesig Mildsein wird in deinem Grimmen
ein Grimm der Hölle nicht von hier.
Ganz rein, ganz planlos frei von Zukunft stieg
ich auf des Leidens wirren Scheiterhaufen,              10
so sicher nirgend Künftiges zu kaufen
um dieses Herz, darin der Vorrat schwieg.
Bin ich es noch, der da unkenntlich brennt?
Erinnerungen reiß ich nicht herein.
O Leben, Leben: Draußensein.                            15
Und ich in Lohe. Niemand der mich kennt.

does it not fill the hands    differently on return:
pure, round its native weight,    it has more.

Ragaz, 24 August 1926

COME, you the last that I shall recognize,
you utter pain* of human tissue: just as
once I burned in the mind, look, I burn
in you; the wood has fought against concurring,
years long, in this flame that you have lit,                5
but now I fuel you and burn in you.
And in your rage my mind's mildness turns
to grim fury from a far hell.
I set myself, pure of plan and future,
to climb pain's chaotic pyre,* secure,                    10
ahead of me nothing to acquire
against this heart's resources, fallen still.
Am I the man, quite unrecognized,
burning there? I drag no memories in.
O life—life: to be outside.                               15
And I'm in flame. Known at the last by no one.

# EXPLANATORY NOTES

OCCASIONALLY reference is made to material included in some of the works of secondary literature listed in the Bibliography, using the surname and short title (e.g. Leisi, *Rilkes Sonette*). Full bibliographic references for quotations from letters are not routinely given, but all the letters referred to are dated so that they may be consulted in one of the volumes listed in the 'Further Reading'. These notes are sometimes indebted to (and suggest corrections to) those in previous editions, selections and translations of Rilke's works (*KA* in particular), but ultimately they always reflect the editor's own opinions and judgements.

## From *OFFERINGS TO THE LARES*

The ninety-nine poems of Rilke's second collection, *Offerings to the Lares*, were in all likelihood written between 1893 and 1895 and published at Christmas of that year (but dated 1896) by a small Prague publisher, Domenicus, with a cover illustration by Valerie von David-Rhonfeld. The collection was dedicated chiefly to the monuments and features of his home city of Prague and to artists and historical figures from the history of Bohemia. The 'Lares' were Roman protective deities, guardians of home and fields, sometimes also of ancestral heroes.

*The Dreamer* (II)

Probably written late autumn 1895, Prague.

3   *Dreams*: dreams and dreaming are a familiar theme in German neo-romantic poetry and this poem has strong affinities with the works of Rilke's contemporary Hugo von Hofmannsthal (1874–1929), most notably with his ghazal 'Für mich' ('For me', 1890).

   *orchids*: delicate and often complex tropical flowers, symbolic of love and perfection, but often used at the turn of the century to suggest decadence and sensuous luxury.

## From *ADVENT*

*Advent* was published at Christmas 1897 by the small publisher Friesenhahn in Leipzig. Most of the poems in the collection were written in Prague and Munich in September and October 1896 and January 1897, but a few were added from the summer of 1897 shortly before publication. Many are dedicated to other poets and to patrons from Munich.

'This my struggle'

Written 18 February 1897, Munich.

> 3 *rootlets*: an early instance of an image that will become extremely impor-
> tant to Rilke, most strikingly in 'Orpheus. Eurydice. Hermes', l. 82
> (p. 81).

## From *IN CELEBRATION OF MYSELF*

*In Celebration of Myself* collects poems written in Berlin and Italy (Arco,
Florence, and Viareggio) between early November 1897 and the end of May
1898. It was published in Berlin by Georg Heinrich Meyer in 1899 with a title
page by the *Jugendstil* artist Heinrich Vogeler—a member of the Worpsweder
colony and a friend of Rilke's. Despite Rilke's later lack of enthusiasm for the
volume, many of the poems in it, inspired chiefly by his relationship with Lou
Andreas-Salomé, are powerful and well crafted.

'Songs I was granted in youth'

Written 28 November 1897, Berlin-Wilmersdorf.

> 5 *Rondeau*: highly structured French poem fashionable in the 16th and 17th
> centuries, usually of 13 lines (in stanzas of 5, 3, and 5 lines) or of 10 (4, 2, 4),
> using two rhymes and featuring a refrain. Rilke's poem has some similari-
> ties with the traditional form, but this (like the sonnet later) is treated with
> some flexibility.

*Prayer*

Written summer or autumn 1898. The ornamental device of centring poems on
the page rather than aligning to the left was popular with *Jugendstil* writers.

> *angel*: this poem is the last in a short series of 'Angel songs', featuring
> early versions of a motif that will become very important to Rilke, espe-
> cially in the *Duino Elegies*. The intimidating aspect of the angel here
> anticipates some of the qualities of the later angels but in its symbolism
> of life beyond the ordinary, routine, and banal here still inhabits a form
> recognizable to ordinary mortals.

> *the weary*: tiredness or languidness is a common motif in decadent
> poetry—the opposite of the will that is evoked in 'Entrance', l. 11
> (p. 25).

'The evening is my book'

Written 20 November 1897, Berlin-Wilmersdorf.

> 7 *damask*: a rich, patterned fabric of cotton, silk, or linen, sometimes of
> wool, nowadays often used for table linen and curtains, or for furniture
> covers.

> *clasps*: large old books (especially Bibles) were often fastened with clasps
> made of brass or other metals.

*dream*: common motif in neo-romantic poetry, marking a farewell to ordinary life and an entry into the realm of the poetic imagination.

### 'I am so afraid of people's words'

Written 21 November 1897 (not 1898, as in *KA* I, 682), Berlin-Wilmersdorf.

*I am so afraid of people's words*: one of Rilke's most explicit statements of the phenomenon of 'language scepticism' that dominated turn-of-the-century German poetry. Here Rilke is distancing himself from the reductive explicitness of the day-to-day language of communication rather than voicing the further-reaching despair at the capacity of language to express the self in any reliable way that is so eloquently articulated (paradoxically) by Lord Chandos in Hugo von Hofmannsthal's paradigmatic text on this problem, 'Ein Brief' ('A Letter', 1902). Cf. Rilke's own essay on 'The Value of the Monologue' (*KA* IV, 121–4).

*and their gardens abut directly on God*: in the German there is an unusually dense pattern of alliteration on 'g'; Rilke remained fond of the device for the rest of his life, sometimes with unintentionally comic results.

*things sing*: an early intimation of Rilke's developing poetics of the 'Dinggedicht' (literally 'thing-poem') that will dominate the *New Poems*.

### 'Shall I name you a rising or a setting?'

Written 2 February 1898, Berlin.

*a rising or a setting*: the aestheticization of evening (and thus symbolically of death) here is an early stage in Rilke's ultimately much more complex ideas about the interdependence of the two realms of light and dark, life and death, but even here the opening line is formulated as a balanced question and eschews the more straightforward death-mysticism of many of Rilke's contemporaries.

### 'What is the furthest I shall reach'

Written 11 January 1898, Berlin-Wilmersdorf.

9 *I'll still be*: expressive of the ideal of a continuum of life that unites humanity (and the poet especially) with nature. It is the faltering and eventual loss of this sense of belonging that will drive Rilke's poetics for much of his life.

## From *THE BOOK OF HOURS*

Rilke's *Book of Hours* is made up of three distinct books, 'The Book of Monastic Life' (whose first version was written between 20 September and 14 October 1899 in Berlin and originally entitled 'The Prayers'), 'The Book of Poverty and Death' (written 18–25 September 1901 in Westerwede), and 'The Book of Pilgrimage' (13–20 April 1903, Viareggio). The whole text was revised in

Worpswede between 24 April and 16 May 1905 and published in December 1905 by Insel in Leipzig. It is dedicated to Lou Andreas-Salomé and was inspired in part by his two visits to Russia with her in 1899 and 1900. The dating of the poems in the notes that follow will identify the individual book in which each features.

### 'So arbitrarily we may not paint you'

Written 20 September 1899, Berlin-Schmargendorf.

9 *arbitrarily*: the art of the Russian icon-painter is to a large extent dictated by traditionally derived and codified rules, in contrast (Rilke suggests) to the more liberal western, predominantly Italian, tradition of individual artists' preferences in the depiction of the saints.

*we*: the voice is that of the monk-narrator of the collection, who is also an icon-painter. In Orthodoxy, the person who crafts an icon is said to 'write' it.

*dense walls*: this is an allusion to the iconostasis, a wall of icons and paintings that divides the nave from the chancel or choir in a church.

### 'We build you with our trembling hands'

Written 22 September 1899, Berlin-Schmargendorf.

*build you*: the motif of building is a common one in the collection, here in the German 'bauen *an*', 'to do building work on' rather than 'to complete the building', underlining the sense of a God that is becoming or being developed rather than pre-existing as an untouchable, infinite, and perfect being.

*trembling hands*: the poet-monk-painter's hands tremble in awe both at God and at the act of creation—the creation of him and of art—that he inspires.

### 'I find your trace in all these things, in all'

Written 24 September 1899, Berlin-Schmargendorf.

11 *your trace in all these things*: a clear expression of Rilke's determination to see God as immanent in the cycles of nature rather than transcendent.

### 'I cannot think that little figure Death'

Written 26 September 1899, Berlin-Schmargendorf.

*that little figure Death*: an unnecessarily threatening externalization of death, in contrast to the concept of 'one's own death' developed later in a poem from the third section of *The Book of Hours* (*KA* 1, 236) and in *Malte Laurids Brigge*. Cf. also 'For we are only rind of fruit, and leaf', l. 2 (p. 19).

*wandering monks*: anticipating the third book of the cycle.

13 *the yellow hand*: pointing to the way the physical body has a degree of
independence from consciousness, and again anticipating a key episode in
*Malte* (*KA* III, 518–21).

'*What will you do, God, when I die?*'

Written 26 September 1899, Berlin-Schmargendorf.

*you have no meaning once I'm dead*: sometimes described simply as blas-
phemous, Rilke's bold statements here are more complex than that; they
articulate in an extreme form one pole of the mutual relationship of man
and God, where the divine is seen as 'the oldest work of art' (from Rilke's
'Florence Diary').

'*Just as the watchman of the vineyard lands*'

Written on or around 1 May 1905, Worpswede (a revision of an earlier poem).

*watchman of the vineyard lands*: referring to the tradition of building
a watch-tower in a vineyard to protect the crop from thieves; cf. Isaiah 5:
1–2 'My wellbeloved hath a vineyard in a very fruitful hill: And he fenced
it, and gathered out the stones thereof, and planted it with the choicest
vine, and built a tower in the midst of it'—where the vineyard represents
Israel and its owner God—and Matthew 21: 33–46 (and parallels in the
Synoptic Gospels), where the crop is taken away from those who expect to
receive it.

'*I lived with the ancient monks*'

Written 4 October 1899, Berlin-Schmargendorf.

15 *narrate you*: the poet-monk-painter tells of a God who is rooted both in
history and the earth.

'*Put out my eyes: I see you still the same*'

Dating uncertain: 18 September 1901 according to the editor of *Sämtliche Werke*;
as early as summer 1897 according to Lou Andreas-Salomé, but unlikely to have
been written earlier than summer or autumn 1899 according to *KA* I, 768.

*Put out my eyes: I see you still the same*: the beginning of an intense
series of contradictory or paradoxical contentions to demonstrate the
strength of the bond with God (or, in this case, perhaps Lou herself rather
than God). The tradition of such paradoxes goes back at least as far as
François Villon's 'Je meurs de soif auprès de la fontaine' ('I am dying of
thirst by the fountain'), a Ballad of Contradictions from the mid-
15th century.

'*You are the future, sovereign morning red*'

Written 20 September 1901, Westerwede.

17 *word silent in your ban*: cf. note to 'I am so afraid of people's words'
(p. 275).

*'The emperors of earth are old'*

Written 20 September 1901, Westerwede.

17 *coin and wheel*: cf. *Sonnets* 2. XIX, another critique of the technological anonymizing of the world.

*'The barberries already ripen red'*

Written 22 September 1901, Westerwede.

19 *barberries*: evergreen shrub related to the Mahonia, with small red berries either round or bar-shaped, with a slightly sour taste; used particularly in Persian cuisine.

*He who is not yet rich*: cf. 'Autumn Day', l. 8 (p. 33).

*'For we are only rind of fruit, and leaf'*

Written 16 April 1903, Viareggio.

*trees from lutes*: cf. *Sonnets*, 1. 1, l. 2 (p. 183).

21 *found it green*: such that it can still ripen and grow and become the 'great death' of line 2, which will be the fulfilment of life.

*'Lord, we are poorer than the poor beasts'*

Written 16 April 1903, Viareggio.

*poor beasts*: cf. *DE* VIII (p. 165).

*less than entirely died*: an incomplete death is an indication of an incomplete life.

*the One*: a combination of Christ and an ideal artist-figure.

*'For see, they will live, flourish, multiply'*

Written 19 April 1903, Viareggio.

23 *they are blessed*: a clear echo of the Beatitudes in the Sermon on the Mount (Matthew 5: 3–12).

*rested hands ... weary*: echoes perhaps of Hugo von Hofmannsthal's poem 'Manche freilich' ('Many it is true'), which contains images of unburdened hands and the tiredness of peoples.

*'But bear them away again from urban evils'*

Written 19 April 1903, Viareggio.

*Has the earth no place for them?*: a reference to urban development encroaching upon the 'real' earth.

*'Cities turn their force full on their own'*

Written 19 April 1903, Viareggio.

*and*: the sequence of eleven lines beginning 'und' in German, with six consecutive such lines in the second stanza, is strongly reminiscent of another poem by Hofmannsthal, 'Ballade des äußeren Lebens' ('Ballad of the Outer Life', 1894), which shares a similar theme, albeit couched in much less trenchant terms.

25 *transient*: the key defect of urban life, in contrast to the permanent and lasting, which are concepts developed subtly for the rest of Rilke's life.

## From THE BOOK OF IMAGES

*The Book of Images*—which could just as appropriately be translated as *The Book of Pictures*—was first published in July 1902 by Axel Juncker in Berlin, with an ink drawing of a fountain surrounded by trees and foliage by Heinrich Vogeler on the title page. It was dedicated to the dramatist Gerhard Hauptmann 'in love and gratitude for *Michael Kramer*' (a play in the Naturalist style about a painter, first performed in December 1900). A second, considerably extended, edition was published in December 1906.

The poems in the first edition were written between 29 September 1898 and 7 November 1901, chiefly in Berlin, with two particularly intensive periods of work in July 1899 and the last third of 1900. Those added in the second were written between 11 September 1902 and 12 June 1906, mainly in Paris. Only a few of the original poems were omitted in the second edition.

### Entrance

Written 24 February 1900, Berlin-Schmargendorf (a diary note of Rilke's specifies 'Dahlemer Straße').

*free their gaze*: cf. 'The Panther' from *New Poems* (pp. 63–5).

*will comes to grasp*: the comprehension of the world is equated with the construction of the world via visual perception and in a characteristically paradoxical Rilkean pairing, full comprehension of the mutability of the world is only completed as 'grasping' is followed by 'releasing'.

### The Saint

Written 1 November 1902, Paris.

*Saint*: the saint in question is usually supposed to be St Geneviève, patron saint of Paris (*c.*422–*c.*500) who saved the city from the invasion of Attila the Hun in 451 by encouraging the inhabitants to fast and pray. Rilke knew a series of paintings by Puvis de Chavannes in the Panthéon that depicts scenes from her life (cf. letter to Clara of 31 August 1902).

27 *the young willow twisted in her hands*: since the 15th century, a divining or dowsing rod, in the form of a Y-shaped willow branch, has been used to try to locate underground water supplies.

### From a Childhood

Written 21 March 1900, Berlin-Schmargendorf.

*Childhood*: a key theme in Rilke's works; cf. *DE* IV (p. 149).

*The Boy*

Written winter 1902–3, Paris. Motivically linked to the depiction of the hero in *DE* VI.

  29  *trumpet*: when giving readings from his poetry, Rilke sometimes explained that these images refer to a fire-engine.

*People at Night*

Written 25 November 1899, Berlin-Schmargendorf.

   *Nights*: the contrast of the distortive light and the protective dark echoes *The Book of Hours*.

*The Neighbour*

Written 1902 or 1903, Paris.

  31  *neighbour*: Rilke's mistrust of neighbours because of the threat they posed to his creative self-sufficiency recurs in *Malte Laurids Brigge* (*KA* III, 572–85) and in letters to Lou Andreas-Salomé (e.g. 18 July 1903).

*Pont du Carrousel*

Written 1902–3, Paris.

   *Pont du Carrousel*: bridge over the Seine in Paris.

   *blind man*: blindness is a motif repeated several times in Rilke's work from *The Book of Hours* to *Malte* and *DE* V, l. 56 (p. 153). Cf. letter to Lou Andreas-Salomé recalling how 'the blind man on the Pont du Carrousel about whose survival I was worried as long ago as the winter of 1902 was still standing in his place, grey and wet' in 1920 (31 December). The 'object'-like nature of the figure here marks the poem as a precursor of the 'thing-poems' of the *New Poems*.

   *just man*: an expression frequently used in the Bible, but also the subject of Plato's *The Republic*.

*Solitude*

Written 21 September 1902, Paris.

  33  *lifts . . . falls*: the complementary movements of rising and falling form a key Rilkean 'figure' analagous to the complementarity of life and death. Cf. the end of *DE* X (p. 181 and note). The rain simile suggests a positive understanding of solitude, rather than a melancholy one, which is often associated with autumn (cf. the following poem).

*Autumn Day*

Written 21 September 1902, Paris.

   *Whoever has no home*: this phrase is often linked with a similar phrase from Friedrich Nietzsche's poem 'Die Krähen schrei'n' ('The Crows are Cawing'): 'Soon it will snow, | Woe to him who has no home.' For a similar formulation, cf. 'The barberries already ripen red', l. 3 (p. 19).

*Evening*

Perhaps written autumn 1904, Sweden.

35 *falls . . . rises*: cf. note to 'Solitude' (p. 280).

*The Three Kings*

Written 23 July 1899, Berlin-Schmargendorf.

> *Three Kings*: also known as the Magi or Three Wise Men, three important figures 'from the East' who (according to St Matthew's Gospel, 2: 1–2) visit Christ shortly after his birth and bring gifts of gold, frankincense, and myrrh. The Bible neither names nor numbers them.

> *a Rex to left, a Rex to right*: the original is also deliberately humorous, so as to demystify a familiar story, render it almost child-like, and bring its significance for ordinary humanity closer.

> 37 *round silver thing*: a thurible or censer, hung from chains, in which incense is burned.

> *azure heaven*: blue is traditionally a royal colour and that of Mary's over-garment in much Christian art—she is the earth, overshadowed by the blue of heaven; many churches have their sanctuary ceilings painted blue.

*The Leper's Song*

Written 1905–6, Paris. The last (although first to be written) in a sequence of nine poems entitled 'Die Stimmen' ('The Voices') completed bewteen 7 and 12 June 1906.

> 39 *one of those the world has abandoned*: outsiders, the sick, and the unwanted form the subject of a number of Rilke's poems from *The Book of Hours* to *New Poems*, and of sections of *Malte*. The world may have abandoned them, but they thereby achieve a form of liberation from that world, which Rilke sees in contrast as increasingly devoid of true poetic significance.

> *leprosy*: a bacterial disease badly affecting the skin and traditionally believed to be highly contagious.

> *rattle*: in the Middle Ages, lepers were made to carry loud rattles when outside their colonies to warn people to stay away from them.

*About Fountains*

Written 14 November 1900, Berlin-Schmargendorf.

> *have knowledge of*: the sudden insight into how an external object reveals truths about the inner workings of the poet himself (cf. l. 16), and thus a precursor of the *New Poems*.

> *trees of glass*: cf. *DE* VI, l. 5 (p. 157), in which the down- and upwards-twisting branches of the fig-tree are likened to the pipes of a fountain, again combining organic and man-made images.

39  *Did I forget*: the motifs of forgetting and the difficulty of remembering that run through the poem are indicative of an aesthetic crisis as Rilke strives to recreate intuitions that were once natural and unforced.

*steep paths*: the German 'Aufstieg' here makes clear the link with the upwardly striving movement of the water in the fountain and the 'rising' of song in the throats of girls in the next two lines.

41  *tumbled-over weight of falling*: the rise and fall of the fountain fascinated Rilke, who once gave the grandson of Princess Marie von Thurn und Taxis a little old-fashioned fountain in which water was circulated thus: 'For Rilke it was something quite magical.'

*End Piece*

Written 1900–1.

43  *End . . . Mid-life*: the title has a dual meaning, announcing the end of *The Book of Images*, but also in ironic tension with the image of the presence of death not at the *end* of our lives but mid-way through.

## UNCOLLECTED POEMS 1906–1908

*'Musing upon legend after legend'*

Written spring 1906.

*you of the bright beauty*: the poem was composed in memory of Baroness Luise Schwerin, who died on 24 January that year. Rilke had met her in Dresden a year before and stayed with her in Schloß Friedelhausen on the River Lahn for some six weeks in the late summer of 1905.

*accumulate you*: the German here is a compound of the word 'sparen', 'to save' or 'put by', suggesting an action of gathering or subsuming the essence of another person or thing, which in this and other compounds expresses a concept important to Rilke throughout his creative life. Cf. *DE* v, l. 103 (p. 157), *DE* vii, l. 58 (p. 163), and (in the form of its opposite), *Sonnet* 2. iv, l. 7 (p. 215).

*Marriage*

Written spring 1906, Meudon.

45  *endowment*: in English underlining the theme of the controlling of male sexuality; in German, 'der Stifter' refers also to the donor or sponsor of a work of art in medieval or Renaissance times, who will usually have been portrayed in the work itself, often kneeling in prayer. Rilke devotes one of the *New Poems* to this figure (*KA* i, 471–2).

*Leaving*

Written June 1906, Paris. One of six poems written for Madeleine de Broglie (1866–1929).

*Grand Canal*: the major waterway through Venice.

*fire*: a major fire in January 1514 that almost totally destroyed the Rialto area.

*ceases to be*: cf. the last line of 'The Panther' (p. 65).

## La Dame à la Licorne

Written 9 June 1906, Paris.

47 *Tapestries in the Hôtel de Cluny*: 'The Lady with the Unicorn' is a series of six tapestries woven in Flanders in the late 15th century. Five are now thought to represent the five senses, and the sixth, 'A mon seul désir', depicts a woman putting a necklace into a box, which is usually interpreted as the renunciation of worldly pleasures.

*Stina Frisell*: the wife of Erik Frisell, a prominent Swedish industrialist, and a cousin of a friend of Rilke's, Lizzie Gibson. She visited Paris with her daughter in June 1906, and Rilke dedicated this poem to her in commemoration of a visit they had recently paid together to the tapestries. He described her to Clara as a 'dear, simple, loyal person' (14 June 1906).

## Marionette Theatre

Written 20 July 1907, Paris. Originally intended for *New Poems*, but removed shortly before their publication.

*Furnes. Kermes*: Rilke visited the town of Furnes (Veurn) as part of a trip to Belgium in the first two weeks of August 1906. He was there at the time of its annual fair (called Kermes). Cf. Rilke's essay on Furnes (*KA* IV, 639–46).

*Behind bars, like animals*: cf. 'The Panther' and Rilke's prose poem 'The Lion Cage' (*KA* I, 392–3).

*they*: the puppets. Cf. *DE* IV (p. 147).

## The Goldsmith

Lines 1–11 written 5 August 1907, Paris; completed late autumn 1925, Muzot.

51 *Goldsmith*: the poem implies a comparison of the work of the goldsmith with that of the poet, allied (above all by the emphasis on 'things') with the *New Poems*.

*All of a sudden*: the final lines enact a characterisic Rilkean 'turning', albeit one in which the poet's *lack* of control over his material is emphasized, which is more characteristic of Rilke's latest works.

## 'In the instrument how they darken and rustle'

Written 10 November 1911, Baden near Vienna. Inscribed in the guest-book of Baroness Gisela von Heß–Diller, whom Rilke visited that day.

## Requiem for a Friend (extract)

Written 31 October to 2 November 1908, Paris, in memory of the painter Paula Modersohn-Becker, who had died on 20 November 1907 in childbirth.

Rilke had met her in 1900 together with his future wife, Clara Westhoff. The whole poem is 271 lines long. The theme of the irreconcilability of motherhood and the calling of the artist is met elsewhere in Rilke's work (such as the *Florence Diary*, in which he states baldly, 'A woman who is an artist no longer has to be creative when she becomes a mother. She has given her aim from within her and may from then on live art in the deepest sense').

53 *mourning women*: the custom of hiring women to mourn loudly at a funeral was widespread in ancient Greece, Rome, and Egypt.

55 *right of possession*: a reference to Rilke's conception of the higher status of unrequited love; cf. *DE* I and *DE* II and notes (pp. 133, 137–9 and 305–6).

*Nike*: winged Greek goddess of victory. The statue known as the Nike of Samothrace (*c.* 190 BCE), in the Louvre, stands on the prow of a ship.

*the woman who no longer sees us*: a reference to Eurydice emerging from the underworld.

## From *NEW POEMS* and *NEW POEMS, SECOND PART*

The *New Poems* were first published by Insel in Leipzig in December 1907. The earliest of them ('The Panther') may have been written as early as November 1902, and their composition then stretched from 1903 until 25 July 1907. The second volume, literally entitled 'The Other Part of the New Poems', was written more quickly, between 31 July 1907 and 2 August 1908, and published in early November 1908. Most of the 189 poems in both parts were written in Paris, although a few were completed during a stay on Capri early in 1907.

The *New Poems* were dedicated to Rilke's friends the banker, writer, and art collector Karl von der Heydt (1858–1922) and his wife Elisabeth (1864–1963), who had met Rilke in 1905. They supported Rilke financially from time to time and Karl wrote a highly positive review of *The Book of Hours* in the influential *Prussian Yearbooks* that contributed significantly to its very positive reception.

The *New Poems, Second Part* were dedicated to the sculptor Auguste Rodin (1840–1917), about whom Rilke had written a monograph towards the end of 1902, and who had employed Rilke as his secretary for some nine months in 1905–6.

*Early Apollo* (MS)

Written 11 July 1906, Paris.

57 *Apollo*: Greek and Roman god of light, the sun, oracles and prophecy, healing, archery, and—most importantly in the context of Rilke's poetry—poetry, music, and the arts. The inspiration for the poem is variously thought to be an Athenian head of a youth, *c.* 530 BCE, or a statue of Apollo or Couros (beardless youth) from Patros, both of which are in the Louvre in Paris.

*fatal*: cf. *DE* I, ll. 4–5 (p. 131).

*rose-gardens*: bearing in mind Rilke's frequent and powerful use of the image of the rose, the rose-garden may stand for the place where art and life may fully unfold.

*eyebrow*: the origins of culture lie between the god's forehead (thought) and his eyes (seeing).

*smile*: cf. note on *DE* V (p. 309).

## Love Song (SR)

Written mid-March 1907, Capri.

*other things*: note the paradox of a love song seeking to move beyond an erotic connection to the beloved to permit a concentration on 'things'. In contrast to the poem that precedes this in the volume, 'Girl's Complaint', this is a reflection on adult love.

*musician*: many editions of Rilke have 'Geiger' ('violinist', 'fiddler'), but 'Spieler' ('player') is now thought to be the correct version.

## The Garden of Olives (MS)

Written May or June 1906, Paris.

59 *Garden of Olives*: Gethsemane, according to the four Gospels, the place where Christ and his disciples prayed the night before the crucifixion. Rilke may be responding to El Greco's *Christ on the Mount of Olives* or *Christ in the Desert* by Ivan Kramskoi (on whom he had received a book from Sophia Schill in February 1900).

*angel*: only St Luke's Gospel recounts the appearance of an angel (22: 39–46).

## L'Ange du Méridien (MS)

Written May or June 1906, Paris.

61 *L'Ange du Méridien*: the title is one of only four in French in the two volumes of *New Poems*. The word 'méridien' is an archaic term for sundial.

*Chartres*: the subject of the poem is the Angel with the Sundial on the south side of Chartres Cathedral. This is the first of a group of six poems about Chartres. Rilke visited Chartres with Rodin and his wife on 25 January 1906 and wrote to Clara of 'the deep smile of [the angel's] cheerfully servient face, like heaven reflected', and of the chill winds that struck them when they turned the corner on which the angel is situated (letter of 26 January 1906). The same visit is recalled in a poem from the French collection *Vergers* in 1924 (*KA* V, 30).

*sceptic*: the German word 'Verneiner' almost inevitably recalls the self-description of Goethe's Mephistopheles in *Faust*, 'Ich bin der Geist, der stets verneint' ('I am the spirit of perpetual negation', trans. David Luke).

*mouths*: the Greek 'angelos', from which both German and English words for angel are derived, means 'messenger', and Rilke's stress here is on the mediating function of the figure.

*The Rose Window* (MS)

Written shortly before 8 July 1906, Paris.

The fourth of the Chartres poems. There are three rose windows in the Cathedral; that on the west front has as its theme the Day of Judgement.

 61 *Inside*: suggesting that the cat in the first part of the poem is in a cage (like the panther, cf. p. 63). The succession of columns in the nave of the cathedral may suggest bars.

*God in the Middle Ages* (SR)

Written between 19 and 23 July 1907, Paris.

The last of the Chartres poems, linked to the first by the theme of time, but the only one that does not have an object or a building as its theme.

 63 *weights*: an image for the weights of a long-case clock driving the pendulum and the striking mechanism, before being transferred to the massiveness of the Gothic Cathedral. Contrast l. 10 of 'L'Ange du Méridien' which refers to 'Gleichgewicht' ('balance'), in which the word for weight ('Gewicht') is contained.

 *let Him pass*: the verbs show the shift between the people's original conception of God—wanting him to act as a measurer and regulator for their existences, rather than content for him merely to *be*—and their terror when his true nature is revealed as not circumscribed by their expectations. The shift marks that between the pre-modern (not necessarily synonymous with 'medieval') and the modern, as the reference to cities in l. 11 indicates.

*The Panther* (SR)

Perhaps written 5–6 November 1902, or in 1903.

Described as 'the first result of my strict, good schooling [at Rodin's hands]' (letter of 17 March 1926 to 'a young friend').

 *Jardin des Plantes*: the Botanical Garden, with a menagerie created in 1793. Rodin also possessed a plaster cast of an ancient carving of a tiger, of which Rilke wrote that he found 'the expression of slinking steps intensified to the highest extent', admiring also 'the circumspection in which all its power is wrapped, this soundlessness' (to Clara, 27 September 1902).

 65 *the curtain in his eye lifts inaudibly*: this is somewhat reminiscent of the action of a camera shutter being opened to let light in. Rilke's panther 'receives images' without 'seeing' any more than a mechanical photographic equipment can 'see'. Rilke's French translator Maurice Betz reports a conversation in which Rilke admired the way in

which cats vanish suddenly 'as if we were only present in their imagination, a shadow that their pupil has not even registered' (quoted in *KA* I, 977).

## The Gazelle (SR)

Written 17 July 1907, Paris.

*Gazella dorcas*: the Latin name for the small species of gazelle known as Dorcas (a word of Greek origin, also meaning 'gazelle') or Ariel gazelle. The inclusion of the Latin name perhaps evokes the animal's situation in the menagerie, where the cages would have been labelled like this. Rilke wrote to Clara of seeing three gazelles in the Jardin des Plantes, a few feet apart from each other: 'just as women look out of pictures, so they seem to be looking out of something with a soundless twist of finality. And when a horse neighed, one of them pricked up her ears and I could see the radiance around her delicate head from the ears and horns' (13 June 1907).

*songs of love*: in chapters 2 to 5 of the Song of Solomon the beloved is frequently compared to a gazelle.

*spring-loaded in the gun*: the word 'Lauf' means both the leg of an animal and the barrel of a gun, so Rilke's metaphor works on two levels simultaneously.

*woodland bather*: suggestive of the myth of Artemis (or Diana) and Actaeon, who in Ovid's *Metamorphoses*, Book III, surprises the goddess bathing and is turned into a stag before being killed by his own hounds. Possibly also inspired by Rembrandt's *Susanna Bathing* (c.1636).

*face*: note the sudden transposition of an image of hearing into one of seeing.

## The Unicorn (SR)

Written winter 1905–6, Meudon.

*Unicorn*: cf. 'La Dame à la Licorne' (p. 47), and *Sonnet* 2. IV (p. 215), and notes. This poem, too, is based on the tapestries *La Dame à la licorne* in the Musée de Cluny.

67 *into space*: the motif of seeing that links this with the two previous 'animal poems' is extended here as the unicorn creates poetic images that exist within a world of their own beyond that of observable reality, and thus anticipates the aesthetic of the *Sonnets*.

*blue*: in each of the six tapestries the unicorn is enclosed within a blue oval.

*saga-cycle*: cf. *Sonnet*, I. XX.

## The Swan (MS)

Written winter 1905–6, Meudon.

*Swan*: this poem has often been compared thematically to Charles Baudelaire's 'L'Albatros' as well as 'Le Cygne'.

67 *things not yet done*: in a general sense, the 'things of life' that remain to be accomplished, but more specifically also the work of the poet that has yet to come. A letter-poem to Rilke's future wife Clara contains the same idea in relation to a swan swimming on dark water ('And it promised us much that has not yet been done', *SW* III, 711).

*The Poet* (SR)

Written winter 1905–6, Meudon.

*the hour*: the moment of inspiration ('kairos' in Greek, as opposed to 'chronos', which denotes measurable, sequential time).

69 *nowhere that is my home ground*: perhaps an echo of Rilke's period of creative crisis in Rome in 1904, when he wrote to Ellen Key, 'Oh, that I have no parental home in the country, nowhere in the world a room with a few old things and a winter' (9 May 1904).

*Blue Hydrangea* (SR)

Written mid-July 1906, Paris.

*green paint left in a jar*: the flower of the poem hardly exists in a botanic sense, with texture and scent; the view of it is overwhelmingly painterly and visual.

*whose blue is not their own*: the hydrangea is a plant whose colour is determined by the mineral content of the ground in which it grows (blue flowers when the soil is acid).

*Then with a start*: the experience of transience that the withered plant had encapsulated suddenly gives way to one of renewal as fresh growth is perceived.

*within one umbel*: Rilke wrote to Clara of the hydrangea that he had in Paris that it had survived the winter and 'has many budding umbels at the bottom of its uppermost leaves' (7 June 1907). The hydrangea has flowers in clusters (or umbels) that resemble the head of a mop.

*The Courtesan* (MS)

Written mid-March 1907, Capri.

*Venice*: this poem is related to a series in the Second Part of the *New Poems* that are set in or related to Venice (beginning with 'Venetian Morning'). The comparison of the city with a courtesan rests on a popular early twentieth-century view of the city as a symbol of decadence, over-refinement, and corruption and is reflected in the sexualized nature of the imagery at some points. Cf. also 'Leaving' (p. 45).

71 *as if by poison*: identifying the courtesan/Venice as a typical fin-de-siècle 'femme fatale'.

*The Orangery Steps* (MS)

Written mid-July 1906, Paris.

> *Versailles*: Rilke visited Versailles with Rodin on 17 September 1905. The orangery is under the south terrace of the palace and the steps lead up to it.

> *towards no place*: this is not literally true of the steps in Versailles but emphasizes Rilke's technique of isolating a detail and considering it for its own sake, specifically divorced from any possible function. Rilke wrote to Lou Andreas-Salomé about seeing a flight of steps leading nowhere because the building to which they had been attached had burned down, and there is a famous passage in *Malte Laurids Brigge* on the same image (*KA* III, 552–6).

*Roman Fountain* (MS)

Written 8 July 1906, Paris.

> *Borghese*: the gardens of the Villa Borghese in Rome. Rilke resided in Rome from September 1903 and from November until June 1904 lived in a garden studio in the Villa Strohl-Fern adjacent to the Villa Borghese. The identity of the specific fountain has been debated.

> 73 *dish*: in the German, the word for dish, 'Schale', occurs at the end of the line but has no matching rhyme-word, and is thus 'orphaned'—a rare feature in Rilke's sonnets, and one which may deliberately underpin the sense of self-sufficiency that the line conveys.

*The Merry-go-round* (MS)

Written June 1906, Paris.

> *Jardin du Luxembourg*: a large park in Paris behind the Luxembourg Palace, now the home of the French Senate. There is still a children's playground in the garden.

> 75 *a circle spun that has no aim*: the central imagery of the circularity of existence, punctuated by the evocative and incongruous 'white elephant', has been interpreted as symbolic either of the meaningless transience of existence or, more positively, of the childlike experience of existential directionlessness and thus of purity. The smile (l. 25), however, is frequently an image of acceptance in Rilke's work, so the more positive reading is more convincing.

*Spanish Dancer* (MS)

Written June 1906, Paris.

> *Spanish Dancer*: shortly before this poem was written, Rilke had seen a Spanish gypsy dancer at a baptismal celebration for the son of a friend, the Spanish painter Ignacio Zuloaga y Zabaleta (1870–1945). She has been identified by Jaime Ferreiro Alemparte (*España en Rilke*, 1966, p. 34) as

one 'Carmela', and her accompanist then was the Catalan pianist and composer Isaac Albéniz (1860–1909). In Rilke's account of this occasion to Clara (26 April 1906), he mentions 'die eng von Zuschauern umstandene Tänzerin Goyas' ('Goya's dancer surrounded by a press of spectators') as being even more 'atmospheric'. *KA* I, 949 and Stahl, *Kommentar*, p. 206, both suggest that he is referring here to a painting by Goya entitled *La ballerina* [sic] *Carmen la gitana* (*Carmen, the Gypsy Dancer*), but there is no painting by Goya with this or a similar title and none that might plausibly be described by Rilke's phrase. Attempts (following Alemparte) to demonstrate that Rilke must be referring instead to a specific work by Zuloaga have proved unconvincing, although Zuloaga did paint a number of gypsy dancers in the late 1890s and early 1900s that Rilke may have seen exhibited in Paris or displayed in the painter's studio; Zuloaga's portraits of Lucienne Bréval as Bizet's Carmen post-date the poem and the letter.

*Orpheus. Eurydice. Hermes* (SR)

Written early 1904, Rome (1st version); autumn 1904, Furuborg, Sweden (final version).

77 *Orpheus. Eurydice. Hermes*: the poem was inspired by an Attic bas-relief of *c*.400 BCE, attributed to Callimachus, unusually depicting Hermes along-side Orpheus and Eurydice (of which Roman copies exist in the Villa Albani in Rome, the Louvre in Paris, and the National Archaeological Museum in Naples; Rilke certainly saw the Naples copy several times). The simple enumeration of the names, with full stops between them, evokes the peaceful, static quality of the figures on the relief. For the Orpheus myth, cf. the notes to the *Sonnets to Orpheus*, esp. p. 317. Hermes was the messenger of the gods in Greek mythology and, as Hermes Psychopompos, guided souls to the underworld.

*porphyry*: brownish-purple, or red, igneous rock, used for columns and monuments because of the association of the colour purple with imperial power.

*blind . . . lake*: possibly Lake Avernus, a volcanic crater lake near Cumae in southern Italy, said by the Romans to be the entrance to the underworld (Virgil's Aeneas descends to Hades through a cave nearby). The grotto of the Cumaean Sibyl is on the shore, and there is a view of Capri from the lake.

*The slender man*: Orpheus; cf. *Sonnets*, I. III, l. 2 (p. 185).

79 *the god of despatch*: Hermes, whose traditional attributes include the caduceus (a short staff or wand with two entwined serpents) given to him by Apollo in exchange for the lyre, a winged hat, and winged sandals (cf. ll. 43–5).

*a world . . . made of mourning . . . reappeared*: cf. *DE* x for the figure of the 'Klage' or 'Lament'. Losing the beloved and turning away from desire are the preconditions of lament, and therefore poetry (as symbolized by the lyre in l. 47).

*Archaic Torso of Apollo* (MS)

Written early summer 1908, Paris.

81 *Apollo*: both parts of the *New Poems* open with a sonnet on the Apollo figure inspired by a classical statue, in this case the torso of a youth from the 6th century BCE in the Louvre. Rilke wrote to Clara about Rodin's torsos, which were deliberately created as fragments of bodies, rather than accidentally broken over time as the classical statues had been: 'it would all be less whole if the individual bodies had been whole. Each of these chunks has an eminently poignant unity and is only possible like that, so that it has no need of completion' (2 September 1902).

*Unheard*: the German means both 'unheard of' in the sense of something astonishing and 'unheard' in the sense of a command or request that goes unfulfilled.

83 *screwed back*: the image is of an old-fashioned branched gas-lamp that could be turned up or down using a screw knob.

*smile*: Rilke interprets the curved lines made by the marble representations of the folds of skin between a man's legs and groin as forming a smile.

*pelt*: an animal skin, perhaps alluding to the tiger-skin worn by Dionysus, who is thus subsumed by Apollo.

*You must change your life*: cf. letter to Thankmar von Münchhausen, in which Rilke asks 'what is our purpose [as poets] if not to provide occasions for change, pure and great and free?' (28 June 1915).

*Leda* (MS)

Written autumn 1907, Paris, or spring 1908, Capri.

*Leda*: in Greek mythology the king of the gods, Zeus, took the form of a swan and raped Leda, wife of King Tyndareus of Sparta, after she had slept with her husband. The unions produced Helen (later of Troy) and Clytemnestra, and the Dioscuri Castor and Pollux (or Polydeuces). Rilke's poem is thought to have been inspired by Correggio's *Leda and the Swan* (*c.*1531–2), which he may have seen in the Kaiser Friedrich Museum in Berlin.

*The Island of Sirens* (MS)

Written between 22 August and 5 September 1907, Paris.

85 *Sirens*: the Sirens were women with human heads and faces but birds' bodies, claws, and wings, in Ovid (*Metamorphoses* V.551) the companions of Persephone who were given wings so that they could search for her over the sea as well as on land after she had been taken down to Hades by Dis. In Book XII of Homer's *Odyssey* they sing to entice the sailors to leap into the sea as they pass the Island of the Sirens, but Odysseus has instructed his men to stop their ears with wax and lash him to the mast to prevent this: the 'he' of this poem is Odysseus. Rilke is alluding here to another tradition, according to which the Sirens threw themselves into the sea and were turned into rocky islands after failing to seduce the Argonauts

(because their song was surpassed by that of Orpheus, who was sailing with Jason). Rilke wrote to Clara from Capri of seeing 'the three islands of the Sirens (strange cliffs, obstructing the passage, that looked as if they had once been gilded), past which [Odysseus] came, bound to his mast and only because of that constraint secure from the invincible force, dissolved in the gentle breeze, sonorous' (18 February 1907).

85  *ringed round . . . by tranquil stillness*: Rilke sees not only the sirens' song but its opposite or 'obverse side' (l. 19), total silence, as the power that cannot be resisted.

*A Prophet* (SR)

Written shortly before 17 August 1907, Paris.

*Prophet*: the artistic inspiration for this poem and the next were perhaps Michelangelo's prophets and sibyls in the Sistine Chapel in the Vatican. This prophet is probably Ezekiel, to whom the Lord appears on a chariot of cherubim and consecrates him a prophet to deliver dreadful tidings, dirges, and intimations of the doom of nations, which mission he obediently fulfils.

87  *dog-like*: a letter to Clara Rilke describes Cézanne sitting in the garden 'like an old dog, the dog of his work that calls to him again, and beats him and lets him starve', making his 'saints' out of such things, 'forcing them to be beautiful' (9 October 1907; *KA* IV, 611), which suggests a parallel between the situation of the prophet and the work of the poet (cf. also the Introduction, p. xxii). Hugo von Hofmannsthal also refers to the poet in his lecture 'Der Dichter und diese Zeit' (published in March 1907) as a beggar in his own house, banished beneath the steps with the dogs to look and listen.

*A Sibyl* (SR)

Written between 22 August and 5 September 1907, Paris.

*Sibyl*: sibyls were prophetesses in the ancient world, between nine and twelve in number, usually associated with a particular place (such as the precinct of Apollo at Delphi).

*counted her . . . by centuries*: the Cumaean Sibyl (cf. above, p. 290) was said to be hundreds of years old (cf. the narrative of her encounter with Aeneas in Ovid, *Metamorphoses*, XIV.101–53).

*The Beggars* (MS)

Written early summer 1908, Paris.

89  *muck*: the harshness of this poem and its uncompromising portrayal of unpleasant physical detail perhaps owes something to Baudelaire's 'Une charogne' ('A Carcass'), which Rilke knew well.

*and spew up*: cf. l. 7 of 'Und deine Armen leiden' ('And these your poor suffer') from *The Book of Hours*: 'und wie in Sonne Faulendes bespien' ('spat on like putrefaction under the sun').

*Corpse-washing* (MS)

Written summer 1908 (before 15 July), Paris.

> *quite unknown*: The light of revelation that is the kitchen lamp reveals unfamiliarity rather than familiarity, which perhaps accounts for 'restlessly' (l. 3).

> *sponge of vinegar*: According to three of the four Gospels (Matthew 27: 48; Mark 15: 36, and John 19: 29), Christ was given a sponge soaked in vinegar to drink from whilst on the cross, echoed in 'nothing more to drink' (l. 13). Cézanne painted *Préparation pour l'enterrement* (*Preparation for Burial*, otherwise known as *The Autopsy*) in 1868, which depicts a man and a woman washing a naked corpse rather than two women, as here, but the body is sometimes thought to be reminiscent of Christ, who was prepared for burial in the tomb by the female disciples (cf. Mark 16: 1).

91 *The night . . . ignored them*: cf. 'The Garden of Olives', ll. 16–17 (p. 59): 'It was the night that came, | leafing indifferently through the trees.'

> *made the laws*: cf. the end of 'Archaic Torso of Apollo' where an existential imperative also derives from a 'body' that can neither see nor speak.

*The Blind Man* (MS)

Written 21 August 1907, Paris.

> *Blind Man*: there is an echo in this poem of Baudelaire's 'Les Aveugles' ('The Blind'), from *Les Fleurs du mal* (*The Flowers of Evil*), which begins 'Contemple-les' ('Watch them') and is also set in the city. Both poems contrast an inability to see the outside world with the growth, or possibility, of inner richness.

> *dark crack . . . cup*: cf. *DE* VIII, ll. 63–4 (p. 169).

*Snake-charming* (MS)

Written autumn 1907, Paris, or spring 1908, Capri.

> *snake-charmer*: referring to the street entertainment popular in the Indian sub-continent and North Africa, in which a performer with a musical instrument appears to charm or hypnotize a poisonous snake from within a basket.

> *rigid*: by this point the sexual connotations of the snake's movement in the poem will be unmistakable.

93 *death*: lines 1–13 form a single sinuous sentence, prolonged by eight relative clauses, echoing the form and movement of the snakes. In French 'la petite mort' ('little death') is a euphemism for orgasm, an interpretative dimension here that is reinforced by the sensations described in the next lines.

> *venom*: the poisonous seductiveness of the East (as represented by 'Indian', l. 12).

*Black Cat* (MS)

Written summer 1908 (before 2 August), Paris.

93  *Black Cat*: this poem, too, has a possible link with Baudelaire's *Les Fleurs du mal*, which contains three poems about cats, albeit somewhat more domesticated ones than Rilke's here. Leisi, *Rilkes 'Sonette an Orpheus'*, 207, claims that the word 'cat' only appears twice in the entirety of Rilke's lyric writing, whereas there are many references to dogs (cf. below, 'The Dog').

   *yellow*: the German 'geel' here is an old form of 'gelb'.

   *amber*: golden-yellow-coloured fossilized tree resin used in jewellery; often containing insects or parts of plants.

*Song of the Sea* (MS)

Written before 26 January 1907, Capri (the earliest poem to be included in the *Second Part* of the *New Poems*). Under the title 'Nacht an der piccola marina' ('Night on the piccola marina'), inscribed in the guest-book of the Villa Discopoli where Rilke stayed between December 1906 and May 1907 as the guest of Alice Faehndrich. Elements of the poem prefigure *Sonnets*, I. III.

95  *Piccola Marina*: a small beach in a bay on the island of Capri.

   *withstand you*: cf. *DE* VII, l. 58 (p. 163) and *Sonnets*, I. V, l. 7 (p. 187) and 2. XIII, l. 4 (p. 225).

   *a fig-tree feels driven*: cf. *DE* VI, l. 1 and note (pp. 157 and 310).

   *up there*: despite the unusual layout of this poem, the final rhymes confirm it as a sonnet.

*Venetian Morning* (SR)

Written early summer 1908, Paris. Another sonnet in an unusual form, with the tercets placed between the quatrains instead of after them, echoing the mirroring theme of the poem.

   *Richard Beer-Hofmann*: (1866–1945); Austrian novelist, dramatist, and poet. Rilke admired his novella *Der Tod Georgs* (*The Death of Georg*, 1900), and borrowed some rare books on Venice from him in November 1907.

   *nymph receiving Zeus*: not an allusion to a specific myth, but to the awakening of an unreflective natural creature to self-consciousness.

97  *San Giorgio Maggiore*: one of the islands that make up Venice, on which a 16th-century Benedictine church by Palladio stands as one of the city's most striking monuments.

*Late Autumn in Venice* (MS)

Written early summer 1908, Paris.

   *new will is rising*: cf. a letter to Sidonie Nádherný von Borutin: 'the palaces . . . made entirely of will, of resistance, of success' (24 November 1907), referring to the precarious situation of Venice on a marshy lagoon.

*admiral*: the Venetian Admiral Carlo Zeno (1334–1418), who defeated the Genoese at the Battle of Chioggia in 1380 and thereby secured Venetian control of the Adriatic.

*arsenal*: the shipyard and munitions depot in Venice.

### The Lute (MS)

Written autumn 1907, Paris, or spring 1908, Capri.

*vaulted lines*: possibly an echo of Hugo von Hofmannsthal's drama *Der Abenteurer und die Sängerin* (*The Adventurer and the Singer*, 1899), set in Venice and based on an episode from the *Memoirs* of Casanova, which contains the line 'This is my all: I am hollowed out like the vaulted body of a lute'. The next poem in the *New Poems, Second Part* is entitled 'The Adventurer'.

*Tullia's*: Tullia d'Aragona, 16th-century Venetian courtesan and poet.

### Rose Interior (SR)

Written 2 August 1907, Paris.

99 *stream out from inner spaces*: the blooming of the vulnerable rose transforms the outer world from within.

### Lady at the Mirror (SR)

Written between 22 August and 5 September 1907, Paris.

*Lady at the Mirror*: possibly inspired by Édouard Manet's *Devant la glace* (*Before the Mirror*, 1876), which Rilke may have seen at an exhibition of female portraits 1870–1900 at the Château de Bagatelle on 4 June.

### The Flamingos (MS)

Written autumn 1907, Paris or spring 1908, Capri.

101 *Fragonard*: Jean-Honoré Fragonard (1732–1806), French painter in the Rococo style, known for his delicate but luminous colours.

*blooming*: Rilke wrote to Clara of a visit to the Jardin d'Acclimatation (rather than the Jardin des Plantes) where 'it was almost painful in this wind to see the pink and red flamingos blooming' (15 February 1906).

*Phryne*: a Greek courtesan from the 4th century BCE.

### Pink Hydrangea (SR)

Written autumn 1907, Paris, or spring 1908, Capri.

*pink*: see note to 'Blue Hydrangea' from the *New Poems* (p. 288), to which this poem is a partner. The pink colour is produced by alkaline soils.

101 *Smile from the air? Do angels wait*: cf. *DE* II, ll. 23–7 (p. 137).

103 *knowing everything*: because it has experienced both life and death.

*The Ball* (MS)

Written 31 July 1907, Paris. A sonnet extended by a third tercet. Rilke reputedly said of this poem, 'I did nothing but utter what is almost unutterable about a pure movement, which is why it is my best poem' (quoted in *KA* I, 1002).

103 *You roundness*: cf. *Sonnets*, 2. VIII (p. 219) and 'For Erika' (p. 269).

*the uncertain fulcrum tilting flight to fall*: cf. 'Dedicated to M. . . .', l. 13 (p. 245) and *DE* V, ll. 81–6 (p. 155) for other examples of these precious, expressive moments of hovering between one state and another, when the positive aspects of both are united.

*The Dog* (MS)

Draft of ll. 1–15 written late June 1907, Paris; completed 31 July 1907, Paris.

*The Dog*: cf. *Sonnets*, 1. XVI (p. 199). Rilke felt an affinity with dogs, 'these beings wholly dependent on us whom we have helped lift themselves to gain a soul, but for which there is no heaven' (letter to N.N., 8 February 1912), and they are an example of the 'animal' that *DE* VIII will explore further.

*image*: this word suggests a reading of the poem as poetological. The poet sometimes explores the possibility of leaving his own somewhat precarious existential state, 'not cast out but not let in', probing the images or representations of a reality other than his own, but he holds back because then he would no longer manage to 'be' (l. 14).

*At times*: 'nur manchmal' is a favourite phrase of Rilke's: cf. 'The Panther', l. 9 (p. 65) and 'Roman Fountain', l. 11 (p. 73).

*Buddha in Glory* (MS)

Written summer 1908 (before 15 July), Paris.

105 *Buddha*: meaning 'awakened one' or 'enlightened one', both a generic name and that of the supreme Buddha, Siddhartha Gautama (6th century BCE). There are also two Buddha poems in the first part of the *New Poems*. 'In glory' refers to the mandorla (see below, note to l. 2).

*cores*: Rilke wrote to Julie von Nordeck, 'Increasingly . . . I am living the existence of the core in the fruit, which arranges everything that it has around itself and from within itself in the darkness of its working. And increasingly I see living like this as my only escape: otherwise I cannot transform the sourness around me into the sweetness that I have long since owed to God' (10 August 1907).

*almond*: the German 'Mandel' means both the nut-like fruit and the 'mandorla', a halo-like 'aura' surrounding a whole figure rather than just the head, used in Christian and Buddhist iconography and formed from two circles overlapping to form an almond shape in the centre, symbolic of wholeness.

*duration*: the key Rilkean word 'überstehen' is the last of this collection; cf. note to 'Song of the Sea' (p. 294), and note the final words of *The Sonnets to Orpheus*.

## UNCOLLECTED POEMS 1912–1922

*'Ah, as we waited for human help'*
Written 11 July 1912, Venice.

*The Raising of Lazarus*
Written January 1913, in Ronda (Andalusia, southern Spain).

107   *Lazarus*: based on the story in St John's Gospel, 11: 1–45. The name means 'God (has) helped' in Hebrew. Lazarus of Bethany, one of Christ's followers, falls ill; Christ is summoned but shows no urgency and arrives four days after his death and entombment. Christ prays before the tomb and calls him out, in front of a crowd of mourners. The resurrection of Lazarus demonstrates Christ's power over life and death.

*his tears flowed*: an echo of the shortest verse of the Bible, 'Jesus wept' (John 11: 35).

*protest at their small distinctions*: Christ's anger in the poem is chiefly at the relatives' limited understanding of the close relationship of life and death, although it begins earlier (l. 9) when he is reproached for arriving 'too late'. Rilke's objections to Christianity were often motivated by its emphasis on the hereafter, on the fundamental division between life and death, and on the need for Christ as mediator between the two.

*stank*: the 'voice' in St John is that of Lazarus' sister Martha, who is sceptical of Christ's power to perform the miracle.

*'Tears, tears breaking out of me'*
Written late autumn 1913, Paris.

109   *Moor*: *KA* ii, 488, suggests that this refers to a statuette or carving of a Moor carrying a tray; these were popular as domestic decorations in the early 20th century. It may be a more precise reference, however, to one of four famous statues in the 'Grünes Gewölbe' ('Green Vault') in Dresden, including the 'Moor with the Emerald Cluster'.

*'So it must surely be the angel, drinking'*
Written late 1913, Paris. From the 'Poems to the Night', a collection of 22 poems put together some time in 1916 (when Rilke was having difficulties writing) for his friend Rudolf Kassner (cf. p. 313). They are thematically and motivically linked to the *Duino Elegies*.

109  *angel*: not yet the dread Angel of the *Elegies*, since apparently attempting to reach out for contact with humanity, but already an inhabitant of a purer sphere than ours.

   *drinking slowly from my features*: cf. *DE* II, ll. 16–17 (p. 137).

'*O leave me, you whom I asked*'

Written late 1913, Paris. From the 'Poems to the Night'.

111  *taste my smile*: there is a parallel here with the 'drinking' image from the previous poem, although the one 'tasting' here is the beloved not the angel.

   *let us forget*: Rilke here dismisses the beloved, somewhat condescendingly. This poem was the eighth in the sequence put together for Kassner and marks a turning-point in the rivalry of angel and beloved, in favour of the former.

   *un-lured*: cf. *DE* I, l. 8 (p. 131) and *DE* III, l. 76 (p. 145).

'*You, beloved*'

Written winter 1913–14, Paris.

   *lost in advance*: from 1912 on Rilke developed the idea of an 'expected beloved', possibly in response to a series of difficulties and disappointments in actual relationships with women in this decade. It may have been partly influenced by an elegy of Klopstock's from 1747, 'Die künftige Geliebte' ('The Future Beloved'), which reworks the myth of Persephone, by two poems with the same title by Hölty (1775), or by a poem by Goethe entitled 'Gegenwart' ('Presence', 1812), beginning 'Alles kündet dich an' ('Everything heralds you'), the manuscript of which Rilke had seen in Weimar in 1911. The beloved in this poem is perhaps a modern version of Eurydice (cf. in this context 'Orpheus. Eurydice. Hermes' from the *New Poems* and contrast its more 'realistic' descriptions of landscape).

   *cities and towers and bridges*: cf. in contrast the buildings and monuments listed in the *Elegies* (VII, ll. 73–4, p. 163, and IX, ll. 31–3, p. 171).

   *mirror-reflections of shops*: perhaps an echo of Mallarmé's poem 'The Demon of Analogy', in which the poet is seen as having an elegiac function, mourning the death of 'la Pénultième' (The Penultimate), another Eurydice figure.

*Turning*

Written 20 June 1914, Paris. Originally a continuation of another poem, 'Waldteich' ('Woodland Pool').

113  *Turning*: in a letter to Lou Andreas-Salomé Rilke said that the poem was called 'Turning' because 'it represents that very turning that will have to happen if I am to live' (26 June 1914).

*Kassner*: the motto is a slight variation on a quotation from Kassner's collection of aphorisms, *Aus den Sätzen des Yoghi* (*From the Sayings of the Yogi*, 1911), a phrase which Kassner claimed was itself written under the influence of a conversation with Rilke in the Café de la Paix in Paris.

*gazing*: in a continuation of his letter to Lou written on 26 June, Rilke reflects 'that a mental acquisition of the world that so completely makes use of the eye, as is the case with me, would be less dangerous for a visual artist because it is comforted more tangibly, by physical results'. He, on the other hand, is 'so hopelessly turned outwards' (cf. *Sonnets*, 2. v, and note, p. 328). 'Some sort of life within me has saved itself from being exposed like this; it has retreated to an innermost place and lives there, like people during a siege, suffering privations and constant anxiety. It makes itself felt when it thinks that better times have come. . . . And between the two, between that uninterrupted addiction to outwardness and this inner existence that is hardly even accessible to me, there are the true habitations of healthy feeling, empty, abandoned and stripped bare.' In other words, this poem denotes a radical aesthetic shift that is intimately linked with Rilke's concerns about his own existential health.

*building them up again*: a reference to the poetics of the *New Poems*.

*stared into it*: cf. 'The Panther' (p. 63).

*children*: children and animals are motifs that will be developed in the *Elegies*, as will that of 'women who love' (cf. next note).

*more slightly, doubtfully visible*: women who love are already engaged with 'heart-work' and not 'work of seeing' (cf. ll. 48–9).

*room*: there are numerous examples in Rilke's work (notably in *Malte Laurids Brigge*) of the oppressive anonymity of rooms not his own, perhaps partly because he spent so much of his life travelling and in temporary, rented rooms.

115  *gazing . . . has a limit*: both poetologically and physically (Rilke complained to Lou on 19 December 1912, whilst in Spain, that his eyes hurt from all the gazing he was doing); as is so often the case with Rilke, aesthetic positions are achieved partly because of physical circumstances.

*inner young girl*: in contrast to the 'expected beloved' (cf. above, p. 298); cf. also notes to *Sonnets*, 1. 11 (p. 318).

## Plaint

Written early July 1914, Paris.

*to whom make plaint*: the poem may be referring to Rilke's failed relationship with Magda von Hattingberg, which ended in May 1914, although Rilke was later to read back into it an intuition of the coming upheaval of the First World War (in a letter to Thankmar von Münchhausen, quoted in *KA* II, 507).

115 *the future, that that is lost*: another suggestion of the motif of the 'expected beloved'.

117 *invisible landscape*: this, like 'You, beloved, lost in advance', is an early example of the creation of mythicized inner landscapes that begins to characterize Rilke's later work.

### 'Almost all things beckon us to feeling'

Written August/September 1914, Munich or Irschenhausen (near Munich).

*Be mindful!*: the German, 'Gedenk!', is the same verb that is used in *DE* I to ask whether we have sufficiently commemorated Gaspara Stampa (l. 46, p. 133): it asks for a more dynamic response than mere memory.

*embracing and embraced*: it has been suggested that this phrase marks a link to Goethe's poem 'Ganymed' (which contains the line 'umfangend umfangen', 'enclosing enclosed').

*world-inner-space*: this phrase introduces for the first time Rilke's famous concept of 'Weltinnenraum', which denotes the result of fleeting, epiphanic moments in which the boundaries of the inner world and the world outside seem no longer to exist. It takes the usual German word for '[cosmic] space', 'Weltraum', and splices it with the word for 'inside'.

*birds*: in a letter to Adelheid von der Marwitz (cf. note to 'Death' below, p. 301) Rilke recalls a night on Capri standing beneath an olive tree and hearing the call of a bird, being forced to close his eyes so that the call 'was simultaneously within me and outside in a single indistinguishable space of perfect extension and clarity' (14 January 1919). The following lines repeat the same sensation.

### 'Cast out, exposed on the mountains of the heart'

Written 20 September 1914, Irschenhausen. Originally intended for the *Duino Elegies*.

119 *mountains of the heart*: one of Rilke's most famous, most carefully expounded 'mythical landscapes'.

*small*: the words (language, poetry) and feeling that humanity has at its disposal are attenuated and fragile within the huge, bleak landscape of doubt, lack of control, and inexpressibility that this poem evokes.

### To Hölderlin

Written September to 25 October 1914, Irschenhausen (ll. 1–6) and Munich.

*Hölderlin*: Friedrich Hölderlin (1770–1843) was a major German Romantic poet and novelist, author of broad, expansive, unrhymed hymns such as 'Bread and Wine', 'The Archipelago', 'The Rhine', and 'Patmos', as well as shorter works and epigrams. He was passionate about ancient Greek culture (and translated Pindar), if somewhat idiosyncratic and idealizing in his understanding of it. In 1806 he was diagnosed as mad, and from the following year spent the rest of his life in a tower-room overlooking the Neckar in Tübingen. His work fell somewhat into obscurity until 'rescued' by the scholar Norbert von Hellingrath (1888–1916), who was a member of the circle around the autocratic poet Stefan George, and whom Rilke met in October 1910. Hellingrath sent him much material on Hölderlin, including the edition on which he was working, and it was onto a blank page at the back of a proof-edition of the late work that Rilke inscribed this poem. Rilke projected onto Hölderlin many of his feelings about himself, but Hölderlin's style, especially his long, fluent, dactylic lines, was an important influence on much of his later work, especially the *Elegies*.

*swoops . . . falling*: perhaps an echo of Hölderlin's poem 'Fate. Hyperion's Song': 'We have no footing anywhere, | No rest, we topple, | Fall and suffer | Blindly . . .' (trans. David Constantine).

*one whole life*: Hölderlin's wholeness of vision stands in sharp contrast to the situation in which Rilke finds himself.

121 *uncounted years*: the years of Hölderlin's madness.

## Death

Written 9 November 1915, Munich.

*cup without a saucer*: a letter to Lotte Hepner written the day before this poem clarifies this image somewhat. In it Rilke laments the way the modern world tries to push death away and demonize it, whilst a writer like Tolstoy was in a condition to 'think from the perspective of the whole, and to write with a feeling for life that was so thoroughly imbued with the finest particles of death that it seemed contained within it, like a strange spice in the strong taste of life'. That is why he can be so utterly scared when he senses that 'pure death' exists somewhere, 'a bottle full of death, or that ugly cup with the broken handle and the stupid slogan on it, "Glaube, Liebe, Hoffnung" ["Faith, Hope, Charity"—the central "theological" virtues of Christianity, cf. l. 6 and I Corinthians 13: 13]' (8 November 1915).

123 *once from a bridge intensely visible*: cf. letter to Adelheid von der Marwitz of 14 January 1919 in which he recalls seeing a shooting star from a bridge in Toledo, which fell simultaneously through outer and inner space 'and the outline of the body that separates the two was no longer there' (cf. note to 'Almost all things beckon us to feeling', p. 300).

*stand*: an attitude to death that contrasts strongly with the 'hanging on' (l. 12) of that evoked in the earlier parts of the poem.

## To Music

Written 11 and 12 January 1918, Munich. Inscribed in a guest-book for Hanna Wolff after a private concert.

*Music*: Rilke was wary of music for most of his life, perhaps intimidated by its wordlessness, and regarded it as a threatening form of seduction.

He described it in a letter to Sidonie Nádherný von Borutin in highly sensuous terms as 'a danger to me' (13 November 1908). This poem may have been influenced by the work of Emerson (cf. Ryan, *Rilke, Modernism and the Poetic Tradition*, 175–80), and is linked to Rilke's 1919 essay 'Ur-Geräusch' ('Primal Noise', *KA* IV, 699–704) about recording sounds on wax cylinders and playing them back.

123   *breath*: perhaps also in the sense of 'inspiration'.

    *language where languages end*: despite his wariness of music as an art, Rilke saw it as the culmination of art, a form beyond words. Note how Rilke moves from defining music in lines 1–2 to addressing it in lines 2–3.

    *time . . . evanescence*: music is addressed as time, which is fundamental to the structures of music, but it is 'upright' (and therefore lasting), in contrast to the human experience of time as flowing away.

    *heart-space grown out beyond us*: an expression of the inner world projected into the outer.

    *other side of the air*: cf. the exposition of the 'other side of the mirror' in *Sonnets*, 2. III, and 'Space's reversal. Design | for inner worlds laid in the open' in 'Gong (II)' (pp. 213 and 265).

    *uninhabitable*: the boldness of the metaphors and the abstraction that dominates from the outset situate this poem as an important precursor of the turn to abstraction in the very latest poems such as 'Mausoleum' and 'Gong (II)'.

### 'It was in Karnak. We had ridden there'

From the collection of poems entitled *Aus dem Nachlaß des Grafen C. W.* (*From the Literary Remains of Count C. W.*), ten of which were written between 27 and 30 November 1920, the remaining eleven in March 1921. Rilke originally proposed to claim that they were the work of a nobleman from past times that he had found in a cupboard, since when he wrote them, straight into final versions, he found his pen 'literally "led" for me, poem by poem' (letter to Nanny Wunderly-Volkart, 30 November 1920). Many of the themes of the *Elegies* and the *Sonnets* are already present in this collection in a recognizable form. This poem is the only one of these that was published in Rilke's lifetime.

    *It was in Karnak*: the poem recalls Rilke's visit to Karnak in January 1911 (cf. *DE* VII, l. 73, p. 163, and *Sonnets*, 2. XXII, p. 235).

    *guide*: the German uses the Arabic word 'Dragoman', meaning official translator and guide. He is also the 'Fellache' of l. 15, which means 'peasant'.

    *avenue of sphinxes*: Karnak is connected to the Temple of Luxor by a three-kilometre-long avenue of sphinxes, of which only a small portion had been excavated when Rilke visited. There is a shorter avenue of ram-headed sphinxes leading between the Precinct of Amun and the Precinct of Mut, and another from the Nile to the First Pylon, which the progression of the poem suggests is the one referred to here.

*Pylon*: a monumental gate in the form of two massive blocks either side of a portal.

*moon-world-wrapped*: moonlight tours of the temple were popular at the time of Rilke's visit.

125 *one column*: cf. l. 31.

*five of them*: the first courtyard in Karnak originally had ten columns forming the Kiosk of Taharqa, five on each side, but only one now remains.

*scarab-sculptures*: the scarab was a dung-beetle that seemed to the ancient Egyptians to emerge from nothing, and was thus a symbol of renewal and regeneration, associated with the sun-god Ra. Here referring to a huge granite scarab erected by Amenophis III near the Sacred Lake.

127 *the world's secret*: cf. letter to Lou Andreas-Salomé of 20 February 1914: 'exactly what I felt in Egypt when faced by the sculptures . . . the laid-bareness of the secret, the secret that is so through and through, and so secret at every point that there is no need to hide it.'

*'Odd, the words: "while away the time"'*

Probably written on 27 November 1920 as the first of the *C. W.* poems.

129 *staying*: the main theme of *DE* II.

*upstanding*: cf. 'To Music', and the vertical axis that is so important to that poem.

## DUINO ELEGIES

The composition of the *Duino Elegies* was a protracted process interrupted by periods of severe poetic and personal crisis but ending in an astonishing burst of poetic creativity. Rilke began the *Elegies* in the third week of January 1912 whilst a guest of Princess Marie von Thurn und Taxis and worked on them intermittently for another ten years, finally completing them on 26 February 1922. There were five main stages of composition:

1. 21 January to March February 1912 at Castle Duino, when I and II were completed with fragments of IX, portions of III and VI, and the first fifteen lines of X.
2. January and February 1913 in Ronda, when lines 1–31 of VI were written (along with the account of a liberating 'Experience' that Rilke had undergone in the park at Duino the year before).
3. September 1913 in Paris, which saw the completion of III, a few lines of VI, and further work on X, of which a first version (later discarded) was finished towards the end of that year.
4. 22–3 November 1915 in Munich: IV.
5. 7 to 26 February 1922 in Muzot: a tremendous burst of activity that included the composition of *The Sonnets to Orpheus*. VII (on 7th), VIII (7th and 8th), IX (9th, incorporating material written in Duino), some of

vi (9th), x (11th, new parts replacing earlier material from line 13 on),
v (14th), and a new ending for vii (26th).

Rilke sent a folder of materials to his publisher, Anton Kippenberg, on 4
November 1918, which he intended to represent the authorized version of the
*Elegies* if he were to die without finalizing them. It contained other poems asso-
ciated with the *Elegies* but not in fact incorporated when they were completed
in 1922. He also made plans for a 'Second Part' to the *Elegies*, for which he
wrote an afterword on 8 February 1922. The material for this was stored in
an envelope marked 'Fragments', which contained a large number of poems
associated with the genesis of the 'First Part' (the *Elegies* as we know them).

131 *From the Castle . . . Taxis-Hohenlohe*: Duino Castle sits on a rocky head-
land of the Adriatic near Trieste. It was built in the 14th century but is
dominated by a 16th-century tower. It became a centre for cultural activity
under the Counts Torre-Hofer Valsassina in the 17th century, and again in
the late 19th century under Countess Teresa and her daughter Marie
(who married a distant cousin, Alexander von Thurn und Taxis, in 1875).
Rilke stayed in Castle Duino from 22 October 1911 until 9 May 1912 as
the guest of Marie.

I

*Angels*: transcendent beings of perfect consciousness, beyond time,
beyond the limitations of physicality, representations of the most intense
beauty. A famous letter from Rilke to his Polish translator, Witold von
Hulewicz, contains as clear a statement of what he understood by the
figure of the Angel as he ever made: 'The "Angel" of the *Elegies* has
nothing to do with the angels in the Christian heaven (indeed has more in
common with the angelic figures of Islam). [. . . It] is the creature in
which the transformation of the visible into the invisible that we are
undertaking already appears completed. For the Angel of the *Elegies* all
the towers and palaces of the past are still existent *because* they have long
since ceased to be visible, and the towers and palaces that still exist today
in our world are for him *already* invisible, even though they still endure
physically (for us). The Angel of the *Elegies* is that being which guarantees
the recognition of a higher degree of reality in the realm of the invis-
ible.—It is therefore "terrible" to us because we, who love and transform
it, still cling to the visible' (13 November 1925).

*beauty . . . dread*: beauty may be seen as the visible world that has been
(trans)formed and shaped (by the poet or by other artists), whilst dread is
the invisible that has yet to be transformed. Cf. 'Early Apollo', ll. 4–5
(p. 57).

*interpreted world*: the world as filtered by human understanding, which is
therefore a reduced and defensive sphere, in which the full extent of
human experiential possibility cannot be realized and which cannot
adequately contain our most meaningful experiences, such as love, death,
and suffering.

*night*: as a component of the mythology of the *Elegies*, night is a space in which the self can expand beyond the boundaries of the merely human, space in which the Angel is at home, beyond the limiting attentions of human reason. In Rilke's 'Poems to the Night' (1913–14), night appears almost as an anthropomorphized partner.

133 *violin*: for the combination of the violin and night, cf. 'The Neighbour' (p. 31).

*mission*: as the letter to Hulewicz explains, mankind's mission is to sustain the essential value of the things of this earth by interiorizing them, making them 'invisible'. Cf. *DE* IX, l. 70 (p. 173).

*lovers*: an example of a 'transitional' form of consciousness between the human and the Angelic. Cf. *DE* II, ll. 37–45 (p. 137).

*hero's*: another example of 'transitional consciousness'. Cf. VI and notes (p. 311).

*Gaspara Stampa*: (1523–54); Venetian poet, whose painfully unrequited love for Count Collaltino di Collalto is reflected in the first part of a posthumously published collection of 311 powerful and assertive verses entitled *Rime* (1554), edited by her sister. Cf. letter to Sidonie Nádherný von Borutin of 7 October 1908. Stampa is one of a number of 'women who love' celebrated by Rilke (others include the Portuguese nun Marianna Alcoforado, the German writer Bettina von Arnim, who corresponded with Goethe, and the French Renaissance poet Louize Labé); cf. letter to Annette Kolb of 23 January 1912, two days after this *Elegy* was completed.

*young dead*: a third example of 'transitional consciousness' (a fourth, the child, appears in *DE* IV, ll. 76–85). Cf. *DE* VI, ll. 11–20 (p. 157), *DE* VII, ll. 31–4 (p. 161), and *DE* X, ll. 47–105 (pp. 177–81).

*exhortation*: the German 'erhaben' can mean both 'sublime' and 'in relief lettering'.

*Santa Maria Formosa*: a church in Venice that Rilke visited with Marie Taxis on 3 April 1911, on whose walls are tablets commemorating the brothers Wilhelm and Anton Hellemans, to which it is thought these lines refer.

135 *either realm*: a reference to Rilke's notion of the 'double-realm' of life and death that is developed in the *Sonnets*.

*Linos*: in Greek mythology, son of Apollo and Calliope, one of the Muses—and thus brother to Orpheus—killed at an early age (possibly in the course of a music contest by Apollo, possibly by Heracles). His name is used to denote a dirge or song of lament (cf. Homer's *Iliad*, XVIII.570).

II

137 *days of Tobias*: a reference to the Apocryphal book of Tobit in which Tobias is sent on a long journey by his father to collect a debt, with the suggestion

that he look for someone to accompany him: 'Therefore when he went to seek a man, he found Raphael that was an angel. But he knew not; and he said unto him, Canst thou go with me to Rages?' (5: 4–5).

137  *Who are you?*: one of the most important motifs of this *Elegy*, the condition of 'being'. Cf. ll. 29, 39, 49, and 63.

*pollen*: metaphor for fecundity.

*mirrors*: in the letter to Annette Kolb referred to above, Rilke writes of God doing to Marianna Alcoforado 'what he consistently does to the angels', turning all that emanates from her back within her, like the action of the self-reflexive mirrors here.

*pregnant women*: an image found in *Malte*, too (*KA* III, 462 and 464), which describes the faces of pregnant women as 'ausgeräumt' ('evacuated').

139  *the other's hands*: an individual can sometimes feel a very attenuated physical echo of a sense of pure mutual awareness in the touch of his own hands, but that is nothing—certainly not the condition for pure 'being'—compared with the intensity of touch experienced during the first moments of reciprocated new love.

*pure duration*: again, new lovers enjoy an intensity of unconditional emotion that is enough to give a glimpse of eternity and the realms inhabited by the Angel. But the next lines suggest that this is an intrinsically short-lived phenomenon.

*Attic gravestones*: 'stelae' are flat stone slabs carved or painted with the names and images of the dead. Rilke wrote to Lou Andreas-Salomé of those he had seen in Naples on which the gestures were of particularly expressive gentleness (10 January 1912).

141  *strip of land . . . between river and rock*: perhaps a memory of Rilke's journey to Egypt in 1911; a combination of the fluid and the static.

*And our gaze . . . greater control*: a statement of the transformative function of art ('pictures') in the modern world, and myth ('godlike') in the ancient.

III

*hidden, guilty river-god of the blood*: sexual drives, as opposed to the more chaste levels of love and affection that are implied by 'the beloved' here. This may be a specific allusion to Freud's concept of the subconscious. Rilke had met Freud in September 1913 at a psychoanalytic convention that he had attended with Lou Andreas-Salomé. Rilke and Lou had corresponded about Freud's ideas, including his contention in *Three Essays on Sexuality* (1905) that, with respect to love, the classical world placed more emphasis on the *drive* ('Trieb') whereas the modern world favoured the *object* of love. However, the vocabulary of this *Elegy* is pre-empted by a passage pre-dating Freud's study, in Rilke's Rodin monograph (1902) referring to 'old secrets that rose from the unconscious, and, like strange river-gods, lifted their dripping heads from the rushing of the blood' (*KA* IV, 409). What is important in the *Elegy* here is the emphasis Rilke places on acknowledging the unconscious (or the 'Dionysian', in mythological or Nietzschean terms) as well as its 'Apollonian' shaping via art (cf. 'the sweetness of your delicate made world', l. 43).

*lifted his god-head*: a phallic image.

*Neptune*: Roman god of the sea, often depicted carrying a three-pronged spear, known as a trident, and a conch shell.

*constellations*: as the face of a human being expresses in visible form the inner self, so the stars in the form of constellations give articulation to the shapeless infinity of space.

*more ancient terrors*: the deepest instinctive levels of the primitive psyche that persist in humanity beneath the level of consciousness.

143 *nightly imaginings*: cf. *Malte*, *KA* III, 505–7 and 570–2, which evoke night-time terrors.

*wilderness . . . wildwood*: images of dense, jungle-like forests are a frequent correlative of the instinctual drives in early twentieth-century German literature, most famously perhaps in Thomas Mann's *Death in Venice* (1912), of which many elements in lines 42–65 are strangely reminiscent, albeit in a very different context. The depiction of Gustav von Aschenbach sitting wretchedly on the steps of a fountain, the victim of his passion for the boy Tadzio (the revenge of Dionysus on an Apollonian writer who has repressed his instinctive nature), makes use of a number of (critical) adjectival nouns akin to 'der Erleichterte' here, and refers to his eyelids half-closed. Earlier, Tadzio smiles at him (cf. l. 61), which prompts the shameful-yet-noble confession 'I love you' (cf. ll. 52–3 and 63–4).

IV

145 *winter*: the elliptical question of the first line may be asking why human existence does not have seasonal cycles, as nature does, but instead a linear progression from birth to death; or it may wonder why 'life's trees', as opposed to nature's, do not give us a proper signal for the approach of the season of decline, such that we are always left unprepared for this.

*agreed*: the German 'einig' can mean 'agreed' (as in the answer to the question in line 1) but also 'one', 'unified', such that this phrase becomes a description of the basic human condition of dividedness.

147 *free space, hunting, home*: the conditions of love (expansion of consciousness, passionate desire, and comforting protection).

*his heart's curtain*: a dramatic model of the human consciousness, which is both the subject and object of reflection.

*parting*: parting and leave-taking are fundamental components of the human condition (cf. *DE* VIII, ll. 70–5, p. 169).

147  *garden*: if this is understood as the Garden of Eden, then the leave-taking is the equivalent of the loss of perfect pre-lapsarian unselfconsciousness.

*the dancer's entrance*: one of the participants in Kleist's dialogue *On the Marionette Theatre* (1810), which Rilke studied carefully in 1913, is a dancer. Dance was frequently felt to be an exceptional mode of immediate self-expression in the early twentieth century, because unmediated by words.

*puppet:* an example of pure corporeality not hindered by reflectiveness. It matches the Angel, who represents pure consciousness unimpeded by physicality. The pairing of the two (cf. l. 57) has been described as that of 'absolute object' and 'absolute subject' (*KA* II, 645).

*the boy with brown eyes and the squint*: a commemoration of Rilke's cousin Egon von Rilke (1873–80), who is also remembered in *Malte* as Erik Brahe (*KA* III, 473) and in *Sonnets*, 2. VIII (cf. p. 219).

149  *toy*: toys are objects saturated with the child's inner nature, as opposed to 'world', which is composed merely of externality. Cf. Rilke's 1914 essay on 'Dolls' (*KA* IV, 685–92) and a passage from his Rodin monograph in which he asks the reader to recall an object from childhood: 'Think about whether there was anything else that was closer, more intimate and more necessary than that thing. About whether everything else was not in a position to hurt you or do you wrong, except that thing. . . . Was it not a thing with which you first shared your little heart, like a piece of bread that had to make do for two?' (*KA* IV, 455).

*measuring-rod of difference*: to make clear just how immeasurably far childhood is from adult knowingness.

v

151  *Hertha Koenig*: (1884–1976); author and art collector, who bought Pablo Picasso's painting *La Famille des saltimbanques* (*The Acrobat Family*, 1905) from the Thannhauser Gallery in Munich in 1914, on Rilke's advice (letter of 4 November 1914). Between June and October 1915 Rilke used her flat in Munich, where the painting was hung. Koenig met Picasso in May 1914; she sold the painting in 1931 and it is now in the National Gallery of Art, Washington DC.

*travelling, transient people*: the acrobats in Picasso's painting are based on Père Rollin's street performers (cf. the 1907 prose poem 'Saltimbanques (Vor dem Luxembourg)', *KA* II, 394–5), but although they are mostly in costume, Picasso's are not actively performing. They stand as a family group against an anonymous, hilly background, the young woman on the right (the mother of the family) sitting almost as if she has been extracted from the group, leaving a gap between the small boy and girl. Two are carrying bags, as if they are on the way somewhere.

*D*: an outline drawn round the main group of acrobats in Picasso's painting would form the shape of a capital 'D', for 'Dastehn' ('standing', 'endurance') in German. Rilke may be referring to the fleeting yet time-less moment of stillness between tricks.

*Prince August the Strong*: Frederick Augustus I (1670–1733), Elector of Saxony and (as Augustus II) King of Poland and Grand Duke of Lithuania. Said to have been of Herculean strength, able to bend a horseshoe with his bare hands.

*rose of onlookers*: the group described in the *Elegy* is far from being a simple transposition of Picasso's painting, which has no onlookers, but has something in common with one of the *New Poems*, 'Die Gruppe' ('The Group'), also based on the Père Rollin troupe, which shares the metaphor of the flower and a focus on spectators (*KA* 1, 544).

*stamping piston*: referring to the acrobats' continual hard landing on the earth.

*pistil*: whilst the English words 'piston' and 'pistil' share several phonetic elements, they are not etymologically related; the German 'Stampfer' and 'Stempel' are, however. In both cases one word poetically generates another with a very different meaning via their similarities.

*widowed skin*: suggesting that this figure corresponds to the grandfather in Picasso's painting, albeit by contrast rather than in imitation (since Picasso's rotund figure still fills out his skin).

153 *the young one . . . son of a neck and a nun*: matching Picasso's figure of the son, on the far left of the painting, a muscular young man, Rilke's expression suggesting a combination of physical strength and naive simplicity.

*boy*: corresponding to the smaller of the two boys in Picasso.

*mutually constructed movement*: the traditional acrobats' pyramid.

*smile*: the youngest of the acrobats acknowledges the 'heavy' nature of the world, with its difficulties and resistances. In a prose commentary on a short poem in Italian written in 1920 ('La nascita del sorriso', 'The Birth of the Smile'), Rilke describes the smile as 'nothing but the consent of the spirit to be within us' (*KA* 11, 184).

*Subrisio Saltat.*: an abbreviation of 'subrisio saltatorum', 'the smile of the acrobats', in a form such as one might find as a label on an apothe-cary's jar.

*darling one*: without a straightforward equivalent in Picasso's painting, since she corresponds neither to the young girl with her back to the viewer nor to the mother figure.

155 *poised*: possibly a reference to a 'balancing artist', such as a tightrope walker, as well as to the scales on which are weighed the 'market-fruit' of public artistic endeavour.

*equilibrium*: the German 'Gleichmut' points both to physical balance and to emotional equanimity, suggesting that the girl is not touched by the mechanistic side of artistic activity.

155 *pure too-little . . . empty too-much*: a pairing that has been likened to the combination of Angel and Puppet in IV (*KA* II, 661), although if the state of 'empty mechanical facility' might match that of the Puppet, that of 'not-yet-being-able' is not wholly appropriate to describe the Angel. A letter from Rilke to Nanny Wunderly-Volkart describes the 'preposterous' ('unsinnig') slick facility of acrobats as a form of compensation for the artist's tortured sense of having to remain approximate or inadequate in so many areas that ideally demand perfection (22 December 1919). Both states are more appropriately seen as characterizing human activity rather than that of the 'alternative consciousnesses' that Rilke offers throughout the *Elegies*.

*Madame Lamort*: personification of death.

157 *stilled carpet*: in contrast to the 'thinner' mat or carpet of lines 9–10, this is the true complex weave of life itself. Cf. *Sonnets* 2. XXI (p. 233).

VI

*Fig-tree*: a complex symbol. In classical antiquity the fig-tree symbolized fruitfulness and indeed superabundance; it also had erotic connotations deriving from its association with the gods Dionysus and Priapus. The fig itself is equally complex, and what is usually known as the fruit is its flower, which forms a so-called 'multiple' or 'accessory' fruit, a soft pulpy stem forming housing for the flowers which are turned inwards and pollinated through a small hole at the bottom to produce hundreds of seeds (which form the fruits proper). It looks, therefore, as if the tree has no flowers and moves straight to fruit. Finally, the word for fig in German, 'Feige', is identical with the adjective 'feige', meaning 'cowardly' but etymologically suggesting 'destined for death', both of which aspects are suggestive in the context of the hero.

*neglect to flower*: 'überschlagen' in the German can mean 'omit', but also 'enclose', both of which senses are appropriate to the fig-tree (see previous note).

*the god become swan*: referring to the story of Zeus who became a swan and sought refuge from an eagle in the arms of Leda, whom he then raped (cf. 'Leda' from the *New Poems, Second Part*, p. 83). One of the children born from the violent union of divine and human was Helen of Troy, who was responsible for heroic—and destructive—action on a grand scale. The link between this and the previous image of water being thrust through pipes to jet upwards in the fountain is the impregnation of Leda by the sperm of the god.

*linger*: if Rilke was thinking specifically of Helen in the context of the previous image, then the choice of the word 'verweilen' here might echo the second part of Goethe's *Faust*, where the beauty of Helen of Troy induces Faust to utter the formula that might end his striving, 'verweile doch! du bist so schön' ('tarry, please, you are so beautiful').

*our flowering*: most of us wish for the self-expressive grandeur of the flower, to make an impression, since the fruit is a stage nearer death.

*bas-reliefs at Karnak*: the decorations on the outer wall of the Hypostyle Hall in the Temple of Amun at Karnak have reliefs of Seti I and Rameses II waging war in Syria and Palestine, including the Battle of Kadesh.

*hero*: One of Rilke's 'alternative consciousnesses', who is untouched by all the difficulties pertaining to human existence that the first five *Elegies* have expounded. His is a powerful will to life, expressed without doubt, reflectiveness, or hesitation, and as with the youthful dead his own death is 'counted in' as part of life from the outset rather than being a source of anxiety. It should be noted that this, the 'hero *Elegy*' as it is sometimes known, shares much of the enthusiasm and optimism of *DE* VII and *DE* IX, which are widely regarded as the only two 'positive' *Elegies*—the difference being that their enthusiasm is for the capacities and potential of flawed mankind rather than those of a rare form of exceptional existence.

159  *boyhood*: cf. 'The Boy' (p. 27), to which sections of this *Elegy* are themat- ically related.

*reading*: Rilke projects himself back into the childhood state of antici- pating the future—not one of action like the hero's but nonetheless one of fulfilment in writing and the imagination.

*Samson*: Samson's mother was barren for many years before his birth was announced by an angel. Many stipulations for his upbringing and predic- tions for his future were made even before he was born.

*pillars . . . breaking out of your body's world*: Samson took revenge on Delilah and the Philistines, who had captured and blinded him, by tearing down the pillars of their temple in Gaza (Judges 16: 18–30). Rilke suggests that this act is prefigured in his determination to be born and that birth and heroic fulfilment are equivalent.

*sacrificed to the son*: it is the fate of women who love heroes to be abandoned by them, as it is often the fate of mothers to be left behind to mourn the death of the son. Cf. also Judges 13: 6–7—it is Samson's mother who, on the advice of an angel, dedicates her son to God.

*storm through the habitations of love*: the hero is not to be detained by being bound in love to another human being any more than he was happy to remain in the comforting protection of the womb.

VII

*wooing*: this *Elegy* is determined that the language of wooing is no longer adequate (cf. the insistence of line 85). Wooing is associated with seeking the kind of love that does not permit the full expression of the self, seeking the attention of another to alleviate fear and isolation. Cf. *Sonnets*, I. III.

159 *voice grown beyond it*: the emphasis on language in this *Elegy* is made clear from the outset with an appeal to a purer expression of life and vitality, without ulterior motivation, like the call of a bird.

*cry pure as the bird*: the call of birds effects an inwardness for Rilke, who noted in 1914, 'we take the song of a bird so easily into us, it seems to us as if we were translating it, perfectly, into our own feeling; for a moment it can even turn the whole world into inner space ["Innenraum"] because we feel that the bird does not distinguish between its heart and the world's' (*KA* IV, 694).

161 *the steps upward*: this section suggests both the rising of the bird into the air and the rising intensity of pure self-expression.

*nights*: cf. note to *DE* I, l. 18.

*not only she*: the poet's voice, with its new intensity, cannot by definition restrict itself to one 'target'.

*more value than childhood*: the 'interred', those who have died young, are always searching for a life that they have not been able to live, whereas what they would have experienced had they survived would have been 'fated', or life with a purpose. The potential crammed into childhood (which they have barely outlived) is worth more than such a life. They have only 'seemingly' ('scheinbar', l. 40) been deprived.

163 *transform it within us*: it is the task of the modern age to transform the outer world into inner. If previous ages have had external objects (domestic, artistic, religious—cf. the temples of line 57) that reliably expressed the true nature of their being, the modern world lacks them and must 'transform' external reality, imbue it with inwardness, and rebuild it in our consciousness—in the case of the poet, using language.

*the external dwindles . . . move across consciousness as an image*: it is the interiorized experience of the external object, here the house, that now guarantees its lastingness.

*vast reserves of power*: ironically an image borrowed from the modern technical age, that of the power station.

*Columns . . . cathedral*: a series of strongly vertical images, each suggesting a reaching upwards, not in order to transcend and leave behind the real world but as symbols of 'standing' or 'duration' (cf. *DE* V and other references to non-load-bearing columns, e.g. p. 251).

*pylons*: probably not in the modern sense of an electricity pylon (which was only gaining currency in the 1930s), but a Greek word designating a monumental gateway, especially as used of Egyptian temples.

165 *window*: a familiar image of a threshold, of a gateway between worlds.

*leaving*: there is an untranslatable play on words in the German, where 'hinweg' as an adverb denotes motion away ('leaving') but 'Hinweg' as a noun means 'path towards'. There follows a similar Janus-faced gesture in the hand that is both calling on and pushing back.

VIII

*Rudolf Kassner*: (1873–1959); Austrian writer and cultural philosopher; friend of Rilke's from 1907.

*the Open*: 'das Offene' is a concept derived from, or at least reinforced by, the visionary mystic Alfred Schuler (1865–1923), some of whose lectures on 'The Essence of the Eternal City' Rilke heard in 1915 and 1917–18. According to Schuler it is a condition of inward-turning, of possession-less freedom, in which the self is at one with the boundless universe in a feeling of 'absolute being', when time stands still and birth, life, and death is experienced as a continuum.

*animal*: like the Angel, an example of an alternative mode of consciousness to that of human beings. It lives its life unconcerned about the prospect of its death, unlike us; unlike children, who are brought up by adults into a different way of seeing things, the animal preserves this state always. Rilke began to develop this idea as early as *The Book of Hours* (cf. 'Lord, we are poorer than the poor beasts', p. 21).

*within eternity*: without the kind of direction or purpose that time imposes on life.

167 *left in stillness*: the German 'im Stilln' here suggests both 'in stillness' and 'whilst breast-feeding'; whilst Rilke is not known for his practical toler-ance of small children, he may have noted from his own observations as a father the expression of almost other-worldly rapture that sometimes occupies an infant's face while feeding at the breast.

*Lovers . . . in the light*: another plaidoyer for the experience of unrequited love as an approximation to the Angelic state of wholeness.

*opposite*: a powerful image of cultural and existential alienation and of the radical split in the human consciousness between subject and object.

*nearer once . . . the first home*: in the womb. What distinguishes the warm-blooded creatures to which Rilke is referring in this stanza from others such as insects is the fact that they are born live. These ideas derive to some extent from correspondence in 1914 with Lou Andreas-Salomé concerning her *Three Letters to a Boy* (published 1918), in which she describes differences between mammals and amphibians.

*Oh bliss . . . to birth*: in contrast to mammals, the insects do not know sepa-ration from the mother's womb; the world *is* the womb as far as they are concerned.

169 *lidded*: an image of the deceased was painted or carved on the lid of an Etruscan sarcophagus such that the individual is both within and outside at the same time. The bird, to which the Etruscan soul is likened, has also been both within (in the egg) and outside (in the world).

*bat*: as a flying mammal, it is 'a creature from the womb that must fly' (ll. 61–2). Rudolf Kassner wrote of the bat that one can tell it does not lay eggs: 'I mean to say that in its somewhat jerky, staggering, ghostly flight there is nothing of the pure line and balance of the egg' (*Zahl und Gesicht* [*Number and Physiognomy*], quoted in *KA* II, 680).

169 *for ever in farewell*: the condition of humanity that knows both of its own mortality (and so is aware that each experience will be over and has to be looked back on) and of its exclusion from the womb: the animal's experience of pure presentness means that it is not forever moving on.

IX

*laurel*: allusion to the myth of Daphne; cf. notes to *Sonnets*, 2. XII (p. 330). The laurel is 'darker' perhaps because it is evergreen (cf. *DE* X, l. 13). It is also traditionally the shrub used as a garland for poets victorious in competition.

*smiling*: cf. note to *DE* V, l. 57.

*pleasure*: with 'Glück' here Rilke is referring to a transient form of happiness, one that is stimulated by material things rather than spiritual upliftedness.

171 *life here is much*: an echo of VII, l. 39, 'being here is glorious'.

*seemingly*: it would be an error to suppose that the earth exists merely as a function of mankind, although the idea that both exist interdependently is not so arrogant.

*the other dimension*: death, albeit one stage only in the process of dying, the other being a kind of apotheosis into the dimension of the stars (l. 27), that of pure spiritual space.

*Not our looking*: Rilke has moved on from the aesthetic of the *New Poems* and their focus on 'Anschaun' ('gazing', cf. Introduction, p. xxi).

*gentian*: a small alpine plant, often used in tonics, but also associated with death. It is unclear why Rilke has chosen this plant, but it may be because of its unusually sharp, clear colour, or because blue and yellow together make the green that has already been referred to (l. 3).

*house . . . window . . . column, tower*: in contrast to the cultural creations of humanity listed in *DE* VII, ll. 73–83, these are mostly modest and even domestic objects, with the column and the tower presented less for their imposing stature than as examples of the furthest extent to which the 'saying' of our world should go.

*crusted acts*: superficial behaviour, without deep-rooted meaning and value, whose essentially meretricious nature is soon exposed. This stanza articulates aspects of Rilke's critique of the modern age, and is supplemented in his letter to Hulewicz (cf. p. xxv) by references to 'Schein-Dinge, *Lebens-Attrappen*' ('fake things, *substitute lives*') that are forcing their way to Europe from America.

173 *simple*: the opposite of the 'fake things', objects with local meaning, personal significance, traditional value.

*rope-maker . . . potter*: crafts, hand-made objects are more valuable than the anonymous products of technology.

*I will*: reminiscent of a response to a proposal of marriage or a marriage vow.

X

175 *paeans of rejoicing*: the final *Elegy* begins with a firmly expressed wish to overcome the period of lament and attain a state where rejoicing and praising can dominate, but it is still a wish rather than a present condition and must wait for fulfilment until Rilke emerges from the dark times of 'fiercest insight'.

*hammer's beat . . . string*: the hammers of a piano, operated by the keys to strike strings inside its case.

*winter-green leaves of the mind*: the German 'Sinngrün' is also the name of a plant (*Vinca minor*), known as periwinkle or creeping myrtle in English. *KA* II, 697 suggests that it is associated traditionally with death, as a decoration for graves and coffins, but although it was commonly believed to grow in paradise, it is better known as a symbol of fidelity and friendship. The Romans thought of it as a dwarf laurel (cf. IX, l. 2). It is one of the many types of flower woven into the tapestries of *La Dame à la licorne*, which Rilke knew well (cf. p. 47).

*Mourning's capital*: this is the beginning of an allegorical journey through the 'interpreted world', literally called 'the city of suffering', the opposite of the 'authentic' places of the previous line.

*marketed comforts*: this is a critique of the way organized religion anaesthetizes its adherents to the reality of death. A letter to Countess Sizzo is more explicit: 'I reproach all modern religions with the fact that they have offered their faithful consolations and palliatives for death rather than giving their minds the means of living with it and coming to terms with it' (6 January 1923).

*jugglers*: the scene is reminiscent of the acrobats in *DE* V: the prose poem that Rilke wrote on the subject of the Père Rollin troupe that inspired it (cf. p. 308) specifically talks of Rollin's appearances at regular funfairs, and *Die Gaukler* is the usual German title for Picasso's *Saltimbanques*.

177 *In her footsteps*: Rilke is here perhaps consciously echoing the relationship of Dante and Virgil in Dante's *Divine Comedy*.

*questioning youth*: one of the youthful dead.

179 *sibyls*: cf. 'A Sibyl' and note (p. 292).

*seers:* the masculine equivalent of sibyls (the German word is a Rilkean neologism).

*Sphinx*: Rilke visited the Great Sphinx of Giza, on the Nile near Cairo, during his visit to Egypt in 1911, spending by his own account almost a whole night lying near it (letter to Magda von Hattingberg ('Benvenuta'), 1 February 1914). The sphinx is a reclining lion with a human head. Cf. VII, l. 73 (p. 163).

179 *owl*: the owl was an Egyptian bird of death. The letter to 'Benvenuta' referred to in the previous note recalls how during Rilke's night with the Sphinx an owl flew from behind its head and swept across its face, touching its cheek, 'indescribably audible', so that 'into my sense of hearing, which had become especially sharpened after hours in the still-ness of the night, was etched the contour of that cheek, as if by a miracle'.

*rim of the crown*: the German uses the Greek word 'Pschent', meaning the double-crown of Upper and Lower Egypt, although this does not resemble the headdress worn by the Sphinx.

*Rider*: cf. *Sonnets*, I. XI.

*Staff . . . Garland of Fruit . . . Cradle*: the meanings of these constellations do not command agreement amongst scholars. These three are perhaps symbolic of the combination of male (phallus) and female (fecundity), producing a symbol of childhood.

*Path*: possibly symbolic of the 'directional' mode of existence of adult human beings.

*Burning Book*: it is almost impossible not to hear in this image an echo of the burning *bush* of Exodus, chapter 3, in which an angel of the Lord appears to Moses in a bush that is on fire but is not consumed by the fire, so the image here may be one of revelation, distorted so as to refer to writing rather than religion.

*Puppet, Window*: cf. *DE* IV, ll. 26–9 (p. 147) and *DE* I, l. 29 (p. 133).

*M*: if one looks at the lines and folds in the palm of a hand when it is slightly cupped, it is usually possible to see a letter M formed by four (sometimes only three) of the deepest. The letter M has five points, corre-sponding to the five southern constellations of line 92. Rilke is fond of such visual interpretative leaps: cf. the 'D' of 'Dastehn' in V, ll. 13–14, and the smile created by the skin folds sculpted in the 'Archaic Torso of Apollo',
ll. 7–8 (p. 83).

181 *catkins . . . the rain that falls*: the two symbols that the earth offers us for an understanding of our situation—Rilke is rarely so explicit about his poetic procedures—the catkins that hang downwards from a bare hazel bush seem to indicate falling and decline but in reality herald the rejuve-nation of the bush after the winter, as does the falling spring rain. Line 110 supplies the context that we are usually inclined to associate happi-ness with images of rising than with those of falling. The fact that rising and falling are not in contradiction here allows us to see, or feel, the inner relatedness of life and death or joy and suffering.

*hazel*: it is tempting to try to read a symbolic dimension into the choice of hazel—which commonly signifies divination, wisdom, and authority, and some say also poetry—but Rilke's first choice here was 'willow', which is where he erroneously believed that the hanging catkins grew. He was corrected by Elisabeth Aman-Volkart in a letter of June 1922.

## THE SONNETS TO ORPHEUS

*The Sonnets to Orpheus* were first published by Insel in Leipzig at the end of March 1923 but Rilke had written all fifty-five in two extraordinary bursts of creative activity in February 1922 in the Château de Muzot, the house in the Valais, Switzerland, that he was sub-letting from Werner Reinhart, a cousin of his friend Nanny Wunderly-Volkart. Part One emerged in almost final form in four days between 2 and 5 February (the original of 1. XXI was replaced with a new poem on 9 February; 1. XXIII was added on the 12th or 13th and 1. VII was rewritten shortly before the 23rd). Part Two was composed between 15 and 23 February, beginning with 2. V and 2. VI and followed then by the remainder of 2. II–2. XV by the 17th; 2. XVI–2. XXIII were composed between the 17th and the 19th, with all the others coming between the 19th and the 23rd, ending with 2. I. Almost more astonishingly these two periods were separated by a week in which the *Duino Elegies* and the 'Letter from the Young Worker' were completed (7 to 15 February). Rilke wrote a few notes to the *Sonnets* (reprinted in *SW* I, 772–3).

183 *Orpheus*: poet and musician in Greek myth, associated with the lyre and song. Said to be the son of the river-god Oeagrus (or sometimes of Apollo) and the Muse Calliope, he was taught to play the lyre by Apollo, and his music was so beautiful that it charmed the wild beasts, the trees, and even the rocks. In some versions of the story of Jason and the Argonauts (not Homer's), Orpheus is responsible for playing music to drown out the Sirens' song, saving the crew of the ship. According to Virgil, at the death of his wife, Eurydice, Orpheus played such beautiful mournful music that the gods took pity on him and permitted him to seek her out in the underworld. His music persuaded Persephone to allow Eurydice to return to the land of the living on condition that Orpheus not look back at her until they both reached the surface. Orpheus turned as he emerged, forgetting that Eurydice, too, had to have reached the light, and lost her forever. Orpheus was torn apart by the Maenads in a frenzy of jealousy (according to Ovid he had spurned the love of women after his wife's death and took only youths as lovers). His severed head, still singing to the tune of his lyre, floated down the River Hebrus until it met the Mediterranean; the tides took it to Lesbos where it was buried. Different accounts vary in many of these details. The *Sonnets* do not treat the death of Eurydice, of which Rilke had written in the *New Poems* (pp. 77–81).

*Wera Ouckama Knoop*: (1900–19); talented dancer and friend of Rilke's daughter Ruth; daughter of the chemist, poet, and novelist Gerhard and his wife Gertrud; died of leukaemia before reaching 20. Even though Rilke barely knew her (he had seen her dance in Munich), news of her death and details of her illness sent to Rilke by her mother profoundly affected him, as letters to Gertrud (4 January 1922) and Countess Sizzo (12 April 1923) movingly demonstrate. He associated Wera with the figure of Eurydice in the Orpheus myth.

PART ONE

I. I

183  *A sudden tree soars*: the motifs of the tree and animals appear in a repro-
duction of an ink drawing by Cima da Conegliano (*c.*1459–1518) that
Rilke's friend Baladine Klossowska had left behind in Muzot when she
departed in November 1921; it was pinned to the wall in Rilke's study.

*hearing*: cf. Introduction, p. xxxiii. The motif is picked up overtly in 1.
XVIII, XX and XXVI, and 2. XVI, XIX, XXIV, XXV, and XXVIII.

I. II

*She was almost a girl*: the 'she' that opens this line is the neuter 'es' in
German, which refers to the girl ('Mädchen', a diminutive and thus
grammatically neuter rather than feminine) and may specifically evoke
Wera. However, it may also contain a reference to the idea of the dual
sexuality of all creative individuals that Rilke first encountered in the
works of Sigbjörn Obstfelder in 1904 and may have come across again in
lectures by the mystic visionary Alfred Schuler between 1915 and 1918.
Cf. the line 'See, inner man, your inner young girl' from the poem
'Turning' (p. 115).

*spring veil*: perhaps a reference to Botticelli's 'Primavera' which Rilke had
seen in Florence in 1898.

I. III

185  *through the narrow lyre*: for the image of the lyre as 'gateway' see
also 1. V.

*crossing*: in the ancient world, wayside shrines dedicated to certain gods
were often erected at cross-roads, but these shrines were usually dedicated
to malign divinities such as Hecate rather than to Apollo.

*Apollo*: cf. p. 284.

*does not pay court*: the notion of 'Werbung', wooing or courtship, is
important in the *Elegies* (cf. the opening of *DE* VII, p. 159).

I. IV

*the breath breathed not for you*: cf. the 'Song of the Sea' (from the *New
Poems*, p. 95), where the wind blows 'not for our sake', alluding to the
familiar Rilkean theme of love unreciprocated (and thus stronger or
more pure).

187  *bow to the arrow*: a reference perhaps to the attributes both of
Amor/Cupid (god of love) and Apollo (god of archery); cf. *DE* I, ll. 50–3
(p. 133).

I. V

*memorial*: *DE* X expresses Rilke's dislike of monumental masonry
(ll. 16–19, p. 175). Orphic song is transformative rather than permanent

and its expressive transience, which is simultaneously an act of transcend-ence, is fittingly expressed in the image of the bowl of roses. Rilke's own gravestone famously refers to the 'pure contradiction' of the image of the rose (see p. 263).

*metamorphosis*: Rilke uses the word 'Metamorphose', derived from the Greek for 'change of form', rather than his more usual 'Verwandlung', with its Germanic root. This suggests an allusion to Ovid's *Metamorphoses*, a narrative poem in fifteen books that is known to have been important to Rilke.

I. VI

189 *both these realms*: life and death, both of which Orpheus has experienced, a duality mirrored in the reference to both branches and roots of the willow.

*willows*: Orpheus is said either to have carried a willow-branch to Hades as a form of 'passport' to the Underworld, or to have touched a willow in a grove sacred to Persephone and thereby received his gifts of eloquence, depicted in famous frescoes by Polygnotus (5th century BCE) in the temple at Delphi, as described by the Greek traveller and geographer Pausanias. Lyres were sometimes carved from willow.

*bread and milk*: in folklore and legend, these were often left as offerings to the dead. In Book X of Homer's *Odyssey*, milk is one of the offerings made to conjure up the spirit of the blind Theban poet Teiresias. Rilke will have recalled, of course, the Christian association of bread with the body of Christ, another of those who have known the realms of both life and death.

*fumitory*: a herb with grey-green leaves, sometimes also known as 'earth-smoke' because it was said in the Middle Ages to be formed from vapours seeping out of the earth. Traditionally used to treat skin conditions (espe-cially scurvy) and as part of exorcism rites, its legendary properties included both making people invisible and making the spirits of the dead visible.

*rue*: an evergreen perennial bush with yellow flowers and blue-green foliage; also known as the herb of grace in English (because of the associa-tion of its name with repentance and regret) and herb of the dead ('Totenkraut') in German; its many properties reputedly included protec-tion against magic spells, the plague, werewolves, epilepsy, and vertigo, and it was said to foster second-sight.

*pitchers, brooches and rings*: everyday objects sometimes used as grave goods during burial services.

I. VII

*Praising*: the first of three consecutive sonnets on the theme of 'praise' for the here-and-now, a theme picked up from the penultimate line of I. VI and echoed in the 'Letter from the Young Worker' written in the

same month as the *Sonnets*: 'Give us teachers who will praise for us
what is here' (*KA* IV, 747). The theme also relates these sonnets to *DE* VII
and IX.

*transient press of an endless wine*: the vocabulary of viniculture (press,
grape, vineyard, wine) represents a transformation process akin to that
practised by Orpheus. The rhyme of 'dust' and 'grape' in the German
reflects Rilke's sense that the fruit is the realization of the essential 'sap' of
life transmitted and transformed via the earth (in which the dead are
buried) and the roots of trees. The references to burial are echoed in
a number of other sonnets.

*tender and sensuous South*: MS is indebted to Stephen Mitchell for this
phrase: he has brought out perfectly the different connotations of 'fühlend'
in Orpheus' intimate and sensory relationship to earthly life and death; he
also reinforces the sensuous transformations of the god by drawing atten-
tion to the texture of sounds in the repeated 's' sounds, as in the original,
and the repeated 'e' where the original uses 'ü'.

I. VIII

191 *Only in the realm of praise*: with personified Grief only permitted to
walk within the 'realm of praise', this sonnet reverses the situation
described in *DE* X, where the 'Joy-Spring' rises in the 'landscape of
Grieving' (cf. p. 179).

*nymph of the spring*: in Ovid's *Metamorphoses* (IX.446–665), the nymph
Byblis falls passionately in love with her brother Caunus, confesses her
love in a letter and is spurned. Caunus flees in horror, but Byblis,
maddened by rejection, follows him on a long journey until she falls,
exhausted and weeping, and is changed into a spring. The 'precipitation'
of l. 3 refers to tears.

*Jubilation . . . Longing . . . Grief*: the personification of these emotions as
three sisters recalls the Hours or Horae of Greek mythology, the three
daughters of Zeus and Themis who supervise the orderly passage of time
or the cycles of life and growth, representing (according to different
traditions) justice, law, and peace or spring, summer, and autumn.

I. IX

It has been suggested (on the basis of a letter to Katharina Kippenberg of
30 June 1926) that Rilke may here be alluding to a poem by Goethe, 'Phenomenon'
from the *West-Eastern Divan*, I, 9: 'Wenn zu der Regenwand | Phöbus sich
gattet' ('When Phoebus mates with a curtain of rain'). The sonnet shares with
Goethe's poem the verse-form (alternating largely dactylic three- and two-beat
lines) and some rhyme-sounds; Phoebus is another name for Apollo, who, with
the theme of metamorphosis, is thematically important in the *Sonnets*.

*poppy-seeds*: poppies are traditionally associated with sleep and death,
partly because they are the source of opium, partly because of their blood-
red colour.

1. X

193 *sarcophagi*: ancient sarcophagi (stone coffins) were often re-used as water troughs or fountain basins, and Rilke was struck by their double connection with both death and life (echoed in the tercets as a contrast between closure/silence, openness/speaking and knowing/not knowing). He wrote other poems on the same theme, including 'Roman Sarcophagi' and 'Graves of the Hetaerae' in *New Poems* (and *DE* VIII has a reference to an Etruscan grave-image, p. 169); the first stanza of this sonnet is also linked to 2. XV.

*transformative*: the German verb 'wandeln' means both 'to walk, to stroll' *and* 'to change, to metamorphose', so the water which is the Orphic song both flows and transforms.

*those lying open*: according to Rilke himself stanza two of this sonnet was prompted by his memory of 'the graves in the famous old cemetery of Allyscamps near Arles that also features in *Malte Laurids Brigge*', and which was famously painted by Van Gogh. 'Les Aliscamps' etymologically means 'the Elysian Fields' where heroes and the virtuous have their final resting place.

1. XI

*Rider*: Whilst there are stars in the constellation of the Ursa Major called the 'Horse and Rider' (Mizar and Alcor), so close together that they are difficult to distinguish with the naked eye, Rilke's constellation in this sonnet has less to do with astronomy than with the action of the imagination in projecting or constructing unity from difference, the partnership of horse and rider being no more a necessary relationship than man's perception of symbolic patterns amongst the stars.

1. XII

195 *spirit*: poetry, the art that constructs connections.

*truly . . . figure-spaces*: note the paradox of finding binding truths in the temporary constructions of the imagination ('figures').

*Antennae*: originally used of insects, but by 1922 in common currency in connection with radio communications. Rilke rarely uses technological imagery, and in this very poem contrasts authentic 'inner time' with that measured mechanically by the hands of a clock (cf. 2. XXVII).

1. XIII

*apple, banana, pear, gooseberry*: Rilke will have known Paula Modersohn-Becker's *Still-Life with Apples and Bananas* (1905, in the Kunsthalle Bremen), which was itself influenced strongly by Cézanne's still-lifes. Fruit was important to Rilke, not only because he was a vegetarian, but because of the significance of the sense of taste in connection with language and poetry. He wrote to Lou Andreas-Salomé, 'if once in a while I tasted a fruit and it dissolved on my tongue, it was like a word from the spirit melting away: the experience of what had been imperishably accomplished within it surged upwards at once in all the visible and invisible vessels of my being' (26 June 1914).

197   *a child's face*: a child's innocent wonder is untarnished by an adult's over-familiarity with everyday experiences such as tastes. For a related image, see *DE* IV, ll. 76–85 (p. 149).

*namelessness*: direct experience replaces that mediated via words and description and the sensation of tasting a product of the earth thus paradoxically gives a glimpse of something timeless. Cf. 1. XI, l. 11, and l. 2 of the next sonnet.

I . XIV

*are they the lords*: this is another of Rilke's open questions (cf. 1. XI, l. 9), casting doubt on the usual priority of the living over the dead in favour of an appreciation of the essential ambiguity of the 'double-realm'.

*this work of surly slaves . . . sleep there with the roots*: there are several striking echoes here of Hugo von Hofmannsthal's 1896 poem 'Manche freilich . . .' ('Many, it is true . . .'), which contrasts nobility and slavery, those 'above' with those 'below' (who 'lie with heavy limbs | at the roots of confused life') and ends with an assertion of the value to life of 'mein Teil' ('my part'; cf. l. 6 of Rilke's sonnet). Cf. also the image of 'the shadow people under the roots of trees' in the fourteenth stanza of Paul Valéry's *Le Cimetière marin*, which Rilke had translated in 1921.

I . XV

199   *Dance*: a form of symbolic (syn)aesthetic expression for the taste of the orange that bypasses words, as l. 13 suggests it must; an echo, too, of Wera Ouckama Knoop's artistic passion. The 'dance' recreates or reinterprets the gustatory experience and is itself recreated in the dense and complex sound-patterning of the original German (with very frequent alliteration on 'w', for example, uniting a characteristic Rilkean pairing of resistance and yielding, and a shift from the 'u' sounds of the first quatrain into the lighter 'ü' sounds of the second and the tercets).

*made itself over*: following the vocabulary of resistance, the German 'bekehrt', 'converted', has overtones of religious conversion, to a free and unfettered form of paganism in contrast to the restrictiveness that Rilke felt characterized Christianity.

I . XVI

*You*: according to a letter to his wife Clara (23 April 1923), Rilke addressed this sonnet to a dog, noting that the 'master' of l. 13 is Orpheus, the poet's master. The dog is ill at ease in the world of words and gestures, like mankind in 'the interpreted world' referred to in

*DE* I (p. 131). Rilke's coat of arms (which is on his gravestone in Raron) features two greyhounds salient. Cf. note to 'The Dog' (p. 296).

201  *Esau*: With a name meaning 'hairy', Esau was the twin brother of Jacob, patriarch of the Israelites, who held on to Esau's heel as he was born. He sold his right to be recognized as the first-born to his brother for a 'mess of pottage' (lentils), but was later deceived by Jacob, who contrived with his mother Rebecca to obtain the blessing of his blind father, Isaac, by covering his own smooth arms and neck in goatskin (cf. Genesis 25: 25–34 and 27). Rilke confuses the names of Esau and Jacob in the letter to Clara referred to in the previous note, but there is no reason to suppose the same confusion in the sonnet: there the 'master's hand' is guided to bypass humanity and bless the hairy, honest 'brother' of mankind.

I . XVII

*ancient*: this sonnet describes a form of autobiographical family tree, charting a development from ancient generations at the tree's 'roots' to the poet himself in the uppermost 'branches' (the imagery of 'above' and 'below' is linked to that of I. 14)—or from a non-Orphic form of existence to an Orphic. Rilke was fond of considering himself the scion of an ancient aristocratic family. The figure of the 'ancient' has plausibly been linked with a poem by Victor Hugo, 'Booz endormi' ('Boas asleep').

*Helmet and hunter's horn*: attributes of lives with a fixed vocation (war, hunting), like those of the quarrelling brothers and the 'lute-shaped' women (whose function is to give birth). Ovid's evocation of the 'Golden Age' in the *Metamorphoses*, I. 98–9, characterizes it as one in which 'non tuba derecti, non aeris cornua flexi, | non galeae, non ensis erat' (there were no straight war-trumpets, no coiled horns, no swords and helmets). These are precursors of the 'machines' of the next sonnet.

*lyre*: symbol of pure, free art; attribute of Orpheus. On 31 January 1922 Rilke had made a small ink drawing of a lyre whose two curved arms are sprouting leaves and turning into the branches of a tree (reproduced in Leisi, *Rilkes 'Sonette an Orpheus'*, 251). This and the reverse trajectory in the sonnet (where the lyre grows out of the tree) both point to the continuity between nature and art or the emergence of art and music out of the 'sap' that flows through the natural world from the earth through the trees. Note the contrast between the triumphant way the lyre 'curves' and the 'ravelled' existence of more primitive mankind.

I . XVIII

*Lord*: the first time that Orpheus is *addressed* in this way (although I. XVI refers to him thus). This usage echoes that of Christian prayer, suggesting that Orpheus is regarded as a god; in I. III and I. XIX Orpheus is more explicitly identified as divine, and although Ovid describes Orpheus as 'born of the god' (*Metamorphoses*, X.89), it is relatively unusual in the classical tradition, although not unknown, to see him as a god himself.

201　*the New*: the first of the *Sonnets* to thematize the modern technological age (cf. also 1. XXII–XXIV, 2. IX, and 2. X).

*machine-part*: soulless technology, wholly alien to Orpheus because in Rilke's view its objects are entirely consumed by their purpose and are without aesthetic value. The noise of machines means that 'nowhere can ears hear', where 'hearing' is part of the closed Orphic circle created by mouth and ear.

*acclamation*: despite his misgivings, Rilke seems to be suggesting that even components of the machine deserve the transforming praise that it is the function of poetry to bestow.

1. XIX

203　*changes*: here and in l. 5, the regrettably rapid pace of modern life, not the celebrated metamorphic transformation that the word 'wandeln' usually signifies in the *Sonnets*.

*prime song*: the German 'Vor-Gesang' can mean both 'primal song' (as sung by Orpheus in a timeless Golden Age) and 'model song' (a form of teaching).

*Not yet*: ll. 9–12 combine regret that humankind has not perfectly understood the basic emotions of the world with satisfaction that this lack of understanding prevents love, suffering, and death from being debased. The delicate balance between the two is akin to the 'untellable point' in *DE* V (ll. 85–6, p. 155) 'where the pure too-little transforms | inexplicably—and leaps veering | into that empty too-much'.

1. XX

*Russia*: this sonnet was inspired by an incident during Rilke's second journey to Russia with Lou Andreas-Salomé in 1900 (cf. a letter to her of 11 February 1922). Rilke describes the poem itself as 'an *ex-voto* for Orpheus', in line with the imagery of dedication in the first and last lines.

205　*stake*: the horse is no longer tethered up and can indulge its natural physical instincts, yet the stake is not wholly shaken off: Rilke may be reminding himself that his current burst of liberated productivity both follows some seven years of frustration and is in a sense the product of this time of creative inhibition.

*sang—and listened*: cf. note to 1. XVIII, l. 7 and the image of the 'circle' in this line.

*cycle of legend*: in Ovid's *Metamorphoses* this is the song-cycle performed by Orpheus three years after the second loss of Eurydice that forms the major part of Book X.

1 . XXI

> *Spring*: deliberately establishing a link to the previous sonnet (l. 3), this poem replaces Rilke's original sonnet, which took up the theme of the machine again.
>
> *set free*: the German 'frei haben' can mean both 'liberated' and 'to have a day off school'.
>
> *play with the children*: Rilke notes in a letter to Gertrud Ouckama Knoop (9 February 1922) that the poem is in a sense a response to a mass he heard sung to a dancing rhythm by schoolchildren during a visit to Ronda in Spain in December 1912.
>
> *stems and roots*: both those of the plant world and those of language and etymology.

1 . XXII

There are numerous echoes of Goethe's *Faust* in this sonnet, particularly in the second quatrain: they include the imagery, the rhythms, and even the rhyme-sounds of the final 'Chorus mysticus' of *Part II* (beginning 'Alles Vergängliche | Ist nur ein Gleichnis' ['All that is transient | is but a metaphor']) and the phrase that in theory seals the loss of Faust's pact with Mephistopheles, 'Verweile doch, du bist so schön' ('tarry, please, you are so beautiful', said to the passing moment); cf. note to *DE* VI, p. 310.

207 *transient*: the main theme of the sonnet is the contrast between the time-lessness of Orphic experience and the pressures of modern life on our experience of time. The same rhyme of 'Treibenden' and 'Bleibenden' appears in 2. XXVII.

1 . XXIII

> *youthful pride*: cf. 1. XXII, l. 11: flight can become an Orphic symbol of poetry only when it transcends excitement at mere technological achieve-ment and the pilot *becomes* what he is doing. This was the age of the aircraft: the Wright brothers made their first flights in 1903, and in 1927 Lindbergh crossed the Atlantic.

1 . XXIV

209 *hard steel*: perhaps another echo of the 'Golden Age' evoked by Ovid in the *Metamorphoses*, Book 1 (which refers to 'harmful iron', l. 141), whose loss is lamented by Rilke here. It contrasts here with the soulless, anonymous modern industrial era in which our relationship with the gods goes unrecognized (or needs to be pinned down with a grid-reference) and direct, purposeful roads (a means to an end) replace gently winding paths (an end in themselves).

> *flames*: contrasting the steam-generators of industrial machinery perhaps with the flames in the domestic hearth or on the votive altar.

1 . XXV

209   *you*: this poem almost explicitly treats the death of Wera Ouckama Knoop (cf. also the reference to 'dancer' in l. 5), and the immediacy of the personal reference may explain why death is treated here in an unusually negative manner (cf. the 'open, comfortless door' in l. 14) rather than as a component of the 'double-realm'.

*cast into ore*: an allusion to Rodin's numerous bronze statues of dancers.

*shadows*: linking the death of Wera with the myth of Eurydice and her journey to Hades.

*natural spring . . . shimmered*: the alternation of decline ('darkness and falling') with such positive moments may reflect the account of Wera's illness sent to Rilke by her mother, in which she speaks of deceptive temporary improvements.

*earth-ore*: the German 'irdisch' can mean 'earthy', 'earthly', or 'made of ore' (which echoes 'Erz' in l. 6).

1 . XXVI

211   *you, divine being*: an address to Orpheus once more, bringing the first part of the cycle full circle and describing his death at the hands of the Maenads.

*order*: Orpheus is associated with Apollo, the representative of order, harmony, reason, and lightness, whereas Dionysus, god of wine, incarnates disorder, intoxication, and frenzy. The two gods are brothers, sons of Zeus.

*gifted with hearing*: cf. Ovid, *Metamorphoses*, XI.10–13, in which the stones thrown by the Maenads are deflected by the beauty of Orpheus' music.

PART TWO

2 . I

*Breathing . . . poem*: the sonnet equates the physical act of breathing with the 'exchange' (l. 3) between inner and outer worlds that constitutes the function of a poem. Breathing is 'invisible', but the creation of the poem is an act of 'making visible' in accordance with the injunction of *DE* VII, ll. 47–8 (p. 163).

*rhythmically*: contrasting sharply with the last poem of Part One and its energetic dactylic pentameters, this is rhythmically the freest of the *Sonnets*, with lines ranging between two and seven stresses (three and fourteen syllables). The verb 'sich ereignen' ('to take place') that is qualified here by 'rhythmic' is very rarely used in the first person and its use like that here is a powerful statement of the poet's self-realization in the act of writing the poem and clothing his inner space in the rhythms of language.

2 . II

213 *pen-stroke*: what is suggested of the visual artist here (Rodin perhaps) may also be applied to a poet. Comparing the final form of this poem with evidence from an earlier draft ironically suggests that Rilke here means that the hasty lines (or the scribbled note) of an early sketch (draft) may prove to be more authentic than the carefully crafted, final version.

*reflection*: in the same way, a casual glance in the mirror when a girl 'feels her way' into the morning may be more authentic than the 'image' she projects to 'real people' during the day. Mirrors are important to Rilke as vehicles for pure, closed circles of Orphic exchange (cf. *DE* II, p. 137).

2 . III

*interstices of time . . . sieve holes*: Rilke conflates time and space: sieve holes are empty nothingness but they have definition and thus meaningful existence because of the wire that surrounds them; similarly mirror-spaces are unreal but are framed by the real and have meaningful conceptual extension; time is measured and delimited in various ways and Rilke posits 'spaces' between units of time that are no more real than mirror-spaces but which are meaningful because more timeless than time itself.

*lustres*: chandeliers.

*sixteen-pointers*: mature stags with antlers that have sixteen 'tines' or points, regarded as especially noble.

215 *Narcissus*: beautiful youth in Greek mythology who spurned those who fell in love with him. The nymph Echo was so wounded by his rejection that she pined away until only her voice was left. He was punished by being made to fall in love with his own reflection one day while hunting; he pined in his turn and died, whereupon a narcissus flower grew where his body lay. Rilke wrote a number of poems on Narcissus, including two in April 1913 (*KA* II, 55–6; cf. also *KA* V, 262 for a poem in French). He may have used Ovid's *Metamorphoses*, III.341–510 as a source. For Rilke Narcissus was less an instance of self-obsession than one of the complete loss of selfhood.

2 . IV

*Unicorn*: mythological creature with a wide range of pagan and religious symbolic associations, although in his note Rilke excludes parallels between this poem and Christianity, suggesting instead that the unicorn represents 'all the love for things undemonstrated, intangible, all the belief in the value and the reality of what our minds have created and elevated through the centuries from within us' (letter to Countess Sizzo, 1 June 1923). Rilke wrote several poems on this subject (two of which are included in this selection, pp. 65–7 and 215) and dedicates several pages of his novel *Malte* to the six tapestries *La Dame à la licorne* in the Musée de Cluny in Paris (*KA* III, 544–9). He saw this creature as intimately linked with the figure of Narcissus.

215   *maid's*: the unicorn was said to be tameable only by a virgin.

2. V

*anemone*: Rilke wrote to Lou Andreas-Salomé of his anxiety over the little anemones in Rome that were open so wide that they could not close again when night fell. He associated them with his own very painful existential condition: 'Ich bin so heillos nach außen gekehrt' ('I am so hopelessly turned outwards'; 26 June 1914). This is the first of a group of three flower poems: flowers are important to Rilke because they are pure and purposeless, blooming as a means of self-realization.

217   *We live the longer*: the anemone may be vulnerable but it contrasts favourably with the forcefulness of humankind, which can rarely display such radical openness.

2. VI

*Ancients*: Rilke thought that the ancient world knew only the eglantine or sweet briar, a rose with five simple flat petals. They also grew near his home in the Valais. (Cf. the French poem 'Gente églantine', *KA*, V, 330.)

*flower of fullness*: the modern rose, cultivated, complex, and many-layered.

*names*: cf. 1. XXV, l. 2 (p. 209).

*glory*: in German 'Ruhm', related to the *Sonnets'* central activity of praise and celebration ('rühmen').

2. VII

219   *warmth of the girls*: suggestive of sexuality. Paradoxically the girls who 'heal the wounds' of the cut flowers by putting them in water only do so by allowing the flowers to lose the warmth that they have received from the girls' own hands. Experiencing 'warmth', being 'picked' (the loss of virginity), is a sin, a step out of timeless purity towards mortality. The image is linked to that of the ball (cf. next sonnet) in the poem of that name in *New Poems, Second Part* (p. 103, l. 1: 'roundness . . . giving away both hands' warmth') and with the ball and sin or guilt in 'Requiem for a Friend' (p. 55).

2. VIII

*banner of the lamb*: explained in a note by Rilke as 'the lamb (in cartoons) that only speaks using a speech-bubble', but also reminiscent of the victorious Lamb of God (the risen Christ), which is often depicted in art as carrying a banner with a cross on it (e.g. Dürer's 'Adoration of the

Lamb' (1496–8) )—the origin of the familiar English pub name 'The Lamb and Flag'.

*falling ball*: perhaps another of Rilke's symbols of the enclosed Orphic loop (like mirrors, fruit, girls, dance, Narcissus, etc.), an object whose upward arc must be completed by a downward fall, a figure of going-away followed by coming-back, and as such representative of Rilke's cousin Egon, who died at the age of 7 (cf. also note to *DE* IV, l. 35), whose life cannot be thought of without his death. Cf. 'The Ball' from *New Poems, Second Part* (p. 103).

2. IX

221 *irons . . . throats*: the iron collar, a medieval instrument of torture.

*tenderness strained and distorted*: Rilke's critique is of the pretensions of the modern age to humanitarian clemency merely because justice no longer takes violent social forms. True mercy paradoxically is more forceful, because more transcendent in its openness.

*more than a wind*: in the context of the reference in the previous line to divine beings, the combination of force and gentleness in the tercets suggests parallels with the Christian idea of the descent of the Holy Spirit in Acts 2: 2: 'And suddenly there came a sound from heaven as of a rushing mighty wind' and Christ breathing on his disciples to bestow on them the Holy Spirit in John 20: 22, although Rilke was keen to distance his work from comparisons with Christianity.

*infinite pairing*: a hint at the figure of Orpheus, born of divine parentage.

2. X

*machine*: the arch-enemy of Orpheus, because entirely consumed by purpose. Cf. 1. XVIII.

*stone*: whilst Orpheus bends or deflects the stones with his singing, and the sculptor (such as Rodin) cautiously shapes them, the machine cuts and shapes them for the purpose of building.

*our existence enthrals us*: this is a powerful counter-attack against the machine with a statement of the continuing magic of true Orphic humanity ('verzaubert' in the German literally means 'enchanted' or 'bewitched').

*music*: Rilke saw music as the extreme form of an art not exhausted by function or purpose.

*unfeasible space*: used positively here. Cf. the note to 2. III, ll. 3–4.

*deified house*: in contrast to the 'resolute building' with which the quatrains finished, a cathedral perhaps, such as those celebrated in some of the *New Poems*.

2. XI

This sonnet is based on an experience Rilke described in a letter to his publisher's wife, Katharina Kippenberg (31 October 1911), watching whilst hunters drove a pale variety of rock-dove out of the caves in Karst regions near Duino by waving canvas strips hung from the entrances, shooting them as they flew out.

223 *permitting*: Rilke wrote of 'im-Recht-seiende Dingen' ('things that are existentially in the right') and of himself being 'völlig im Unrecht' ('completely in the wrong') in letters to Lou Andreas-Salomé (19 February and 16 March 1912), in other words of being 'out of kilter' with the world. This sonnet seems to recollect that feeling and restore some equilibrium by finding a context for, and thus coming to terms with, an event that must originally have been somewhat shocking to Rilke.

2 . XII

*changed*: the sonnet is a hymn to transformation or metamorphosis, exemplifying its virtues using examples from the four elements in each stanza in turn (fire, earth, water, and air).

*leaves your reach*: this is a key moment in transformation, the point when a thing leaves the state of being present and possessed to enter that of absence and relatedness.

*point of the turn*: for Rilke, this was the ineffable moment of transformation, the indefinable point between one state and another and more meaningful than either, the point of self-realization.

*wellspring*: allusion to the myth of Byblis (cf. note to 1. VIII, l. 2).

225 *Daphne . . . laurelling*: in Greek myth a nymph pursued by Apollo, whose passion for her had been deliberately inflamed by Eros. Determined to preserve her virginity, she prays for help and is transformed into a laurel tree (cf. Ovid, *Metamorphoses*, 1.452–567). The figure of Daphne combines two motifs of great importance to Rilke, the virgin girl and the tree.

2 . XIII

This sonnet was repeatedly described by Rilke as the most significant of all the *Sonnets to Orpheus* (e.g. in letters to Katharina Kippenberg, 2 April 1922, and Gertrud Ouckama Knoop, 18 March 1922).

*dead in Eurydice*: this represents the only direct mention of Eurydice in the cycle.

*this time*: the uniqueness of the opportunity of the fulfilment of human existence is often stressed by Rilke (cf. *DE* IX, ll. 12–15, p. 171, where the phrase '*Ein* Mal', 'once and no more', is repeated six times).

*annul the amount*: the paradox of 'adding yourself' to the total sum and then 'annulling' all addition or counting is a version of the paradox of realizing one's individuation by losing it in the totality. Cf. the image of the ringing glass, l. 8, and *DE* V, ll. 85–6 (p. 155), which are all examples of the simultaneous coexistence of 'being' and 'non-being'.

2. XIV

*fate . . . their regret*: we, humankind, impose the concept of fate on nature so it is up to us to enact regret when the 'fate' of the flowers is accomplished, because they cannot and should not have to. Fate in this sense is similar to a consciousness of passing time.

*exhausting teachers*: the verb 'zehren', to 'sap, drain, debilitate', is a strong word in Rilke's vocabulary, expressing the inappropriate demands that mankind makes on nature. The figure of the teacher, who puts an end to play and childhood by imposing tasks and purposes, is equally negative, perhaps unsurprisingly given his experiences of education.

2. XV

227 *fountain-mouth*: it is usually assumed that Rilke was writing of the fountain outside the Basilica of Santa Sabina in Rome which has a marble mask (Leisi, *Rilkes 'Sonette an Orpheus'*, 152, and *KA* II, 756), but between the 1870s and 1936 this fountain was in storage. Rilke's fountain is more likely to be the Fontana del Mascherone (Fountain with the Grotesque Face) on the via Giulia, which draws water from the Acqua Paola aqueduct; the water pours from the face into a half-round basin below (the 'ear' of l. 10).

*giving*: cf. 1. 12, l. 14: 'Earth *bestows*'.

*for her own hearing . . . interrupting*: the speaking and the hearing, representing and represented by the flow of the water from the earth (in the hills above Rome) back to the earth (into the drain of the fountain), are a self-enclosed natural process that mankind spoils by interrupting (cf. 2. XVII, l. 14).

2. XVI

*Torn open . . . dispersed*: a reference both to the dismemberment of Orpheus by the Maenads (cf. also 1. XXVI, l. 13, p. 211) and to the image of mankind's interruption or disturbance of nature with which the last sonnet ended. Orpheus, in contrast, represents wholeness.

*sharp*: humanity's sharpness is linked to the sharpness of the stones that were thrown at Orpheus (1. XXVI, ll. 6–7, p. 210).

2. XVII

The evocation of a mythical realm of fruitful gardens tended by hidden gardeners and watched over by angels is a Rilkean version of the Garden of Eden, albeit not a Judaeo-Christian one. Mankind cannot reach it, although we may perhaps find evidence of its existence in our own impoverished lives (the single fruit of l. 4). It is even suggested that we are responsible for our own exclusion, as the word 'Benehmen' in l. 13 can mean 'behaviour' or 'conduct', suggesting a secularized—or rather 'Orphicized'—'Fall of Man'. The theme of 'timely' behaviour (neither 'premature' nor 'withered') echoes the opening of *DE* IV (p. 145).

2. XVIII

229 *Dancer*: addressed to the dedicatee of the *Sonnets*, the motif of dance may here also have been inspired by images of dancers on antique vases seen many times in Rome (cf. l. 11) or by Paul Valéry's dialogue 'L'Âme et la danse', which Rilke read in 1921 and translated in 1926.

231 *whirl at the end*: a pirouette, which combines both motion and stasis and in that sense is like a 'tree grown of motion'.

*bore fruit*: both in the obvious sense of the fruit produced by a natural tree, an important Rilkean motif, but also in an artistic sense, the depictions of dancers in movement on vases, which—because the artist's dark pen-strokes remind us of her dark eyebrows—brings the poem full-circle back to the dancer.

2. XIX

*gold*: when raw material of coinage is in the earth, it maintains its essence, but when it is made into money it becomes functional and paradoxically loses its value. Cf. from *The Book of Hours*: 'The ore is sick for its origins | and leaves behind it coin and wheel | that teach only the petty life' (p. 17).

*beggar*: when money touches the hand of the beggar (i.e. leaves the cycle of capitalism because it is freely given not exchanged), it is effectively consigned to oblivion. Rilke's work often focuses on poverty, celebrated as 'ein großer Glanz aus Innen' ('a great shining from within'; *Book of Hours*, *KA* I, 244).

*money*: cf. *DE* X, ll. 29–33 (p. 175). Capitalism is another attribute of the modern age that the *Sonnets* so often lament.

*close*: cf. the anemone of 2. VI and the symbolism of openness in contrast to the closed cycle of capitalism.

2. XX

233 *unthinkably far*: the paradox that two human beings, in close proximity, may actually be worlds apart and unable to communicate meaningfully.

*Fate*: cf. note to 2. XIV (p. 331).

*can it be spoken without them*: the non-existent 'language of fish' conjures up a mode of communication beyond what is banally familiar to mankind. Cf. the end of Hugo von Hofmannsthal's fictional letter from Lord Chandos to Lord Bacon ('Ein Brief', 'A Letter'), in which a gifted writer who has lost the capacity to speak imagines a 'language in which the dumb things of the world will speak to me'.

2. XXI

*you have never known*: cf. the paradox in 2. IV, l. 1: 'This beast does not exist' (p. 215).

*Shiraz . . . Isfahan*: ancient Persian cities famous for their gardens, Shiraz for roses in particular, Isfahan for its irrigation system.

*sing and praise them*: cf. *DE* I, l. 36 (p. 133), *DE* III, l. 1 (p. 141), *DE* IX, l. 52 (p. 173), and *DE* X, l. 2 (p. 175).

235 *carpet*: an image of a textured whole, in which beauty and pain are inextricably interwoven. 'Teppich' may also refer to tapestries, such as those that partly inspired 2. IV.

2. XXII

*abundances*: the timeless monuments of past cultures, often fragmentary but conjuring up a wholeness that the modern world has lost. In a letter to Simone Brüstlein written shortly before the *Sonnets* were begun (13 January 1922), Rilke blames the war for the fragmentation of modern life and laments mankind's inability to put back together what has been blown asunder. 'Nur die ganz uralten Bruchflächen haben recht, die die Natur anerkannt hat, – die Tempelmauern von Karnak, die Fragmente der Sappho, der Pont d'Avignon' ('Only the ancient fractured things that nature has recognized have any validity: the walls of the temple at Karnak, the fragments of Sappho, the Pont d'Avignon').

*Karnak*: near Luxor, a cluster of semi-ruined temples containing the Kiosk of Taharqa, in which only one of ten original huge columns 21 metres high remains. Cf. 'It was in Karnak' (pp. 123–7).

*surpluses*: the cultural achievements that once existed in generous profusion ('Überflüsse') are now surplus to requirements ('Überschüsse'), additional extras that rush past us in our hectic lives. The former 'outlive', the latter 'disperse'.

*over-lit nights*: an image for the modern city, linked with other regrettable technological innovations such as the aeroplane. The last line (and the image of the curve, usually a positive one in Rilke) seems to suggest that even these have a small claim for durability because they pass through our thoughts.

2. XXIII

*Summon me*: Rilke himself notes that this poem is addressed to the reader, presumably by the poet.

*We are free*: this freedom seems to be constituted paradoxically by those frustrating moments when we just fail to grasp what we think we were on the brink of holding or understanding, when a greeting turns out to be a parting, when we are neither young enough nor old enough for what we seek.

237 *bough and blade*: perhaps a reference to cutting off the branch on which we sit, another uncomfortable image of frustration, as the 'alas' indicates.

2 . XXIV

237 *So little help they had*: a celebration of human endeavour, which maintains
its energy even when virtually unsupported by others.

*We*: throughout the poem the speaking voice, that of the poet, associates
himself with mankind and its development and potential in contrast to his
more critical stance in other sonnets.

*surpass and shatter*: an image of fulfilment. Cf. the ringing glass in 2. XIII,
l. 8 (p. 225).

2 . XXV

*human rhythm*: another reference to the seasons, nature's ordered progress,
and man's place within it, but also an evocation of the repetitive, rhythmic
physical work of cultivation.

239 *Every hour that passes grows young*: possibly an echo of the Hours in Greek
myth (cf. 1. VIII), but also an expression of timelessness created by
progression simultaneously forwards and backwards.

2 . XXVI

*the bird's cry*: this sonnet distinguishes between two types of cry, that of
the bird, an expression of creaturely necessity (cf. *DE* VII, l. 2 (p. 159):
'though you cry pure as the bird'), and that of the children here, who
shout for attention rather than as an act of self-expression. Only the first
is truly Orphic.

*Chance they cry*: Rilke was notoriously intolerant of children's noisy play,
seen as articulating disorder.

*Order the criers*: cf. the cry of the Maenads in 1. XXVI, l. 3, which is
'drowned out . . . with order'. Even if the famous cry of the first line of
*DE* I (p. 131) is akin to the cry of the bird, and thus an authentic form of
self-expression, the 'orders of angels' would perceive it as akin to the
disruptive cries of children.

*singing God*: Orpheus, here explicitly associated with order, which is in
turn represented by singing, and for which 'the head and the lyre'
are guarantors (as they are in 1. XXVI, l. 5, despite the attacks of the
Maenads).

2 . XXVII

241 *demiurge*: in Platonism, the maker or creator of the world; in Gnosticism,
a being subordinate to the Supreme Being, sometimes the author of evil.
Here time is the demiurge.

*we drift in a transient course*: humanity is characterized by transience,
which is why time is felt to be hostile towards it. In the Orphic world,
however, time is suspended, and there is no distinction between 'being'
and 'becoming', so the sonnet questions whether our 'evanescence' is
really as negative as 'fate' (which is essentially teleological) would have us

believe: Orpheus has a 'divine use' for it, and as l. 5 of the following
sonnet suggests, in our transience we actually even surpass nature.

2. XXVIII

*come and go*: cf. 1. V, l. 6, p. 187: '[Orpheus] comes and goes', another
example of the *Sonnets*' alternating rhythms and necessary complement-
arity of opposites. The sonnet is addressed to Wera Ouckama Knoop, who
is fully assimilated into the Orphic world as she, too, 'comes and goes'.

*centre still unheard*: like the 'whirl' of 2. XVIII, l. 3, one of the points that
for Rilke unites motion and stillness (cf. also note to the 'point of the turn'
in 2. XII, l. 4, p. 223).

*friend*: the poet, who hereby claims Wera as his inspiration for the cycle.

2. XXIX

Rilke's note states that this sonnet is addressed to 'a friend of Wera's', and
critical opinion is divided as to whether this means Orpheus or the poet (in
dialogue with himself or with Wera). It is hard to see these possibilities as
mutually exclusive, however, and this sonnet may be the point at which Rilke
feels most at one with his poetic god.

243 *breath*: this sonnet returns to the principal motif of 2.1.

*Move . . . in and out of transformation*: another formulation of the principle
articulated in 'come and go' in the previous sonnet and elsewhere.

*I am running . . . I am*: the last lines of the cycle fuse motion and stillness
once again as the essence of Orphic self-realization. The last words can be
read as an answer to the question posed in 1. III, l. 8 ('when are we actual?').
The affirmation of being is perhaps not coincidentally an echo of, and a
response to, the last word of Ovid's *Metamorphoses*, 'vivam' ('I shall live'),
which asserts the poet's place in posterity; for Rilke, however, the Orphic
ideal is self-realization beyond time, but within poetry.

## UNCOLLECTED POEMS 1922–1926

*Odette R . . .*

Written 21 December 1922, Muzot. The dedicatee is the painter Odette Ruffy
(1892–1915), and the poem was written for her sister, Marguerite Masson-
Ruffy, inscribed in a copy of *Malte Laurids Brigge*.

245 *once fully risen descends*: cf. the end of *DE* x (ll. 110–13, p. 181).

*Dedicated to M . . .*

Written 6 and 8 November 1923, Muzot. The dedicatee is Baladine Klossowska
(known as Merline) and the poem was inscribed for her in an example of the
*Duino Elegies*.

*turning-point of gravity*: another of Rilke's indefinable moments of
'Umschlag' or 'flipping over' from one state into another.

245  *how new!*: the poem was written in the winter after Rilke translated
Valéry and may be read as anticipating a new creative period as a result,
one in which poetry was conceived of in the Mallarméan tradition as
akin to magic.

247  *second semi-circle*: the two half-measures of joy, the to-and-fro of the
swinging motion, make a semi-circle that is mirrored in the poet's mind
to form a circle, an image of wholeness.

   *departure*: the necessary returning movement of the swing becomes
a farewell to the self that continues in the imagined whole, and is thus
a metaphor for death and the 'double-realm'.

### *For* Nike

Lines 1–11 on 31 January or 1 February 1922 and immediately thereafter; ll.
12–20 before Christmas 1923, Muzot. The dedicatee is Nanny Wunderly-
Volkart and the poem was inscribed in her copy of the *Elegies*.

   *the god*: Orpheus (the poem was conceived immediately before the com-
position of the *Sonnets*).

   *the word soars to the conjuring*: cf. note to the previous poem, l. 16, and the
idea of poetry as magic.

### *The Magician*

Written on 12 April 1924, 'around midnight', Muzot. There is a French version
of this poem, written on the same day (*KA* v, 204).

249  *Magician*: the poem is almost a programmatic statement of Rilke's new
conception of poetry after the completion of *The Sonnets to Orpheus*.

   *the Other*: cf. 'Dedicated to M. . . .', l. 16: the 'other' is the object of the
magician's incantatory art, wholly distinct from him.

   *midnight*: indicative that even a successful act of conjuration does not
provide insight into the 'other'; the 'knot' that is fastened binds both the
'other' and the poet.

### *Eros*

Written mid-February 1924, Muzot.

   *Eros*: Greek god of sexual love.

   *Masks*: conceived of here as protective against the power of Eros.

251  *Life . . . destiny*: the result of the divine pairing that produces Eros is the
loss of open-ended, targetless life and the substitution instead of fate,
which is life understood as the product of a teleology.

### *Transience*

Written late February 1924, Muzot.

   *Sand-shift of hours*: an image of an hourglass, or of the desert sands
recalled from Rilke's visit to Egypt in 1911.

*columns jut*: the non-load-bearing column features frequently in Rilke's verse (cf. 'It was in Karnak', ll. 14–15, p. 125; 'Gong (II)', l. 19, p. 265; *Sonnet*, 2. XII, l. 7, p. 223).

*change*: the German, 'Wandel', echoes the major theme of the *Sonnets* and suggests a positive interpretation of the changes evoked here rather than a melancholy one.

*seeing head*: an echo perhaps of 'Archaic Torso of Apollo' (p. 81).

### 'Do you remember: falling stars that leapt'

Written 1 June 1924, Muzot, after a walk to Corin-La-Chapelle between Sion and Serre with Nanny Wunderly-Volkart.

*falling stars*: the motif of the falling star in Rilke is an image of mediation between the cosmos and the earth (cf. the 'Elegy for Marina Tsvetaeva', *KA* II, 405), and of self-realization in death, since a meteor only becomes visible as it burns up (cf. 'Death', l. 18, p. 123). Rilke's famous letter to his Polish translator, Witold von Hulewicz, speaks of 'some stars [that] are immediately intensified and consumed in the infinite consciousness of the angel'.

### Wild Rose

Written 1 June 1924, Muzot.

*Wild Rose*: Rilke's preference is almost always for the complex, cultivated rose over the natural wild rose.

253 *look at me*: the rose is an image of openness and honesty, self-sufficient and unhampered by any form of 'purpose'.

### 'World was there in my beloved's face'

Written mid-July 1924, Ragaz (a small spa town in the Swiss canton of St Gallen).

*poured and emptied*: the image of the world as liquid, with the face of the beloved as the vessel from which world is drunk.

*running over*: 'übergehen' here has the dual meaning of 'overflowing' and 'flipping over', and as such represents an ineffable Rilkean turning-point, here between empty insufficiency and over-fullness.

### 'Overturn nothing that stands!'

Written mid-August 1924, Muzot.

*born through us more*: this and the other unusual comparatives in the poem (e.g. ll. 2–3) suggest a process of huge intensification that the static world undergoes under the gaze of the observer until it bursts forth, as if new-born and laden with the dynamic tensions of its various relationships.

*'Night's constellations'*

Written late September 1924, Muzot.

255 *overleap*: cf. 'Night. O you so deeply freed face' for the idea of the self being small faced with the hugeness of the night.

*bishop*: the correspondence with Mitterer makes some use of the chess-board metaphor (cf. *KA* II, 358).

*Palm of the Hand*

Written on or about 1 October 1924, Muzot.

*Palm of the Hand*: André Gide reported a conversation with Rilke in which he expressed his astonishment that German has no satisfactory word for the palm of the hand (he knew 'Handfläche', 'flat of the hand', and found the unusual word 'Handteller', literally 'plate of the hand' in Grimm's etymological dictionary, but was dissatisfied with both). The word for 'back of the hand' was in common usage, which suggested people were interested in this, 'the impersonal, un-sensual, rough outside', preferring it to the 'lukewarm, caressing, soft interior of the hand, which expresses all an individual's secrets!' (quoted in *KA* II, 842–3).

*wanderers*: cf. note to *Sonnets*, I. x, l. 4 and lines 9 and 12 of this poem.

*alterer*: the transforming process that the hand enacts is also a creative one (cf. the verb 'schöpfen' in line 7, which means both 'to draw' or 'scoop', of water, and to 'to create'; cf. line 7 of the next poem): the hand is a creator of poetry.

*'Night. O you so deeply freed face'*

Written 2 and 3 October 1924, Muzot, written under the night sky over two evenings, according to a letter to Nanny Wunderly-Volkart from the following day.

*Night*: the use of a single word or short verbless phrase to open a poem (sometimes referred to by critics as an 'evocative') is characteristic of a number of Rilke's works from this period, including 'Palm of the Hand', 'Transience', 'Eros', etc. Such openings are conjurations, almost magic formulae, without case or tense, approximations to a form of 'language made of word-kernels' (as Rilke called it in a letter to Nanny Wunderly-Volkart of 4 February 1920).

257 *yet*: a characteristic expression of 'pulling back', when Rilke asserts mutuality or unity after having evoked an imbalance (in this case of the hugeness of night over the insignificant self).

*Gravity*

5 October 1924, Muzot.

*gravity*: a metaphor for existential and poetic forces rather than a physical condition.

*flying . . . standing . . . sleeping*: three different modes of being, each artic-
ulating a different perspective on being affected by gravity.

## Mausoleum

Written October 1924, Muzot.

*Mausoleum*: a form of tomb, built above the ground (as opposed to a
subterranean crypt), named after the tomb of Mausolus at Halicarnassus,
one of the Seven Wonders of the Ancient World, although it is not likely
that Rilke is referring to this monument specifically here.

*Balsam fruit*: there are several types of balsam but Rilke may have in
mind the biblical phrase 'Balsam (or balm) of Gilead', which refers to the
resin of a tree of the genus Commiphora native to Palestine and Israel.
Balsam was highly valued for its medicinal properties and as a luxurious
perfume.

*heartnut*: whilst there is a tree of the genus Semecarpus that produces fruit
sometimes known as the 'heartnut', once believed to prolong life, it is
likely that Rilke is more interested in the suggestive properties of the word
than those of the fruit itself. It exists in a chiastic relationship with the
word for 'King's heart' that opens and closes the first stanza.

*Poppy-head urn*: a funerary urn shaped like the seed-head of a poppy, asso-
ciated with sleep and death. If, as seems likely, this poem is to be associ-
ated with Rilke's memories of Egypt, these may be the canopic jars used
by the Egyptians to preserve the internal organs of the person whose body
is then mummified.

259 *gentle girl*: it has been suggested that this might refer to Queen Nefertiti,
wife of Amenophis IV-Akhenaten, whose image Rilke saw on reliefs in
a museum in Cairo in 1911. Lotti von Wedel had sent him several
photographs of a bust of Nefertiti in January 1922.

*wing-velvet*: the 'Florflügel' in the original refer to the delicate wings that
an insect protects with wing-cases. Rilke uses it in another poem written
at the end of January 1922 (*KA* II, 195).

*sang them to oneness*: the Queen's heart is not with the King's, in the urn,
'mid-placed mid-building' and the poet 'sings them together', an image
of the unity created by poetry in a poem shot through with images of
separation and distance.

*wind's within-ness*: an image of internalization perhaps even more intimate
than that of the 'palm of the hand' (p. 255). The wind, and specifically
moments when the wind seems to cease, when the elements 'pause for
breath', are associated with Rilke's memories of Egypt in a letter to Lotti
Wedel (28 January 1922) in which he writes of just such an intake of
breath, metaphorically describing a cultural shift at the time of Amenophis
IV-Akhenaten. It has been suggested that the unusual punctuation in this
poem articulates similar 'pauses for breath', or tipping-points like the
fulcrum of a see-saw, and that Rilke is reflecting on a change of direction

in his writing towards the principle of 'complementarity' (cf. *SW* II, 771–2).

*'Waters that plunge and the quick-sliding'*

Written mid-October 1924, Muzot.

259   *gaily*: water, especially the water of flowing streams, is often associated with happiness in Rilke's verse (cf. 'Heitres Geschenk von den kältern | Bergen'; 'Happy gift from the colder mountains', *KA* II, 363). Water itself is an ancient symbol of life.

      *mingled . . . dividing*: in a poem written a few months before this one, in June 1924, Rilke uses similar images of separation and mixing ('Mädchen ordnen', 'Girls order', *KA* II, 326).

*'Somewhere the flower of farewell blooms'*

Written mid-October 1924, Muzot.

Although Rilke never wrote a haiku proper this and his own epitaph (p. 263) are fruits of his late interest in this most condensed of forms.

*'Urn, opium-poppy ovary'*

Written late October 1924, Muzot (incomplete).

261   *Urn, opium-poppy*: Rilke seems to have taken an image from line 3 of 'Mausoleum' (p. 257) and experimented with its potential as a metaphor of transience, very differently from its function in the slightly earlier poem.

*Autumn*

Written late autumn 1924, Muzot.

      *the sky—which does not know us*: the comforting experience of the tree (which is both seen and seeing) when it has its leaves in summer turns into a sense of vulnerability as its (and our) inner self is exposed to the cosmos.

263   *search for reference*: the self has no defining boundaries.

*'Rose, O pure contradiction, delight'*

Written 27 October 1925, Muzot (in Rilke's will, where he specified that it should be used on his gravestone). The French prose poem 'Cimetière' ('Cemetery') was written immediately before it, and ends 'sommeil de personne sous tant de paupières' ('no-one's sleep under so many eye-lids', *KA* v, 290).

      *Rose*: the cultivated rose that features in so many of Rilke's poems (contrast 'Wild Rose', p. 251).

      *oh*: a combination of celebration and regret.

      *eyelids*: the German 'Lider' is homophonous with 'Lieder' (meaning 'songs' and thus by extension 'poems'). Rilke uses the image of eyelids for rose-petals elsewhere, too.

*Idol*

Written in summer 1925 (first line) and November, Paris and Muzot.

> *cats*: another poem associated with Rilke's memories of Egypt, here the Egyptians' reverence for cats. The reference to 'crypt' in line 5 may also be related to Egypt.

> *ripe eye-berries*: cf. 'Archaic Torso of Apollo', l. 2 (p. 57), for the image of the ripened eyeball.

> *juice of the grape of seeing*: an extraordinary image, not just evoking the visible or the action of seeing but trying to convey sight itself as if in tangible terms via a synaesthetic link with taste.

> *gong! gong!*: another indication of Rilke's progress to a new form of writing: not sound used to structure, underpin, or reinforce meaning but sound for its own sake.

> *other gods . . . god of wiles*: Rilke has moved from his earlier mythic beings (the Angel, Orpheus) to a new set of divinities for his last phase of writing.

*Gong*

Written late October 1925, Muzot. A fragment, evidently a draft for the next poem.

*Gong* (II)

Written November 1925, Muzot.

265 *No more for our ears . . .: sound*: the foregrounding of sound in this poem, and the frequency with which Rilke uses a series of rhetorical figures such as chiasmus, parallelisms, antitheses, etc., is the basis on which Paul de Man uses this and related poems to support his claim that Rilke's poetry fails to move beyond his own obsession with poetic language itself and rhetorical structures and has no valid purchase on the world (see *Allegories of Meaning*).

> *seem the hearers*: in contrast to the *Sonnets*, where hearing is paramount, we are now being heard rather than hearing.

> *Design for inner worlds laid in the open*: contrast the 'interiorization' of the world, the transformation of the outer world into 'the inner' in Rilke's previous poetry.

> *gong!*: the sound is now the space in which the gods are dissolved entirely, despite their resistance.

> *newly re-poured star*: the stars of Rilke's earlier poetry, distant and beyond all human intervention, models of poetic structures, are now recast, remoulded, subject to the dissolving action of sound.

> *bearing column*: another reversal of a key image: cf. the note to 'Transience'.

265 *betrayal of all things*: Rilke's previous poetics used things as means of articulating human subjectivity, which is now seen as a betrayal and impossible in the non-human sound-universe of 'Gong'.

### *A Sequel to the 'Bowl of Roses'*

Written 15 February 1926, in a sanatorium at Val-Mont near Montreux, and inscribed as a dedication in a copy of *New Poems* for a fellow patient, Paula N. Riccard.

> *Bowl of Roses*: the last of the first book of *New Poems*, celebrating the richness of life and containing a key image of rose-petals likened to eyelids (cf. Rilke's epitaph, p. 263).
>
> *so tender a killer?*: the falling rose-petals are, like the dying poet, a victim of the passing of time, which here is celebrated for its tenderness.

### *Arrival*

Written early June 1926, Muzot.

267 *Arrival*: anticipating the image of pregnancy and birth in the poem, and an allusion to the Christian season of Advent (and thus to Rilke's own earlier collection of verse with that title, published in 1898).

> *bed*: the locus both of sexual union and of birth; the image of swimming in the next line has been seen as a reference to the sperm and impregnation.
>
> *then only shall I be*: the nine months of pregnancy are symbolic of the incalculable time it will take for a rebirth of the poet into the condition ('being') that his earlier verse was most concerned with. Rilke repeatedly linked the idea of poetic creativity with the images of the pregnant woman and giving birth.
>
> *two millennia*: a reference to ideas adumbrated in much earlier work (*The Book of Hours* and the *Florentine Diary* from the late 1890s and the *Letters to a Young Poet* of 1903) according to which artists were the precursors of 'das werdende Gott' ('the god of becoming'), a kind of messiah, who would replace the two-thousand-year age of Christianity.
>
> *facing you*: the German enacts the image of confrontation by idiosyncratically splitting the preposition 'gegenüber' ('opposite') into two parts, surrounding the word for 'you'.

### *Written for Count Karl Lanckoroński*

Written 18 August 1926, Ragaz. This is Rilke's last major poem, and may consciously owe something to his reading of Goethe's late poetry, since the six-line stanzas rhyming AABCCB match those of 'Vermächtnis' ('Legacy') and 'Eins und alles' ('One and All'), although with five stresses Rilke's lines are longer than Goethe's.

> *Count Karl Lanckoroński*: (1848–1933); Viennese writer, art collector, and patron of the arts, who stayed in Ragaz at the same time as Rilke in 1926.

*Spirit and fervour . . . lose*: this is a line from a poem by Lanckoroński contained in a manuscript of his own poetry that he gave to Rilke whilst in Ragaz.

269 *shepherd*: an image of the poet.

*death . . . or life*: the last in a whole series of apparent opposites, beginning with 'spirit and fervour', via 'the gentlest things' and 'the starkest force', 'sleep' and 'watching', 'sob' and 'laughter', that the poem seeks to bring together and balance.

*the angle of the bent knee*: a characteristically concrete image for a much more abstract thought, the 'new measure' of the world that those who are 'chosen' (l. 3) will apply.

*For Erika*

Written 24 August 1926, Ragaz.

*Erika*: the young Austrian poet and dramatist Erika Mitterer (1906–2001). Rilke's exchange of epistolary poems with Mitterer began in May 1924, when she sent him two poems in response to *The Sonnets to Orpheus*. She visited Rilke in Muzot from 21 to 23 November 1925 and their correspondence, in which Rilke displayed a greater personal openness than usual, lasted until August 1926. This is the last poem in the correspondence and imitates an ancient ode-form where the lines consist of two half-lines with a strong caesura between them, each half-line containing one dactyl (– ⌣ ⌣) and one cretic (– ⌣ –).

*In celebration of praise*: the word 'Rühmung' here picks up the same word in the last line of Mitterer's previous letter-poem, which reports a successful outcome to a serious operation.

*best sheltered*: the dove stands in some respects for the human heart and expresses the paradox that the dove (or heart) least exposed and with most overt protection will not have had the opportunity to experience tenderness.

*the thrown ball*: cf. *Sonnets*, 2. VIII and notes.

*'Come, you the last that I shall recognize'*

Written mid-December 1926, Val-Mont. Rilke's last poem, and the last entry in his diary.

271 *pain*: despite the proximity of this poem to Rilke's death on 29 December, at the age of 51, the subject of the poem is pain rather than death. His doctor, Dr Haemmerli, wrote to Princess von Thurn und Taxis that he only truly realized he was going to die some three days before the event.

*pyre*: the comparison is with being burned at the stake.

# INDEX OF GERMAN TITLES
# AND FIRST LINES

*Abend*                                                          32
Ach, da wir Hülfe von Menschen erharrten                        106
*Advent*                                                          2
Alle die Stimmen der Bäche                                      246
Alles Erworbne bedroht die Maschine, solange                    220
Als ihn der Gott in seiner Not betrat                            82
Also, das tat not für den und den                               106
*An die Musik*                                                   122
*An Hölderlin*                                                   118
*Ankunft*                                                        266
*Archäischer Torso Apollos*                                       80
Atmen, du unsichtbares Gedicht!                                 210
Auf einmal weiß ich viel von den Fontänen                        38
*Auferweckung des Lazarus*                                       106
*Aus einer Kindheit*                                              26
Ausgedehnt von riesigen Gesichten                                84
Ausgesetzt auf den Bergen des Herzens                           118

*Blaue Hortensie*                                                 68
Blumen, ihr schließlich den ordnenden Händen verwandte          216
Blumenmuskel, der der Anemone                                   214
*Buddha in der Glorie*                                           104

Da drin: das träge Treten ihrer Tatzen                           60
Da oben wird das Bild von einer Welt                            102
Da steht der Tod, ein bläulicher Absud                          120
Da stieg ein Baum. O reine Übersteigung!                        182
*Dame vor dem Spiegel*                                            98
*Das Buch der Bilder*                                          24–42
Das Dunkeln war wie Reichtum in dem Raume                        26
*Das Einhorn*                                                     64
Das ist mein Streit                                               2
*Das Karussell*                                                   72
*Das Lied des Aussätzigen*                                        38
*Das Rosen-Innere*                                                98
*Das Stunden-Buch*                                             8–24
Das Volk war durstig; also ging das eine                         24
Das war der Seelen wunderliches Bergwerk                         76
Daß ich dereinst, an dem Ausgang der grimmigen Einsicht         174
Denn sieh: sie werden leben und sich mehren                      22
Denn wir sind nur die Schale und das Blatt                       18
Der Abend ist mein Buch                                           6

| | |
|---|---|
| Der Abend wechselt langsam die Gewänder | 32 |
| *Der Ball* | 102 |
| *Der Blinde* | 90 |
| Der blinde Mann, der auf der Brücke steht | 30 |
| *Der Dichter* | 66 |
| *Der Goldschmied* | 50 |
| Der Heilige hob das Haupt, und das Gebet | 64 |
| *Der Hund* | 102 |
| *Der Knabe* | 26 |
| *Der Magier* | 248 |
| *Der Nachbar* | 30 |
| *Der neuen Gedichte anderer Teil* | 80–104 |
| *Der Ölbaum-Garten* | 58 |
| *Der Panther* | 62 |
| *Der Schwan* | 66 |
| *Der Tod* | 120 |
| Der Tod ist groß | 40 |
| *Der Träumer* (II) | 2 |
| *Dich* aber will ich nun, *Dich*, die ich kannte | 208 |
| *Die achte Elegie* | 164 |
| *Die erste Elegie* | 130 |
| *Die Bettler* | 86 |
| *Die dritte Elegie* | 140 |
| Die Einsamkeit ist wie ein Regen | 30 |
| *Die Fensterrose* | 60 |
| *Die Flamingos* | 100 |
| *Die fünfte Elegie* | 150 |
| *Die Gazelle* | 64 |
| *Die Heilige* | 24 |
| *Die Heiligen Drei Könige* | 34 |
| *Die Insel der Sirenen* | 84 |
| Die Könige der Welt sind alt | 16 |
| *Die Kurtisane* | 68 |
| *Die Laute* | 96 |
| Die Nächte sind nicht für die Menge gemacht | 28 |
| *Die neunte Elegie* | 168 |
| *Die sechste Elegie* | 156 |
| *Die siebente Elegie* | 158 |
| *Die Sonette an Orpheus* | 182–242 |
| Die Städte aber wollen nur das Ihre | 22 |
| *Die Treppe der Orangerie* | 70 |
| *Die vierte Elegie* | 144 |
| *Die zehnte Elegie* | 174 |
| *Die zweite Elegie* | 134 |
| Diese Mühsal, durch noch Ungetanes | 66 |
| Dir aber, Herr, o was weih ich dir, sag | 202 |
| Du aber, Göttlicher, du, bis zuletzt noch Ertöner | 210 |
| Du bist die Zukunft, großes Morgenrot | 16 |
| Du entfernst dich von mir, du Stunde | 66 |

Du im Voraus 110
Du, mein Freund, bist einsam, weil . . . . 198
Du Runder, der das Warme aus zwei Händen 102
Du wußtest nicht, was den Haufen 86
*Duineser Elegien* 130–80

*Ehe* 42
Ein Gespenst ist noch wie eine Stelle 92
Ein Gott vermags. Wie aber, sag mir, soll 184
*Ein Prophet* 84
*Eine Folge zur ›Rosenschale‹* 264
*Eine Sibylle* 86
Eines ist, die Geliebte zu singen. Ein anderes, wehe 140
*Eingang* 24
*Einsamkeit* 30
Einst als am Saum der Wüsten sich 34
Einst, vor Zeiten, nannte man sie alt 86
Er ging hinauf unter dem grauen Laub 58
Er ruft es an. Es schrickt zusamm und steht 248
Ernster Engel aus Ebenholz 4
*Eros* 248
Errichtet keinen Denkstein. Laßt die Rose 186
Es winkt zu Fühlung fast aus allen Dingen 116
Euch, die ihr nie mein Gefühl verließt 192

Feigenbaum, seit wie lange schon ists mir bedeutend 156
Flugsand der Stunden. Leise fortwährende Schwindung 250
*Fortgehn* 44
Frau und Erlauchte: sicher kränken wir 46
Fremde Geige, gehst du mir nach? 30
*Früher Apollo* 56
Frühling ist wiedergekommen. Die Erde 204
*Für Erika* 268
*Für Nike* 246
Fürstlich verwöhnte Fenster sehen immer 94

*Gebet* 4
*Geschrieben für Karl Grafen Lanckoroński* 266
Gestirne der Nacht, die ich erwachter gewahre 254
Giebt es wirklich die Zeit, die zerstörende? 238
*Gong* 262
*Gong* (II) 264
*Gott im Mittelalter* 62
Gott oder Göttin des Katzenschlafs 262

*Handinneres* 254
Heil dem Geist, der uns verbinden mag 194
*Herbst* 260
*Herbsttag* 32

Herr: es ist Zeit. Der Sommer war sehr groß                    32
Herr: Wir sind ärmer denn die armen Tiere                      20
Hinter Stäben, wie Tiere                                       46
Hinweg, die ich bat                                           110
Hörst du das Neue, Herr                                       200

Ich bin die Laute. Willst du meinen Leib                       96
Ich finde dich in allen diesen Dingen                          10
Ich fürchte mich so vor der Menschen Wort                       6
Ich kann nicht glauben, daß der kleine Tod                     10
Ich möchte einer werden, so wie die                            26
Ich war bei den ältesten Mönchen                               14
*Idol*                                                        262
Im Sturm, der um die starke Kathedrale                         60
Immer wieder von uns aufgerissen                              226
In einer Rose steht dein Bett, Geliebte. Dich selber          266
In Karnak wars. Wir waren hingeritten                         122
In Spiegelbildern wie von Fragonard                           100
Innres der Hand. Sohle, die nicht mehr geht                   254
Irgendwo blüht die Blume des Abschieds                        260
Irgendwo wohnt das Gold in der verwöhnenden Bank              230
Ist er ein Hiesiger? Nein, aus beiden                         188

Jeder Engel ist schrecklich. Und dennoch, weh mir             134
Jetzt reifen schon die roten Berberitzen                       18

Kann mir einer sagen, wohin                                     8
*Klage*                                                       114
Klang, nichtmehr mit Gehör                                    262
Komm du, du letzter, den ich anerkenne                        270
Königsherz. Kern eines hohen                                  256

*La Dame à la Licorne*                                         46
*L'Ange du Méridien*                                           60
Lange errang ers im Anschaun                                  112
*Larenopfer*                                                    2
*Leda*                                                         82
*Leichen-Wäsche*                                               88
*Liebes-Lied*                                                  56
*Lied vom Meer*                                                94
Lösch mir die Augen aus: ich kann dich sehn                    14

Manche, des Todes, entstand ruhig geordnete Regel             222
*Marionetten-Theater*                                          46
Masken! Masken! Daß man Eros blende                           248
*Mausoleum*                                                   256
Meine frühverliehnen                                            2
*Menschen bei Nacht*                                           28
*Mir zur Feier*                                               2–8

Mit allen Augen sieht die Kreatur 164
Mit einem Dach und seinem Schatten dreht 72
Mitte aller Mitten, Kern der Kerne 104
Mitte, wie du aus allen 256
Musik: Atem der Statuen. Vielleicht 122

Nacht. Oh du in Tiefe gelöstes 254
Nenn ich dich Aufgang oder Untergang? 6
*Neue Gedichte* 56–80
'*Nicht Geist, nicht Inbrunst wollen wir entbehren.*' 266
Nicht mehr für Ohren . . . : Klang 264
Nicht um-stoßen, was steht! 252
Nun treibt die Stadt schon nicht mehr wie ein Köder 96
Nur im Raum der Rühmung darf die Klage 190
Nur nimm sie wieder aus der Städte Schuld 22
Nur wer die Leier schon hob 190

*Odette R . . . .* 244
O Bäume Lebens, o wann winterlich? 144
O Brunnen-Mund, du gebender, du Mund 226
O diese Lust, immer neu, aus gelockertem Lehm! 236
O dieses ist das Tier, das es nicht giebt 214
O erst *dann*, wenn der Flug 206
O ihr Zärtlichen, tretet zuweilen 184
O komm und geh. Du, fast noch Kind, ergänze 240
O trotz Schicksal: die herrlichen Überflüsse 234
Oh hoher Baum des Schauns, der sich entlaubt 260
*Orpheus. Eurydike. Hermes* 76

Plötzliches Fortgehn; Draußensein im Grauen 44
*Pont du Carrousel* 30

Reich war von ihnen der Raum, immer voller und sätter 264
*Requiem für eine Freundin* (Auszug) 52
*Römische Fontäne* 70
*Rosa Hortensie* 100
Rose, du thronende, denen im Altertume 216
Rose, oh reiner Widerspruch, Lust 262
Rufe mich zu jener deiner Stunden 234
Rühmen, das ists! Ein zum Rühmen Bestellter 188
Rühmt euch, ihr Richtenden, nicht der entbehrlichen Folter 220

Schaukel des Herzens. O sichere, an welchem unsichtbaren 244
*Schlangen-Beschwörung* 90
*Schlußstück* 40
Schon, horch, hörst du der ersten Harken 236
*Schwarze Katze* 92
*Schwerkraft* 256
Sei allem Abschied voran, als wäre er hinter 224

Sein Blick ist vom Vorübergehn der Stäbe                                    62
Sie hatten sich an ihn gewöhnt. Doch als                                   88
Sie ist traurig, lautlos und allein                                        42
Sieh den Himmel. Heißt kein Sternbild ›Reiter‹?                            192
Sieh, er geht und unterbricht die Stadt                                    90
Sieh ich bin einer, den alles verlassen hat                               38
Siehe die Blumen, diese dem Irdischen treuen                              224
Singe die Gärten, mein Herz, die du nicht kennst; wie in Glas             232
Sinnend von Legende zu Legende                                             42
So, nun wird es doch der Engel sein                                        108
So starbst du, wie die Frauen früher starben                               52
So wie das letzte Grün in Farbentiegeln                                    68
So wie dem Meister manchmal das eilig                                     212
Sollen wir unsere uralte Freundschaft, die großen                        208
*Spanische Tänzerin*                                                       74
*Spätherbst in Venedig*                                                    96
Spiegel: noch nie hat man wissend beschrieben                            212
Stiller Freund der vielen Fernen, fühle                                   242


Tänzerin: o du Verlegung                                                  228
Taube, die draußen blieb                                                  268
Tränen, die innigsten, *steigen*!                                         244
Tränen, Tränen, die aus mir brechen                                      108
Träume scheinen mir wie Orchideen                                          2


Und fast ein Mädchen wars und ging hervor                                182
Und sie hatten Ihn in sich erspart                                        62
Uraltes Wehn vom Meer                                                     94
Urne, Fruchtknoten des Mohns—                                            260


Venedigs Sonne wird in meinem Haar                                        68
*Venezianischer Morgen*                                                   94
*Vergänglichkeit*                                                        250
Verweilung, auch am Vertrautesten nicht                                  118
Verzauberte: wie kann der Einklang zweier                                 64
Voller Apfel, Birne und Banane                                           194
*Von den Fontänen*                                                        38


Wandelt sich rasch auch die Welt                                         202
Warte! Langsam! droh ich jedem Ringe                                      50
Wartet . . . , das schmeckt . . . Schon ists auf der Flucht              198
Warum, wenn es angeht, also die Frist des Daseins                        168
Was wirst du tun, Gott, wenn ich sterbe?                                  12
Wasser, die stürzen und eilende . . .                                    258
Weißt du noch: fallende Sterne, die                                      250
Welt war in dem Antlitz der Geliebten                                    252
Wem willst du klagen, Herz? Immer gemiedener                             114
*Wendung*                                                                112
Wenige ihr, der einstigen Kindheit Gespielen                             218

Wenn auf dem Markt, sich wiegend, der Beschwörer          90
Wenn er denen, die ihm gastlich waren          84
Wer aber *sind* sie, sag mir, die Fahrenden, diese ein wenig          150
Wer du auch seist: am Abend tritt hinaus          24
Wer nahm das Rosa an? Wer wußte auch          100
Wer, wenn ich schriee, hörte mich denn aus der Engel          130
Werbung nicht mehr, nicht Werbung, entwachsene Stimme          158
Wie der Wächter in den Weingeländen          12
Wie dunkeln und rauschen im Instrument          50
Wie ergreift uns der Vogelschrei . . .          238
Wie in der Hand ein Schwefelzündholz, weiß          74
Wie in einem Schlaftrunk Spezerein          98
Wie Könige die schließlich nur noch schreiten          70
Wie manches Mal durch das noch unbelaubte          56
Wie soll ich meine Seele halten, daß          56
Wie steht er da vor den Verdunkelungen          250
*Wilder Rosenbusch*          250
Wir bauen an dir mit zitternden Händen          8
Wir dürfen dich nicht eigenmächtig malen          8
Wir gehen um mit Blume, Weinblatt, Frucht          196
Wir kannten nicht sein unerhörtes Haupt          80
Wir sind die Treibenden          206
Wo, in welchen immer selig bewässerten Gärten, an welchen          228
Wo ist zu diesem Innen          98
Wolle die Wandlung. O sei für die Flamme begeistert          222
Wunderliches Wort: die Zeit vertreiben!          128

Zu unterst der Alte, verworrn          200
*Zueignung an M . . . .*          244
Zwei Becken, eins das andre übersteigend          70
Zwischen den Sternen, wie weit; und doch, um wievieles
          noch weiter          232

# INDEX OF ENGLISH TITLES
# AND FIRST LINES

A ghost persists, something like a locus                          93
A god can do it. But how may a man follow                       185
A sudden tree soars. O sheer exceeding!                         183
*About Fountains*                                                 39
*Advent*                                                          3
Aeons ago people called her old                                  87
Age-old wind, blowing                                            95
Ah, as we waited for human help, angels climbed                107
All this pushing through things not yet done                    67
All we have won the machine imperils, by                       221
Almost all things beckon us to feeling                         117
Along with roof and shadow, it rotates                          73
And she was almost a girl, appearing out of                    183
And so you died, as women used to die                           53
And they had saved Him up inside themselves                     63
Answering, when they sat at evening                             85
*Archaic Torso of Apollo*                                        81
*Arrival*                                                       267
As sometimes when the fullest spring morning                    57
*Autumn*                                                        261
*Autumn Day*                                                     33

*Ball, The*                                                     103
Be ahead of all parting as though you found it behind          225
*Beggars, The*                                                   87
Behind bars, like animals                                       47
*Black Cat*                                                      93
*Blind Man, The*                                                91
*Blue Hydrangea*                                                69
*Book of Hours, The*                                           9–25
*Book of Images, The*                                         25–43
*Boy, The*                                                      27
Breathing, you invisible poem!                                 211
*Buddha in Glory*                                              105
But bear them away again from urban evils                       23
But you, divine being, you who sang to the end                 211
By now they had grown used to him, but when                     89

Cast out, exposed on the mountains of the heart                119
Centre of all centres. Core of cores                           105
Centre-core, how you draw yourself                             257
Cities turn their force full on their own                       23

Come, you the last that I shall recognize 271
*Corpse-washing* 89
*Courtesan, The* 69

Dancer, O you translation 229
*Death* 121
Death is mighty 41
*Dedicated to M . . . .* 245
Desire to be changed. O be alive for the flame 223
Do not boast, judges, that you dispense with torture 221
Do you remember: falling stars that leapt 251
Does time truly exist? And annihilate? 239
*Dog, The* 103
Dove, so long gone from us 269
*Dreamer* (II), *The* 3
Dreams: as vivid in my eyes as orchids 3
*Duino Elegies* 131–81
Dull and rough these leaves, like vestiges 69

*Early Apollo* 57
*Eighth Elegy, The* 165
Enchanted creature, how can the twinned tuning 65
*End Piece* 41
*Entrance* 25
*Eros* 249
*Evening* 33
Every Angel is dread. And yet, alas 135
Every voice of the streamlet 247

*Fifth Elegy, The* 151
Fig-tree, how long you have held this meaning for me 157
*First Elegy, The* 131
*Flamingos, The* 101
Flower-muscle of the anemone 215
*For Erika* 269
*For* Nike 247
For see, they will live, flourish, multiply 23
For we are only rind of fruit, and leaf 19
*Fourth Elegy, The* 145
*From a Childhood* 27
Full-ripe fruit: apple, banana, pear 195

*Garden of Olives, The* 59
*Gazelle, The* 65
*God in the Middle Ages* 63
God or goddess of cats' sleep 263
*Goldsmith, The* 51
*Gong* 263
*Gong* (II) 265

Grave angel of ebony                                            5
*Gravity*                                                      257
Greetings I bear you, who endure in my feeling               193

Hand's interior. Sole that walks the surface                 255
He calls to it. It startles, halts and stands                249
He walked up under the grey leaves, just                      59
Heart, to whom make plaint? Ever more shunned                115
Heart's swing. O safe swinging, from what invisible bough    245
His eyes have grown so tired with the passing                 63
His eyes—wide open to his vast visions                        85
How far the stars are apart; and yet how much further        233
How may I hold my soul that it refrain                        57
How we are seized by the bird's cry . . .                    239

I am so afraid of people's words                               7
I am the lute. If you should think to describe                97
I cannot think that little figure Death                       11
I find your trace in all these things, in all                11
I lived with the ancient monks                                15
I want to be one of those who drive their wild                27
I will remember you now one last time                       209
*Idol*                                                       263
*In Celebration of Myself*                                   3–9
In reflections resembling Fragonard                          101
In the instrument how they darken and rustle                  51
Inside a rose your bed, beloved. You yourself                267
Inside, the lazy padding of their paws                        61
Is he from here? No, for his full                            189
*Island of Sirens, The*                                       85
It is one thing to sing the beloved, but another, alas       141
It was in Karnak. We had ridden there                        123

Just as a quick sheet of paper sometimes                     213
Just as the watchman of the vineyard lands                    13

King's heart. Core of a high                                 257

*La Dame à la Licorne*                                        47
*Lady at the Mirror*                                          99
*L'Ange du Méridien*                                          61
*Late Autumn in Venice*                                       97
*Leaving*                                                     45
Leaving suddenly. Standing in the grey                        45
*Leda*                                                        83
*Leper's Song, The*                                           39
Like a match struck in the hand, white                        75
Like kings who in the end no more than stride                 71
Like spices in a sleeping draught she slips                   99

Lingering, even with the most intimate                                119
Listen, already you can make out the first                            237
Long he had won it through gazing                                     113
Look among the stars. Is there no 'Rider'?                            193
Look at me: one of those the world has abandoned                       39
Look at the flowers, these living things loyal to the earth           225
Look: here is death, this faintly blue decoction                      121
Look how it stands, against the darkening glooms                      251
Lord, have you heard the New                                          201
Lord, it is time. The summer was immense                               33
Lord, we are poorer than the poor beasts                               21
*Love Song*                                                            57
*Lute, The*                                                            97

*Magician, The*                                                       249
Make no memorial. Simply let the roses                                187
Man, you resolved to hunt, striving to subjugate                      223
*Marionette Theatre*                                                   47
*Marriage*                                                             43
Masks! Bring masks! For we must shade his gaze                        249
*Mausoleum*                                                           257
*Merry-go-round, The*                                                  73
Mirrors: no one has consciously told                                  213
Music: breath of statues. Perhaps even                                123
Musing upon legend after legend                                        43

*Neighbour, The*                                                       31
*New Poems*                                                         57–81
*New Poems, Second Part*                                          81–105
Night. O you so deeply freed                                          255
Nights are not created for crowds                                      29
Night's constellations, here in my woken awareness                    255
*Ninth Elegy, The*                                                    169
No more for our ears . . . : sound                                    265
No more of wooing, O voice grown beyond it, no more let               159

O fountain-mouth, you giving one, you mouth                           227
O high tree of looking: now in leaf-fall                              261
O only *then* when this flight                                        207
O our existence's wondrous abundances                                 235
O this renewing joy of our loosened clay!                             237
O trees of life, when is your winter? Ours                            145
O you tender ones, step now and then                                  185
Odd, the words 'while away the time'                                  129
*Odette R . . . .*                                                    245
*Offerings to the Lares*                                                3
Oh come and go. You, all but child, augment                           241
Oh leave me, you whom I asked                                         111
Once, upon the deserts' edge                                           35

Only he raising the lyre                                                191
Only in the realm of praise may Grief                                   191
*Orangery Steps, The*                                                    71
*Orpheus. Eurydice. Hermes*                                              77
Overturn nothing that stands!                                           253

*Palm of the Hand*                                                      255
*Panther, The*                                                           63
*People at Night*                                                        29
*Pink Hydrangea*                                                        101
*Plaint*                                                                115
*Poet, The*                                                              67
*Pont du Carrousel*                                                      31
Praising is everything! Appointed to praise                             189
*Prayer*                                                                  5
Princely-fastidious windows own the scene                                95
*Prophet, A*                                                             85
Put out my eyes: I see you still the same                                15

*Raising of Lazarus, The*                                               107
*Requiem for a Friend* (excerpt)                                         53
Richly they drenched the room, hourly fuller and stronger               265
*Roman Fountain*                                                         71
Rose enthroned, to the Ancients you were simply                        217
*Rose Interior*                                                          99
Rose, oh pure contradiction, delight                                    263
*Rose Window, The*                                                       61

*Saint, The*                                                             25
Sand-shift of hours. Persistent, quiet dissolution                      251
*Second Elegy, The*                                                     135
*Sequel to the 'Bowl of Roses', A*                                      265
*Seventh Elegy, The*                                                    159
Shall I name you a rising or a setting?                                   7
She is silent, melancholy, alone                                         43
Should we be breaking our ancient bond with the great                   209
*Sibyl, A*                                                               87
Sing, my heart, the gardens you have never known                        233
*Sixth Elegy, The*                                                      157
Slowly the evening changes its array                                     33
*Snake-charming*                                                         91
So arbitrarily we may not paint you                                       9
So, for them all, this was something needed                             107
So it must surely be the angel, drinking                                109
*Solitude*                                                               31
Solitude is like a rain                                                  31
Some day, when I emerge from the fiercest of insights                   175
Somewhere deep in the bank is the indulgent home of gold                231
Somewhere the flower of farewell blooms, and scatters                   261

*Song of the Sea* 95
Songs I was granted in youth 3
*Sonnets to Orpheus, The* 183–243
Sound, no more in our ears' 263
*Spanish Dancer* 75
'*Spirit and fervour: these we would not lose*' 267
Spring has come round again, and the Earth 205
Still friend of places too far-flung to number 243
Strange violin, are you following me? 31
Suddenly I have knowledge of the fountains 39
Summon me to that hour of all your hours 235
*Swan, The* 67

Tears, tears breaking out of me 109
Tears, the tenderest, *rise*! 245
Tell me, who *are* they, these travelling, transient people, more so 151
*Tenth Elegy, The* 175
That was the unearthly mine of souls 77
The ancient, the undermost, ravelled 201
The barberries already ripen red 19
The blind man stands there on the bridge, grey 31
The city now no longer works like bait 97
The darkness was like riches in the room 27
The emperors of earth are old 17
The evening is my book. Its fine 7
The people thirsted; seeing them, the only 25
The saint raised his head, and prayer fell 65
The sun in Venice will prepare here 69
*Third Elegy, The* 141
This beast does not exist. And they, not knowing 215
This my struggle 3
Though the world changes fast 203
*Three Kings, The* 35
*To Hölderlin* 119
*To Music* 123
To that spirit who seeks our reference, hail 195
Torn open by our fingers, over and over 227
*Transience* 251
*Turning* 113
Two basins, one above the other, rising 71

Unheard—his unimaginable head 81
*Unicorn, The* 65
Up there, the image is a world of looking 103
Urn, opium-poppy ovary 261

*Venetian Morning* 95

Wait! Slow down! my growl to every ring 51

Wait . . . that tastes good . . . and is on the move          199
Watch: he walks, a fissure through the town                  91
Waters that plunge and the quick-sliding . . .               259
We are the transient ones                                    207
We build you with our trembling hands                          9
We handle flower and fruit, and the vine leaf                197
What is the furthest I shall reach                             9
What shall I dedicate to you, Lord?                          203
What the heap was, there was no telling                       87
What will you do, God, when I die?                            13
When he assumed the swan, driven by need                      83
When storm assaults the indomitable cathedral                 61
When the snake-charmer at the market                          91
Where and in which ever happily watered gardens, on which    229
Where is the exterior                                         99
Who, if I cried out, would hear me among the orders          131
Who of us guessed this pink? Who was aware                   101
Whoever you may be: at evening step forth                     25
Why, when we could live out our span of existence            169
*Wild Rose*                                                  251
With all its eyes the natural world looks far                165
Woman and noblewoman: often we injure                         47
World was there in my beloved's face                         253
*Written for Count Karl Lanckoroński*                        267


You are the future, sovereign morning red                     17
You, beloved                                                 111
You few playmates of a bygone childhood                      219
You flowers, akin, after all, to hands that bring order      217
You my friend are lonely, because . . . .                    199
You roundness, high in flight, giving away                   103
You, the hour, are deserting me                               67

American Literature

British and Irish Literature

Children's Literature

Classics and Ancient Literature

Colonial Literature

Eastern Literature

European Literature

Gothic Literature

History

Medieval Literature

Oxford English Drama

Poetry

Philosophy

Politics

Religion

The Oxford Shakespeare

A complete list of Oxford World's Classics, including Authors in Context, Oxford English Drama, and the Oxford Shakespeare, is available in the UK from the Marketing Services Department, Oxford University Press, Great Clarendon Street, Oxford OX2 6DP, or visit the website at www.oup.com/uk/worldsclassics.

In the USA, visit www.oup.com/us/owc for a complete title list.

Oxford World's Classics are available from all good bookshops. In case of difficulty, customers in the UK should contact Oxford University Press Bookshop, 116 High Street, Oxford OX1 4BR.

A SELECTION OF    **OXFORD WORLD'S CLASSICS**

|  |  |
|---|---|
|  | **Eirik the Red and Other Icelandic Sagas** |
|  | **The Kalevala** |
|  | **The Poetic Edda** |
| LUDOVICO ARIOSTO | **Orlando Furioso** |
| GIOVANNI BOCCACCIO | **The Decameron** |
| GEORG BÜCHNER | **Danton's Death, Leonce and Lena,** and **Woyzeck** |
| LUIS VAZ DE CAMÕES | **The Lusiads** |
| MIGUEL DE CERVANTES | **Don Quixote**<br>**Exemplary Stories** |
| CARLO COLLODI | **The Adventures of Pinocchio** |
| DANTE ALIGHIERI | **The Divine Comedy**<br>**Vita Nuova** |
| LOPE DE VEGA | **Three Major Plays** |
| J. W. VON GOETHE | **Elective Affinities**<br>**Erotic Poems**<br>**Faust: Part One and Part Two**<br>**The Flight to Italy** |
| JACOB and WILHELM GRIMM | **Selected Tales** |
| E. T. A. HOFFMANN | **The Golden Pot and Other Tales** |
| HENRIK IBSEN | **An Enemy of the People, The Wild Duck, Rosmersholm**<br>**Four Major Plays**<br>**Peer Gynt** |
| LEONARDO DA VINCI | **Selections from the Notebooks** |
| FEDERICO GARCIA LORCA | **Four Major Plays** |
| MICHELANGELO BUONARROTI | **Life, Letters, and Poetry** |

A SELECTION OF    **OXFORD WORLD'S CLASSICS**

PETRARCH

**Selections from the Canzoniere and Other Works**

J. C. F. SCHILLER

**Don Carlos and Mary Stuart**

JOHANN AUGUST
STRINDBERG

**Miss Julie and Other Plays**

A SELECTION OF    **OXFORD WORLD'S CLASSICS**

|  | Six French Poets of the Nineteenth Century |
|---|---|
| Honoré de Balzac | **Cousin Bette**<br>**Eugénie Grandet**<br>**Père Goriot** |
| Charles Baudelaire | **The Flowers of Evil**<br>**The Prose Poems** and **Fanfarlo** |
| Benjamin Constant | **Adolphe** |
| Denis Diderot | **Jacques the Fatalist**<br>**The Nun** |
| Alexandre Dumas (père) | **The Black Tulip**<br>**The Count of Monte Cristo**<br>**Louise de la Vallière**<br>**The Man in the Iron Mask**<br>**La Reine Margot**<br>**The Three Musketeers**<br>**Twenty Years After**<br>**The Vicomte de Bragelonne** |
| Alexandre Dumas (fils) | **La Dame aux Camélias** |
| Gustave Flaubert | **Madame Bovary**<br>**A Sentimental Education**<br>**Three Tales** |
| Victor Hugo | **The Essential Victor Hugo**<br>**Notre-Dame de Paris** |
| J.-K. Huysmans | **Against Nature** |
| Pierre Choderlos de Laclos | **Les Liaisons dangereuses** |
| Mme de Lafayette | **The Princesse de Clèves** |
| Guillaume du Lorris and Jean de Meun | **The Romance of the Rose** |

| | |
|---|---|
| GUY DE MAUPASSANT | **A Day in the Country and Other Stories** |
| | **A Life** |
| | **Bel-Ami** |
| | **Mademoiselle Fifi and Other Stories** |
| | **Pierre et Jean** |
| PROSPER MÉRIMÉE | **Carmen and Other Stories** |
| MOLIÈRE | **Don Juan and Other Plays** |
| | **The Misanthrope, Tartuffe, and Other Plays** |
| BLAISE PASCAL | **Pensées and Other Writings** |
| ABBÉ PRÉVOST | **Manon Lescaut** |
| JEAN RACINE | **Britannicus, Phaedra, and Athaliah** |
| ARTHUR RIMBAUD | **Collected Poems** |
| EDMOND ROSTAND | **Cyrano de Bergerac** |
| MARQUIS DE SADE | **The Crimes of Love** |
| | **The Misfortunes of Virtue and Other Early Tales** |
| GEORGE SAND | **Indiana** |
| MME DE STAËL | **Corinne** |
| STENDHAL | **The Red and the Black** |
| | **The Charterhouse of Parma** |
| PAUL VERLAINE | **Selected Poems** |
| JULES VERNE | **Around the World in Eighty Days** |
| | **Captain Hatteras** |
| | **Journey to the Centre of the Earth** |
| | **Twenty Thousand Leagues under the Seas** |
| VOLTAIRE | **Candide and Other Stories** |
| | **Letters concerning the English Nation** |